THE BLACK
LOTUS

NIGHT FLOWER BOOK ONE

CLAIRE WARNER

<u>Also by Claire Warner:</u>

Night Flower:
Blood Orchid

Faded Rose (in progress)

Coils of Copper and Brass:
Amber Sky (in progress)

<u>Also by Claire Warner:</u>

Night Flower:

Blood Orchid

Faded Rose (in progress)

Coils of Copper and Brass:

Amber Sky (in progress)

For my parents

For my partner Steve. Love you.

To all the girls on the 7.45 bus to Peterborough. Without you I wouldn't have started, much less finished this. Thanks Sarah, Rachel, Emma, Sarah and Tracey.

PROLOGUE

15ᵗʰ June 1752

The floor was cold. That mundane thought floated through her mind as the deep dark of unconsciousness ebbed away. The unyielding surface sent small stabs of pain through her limbs as confusion set in. Her head felt heavy and somewhat hollow as she struggled to remember how she had fallen. She managed to blink, the simple task rendered difficult by the lassitude swamping her. As she struggled closer to full awareness, she became aware of something clasped in her hand. Its surface was smooth, shaped like a flower but, as she traced her fingers over the surface, it seemed to spark a wary, almost sick sensation of worry.

"I think she's waking up,"

A voice, feminine and vaguely familiar, sounded close to her head. She tried to move, to turn her head to stare at the speaker, but her body refused to cooperate, still caught in the spell of near insensibility.

"Yes, I can see that," Another voice, male and disapproving, spoke from further away. "You need not sound so thrilled; I doubt she will welcome you when she opens her eyes."

"Oh, Hugh darling, how can you say that?" Petulant yet teasing notes flowed through the woman's light lilting speech and she longed to see the face that it belonged to. Those tones invoked cautious recognition, a recognition which did not bring her any sense of peace.

"Because it is the truth," The man shifted position and walked closer to her prone figure. "Why on earth did you do it?" The voice dropped lower, becoming accusatory in tone and timbre. She wondered at this, struggling with tattered threads of memory that refused to make sense.

"It solved a problem,"

"I beg to differ," He was stood over her now; she felt the tips of his toes against her side. "Do you think that Justin will thank you?"

Justin, that name caught at her mind, dragging it free from the sludge her memory had become. She knew that name, the feelings it provoked were soft and wondrous. Once again the memories fluttered close to the surface yet she was still not awake enough to make sense of it all

"He should," The voice argued, louder and less teasing than before, "This solves all," She felt the woman move, the edge of a skirt brushed against her side and she wondered how long they were going to stand and argue over her.

"Really?" There was a bark of incredulous laughter. "Our Justin, who promised never to curse another," Her eyelids opened slightly and she focused blearily on the rich brocade silk that tickled her nose. "Do you honestly think he would be happy that you damned someone else?" From her position on the floor, she could see the man's calves and a pair of silver buckled shoes.

"Yes Hugh," The skirt rustled as the woman stepped away from her side to argue with the man before her. "The chit is now safe. John will not be able to hurt her," Another memory tugged at the edges of her mind and this one sent a thrill of fear through her. "And Justin..," The woman laughed shortly, bitterly, "Justin will not spend the next fifty years in depression because he had to leave her,"

"Don't try to claim that you did this for him," The man knelt down now and she felt his hand close about her wrist. Her limited vision took in a rose pink satin frock coat and embroidered lavender waistcoat. "You did it for yourself. You've always felt like the youngest and now you're not," His other hand reached down and settled in the small of her back. "Come on now Melissa, let me help you up," She did not question her name, for she remembered that at least.

With sure movements, he helped her to her feet. Her eyes opened fully and she took in her surroundings. She was in a parlour, mahogany wainscoting covered the walls and a thick blue rug topped the parquet floor. Several chairs stood round a card table in the corner of the room and a fire was burning brightly in the hearth. Behind her lay a closed door and she could hear conversation and music from beyond. As the man guided her to a cushioned chair, she glanced up, taking in the extravagant clothing that seemed totally at odds with the serious cast marred his features.

"You'll be a little disorientated at first," She could see pity in his eyes and she wondered at it. "It'll pass," He reached out to one of the small tables in the corner of the room and picked up a glass of amber liquid. "Take a snifter of that, it'll strengthen your nerves," The scent of brandy filled her nostrils and she took a deep gulp. The liquid burned her throat as she swallowed and made her splutter. As she controlled her coughs, her eyes took in the form of the woman. Taller than her, the woman had blonde ringlets worn in an elaborate style and powdered. An expensive dress of dark blue brocade covered her form and blue eyes sparked with mischief or malice.

"What happened?" She asked, staring at the pair of them in confusion. "Did I faint?"

The man sighed and knelt down, staring at her with sorrowful eyes. "I'm sorry my dear, but," He held out his hand and she looked down at the small snuff box before her. Set into the lid was a black enamel locket in the shape of a lotus flower. The smooth planes of the bloom filled her vision and she stared at it in utter shock. As horrified

recognition raced through her, the man continued to speak. "You have one of these now and I'm so very sorry,"

It was then that she looked down, at the item clasped between her fingers. It was a lotus flower locket, a veritable twin to the one on the box. The sight of it finally sparked her memory and she remembered what it stood for. Her head snapped up and she stared at the blonde woman, hatred replacing shock as her mind finally filled in the gaps of her memory.

"You bitch,"

CHAPTER 1
5 MONTHS EARLIER

Melissa entered the panelled room with hesitant steps. Music and laughter engulfed her, the loud raucous sounds making her flinch. A shadow to the right attracted her attention and she gazed into the mirror, noting with some nervousness the change in her appearance. The girl she knew had fled and in her place stood a woman in rustling green brocade and emeralds. A powdered, made up creature that bore no resemblance to Melissa De Vire. Even her earrings were different to the usual. Waterfalls of tiny emeralds and gold fell from her ears and a matching hung about her throat. Her father moved to her side and squeezed her hand reassuringly as a tall man dressed in lavender stepped forward.

"Edward. So glad you could make it," He held out his hand to her father. "I was about to send out my groom to make sure that you hadn't got lost on the road. I know how you despise coming to town," His voice was affected, even lisping, the antithesis to her father's strong tones. Not normally the type she saw her father associate with at all. Melissa watched the exchange carefully, wondering if her father could contain his sardonic asides.

"Ah Montjoy, This is the cost of having children," Edward De Vire took hold of the offered hand and shook it briskly. "We must all make sacrifices for their futures," Melissa glanced at her father in surprise, wondering where he had gained this bantering light manner, for he rarely displayed it at home. At her left elbow, her mother smiled politely, waiting for introduction.

"You have met my wife?" The conversation was moving along and Melissa dragged herself from the strangeness of her parents among strangers. They did hold balls at their home in the city and parties at their estate, but this was the first time she had been allowed within one floor of the action. Until this evening she had been exiled to the children's playroom with the promise of candied fruits for good conduct. She focused in on the conversation now, knowing that her father would soon be introducing her and sure enough, after several moments of light banter, her father waved her forward.

"So this is the lovely Melissa?" The man faced her

head on and his voice buzzed lightly in her ears. "I was wondering when we were going to meet this daughter of yours," Melissa looked up into a jowly face beneath an overly elaborate wig. His watery blue eyes appraised her carefully, bringing a slow blush to her powdered skin. The gaze was too frank and approving to be polite, it felt as though he were slowly removing the green gown she wore piece by piece. She did not feel flattered, his attention was disturbing and she struggled to keep her discomfort from her face.

"My dear Edward you failed to mention how stunning she was," He stepped forward, drawing her hand towards his lips and kissing her skin with dry papery lips. Melissa feigned a smile and bobbed lightly as she had been instructed before dropping his hand as soon as decorum allowed.

"Oh indeed she is stunning but she is also my daughter," Her father's tone was light, jovial even, yet she caught the warning within the smiling tones. Montjoy gave a smile and stepped back, removing his eyes from the inspection of her form with a light wave.

"And so… let us enter, your daughter will be presented and then she will join in the festivities. I feel this night will be the most talked of event in the season and not least for the appearance of your daughter. She will be the belle of the event,"

"Thank you sir," She couldn't help but reply in a soft, nervous whisper, unused to such lavish compliments and wondering if all of the attendees would be like this. She watched Montjoy turn and remove a glass of canary from the nearest footman as she fervently began hoping that there would be others nearer her own age within, she didn't think she could stand any more exposure to this fop. Her mother's delicate hand descended on her shoulder and her light bright voice spoke up.

"Well Edward, I shall leave you and Montjoy to your talks, I'm not going to have Melissa spend her first ball sitting in a study and she must meet the King. Come along,"

Melissa waved farewell with a relieved heart as her mother walked her towards the end of the room.

"Now I know you don't need to be told, but do not find yourself alone with him," Her mother's voice held a soft note of warning. "He's not above ruining young women," Melissa nodded, not trusting herself to speak and wondering why her father was friends with such a cad.

"You'll do fine, come along," Melissa felt her mother's fingers grasp her shoulder and lead her forward. Soon she stood before the King and her mother was announcing her, a curtsey, a smile and she was away, hardly aware that she had just met the most powerful man in all of England.

"Was that it?" She whispered to her mother as they moved away from the main hall and towards the ballroom.

"Hmm.. what were you expecting my dear, fanfares? The King is not a young man, time when you could have tilted your head at royal fare is long past," Her mother glanced down at her daughter, "Unless you fancy the role of royal mistress," Melissa looked up with shock, unable to find an answer to her mother, who chuckled and led her towards the closed double doors. As they neared the ballroom, they were opened by black liveried lackeys and the noise swelled as they passed through the heavily engraved portals into the room beyond.

A wave of warmth and sensation struck her as they moved beyond the doors and into the loud, golden space. The air was warm, stuffy from numerous candles and people, myriad odours assailed her nostrils, from cologne to powder and she sneezed once as her feet carried her over the threshold. As the ambience of the scene hit, she was swept away by what she saw. Her troubling thoughts about the episode in the hallway, the king, her mother's speech and Montjoy were driven from her mind by the scene before her.

"Well, what do you think?" Her mother muttered as she smiled at Melissa's awestruck face. The ballroom was a vision in white and gold, crystal chandeliers swayed delicately from the ceiling housing hundreds of candles and casting a gold glow about the room. From the gold urns on either side of the floor roses spilled free, scenting the air with heady fragrance. Melissa stared open mouthed at the sight before her, watching the couples move in elegant step to the music, their clothes a collage of silks, taffetas, lace and brocade. For several moments, she could not speak, the surprise freezing her voice.

"Whatever else you may say about him, he plans a good event," her mother said as she led her awestruck daughter onto the dance floor

"Ah Lady DeVire, I presume this is Melissa," A short,

rotund man declared as he kissed her mother's hand. "Oh she's going to break hearts," He turned to face her and held out his hand. "Roland Montcrief. It's a pleasure to see you again. You weren't nearly as attractive the last time I saw you," Melissa looked at her mother, she didn't recall the fat man before her and though he wasn't as slimy as Lord Montjoy, she wasn't too impressed with her mother's seeming inattention to men of her own age.

"Oh don't tease her," Lydia De Vire had not missed the barely concealed expression of panic in her daughter's eyes. "Roland met you as a small child,"

"You and your miscreant older brother were making mud pies and terrorising your governess as I recall," The man said with a cheery laugh, making Melissa cringe at the unwanted memory, the last thing she wanted to be reminded of was that. What if this was the only impression she raised, that of a small child covered in mud? Her eyes sought out her mother's and she was rewarded by a gently encouraging smile.

"I've grown up since then," She replied, putting as much strength into her voice as possible, trying to still the whispers of unease that fluttered through her head like butterflies. She fervently hoped that this flabby, embarrassing old fool wasn't going to keep her occupied all night with stories of her childhood.

"I can see," Roland replied with a smile. "Well I don't want to hold up your conquest of the room and I'm sure you wish to find others closer to you own age," He kissed her hand again and straightened up. "Have a pleasant night," He bade her mother farewell, turned on his heel and drifted back into the crowd. Melissa managed to hold the sigh of relief that was teetering on her lips as she watched the almost puce coloured velvet clad back disappear into the crowd.

"And may I present Edward Danvers," Melissa had barely enough time to process that conversation before she was introduced to another man and then another. Moving like some social whirlwind, Lydia De Vire presented her daughter to the room.

Once the bewildering round of introductions had been concluded, her mother finally left her side. Reeling from her whistle stop tour of the room she was finally stopped by a young man in plum and rose brocade. His eyes were a periwinkle blue and they twinkled merrily as she looked up at him.

"Do my eyes deceive me?" He declared in an overly dramatic tone. "Such a vision of beauty and loveliness. I am dazzled by your face," As he finished speaking, he lent forward and kissed her hand. "Rupert Avery at your service," He dipped into a low bow and moved forward, looking down at her with a delighted gleam in his eyes. "I would be honoured if you would give me the next dance,"

Melissa gave a smile as she offered Rupert her arm and allowed him to sweep her onto the dance floor. The night progressed smoothly after that. She was a novelty, fresh to the scene and therefore of interest. As soon as the dance ended with Rupert declaring undying love, the next suitor had appeared. In a whirl, she moved from suitor to suitor hardly knowing their names but hearing them declare themselves in awe of her beauty. It was an exhilarating yet terrifying experience, several of these bravos had been known to duel for the affections of a lady and she was not experienced enough to play the tease. Melissa felt somewhat sorry for the gallants who promised her the stars, for she only felt a passing affection for some of them. In truth after the third or fourth declaration of love, she felt bored with the whole affair. It all sounded false as though it were the form to be so extravagant. Of course the point of such affairs was to snare an acceptable husband. Flamboyant though it may be, these overly elaborate events were essential to barter her out to the mode. Though she had been brought up for this, she could not quite suppress the dissatisfaction with her lot.

"Do you want me to take you away from all this?" A humour filled masculine voice intruded on her thoughts. Melissa glanced up at the speaker with her first genuine smile of the evening.

"Marcus," She gave her older brother a relieved hug and allowed him to take her onto the dance floor. "I was beginning to get overwhelmed.. Does this always happen?"

Her brother smiled and chuckled. "Oh fairly frequently, it's de riguer you know to over indulge in emotion," Melissa smiled as her brother steered them towards the middle of the room. Beneath the laden chandelier, her brother led her through the steps of the dance, his footsteps sure and steady. It was strange, Melissa concluded, to see him in this setting. Marcus could dress well when the occasion demanded, but he usually preferred riding attire when he resided at home. To see him in powder and court dress gave her an eerie unsettled feeling. He seemed almost unreal. In this attire, he was a member of the court and not the brother who teased her mercilessly.

"But would they really…," She began, wondering just how much she could ask and not cause a fuss. "You know.. um.. duel for my honour?"

"If they thought it would impress you," Marcus replied with a serious note to his voice. "Though technically, you're not supposed to know about it and I'm supposed to keep the more impassioned ones away from you," Melissa rolled her eyes as they executed a perfect turn.

"Because of course I can't deal with the annoyance myself," A small note of impatience crept into her voice.

"My sister, you could take care of yourself, I taught you how to fire a pistol personally, against our father's instruction and I trust you would use it, but you have to think about your reputation," He looked down at her with a very serious look on his face. "Your reputation is fragile and easily bruised; these young bucks could cause a scandal and leave the capital for a few months. When they return their scandal is forgotten, any breath of scandal attached to you would not be," Melissa nodded; she had heard variations on this speech numerous times before from both her parents. A man could shot his rival in a duel, lose his fortune, elope with a woman and get away with it, a woman could not. She sighed and looked away; depressed at the direction their conversation was taking.

Her gaze roamed around the room, past chattering ladies and laughing men. This was to be her world for the next few months or longer if she were unlucky. The point of all of this was to snare a husband, for without that, she was lost.

"I understand," She answered her brother with only the merest touch of heat to her words. "Mother and Father have instructed me endlessly on this point. You don't need to add to it," It was infuriating, this constant harping about good behaviour and consequences. She knew the difficulties, why did they feel the need to keep on at her?

"Force of habit sister mine," Marcus replied with a laugh. "Father would pitch a fit if I didn't keep an eye on you," He looked down at her with a comradely smile. "We're on the same side you know,"

"I know," She allowed a smile to touch her lips as he swept her past a planter of roses, the heady fragrance tickling her nose. Another couple swept past and Melissa found her eyes wandering again. An orchestra played in the corner of the room and before it, across the floor; the crowd were dancing and laughing. It all combined together in one glorious medley of sound and colour. She kept looking, drinking in the experience yet bewildered by it at the same time. Still her eyes roamed, beyond the punchbowl and open doors to the garden until finally they found the one still point of the room. Melissa almost stopped dancing at the sight that greeted her gaze.

Standing in the corner of room, a glass raised to his lips, was a young man. Impeccably and dramatically dressed in dark blue and gold he stood aloof from the crowd, watching the proceedings with little interest.

"Marcus," She nodded towards the corner. "Who is that?"

Marcus glanced up and across the room, his eyes falling on the young man with what seemed to be concern.

"That is Justin Lestrade.," He answered her calmly as he drew her through the crowd, away from the man and towards a pair of chairs.

"I've heard of him," Melissa felt disappointed. That handsome young man had one of the worst reputations in London. Barely a week went by without some scandal or other. Sensible women did not vie for his attention yet he never seemed to lack female company.

"I'm not surprised," Marcus murmured as he guided her to sit. "He has a poor reputation though and I do not believe that father would ever admit him to his company,"

"Oh," Melissa gazed across the room again, yet several dancing couples obscured her view of the corner.

"If you must find someone to moon over," Marcus began, noting her roving eyes. "I would hope that it would be someone other than him,"

"I won't moon over him, I'm just curious," She drew her attention back to her brother and smiled.

"Ah yes but we know what curiosity did and I'm just warning you that Father would have a fit if you turned up on Lestrade's arm," Marcus held her gaze and she saw warning within there. "So save your curiosity for more worthy types,"

Melissa pursed her lips in frustration but said nothing. Her thoughts seethed with questions and though she adored her older brother, she could not make him aware of them. Father was friends with Montjoy and he was hardly what she considered gentlemanly. How could he be friends with one person with a low reputation yet ostracise another? And how could Marcus feel that she would fling herself on a complete stranger just because she asked his name?

"I didn't mean to preach," Marcus said finally as the silence lengthened. "But it's best you hear this from me and not father," He patted her gently on the arm and stood up clearly feeling that the conversation was finished. "Are you alright here?" She nodded and watched her brother move away across the floor.

For several moments she sat quietly, watching the dancers sashay past her and across the floor. Taking a glass of canary from the silver tray of a lackey, she let her gaze drift past Rupert dancing with Emmeline Marsters, away from the blue eyed flirt that was Mary Westbury and into the corner of the room where Lestrade stood. Slowly the dancers parted and she allowed her eyes to drink their fill. He was moderately tall beneath his powdered hair and dressed in a midnight blue coat. The heavy velvet was embroidered extravagantly with gold thread and jewels. Beneath that he wore a waistcoat of gold brocade over a white silk shirt. At his throat, a blue silk cravat fixed with an enamelled cravat pin in the unusual design of a black lotus completed the ensemble. It was a rich dress, signifying much personal wealth yet that was not what called to her. His face drew her attention like nothing else had. She didn't wish to stare like some yokel, yet she couldn't drag herself away. The young man, for he was clearly not that much older than she, was looking at the crowd with an expression of unfathomable humour. A mocking yet slightly sad expression creased his brow and though she could not tell the direction of his stare from this distance, she was sure that they were not watching the soiree with any great interest. He was handsome, she realized as her gaze traced his features and his figure was lean and muscular beneath the rich clothing. As she trailed her eyes over his profile for the second time, he turned his head and his eyes locked with hers. Blushing furiously beneath the powder caking her face, Melissa immediately tore her eyes away and glanced down at her feet, embarrassed to have been caught staring. Feigning an overwhelming interest in the embroidery on her shoes, she hoped to divert his attention. So concerned she was with faking disinterest, she missed his slow walk through the crowd towards her and was unprepared when his shadow fell over her and drew her attention.

"May I join you?" His voice was smooth and well modulated with a teasing note in its depths, she started and looked up into eyes of hazel that looked through her with a directness she found disturbing yet strangely compelling.

"Please," She couldn't refuse now she had been caught staring at him so efficiently and she indicated the empty seat opposite. Her brother would not approve, but she was only going to be talking to him, it wouldn't do to be impolite, she ignored the little voice that murmured that she was curious and attracted to his looks. With smooth movements he sat before her and his eyes travelled over her features carefully. Melissa felt herself flush as the intense gaze returned to her eyes and he smiled. Face to face, he was even more compelling and she felt strangely naked beneath his gaze as though he could see everything that she was trying to hide.

"I'm Justin Lestrade, I'm sure you've been told about me," In his warm voice she could hear suppressed laughter and she smiled, answering his amusement with some of her own. Even so, she wondered at the reason for the hidden humour for she felt that it was not directed toward the conversation but at something she couldn't quite understand.

"My brother did mention you,"

"Of course he would have done," Amusement continued to thrum through his voice and she was sure that he was quite aware of her brother's warnings. "And you would be Melissa De Vire?" Despite being phrased as a question, Melissa was certain that he knew exactly who she was. "I've heard quite a bit about you. You're the toast of the room," The laughter spilled from his voice and spread across his face, it made his features look less jaded, more human. There was something magnetic about his voice; it held a confidence beyond the norm for a man his age and a mildly derisive humour that she couldn't fathom.

"Only because I'm a fresh face," Melissa replied, a soft smile touching her lips. "I got the impression that I was a shiny new toy," She took a sip of the sweet wine and relaxed a little more.

"Well that silk does suit you well," Justin responded, the compliment falling easily from his lips. "Green is your colour," He beckoned a waiter carrying a laden tray forward and removed a small glass of canary. Dismissing the servant with a wave, he turned his attention back to Melissa. "I daresay shiny new toy is the best description for you at this point. It's your first night in society; people are supposed to be curious and intrigued,"

"Intrigued?" Melissa asked, her eyes shifting from his handsome face with required modesty.

"You are an unknown. And the unknown is always to be explored," His eyes sparked as he regarded her and he smiled. Melissa felt her breath catch as he turned that devastating smile full on her. There were layers to his conversation, meanings that she knew were not for a lady or at the least were meant for someone more versed in the arts of seduction. Ordinarily such a conversation would leave her tongue tied and stammering, yet he put her at such ease that she felt confident in replying.

"Perhaps the unknown is best left a mystery," She answered finally, her fingers sliding over the smooth glass in her hands as she stared at him.

"Perhaps," He conceded, "but exploring a mystery is a wonderful venture," He lifted the glass to his lips and delicately took a sip. Melissa followed the motion, drawn to his mouth and its sensual twist with an interest that could not be considered academic.

"What if the unknown wishes to remain unexplored?" It was a bold question and one she should not even be thinking of asking, yet his manner seemed to draw it from her. His rakish smile encouraged indiscretion and for once in her ordered existence she revelled in the opportunity to be free with her thoughts.

"Does the unknown have a choice? What if the explorer decides to find out all he can?" His voice was honey soft and seductive.

She met his eyes boldly. "Then perhaps the unknown will poison him unexpectedly," Shock flickered through his gaze like summer lightning at her daring and for a second, their conversation stuttered to a halt. Melissa did not drop her gaze as a modest lady should and they both stared at each other. Melissa's frank gaze meeting his startled one as the room gossiped and danced around them.

Justin laughed; a low chuckle that broke the unnatural silence and relaxed the tension surrounding them. "This explorer always treads carefully," He conceded finally as the chuckles subsided. "And chooses the safe path," He sipped the canary and sat back, regarding the girl before him with more interest than before. "What has your brother imparted about me?" His eyes laughed as he looked down at her. "All bad I daresay,"

"Yes," Melissa blurted out without thinking, "he says you're a seducer of innocents, a gamester and a cad,"

"Then you're quite safe," He replied smoothly, taking another sip of canary. "For I doubt an innocent would talk so frankly about my foibles in public,"

Melissa felt her face flare scarlet and she drew her hand to her lips, mortified at her faux pas. "I.. I'm sorry,"

Justin smiled, warmth touching the corners of his eyes as he reassured her. "Don't worry, I won't report you to the room," He moved closer and whispered. "Your indiscretion is safe with me,"

"Oh if only I could believe that," Melissa replied and once again, she wondered why she was speaking so freely.

"Your brother has really taken me to task," He chuckled, "Should I be wary of being invited to a duel?"

"He hasn't said so much, but your reputation," Melissa babbled out, wondering if she would ever talk her way out of this mess.

"Ahh yes, my reputation," Justin glanced over his shoulder and whispered conspiratorially. "I have to admit that my reputation is exaggerated. I am much maligned,"

"I'm sure," Melissa noted with no small amount of sarcasm, "but as my grandmother noted, where's there's smoke there's fire,"

"Not strictly true," Justin said, adjusting the enamel brooch at his neck as he spoke. "Damp logs don't burn, they smoke,"

"Semantics," Melissa fired back, enjoying the repartee that was building between them.

"Perhaps," Justin removed his fingers from the brooch and Melissa found her eyes following the movement of his hand as it drew a handkerchief from the cuff of his jacket. "How are you finding court so far?"

"Overwhelming," She breathed, troubled by the shift in

conversation. "It's not what I expected,"

"Are you not finding it exhilarating?" He smiled again and she was once again struck by the perfection of his teeth. It was not something she was used to, most people had severe decay or had lost their teeth to rot and were sporting replacements. Even those who had most of their own teeth could not claim such well kept specimens.

"I suppose it is," She answered honestly, disconcerted by his glimmering smile and perfect teeth. "Or it was at the start of the evening," A couple swept past her and she followed their movements, tearing herself from his visage. Behind him and to the left she could see her brother; he was wearing his court face, a mask of false pleasantry and laughter. The sight made her shudder, Marcus at court was different to that at home, his voice was louder and sentiments cruder.

"And now?" Justin's voice prompted, dragging her from her reverie. She glanced back at him, at the curiosity that she now saw in his eyes.

"Now?" Her voice was small, a thousand leagues from the poised responses of a few moments ago. "Now I feel as though I'm in a charade, that no one here is what they seem," Katherine Devereux drifted across her vision, her arms locked about the form of Walter Pilkington, a fixed rictus of a smile clued on her face. Behind them stood Emily Saint-Clair, the young blonde widow of Lord Edward Saint-Clair. With puzzlement, Melissa noted that Emily's gaze was fixed on them.

"You're quite right there," She blinked at the softly

spoken words and returned her attention to Justin. "None of us here are real," He waved an elegant hand at her. "Take yourself as an example, you are not what you seem, you primp and smile and make polite conversation, but it is all an act," He moved closer, his words soft, compelling as he leant in. "You can never show your real face and I wonder,"

"What?" Scarcely breathing, she stared up at him. "What is it you wonder?"

Carefully he reached forward and captured her hand. "I wonder," His voice was soft, compelling and she raised her eyes back to his. "Just what lies behind your smile?"

"Do you?" Disconcerted by the strangely direct gaze, she pulled back slightly. "Do you really wish to know about my thoughts?"

"I do," He drew her hand to his mouth and gently kissed the tips of her fingers. "I wonder what lies behind that polite, perfect façade you present,"

Melissa drew her hand away in flustered confusion. Even with the overcooked declarations of love she had been receiving all night, she was still unsure of how to handle such seduction. His desire to know her seemed sincere, yet she knew of his reputation. Her fingers tingled where his lips had pressed and she spoke rapidly, nervously.

"I feel like a prime specimen of beef at a meat market," Unbidden and dangerous, words spilled from her lips. "One that's about to be sold for slaughter," She shook her head and stopped speaking, aware that she was crossing the lines for polite behaviour. One did not discuss innermost feelings at such soirees. He glanced at her swiftly as though daring her to continue with her words.

"In a way you are," He replied finally, sipping the drink slowly as he sized her up. "So you dislike the court then?"

"Oh not really… it's just so big," She answered softly, trying to bring words to her sense of bewilderment. She shook her head and pushed away the introspection, such behaviour was not considered seemly in a lady. "So what brings you to London?" Once again she retreated to the norm, her words mild and polite; the expected behaviour for a lady in society. Justin lowered the glass from his lips and regarded her carefully, his dark eyes flashing in brief disappointment before a mocking gleam slid over their surface.

"The court, the King and beauty such as yours," He answered carelessly as he swirled the canary in his glass. Melissa felt her stomach clench as his manner changed. Gone was the gentle questioner of a few moments ago and in his place was an insincere cad. Anger at his inattention and her own failure to see his manipulation made her blood boil.

"My, how insincere of you," Without stopping to think, her words sizzled between them, angry at his flippancy and superior attitude. "And is this how you speak to all the women?"

"And is this how you address your suitors?" He retaliated, startled by her boldness. "Not the way to find yourself a fine match," He quaffed the rest of his drink in a single gulp and smiled at her, a charming smile that further stoked her anger.

"Ah yes, the fine match," her words hissed between clenched teeth. "the ultimate goal of my life because of the misfortune of being born a member of the fair sex," She moved closer, her voice dropping lower as she leant forward. "So I should be grateful for the insincere flattery of a philanderer and happy with being passed about like a prize for the highest bidder?" A sweet, sickening smile flowed across her features. "Such an honour don't you think?" She pulled back, her voice dripping with sarcasm and repressed anger. "If you will excuse me, I shall find other company and leave you and your insincerity to amuse someone else," She stood and started to walk away. With the speed of a striking snake, Lestrade's fingers found her wrist.

"Wait," The smile had gone from his face now and in its place was a strange mixture of apology and interest. "I'm sorry for my inattention. It was rude and beyond the pale," He got to his feet and stared at her full in the face. "Give me a chance to make up for it,"

She looked down at his fingers locked about her wrist and then up at him. When she spoke, her voice was coolly polite and devoid of the anger that had fuelled her earlier words. "Release my arm sir," With a reluctant nod, he slowly retracted his hand and she pulled away. "My brother appears to have been right about you sir, it would be foolish of me to associate with you further. Good eve, Mister Lestrade,"

With a flounce of her head, she moved away from the

table and into the gaming rooms. Behind her Justin stared after her as though confused and across from her, Emily Saint-Clair watched her leave with a bemused smile. She moved through the throng in a cloud of anger. Trying to forget Justin's behaviour, she joined a game of Quadrille and in her flustered state, proceeded to lose in a spectacular fashion.

"I'm sorry," A low, contrite voice at her elbow drew her away from the game and she stared up into green flecked hazel eyes. "I was terribly rude," Justin murmured, oblivious to the stares and chuckles from the dames around the table. "Forgive me,"

Melissa stared up at him, her own anger reducing as she heard the utter truth in his voice.

"I forgive you for your attitude," She said finally, collecting her tokens and playing the next hand. "But I know little but ill of you sir and forgive me but you have not shown yourself to be courteous,"

"All I can offer is my apology and this," He tilted his fingers somehow and a small flower appeared between his fingers. Melissa looked at the bloom, smiling despite herself as she took it from his fingers and held it to her nose, sniffing the delicate scent with pleasure.

"It's lovely," She conceded finally, "but it'll take more than a conjuring trick to adequately apologise for your behaviour," His fumbling attempts at an apology were a start, but she was not ready to forget her impression of him.

"I was unforgivably rude," He said, crouching down to

her level. "And I apologise for any hurt I may have caused you," His voice was soft and entreating and she felt herself smile despite her anger. "I have no excuse for my behaviour and you have no reason to offer forgiveness, but I do ask it of you,"

"My forgiveness will not be immediate, for you were extremely offensive," Steeling herself against his charms, she finally forced herself to speak. "Particularly as this was our first conversation,"

"Then may I make it up to you?" He implored, "Perhaps a dance and maybe we can start again?" He held out his hand and against all her better judgement she felt a strong desire to take it.

"I am committed to this hand," She nodded at the table and smiled apologetically. "And my father would still kill me if I danced with you,"

"Perhaps," He answered, "but I think you dance to your own tune. I would like your company lady," With a soft smile, he left her side and moved back into the room, leaving Melissa to stare after him in some shock. In a strangely preoccupied mood, she played the rest of the hand. She didn't know why she thought of him, he had just insulted her and he had a reputation that could not be denied and yet, she looked dreamily at the counters on the table, he haunted her. He had not called her 'his angel' or compared her beauty to jewels or the morning sun, like so many others had this evening. His eyes were unfathomable and mysterious; she could see depths in them that he seemed to take pains to hide behind wit and sarcasm. Despite his seeming inattention, she knew he had meant his apology. She drew the next card and played it without comment, her thoughts on the strange, beguiling nature of Justin Lestrade.

"You should go after him dear," One of the women at the table said as she picked up her winnings and stood. "So he may be a poor choice for a husband, but for a night's dancing, you could do worse,"

"I don't know who you mean," Melissa blurted out, shocked that her daydreams were so apparent.

"Of course you do.. just as long as you believe nothing he tells you and keep your head. I see no problem with just a dance. As long as you know that he is overly charming rogue,"

Melissa nodded, watching as her small group returned the cards to the deck and prepared to deal again.

"Are you in on this hand?" She shook her head, watching them smile as they returned to their cards. Moving away from the card table, Melissa smoothed out the creases in her skirts and walked back into the ballroom, her eyes alive as she searched for the midnight blue coat. The small voice within her wondered why she was looking for someone with such an unsavoury reputation and one who had clearly dismissed her, but uncharacteristically she ignored it and continued to navigate the floor.

It didn't take long to locate Justin. He was walking through the one of the doors to the gardens beyond, his arm locked together with Mary Westbury, a known flirt. Justin was leaning close to her and they were both laughing.

Melissa stood stock still for a few moments, cursing herself for a fool; of course she was no one special to him. It hadn't taken him too long to throw himself at the pretty, silly and generally annoying Mary. Trying not to allow irritation to show on her face, she picked up another drink and headed to the buffet.

CHAPTER 2

"Melissa," She turned at her name being spoken and looked directly into a pair of laughing clear blue eyes.

"Sarah," She reached forward and greeted the other girl with a genuine smile, their families had been friends for many years and they had practically grown up together. Sarah had been presented several months previously and had been designated incomparable, which of course meant that she had gained a vast array of admirers. "I didn't know you were here,"

"I was taking the air with John Hansombe," Sarah replied with a demure smile as she tucked her arm in Melissa's. "He's declared that he will shoot himself if I don't accept his suit,"

"Oh dear," Melissa replied with a smile, it was the kind of offer that she had been hearing all night, as though she would like nothing better than brain matter for proof of love.

"Oh, don't worry I don't think he means it, I think he just wants to follow the mode," Sarah replied as she reached forward and snagged some food from the buffet table. "I think he's rather sweet,"

"Oh you would," Melissa answered readily enough, yet her eyes were drawn to the parlour doors and the darkness outside. A strange hot feeling coursed up and down her spine.

"Forgive me for wanting to have fun. You're just going to stand here and mock it all, which I think is incurably dreary," Sarah looked closely at her friend and a puzzled look crossed her face. "What are you looking at?" She exclaimed suddenly as she realised her friend's attention had wandered.

"Oh..," Melissa jumped guiltily, as she wondered how to explain herself. She had always been the more mature of the two and Sarah would tease her mercilessly for her thoughts about Justin. For several moments she struggled to offer an explanation only to be caught on the hop as Emily and Justin walked back into the room.

"Oh ho," Sarah crowed as she saw the direction of Melissa's glance and immediately comprehended the situation. "You're mooning for Lestrade,"

"No…" Melissa protested feebly, wondering why Sarah had chosen this particular moment to join her. She would invariably lock onto the most insignificant detail and magnify it out of all proportion. By the end of the evening, Sarah would have her eloping with Justin on a black charger.

"I'm not mooning for him,"

"Don't lie, I can always tell when you're lying because your nose wobbles,"

"That's because I'm speaking idiot, it always wobbles when I talk. There is nothing between me and Lestrade,"

"But you want there to be?" That was Sarah all over; she couldn't let a subject lie. She was only lucky that the older girl hadn't marched over and announced that Melissa was missing him. "I mean he is extremely attractive and he definitely knows it,"

"No! I just…" Melissa sank into a nearby chair and tried not to panic. If Sarah had her way, the rumour that she liked Justin would be all over the room in minutes. She could just hear her brother's fury to that news, he'd probably haul out his pistols. "Look you can't just say that. You don't know anything about it,"

"Well I would if you told me," Sarah said with immense practicality as she sat and stared at her friend. Her fingers smoothed down her gown of periwinkle silk and she looked at Melissa with a stern, querying look on her face. "So.. are you going to tell me why you're taking a break from being sensible and mooning after the most unsuitable man in the room?"

Melissa breathed slowly and then began to speak. She left nothing from her story, even though there was not much to tell. With rare patience, Sarah left her to finish before jumping onto her tale.

"So.. he insulted you and then handed you a flower by way of a conjuring trick straight out of the theatre as an apology. Is that about it?" Her voice was full of interest and outrage, interest because her friend was notorious at thinking things through and outrage that she had not witnessed the event.

"I think you've covered it," Melissa sat back, hoping that Sarah wouldn't fly into a creative frenzy about this. Her friend had been known to concoct bizarre, unworkable plots to attain the heights of romance that she felt her friend was lacking, or, more simply put, she interfered wholesale in Melissa's life.

"And you're fascinated why?" A look of complete incredulity crossed her face as Melissa looked at her shoes. "I mean, he didn't promise to fight a duel for your honour, he didn't threaten to kill himself. He didn't even call you his moon and stars and I got that from the most romantically inept person in the room. And you fall for that?" Melissa looked at Sarah in shock; she had not anticipated this response. For the last few months any pretty face made her friend into putty. When overwrought declarations of love were flying about, Sarah made certain that she caught them. Love and related drama was meat and drink to her, it felt strange that she wasn't concocting vast plots to get her and Justin alone and for the briefest of moments she felt upset that she wasn't getting this response.

"I didn't fall for him, I'm just interested. I don't like all that over the top stuff. I'm not a prize to be wooed like that,"

"So instead you prefer a boorish fool who insults you. Well that makes perfect sense to my romance addled brain,"

"I didn't say I preferred him, I just said he interested me," Melissa was getting angry now; she'd supported Sarah through far worse choices. Twisted a piece of the green taffeta between her fingers, she stared at the gold embroidery for several moments, taking the time to calm herself down.

"I wasn't contemplating matrimony,"

"Oh I'm glad to hear it. He has a terrible reputation. He ruins women," Sarah's voice was getting louder and angrier as she spoke. "Not only that, he is a gamester and a cad,"

"Sarah please," Melissa finally held up a hand to forestall the flood of words. There was nothing in that speech that she did not agree with and her friend was right, Justin Lestrade had one of the worst reputations in London, especially worrying since he was so young. He frequently had to leave the capital through one scandal or another. Duelling, wenching or gaming, he was reputed to be quite the terror and yet Melissa could not stop thinking about him. Despite her anger earlier, there was something about him that called to her.

"I know all this about him and I don't love him or anything silly like that. For heaven's sake there wasn't enough time for any of that to happen. I just feel I should know him better,"

"That's the way it starts," Sarah murmured with a wisdom that seemed strange coming from her lips.

"Well. I don't think I will get to know him better. He couldn't even wait for me to finish a hand of Quadrille before he found another," Her voice was hard, determined, and so different from the clamouring in her heart. Yet she had to say it, there was no other way of putting Sarah off. "So you have nothing to worry about, I doubt I will be eloping with Lestrade at any point in the future,"

"Hmm," A suspicious glance swept over her, before Sarah sighed and decided to let the subject drop. "Anyway, did you note Anna's dress? It was positively indecent; I swear that her abigail doesn't like her one bit,"

Melissa sighed with relief as life returned to a more regular footing, she still thought about those hazel eyes but, as Sarah pointed out, why would she be attracted to a boorish fool with a terrible reputation.

"You did well with your dress tonight, green suits you,"

"It's just a shame about the powder, I prefer my real hair to this powdered mummery,"

"I'll tell the court that shall I," Sarah laughed at the look on her friends face. "This is only the height, nay the pinnacle of fashion and you scorn it. For shame girl,"

Melissa shook her head at the mock outrage on her friends face and joined in the general sense of laughter. "So I saw the King tonight," she finally stammered out, desperate to draw the subject away from Justin and any other men in the room.

"Yes, I saw him too, he's barely awake half the time," Sarah said with a lightly bored tone. "There are far more interesting things to look at," She unsheathed her fan and lightly tapped her hands with it. "So.. have you heard about the murders?"

"Murders?" Melissa queried wondering at the change in conversation but not overly shocked by it. Sarah's mind flittered sometimes from subject to subject and it was hard to keep up unless you were used to it.

"Yes the murders. I heard Papa talking about them to Lord Turnville. Apparently there's been a rash of murders in the lower districts…"

"Sarah there's always killings amongst the lower district,"

"Ahh but not like this," Sarah said with a distinctly annoying tone of voice. "A fair few of them are of our class. Apparently they were taken from their beds and brought to London. My father's spent a fortune putting locks on my shutters. It's almost impossible to sleep at night,"

Melissa exclaimed, an incredulous note to her voice. "The talk would be all over the capital and I would have heard about it from Papa," She rolled her eyes and continued. "If only as a warning,"

"You would have heard if the news was being spoken of openly, but its not. You see most of the girls were…" She considered and drew Melissa closer, lowering her voice to a confidential whisper. "Well not particularly modest or well brought up. Known for indiscretion they were, just the type to leave their beds in the dead of night and follow a rake. My father believes that they left home and ran into trouble on the streets," Sarah gave a wry smile. "My father's using it as an object lesson in following the rules of good behaviour,"

"Sarah," Melissa protested with a smile. "You're not overly silly, you wouldn't sneak out to follow some foolish gallant,"

"Oh and how would you know?" She gave a careless toss of her head, making her wig wobble dangerously. Throwing a mysterious smile at her friend, she continued. "You don't know all my secrets,"

"Really?" With a bark of surprised laughter, Melissa stared at Sarah. "Do tell,"

"Not on your life," Sarah glanced over Melissa's shoulder and smiled broadly at the sight behind her before turning an apologetic glance towards her friend.

"I'm sorry but I promised Lord Carlson the next dance," She was already moving as she spoke to reach the side of her latest flame. "We'll talk later I promise," And with that she was swept back into the crowd, leaving Melissa alone in the corner watching the dancing couples with a wry smile on her face. She might have known that Sarah would not stay with her long.

"May I have the next dance?" A richly dressed young man held out his hand toward her and after a moment's hesitation, she took it. Leaving behind her thoughts about Lestrade for the time being, she threw herself back into the ball. She danced, flirted, smiled and accepted invitations. At least twice she saw Justin on the edges of the crowd, yet he was talking with Mary and did not look towards her. Irritated by his lack of regard, she moved away from him and inwardly fumed at his attitude and her willingness to see good in him.

"May I cut in?" She started as Lord Montjoy spoke at her elbow, his pale eyes regarding her partner with a mild curiosity. Blanching slightly, the callow youth on her arm moved aside, leaving Montjoy to catch hold of her.

"I was hoping to get a dance," His voice was sibilant in her ear and her skin crawled at the suggestive notes that flowed across his words. Still, he could do nothing untoward in the middle of such a crowd and she didn't want to make a scene. A polite smile edged over her features, hiding the revulsion she felt at his touch as they began to dance.

"You've been extremely well received," he murmured against her ears as they moved through several complicated steps. "You are a goddess here you see," The words which she had heard from gallants the whole night sounded ominous falling from his lips and she suppressed a shudder. He manoeuvred her through the crowd, his steps sure and strong as the music dragged on prolonging Melissa's discomfort. Throughout the dance, Montjoy kept whispering in her ear and though she managed to kept her distaste from him, she still froze inwardly every time he opened his mouth. They had been dancing for perhaps two minutes, when Melissa became aware that he was subtly moving them away from the main hallway and its throng of people and toward the gardens.

"Excuse me," She spoke politely and tried to pull away,

mindful of her mother's warnings. She didn't want to be caught alone in the gardens with Montjoy. One glance at the hot, intense gaze in his eyes told her that his intentions were anything but honourable.

"I'd prefer to stay within," Swallowing the panic that threatened to overwhelm her, Melissa came to a stop and tried to move away from him.

"But it's quite loud and over-populous in here," Montjoy's voice slithered over her objections and he kept walking towards the door. "We can't conduct proper conversation in this crowd," In response to her feeble efforts for freedom, his hand tightened on her wrist and he pulled her forward. It would now take a strong wrench of his arm to pull free and that would create a fuss she could little afford. In desperation, she flicked her eyes over the crowd hoping to catch someone's eye, yet Montjoy had placed his body between her and much of the soiree and no one came to her rescue.

"I have another dance sir, I do not wish to be late," She spoke more forcefully, trying to pull her hand away yet his grip was strong and he still drew her onward, towards the yawning doors and the dark gardens beyond.

"It won't take a moment; there is something I wish to show you," His arm dropped to her waist and slid about it with a creeping familiarity. His fingers settled beneath her ribs and as the shock of his audacity flooded her veins, Melissa ceased her attempts at politeness. Anger boiled through her. How dare this abhorrent rake place his hands on her? Scarcely taking the time to think, she rounded on him, bright spots of vivid colour shining through the powder on her cheeks.

"LET ME GO," Her voice snarled out between her lips with a volume that surprised even her. Even as the words left her mouth, she was pulling her hand back to shoulder height and as her shout reverberated around the room, she let fly. With a loud crack, her hand connected with his cheek as she slapped him with as much power as she could muster. "I do not wish to walk in the gardens with you," The sound of flesh striking flesh and her loud exclamation echoed through the hall and drew the immediate attention of the soiree. People near them stopped dancing, their eyes fixed on the spectacle with shock and interest. Near the buffet, Sarah looked up and stared at Melissa with a troubled look on her face. Several of her gallants from earlier began pushing their way through the room towards them and out of the corner of her eye, she saw Justin, The blue clad noble was stood near the main doors, his hand on Mary's arm and his eyes fixed on her. His face was hard to read, yet his eyes never left her even as Mary muttered something in his ear.

"You she-devil," Montjoy hissed as he raised a hand to his reddened cheek, his eyes blazed, wounded pride and anger battling in his watery gaze. "I'll teach you.," Oblivious to the scene around him and angry, he raised his fist against her and struck downwards only to have the strike thwarted by a strong hand.

"You dare raise your vile hand to my sister?" Marcus' voice was low and shot through with menace as he painfully twisted Montjoy's arm. Around them, the crowd was still, everyone watching the action with shock. "You even conceive of it? How dare you sir,"

"She...," Montjoy stammered, looking at the deadly gleam in Marcus' eyes and realised his error. A panicked look about the room revealed his lack of allies. Several of Melissa's dance partners from earlier stared at him with something akin to hatred and most of the other ball goers whispered about him.

"For this insult to her honour I will meet you on the morrow," He released Montjoy's wrist and stared at him full in the face. "Unless you are too craven to attend,"

Montjoy's eyes glittered and he nodded slowly, casting a vicious glance in Melissa's direction as he strode from the ball.

"Did Father not warn you of him?" Marcus watched Montjoy leave before he turned to face his younger sister. "The man's a blight on polite society. He's a villain of the highest order and you put yourself in his path. What the deuce were you thinking?"

"I only danced with him to be polite," Melissa protested at the tone in her brother's voice. She had not anticipated this turn of events and she still felt shaken. The thought that Montjoy would try to manoeuvre her forcibly from the events had not occurred to her and her fingers still stung from slapping his cheek. Her gaze flickered over the crowd, it was also clear that she would be the talk of the town for this little episode,

"Well you shouldn't have," Marcus' voice dragged her

back from her thoughts and he looked down at her with a disapproving expression on his face. "You don't have to dance with all that crave your company. I fancy my dear sister that you have a good deal to learn about society. Maybe you should talk to your friend; she knows how to deal with those of that sort,"

"Perhaps if she'd spent more than ten minutes with me I would have learnt something," Melissa snapped back at him, angry at herself for not realising that she could have turned the man down and angry at Marcus for pointing it out. She had only been polite, why was Marcus turning this into her fault. Angry tears pricked at her eyes and she blinked furiously, determined not to cry.

"And stop acting as though it were my fault, I didn't ask you to play my saviour,"

"Nevertheless sister dearest, I am honour bound to defend your good name. He would have struck you, should I have let him?"

"No of course not but…"

"Then don't be so stupid. I will meet Montjoy on the morn and he will learn manners on the end of my blade,"

That's if he doesn't strike you first

"Now I think we've caused enough upset, I think it's time to go," He captured her hand and they walked towards the doors.

"Do we have to tell Papa?" Melissa asked as they reached the hallway and moved through the crowd.

"Well we can hardly keep it secret," Marcus nodded at a small group of women gossiping in the corner. "You're the talk of the night? I think mama will want to keep you home for several days until the scandal has died down,"

"Not what I wanted to be noted for.," Melissa sniffed as they reached the study and her father. "And where is Sarah?" She looked about her, wondering why her friend had chosen this moment to abandon her.

"I don't know, but I'm not looking for her," Marcus walked into study and crossed the crowded room, heading for their father.

Melissa glanced around the hall, feeling the eyes on her as she waited. It was uncomfortable and she knew that she was the subject on everyone's lips. Trying to ignore the stares, she gazed into the study and watched Marcus reach her father's side.

"Oh I can't believe you did that," She turned at the words and looked at Sarah with a grateful smile. "I mean he did deserve it, but he would have struck you,"

"I wasn't going to let him take me out there," Melissa retorted, remembering the anger that coursed through her as she realised what he meant to do. "Did you want me to meekly go with him?"

"Of course not, but why didn't you just excuse yourself?"

"I tried but he was pinching my arm," She held up her wrist and showed the reddened marks made by his fingers. "Perhaps I should have called for help from another, but I barely know some of these men and why should I have to?" A great sense of injustice flowed within her. "I slapped him for heaven's sake and now Marcus is going to duel him tomorrow,"

"Yes I wouldn't worry about that," Sarah replied. "Montjoy is a poor duellist. Your brother will mark him and then that odious individual will leave court for several years! I would worry more about your own future," Her friend's face took on a more concerned cast. "That little burst of anger will cost you dear, I saw several potential suitors for you turn their eyes away in disgust,"

"Sarah," Melissa protested; worry flooding through her in an instant.

"Well it's true, you just demonstrated conduct unbecoming for a lady and as it is your first day on the scene it hasn't helped. You have to be demure,"

"I know that," Melissa's voice was wrung with agony as she realised the enormity of what she had done.

"You should have had the vapours or fainted," Sarah persisted, seemingly determined to lay salt on the wound.

"I know," In a paroxysm of misery Melissa bent her head back into the lace handkerchief, wiping the hot salty tears into the white fabric.

"Melissa," Her father's voice drew her attention and she looked up as Edward De Vire walked towards them.

"Well I guess he knows," She stepped forward and hugged Sarah farewell, feeling her anxiety rise even further. "Hopefully I'll see you tomorrow,"

"Of course," Sarah replied, stepping away as Melissa's father approached the door.

"We're going home," Edward announced in a voice like thunder as he reached the threshold. In a stony silence, her father led her from the Palace and out into the cool night air. Melissa did not attempt conversation; her father's anger was a palpable force that she feared to test. As she waited for Marcus and her mother to leave the building and as a distraction from her father's raw fury, Melissa turned her head to stare back at the Palace. A lone figure detached itself from the shadows by the exit and walked into the illumination from the carriage lamps. The light bouncing off powdered hair and a bejewelled coat drew her attention. Justin's eyes met hers and he took a hesitant step forward. His face was softer, less mocking than it had been within the ball and he seemed all the more attractive for it. At that moment, her mother and brother left the palace and walked towards them. Her mother was thin lipped and angry and barely spared her a glance as she walked past her towards the waiting coach.

"Into the carriage," Melissa ducked her head and climbed into the coach. She sat and stared out of the curtained window. Justin still stood there, face in shadow beneath the glare of the light. As her mother and Marcus stepped through the doors, he was joined by Mary Westbury and she drew him away towards the Palace. As they pulled away she took one last look at his dark form before he faded from sight. Behind her Justin watched her leave, an enigmatic gleam deep within his eyes as the carriage disappeared from view.

They rode home in silence, Melissa glancing at her father surreptiously as the carriage rumbled over the cobbled streets. Marcus attempted idle banter but his voice sounded thin, lost in the uncomfortable silence caused by their Fathers' displeasure. After a long tense ride, the carriage clattered to a stop before the large town house they rented for the season. As the servants rushed to lower the steps, Melissa risked a glance at her father and she was not cheered by the stony look on his face.

"In the parlour," Melissa's father snapped at her as they moved through the house doors and into the candlelit hallway. Swallowing nervously Melissa moved into the parlour. The fire had been lit in the grate and her father stood before it, his face forbidding in the shadows cast by the orange flames.

"What do you have to say about that disgusting display of poor breeding?" Edward DeVire wasted no time and his voice lashed across the room, pitiless and cold.

"He was rude to me Father…" Melissa stammered out but Edward's upraised hand stopped her.

"I have never felt so ashamed of you. You are a member of the quality and you behaved with all the social grace of a common housemaid. How dare you act like a vicious wildcat on heat? Whatever his offences, you had no reason to strike him and even less reason to be in his company," Melissa tried once again to speak, yet his voice drowned her out. "I am ashamed to have brought you out. You have humiliated your family and yourself. Clearly you are not ready for the season. After Marcus' duel tomorrow we are returning to the country and you will figure out your priorities. Now get out of my sight,"

Repressing the tears of anger that threatened to spill down her cheeks, Melissa ran out of the room, past the parlour maid and up the wide stairs. Her taffeta gown rustled like fallen leaves as she raced to her room. Slamming the door she behind her, she reached her dressing table and stared at her angry reflection. Tears of white hot fury spilled down her cheeks, making runs in the perfect white lead mask. Beneath her pale and fuming face, the emeralds in her necklace winked in the light.

"How dare he?" She seized hold of the chain and pulled the glimmering necklace from her neck, scoring a thin red mark across her skin as she did so. With a flick of her wrist she threw it across the room. It hit the wall with a heavy thunk and slid to the floor behind one of the armoires. She then flung herself across the bed and sobbed bitterly into the thick damask pillows.

"Melissa?" Her brother had followed her into the room. She felt the bed sink as he settled his weight onto it. "Don't worry about Father. He will forgive you,"

"I should not need forgiveness," Her voice, muffled by the pillow, was hard and full of anguish. "Why is it my fault for him trying to force me from the room? He bruised my wrists as he tried to drag me out of there. Why am I being punished for defending myself?" Marcus opened his mouth to speak, but Melissa hadn't finished. "I wish I had been born a man, then I could duel the bastard myself,"

Marcus sighed once and rested his strong fingers on her shoulder. "I understand how you feel…"

"No you don't," She pulled herself out of the pillow and stared at him, her face flushed and smeared with powder and tears. "You have freedom that I can only dream about,"

She pulled a handkerchief from a pocket and blew her nose. "If you wish to go to the theatre you can go. If I wish to go to the theatre, I have to wait for a chaperone," Marcus nodded and once again tried to interrupt, but Melissa's voice overrode him. "If you wish to drive through St. James you can, I am not even allowed on the street accompanied or not," Pulling the handkerchief from her face, she turned bright angry eyes on her brother. "But I can be blamed for a man's behaviour. I can be assaulted and have it be my fault. You don't walk in my shoes brother, so how can you understand?" She turned away from him and flung herself back onto the pillow. "Get out of here Marcus, I don't want to talk to you right now,"

Marcus looked at her for several long moments as his mouth worked soundlessly. What could he say? He hesitated for a moment and gently pressed her shoulder, feeling the sobs ripple through her skin.

"Get some sleep Melly," She did not answer yet he hadn't expected one. Getting to his feet, he crossed the room and picked up the necklace. The clasp was broken and useless and he placed it in his pocket. "I'll have this fixed for you," He murmured as he headed for the door. "I know I can't understand fully, but I am here for you," And with that, he walked through the door and closed it quietly behind him.

CHAPTER 3

In the early hours of the morning, a lone rider made his way towards Maybury Hall. The old edifice had become occupied only recently and the building was not fully habitable. Parts of the structure still lay in ruins and blackened stone told of some distant fire. Justin Lestrade rode his horse into the stables and roused the groom, a small close mouthed individual, who took the reins without comment. Leaving the horse in the capable hands of his servant, Justin strode into the courtyard and stared up at the house. A mainly medieval structure, the manor house loomed over the solitary figure. Its battlements stood stark and ruined against the moonlit night. Lights shone in few of the windows, indicating sparse occupation and the door did not open at his approach. Servants were few and far between within the walls of this house, in fact there was only one in residence. Striding through the newly restored hallway, Justin removed his riding cape and gloves and tossed them on the stairs. Poking his head into the parlour, he glanced at the empty armchair beside the fire with a troubled gaze. It was the fifth night in a row that he had come home to this scenario. Turning back into the hall, he strode back out into the night. In the stables, he found Coll rubbing down the bay mare he had rode in on.

"Is my brother about?" He asked as Coll looked up at him.

"He went out Master Lestrade," Coll's voice was deep and gentle, the kind of voice that people stopped to listen to, the kind of voice that people trusted.

"When?"

"Not half hour after you went. I saddled Thunder for him,"

Justin considered this. His brother showed little interest in courtly amusements, yet he did not know where he went. His brow furrowed in thought as he ran through possibilities in his mind. Alistair didn't have a fancy as far as he knew and he had given gaming houses up recently.

"Send him to me when he returns. Tell him I'll be in the parlour,"

"Very good sir,"

Justin left the stables and returned to the house. The acquisition of this ruin troubled the cream of London, yet to him it was home, even more so than the fine modern accommodation he had secured in the capital. Most people would not understand how much this near ruin meant to him. None were allowed to visit him here; this was his hideaway, the small piece of his past that would always be home, no matter how long he stayed away. He crossed the hall, the noise of his steps echoing to the gallery above. This part of the house was the newest; the wooden balustrade above was all that remained of the large minstrel's gallery and the staircase now led to the only liveable apartments in the old place. Much of the house had been destroyed by fire a century or so before and restoration was slow work.

He sat in the chair and stared at the flames dancing in the fireplace and turned his mind back to the evening and the distractions he threw himself into. There was precious little entertainment to be had at court and it was a diversion he sorely needed. His situation demanded it, if he didn't have his diversions, he would surely go mad.

He stretched out his foot to the flames and picked a stray thread from his sleeve as his thoughts roamed over the ball's occupants. His current flame was Mary Westbury, an overly clingy female who was quite ready to run off with him to Gretna. He was giving serious thought to ending the relationship, but who would he take in her stead? Elinor Marling was available and more than once her eyes had sought him out on the dance floor, yet Elinor would bore him, he could see that without even attempting to woo her, the unfortunate girl held no more interest than a pail of pump water. Sarah Davenport was a good choice, she had cast her spell on most of the young man around her, yet she knew a good deal and was far too sensible, she also giggled incessantly. It was no fun seducing one who would annoy him beyond all reason. His fingers ran over the smooth surface of the bottle as he discarded female after female, he was beginning to wonder if his boredom was more pervasive than he initially thought.

Melissa

The girl's name burst into his thoughts and his mouth opened in shock, he had almost forgotten her, strange as it seemed. Her first night in society had proven to be the most interesting night he'd had there in years. His mind's eye ran over his image of her, a vision in stunning green. Her eyes had trapped him and the intelligence and strength he had seen within beckoned to him. She was a force to consider, she had caused a huge stir, her beauty had dazzled the room, yet he could feel that there was more to her than that. It was this feeling that had driven him to seek her out, yet he had not charmed her. He recalled his words with a shudder of regret, wondering what had driven him to answer so poorly. Melissa De Vire had something to her, beyond that of a usual social butterfly; he had seen something in her eyes something that intrigued him and yet he had pushed her away. He ignored the thought that he had found someone who could understand him and turned to her altercation with the odious Montjoy. The rake deserved more than the slap she had dealt him and he hoped that her older brother would deliver the chastisement needed. The girl had verve; he couldn't imagine any other woman reacting to Montjoy's attentions with such spirit. He smiled at the image of Melissa's fingers striking the man's face and he regretted his flippant approach to her. He had damaged his chances, but he could have her should he wish it. He hesitated at the thought. Did he really want to seduce her as all the others?

He swallowed another slug of the whisky and considered the problem. Melissa had something more to her; there was something in her eyes that held him. She had smiled at him and his thoughts had muddied, confused by her. In his bewilderment, words had snarled free, speaking his thoughts as though called by her clear gaze. And she had answered him back, her own temper rising above the politeness required by her station. He smiled at her audacity and wondered if it had been that which had triggered his uncharacteristic apology. Ordinarily he would chalk up the loss and return to the room, yet he had felt compelled to apologise. He had used words that had been sincere and from the heart and then he had left, worried by the way her smile tugged at him. He had not returned to claim a dance, preferring Mary and her uncomplicated company. Yet he could not banish her from his thoughts. He needed to talk to her again. She would undoubtedly hold his failure to return against him, yet he was confident in his powers of persuasion. As he knocked back another slug, he ignored the small voice that was telling him to leave the girl; that thinking of her was dangerous and tempting him to break a vow. He also ignored the even smaller voice that suggested that Melissa could handle the secrets that he carried on his shoulders like weights. With a sneer at his old romantic notions that could only come to naught, he lifted the bottle again to his lips.

He drained the last dregs of the bottle and threw it into a corner where it smashed into pieces. Justin did not notice the sound of glass breaking as he stared into the blazing fire, his thoughts drifting back along the years, back further than anyone would have thought. Everyone who met him alluded to his maturity, how much older he seemed to be than his looks. Men and women commented on his cynical and jaded approach to life, some seeing it as an affectation that he had taken to displaying yet the truth was far stranger and much more tragic. As he sometimes did at times like this, he touched a finger to the enamel flower at his neck and wondered once again how his life should have gone and why he spent nights following the fashion in the capital and thinking up new ways to amuse himself. He wanted to tell someone about the nightmare of his life, yet there was no one who would understand. Even if he did dream about confiding in a girl like Melissa, what could she do about it? He hadn't found a solution even after all this time. How much use would she be?

The fire popped and drew him from his brooding thoughts. He glanced at the clock on the mantle and pursed his lips, Alistair was exceptionally late and while he didn't keep tabs on his brother, he did worry about him. It was a habit that he hadn't been able to break even after all these years. Alistair would not thank him for his worry; in fact he would probably feel a perverse sense of satisfaction that Justin had spent an evening in concerned silence. He sighed and stood, his fine evening wear was crumpled and his valet was currently installed at the far more proper town house. He struggled out of the fine garments and pulled on different ones, more comfortable garb for relaxing in his parlour. His fingers pulled off the brooch and he placed it on the mantle where it brooded darkly. It was late and he couldn't drag his mind away from the nightmares in his past. The lotus reminded him of his folly and when it did not, his brother filled the gaps. He sank back in the chair and pressed his hands over his eyes. This nightmare had to end, one way or another, despite his efforts to divert himself from the horror he lived in, he still felt it late in the night. Sat in the chair, with the warming affects of alcohol flowing through his veins, he drifted off into an uneasy doze, the only sleep he ever managed these days.

Something cold pressed against his neck and his eyes jerked open. Standing above him, shadowed by the light of the fire, was his brother. A thin bladed knife rested lightly in Alistair's hands and the cool metal pressed against the thin skin of his throat.

"Evening Alistair," Justin's voice was light and untroubled; he ignored the pressure of the knife at his neck as he looked upwards at his brother's form. Alistair had darker hair and his eyes were a warm brown, yet of late they held all the appeal of the grave. Alistair had not adjusted well to their new existence and from time to time Justin worried about his once happy and kind brother. Still given what the others had done with their time, it could have been worse.

"Was your night entertaining?" He stared at the heavy lace on the cuffs of Alistair's shirt and wondered briefly why he was being civil.

"About as usual," Alistair Lestrade stared at his older brother with a sneer. He did not lose his hold on the knife and a thin bead of blood escaped from the skin at Justin's throat. "Were you waiting up for me brother?"

"Not so you'd notice," Justin sent his brother an irritated smile. "Do you mind moving the knife? I don't want blood on this jacket," Alistair sighed and stepped back, his dark eyes observing his brother with cool detachment.

"So have you managed to find the answer to our predicament in the arms of some blue blooded wench?" There was a bitter note to his laughter and Justin winced inwardly at the change in his brother's manner. He glanced at the knife, at the enamel lotus set into the handle.

"I hope you're not planning to stab anyone with that," He indicated the knife and stood up. Crossing to the fire, he poked the glowing embers into sullen life. "Murder would be awkward to deal with,"

"If stabbing you would get me results I would have done it years ago. Unfortunately we both know that it won't work," He pointed at the enamel brooch on the mantle. "I notice that yours is still filling the role of jewellery,"

"I like it close," Justin reached over to the table and hefted another bottle, with a quick motion he threw it towards Alistair. His brother caught it one handed and took a long drink.

"So how about you?" He leant against the edge of the

sideboard and regarded his sibling with a curious look. "Has your night-time roaming come up with anything substantial?"

"Of course it hasn't," Alistair snapped back. "When you get us in trouble, you manage to really do it thoroughly,"

Justin ignored the words, he had listened to hundreds of variations on this speech and he could recite each word in his sleep. It didn't help that Alistair was right, had he been sensible, or at the very least cautious, they would not be in this predicament. Still, he hated to be reminded of his follies by his brother.

"So glad I could oblige," He took another long drink and regarded his brother's angry features. "Have you spoken to the others recently?"

"No," Alistair took a swig from the bottle in his hand and stared at the floor distractedly. "I haven't seen any of them for a number of years now," Alistair glanced up at his brother and raised an eyebrow. "Have you?"

Justin nodded, placing the bottle back on the sideboard, "I see Emily from time to time," He stared down at the faded glory of the sideboard, cracks from age and misuse had destroyed the heavy but once beautifully carved piece of furniture. "She's still passing herself off as the bereft widow of an elderly noble," He absently traced his finger across the whorls in the wood, memories of a long dead past threatening to choke him.

Alistair chuckled mirthlessly. "That's our Emily, the noble whore..,"

"Don't start Alistair," Justin turned back to his brother

with a sigh, "Emily has fewer options than we do,"

"Yes and one more crime to lay at your door," Alistair snarled back, slamming his bottle down onto the table as though to punctuate his words. "She must think she has entered hell,"

"Actually, she is doing fine," A loud, amused voice echoed through the room, cutting across their conversation. Justin pushed himself away from the sideboard, reaching for the rapier he kept in the corner as his brother whirled to face the door, dagger held tightly in his fingers.

"Now now boys; is there any need for that?" Leaning against the doorframe with an expression of amused nonchalance on her delicate features, was Emily Saint-Clair. In contrast to the immaculately coiffered temptress of earlier, she was clad in man's breeches teamed with a frilled shirt and long waistcoat; her blonde hair was tied at the nape of her neck beneath a man's tricorn hat and a riding crop twirled idly between her fingers.

"Very nice," Justin noted as his gaze swept across her form with a deliberate leer, "you look," He settled against the sideboard, his rapier falling to the floor. "delectable,"

"You're looking particularly fine yourself," She answered his sensual gaze with one of her own as she pushed herself away from the doorframe and stepped forward. "Quite desirable," She purred the words as she walked further into the room.

"Heaven forefend," Alistair rolled his eyes and replaced the dagger in his belt. "Don't you get enough of this empty flirting at your.," His mouth twisted into a grimace as he spoke. "parties,"

"Oh good gracious no," Justin smiled and winked at the blonde. "It helps make life bearable," He turned his gaze back to his brother and his smile froze. "Much as empty religious mouthing does for you," Alistair lunged forward, only to have his arm seized by Emily.

"Enough," She hissed, her voice no longer playful, "This isn't why I travelled here tonight," She glowered at Justin, who shrugged and leant back against the sideboard.

"Why did you come here?" Alistair snarled, pulling his arm free and retreating to the far side of the table. "I thought you were cultivating another husband,"

"Yes I heard you," She walked forward and sat on the sideboard. "I can cultivate my next match and still keep in touch with you two," Her fingers trailed onto Justin's upper arm. "We all need to stick together and besides you two are my favourites,"

"Maybe that's even true," Justin allowed her to stroke the back of his neck. "but you never come here without a good reason,"

"Darling you wound me," Her fingers reached into his hair and he closed his eyes, savouring the sensation as she gently massaged his scalp. "Can you not just accept that I like your company?" She moved closer, her lips brushing his cheek. He shivered at the contact, familiarity not diluting the impact of her touch.

"Oh I can accept it," He turned his head and felt her breath drift over his lips. "and I must admit that your company has a certain charm," He could almost feel her smile as she reached forward.

"I can't believe you two," Justin's eyes snapped open and he turned to face Alistair. His brother's face was crimson with pent up rage and he was spluttering incoherently. "Have you no shame?"

"If this bothers you," Emily noted with no small amusement, "then don't look," Her fingers slid across Justin's face and she drew him closer. He wet his lips and leant in for a tender kiss. From the corner of his eye, he watched as his brother stomped towards the door and out of the room. Suppressing the desire to laugh, he held the kiss for a few more seconds before pulling back and away from Emily.

"You're a very bad girl," He noted with a wry laugh. "What would you have done if he had stayed?"

"Kissed you some more," Her voice was matter of fact, a far cry from the kittenish seductive tones of earlier. "He wouldn't have stayed,"

"Surely there are easier and less obvious ways of getting me alone?" He returned to his chair and sat down.

"Justin," She chided, her lips pursing into a mockery of a pout. "I thought you liked my kisses,"

"Oh I do," He levered his legs onto the table and relaxed, "but you only play like this when you want something," He raised his hand and beckoned her forward. "What do you want this time?"

"I was thinking about this evening," She reached the table and sat down, nonchalantly playing with the riding crop between her fingers, "and one part of it intrigued me above all the others,"

"Oh?" Justin rested his head on the back of the chair and stared at her, "Which part?"

"My darling Justin, you know which part," The riding crop briefly tapped against his legs in gentle chastisement.

"You're going to have to be specific; after all, it's been a busy night," With a smile, he leant forward and tugged the crop from her fingers. "And you can't expect me to remember all of your amorous adventures," He laid the whip across his knees and smoothed down his shirt.

"Don't be a bore my darling," Emily's eyes flashed with annoyance and she nearly reached for the crop. Thinking better of it, she rested her hands on her chin. "I'm not talking about myself, but rather that charming hellcat you were talking to," With a careless hand, she removed the hat and let it fall to the table. He watched it settle against the satiny wood before returning his attention to her blue gaze.

"Really and why is that?" A troubling thought flowed through his mind as he regarded the blonde. Emily was no slouch in the brains department and if anyone could figure out his interest, then it would be her.

"Well not many women would slap a man during their debut, but my interest has been piqued about you," Justin sighed inwardly and stood up, taking the crop with him.

"And what, precisely, has captured your interest?"

"Well," She turned to follow him, reaching his side with delicate movements. "You spoke with her, turned on the charm and then," She waved her hands before him, "and then, nothing. No dance, no kiss," Emily turned away and paced towards the door. "You're never this inept, I was watching her face, you had her eating out of your hand and then," She looked back at him and shrugged. "Nothing," A tiny laugh, amused yet somehow disbelieving, escaped her lips. "I don't believe I've ever seen you fail before,"

Justin sighed and pushed himself away from the sideboard. "Well thank you for the boost to my ego. It's a pleasant observation but hardly accurate. I don't win all the time you know,"

Emily smiled a strange catlike grin that spoke volumes. "Nice try darling," She walked forward and pressed a hand against his chest. He stilled as she moved in again. "You like her," It wasn't a question, Justin felt his guts clench at the sure clear knowledge in her gaze.

"That's an interesting insight on the strength of one solitary meeting," He tapped the riding crop against his leg, the slight movement giving him focus and chance to think. Her fingers were splayed against his chest and he stared down at her fine hand, wondering if pulling her in for a kiss would put her off. A long moment of silence passed between them before he finally spoke. "She wasn't my type," Stepping back, he watched her hand fall back to her side and he took a breath. "She was too much of an innocent,"

"That's never dissuaded you before," Sultry, teasing notes laced her words. "You can tell me,"

"No Emily," The words snapped across the space and she stared at him, watching the motion of the crop against his thigh with interest. "I have no interest in Melissa De Vire, beyond the realisation that she is desirable, please leave it at that," He held out the crop and pushed himself away from the sideboard. "Now unless you have anything else of substance to tell me, I'm going to bed,"

"Do you want company?" Emily took the crop and retreated back into flirting, sensible enough to know when she was entering dangerous territory.

"Not tonight," Justin answered, grateful that Emily had let go of the subject. He wasn't entirely sure of what had happened with the De Vire girl, and he didn't want Emily spreading unfounded gossip.

"Pity," Emily reached for her hat and placed it on her head. "Well I shall see you at Lord Carson's," She reached his side and kissed him lightly on the cheek and his skin prickled pleasurably at the sensation. "Though I do think you are lying," Her voice whispered, tickling as it drifted across his ear. "Have a pleasant evening darling," She called as she pushed herself away from him and headed for the door.

"Good night Emily," Justin responded, not stopping the irritation from filling his voice. "and try to keep your theories to yourself,"

"I'll try darling," Emily carolled as she headed out through the door and into the hall. Justin could hear her shouting farewells to Alistair as she headed down the hall and he swore under his breath. Emily saw far too much and this was one thing he didn't want to reach the others.

"She's not spending the night then," He turned to see

Alistair standing at the door. "At least you have some morals,"

"I'm not in the mood brother," Justin replied. "I'm tired,"

"Well we both know that's a lie," Alistair sneered as he let Justin go past, "But I'll let it go this time,"

"Thank you for you forbearance," Justin rolled his eyes and walked into the hall. "Don't look for me tomorrow as I'm heading into the city, now my house is established properly I should be available,"

"Still playing the court, is this going to be the rest of eternity for you? Stood in rooms filled with vapid ladies and boring men?"

"Well it beats sitting in draughty halls bemoaning my fate," He turned away from his brother and headed for the stairs, not even bothering to check the damage to his throat as he passed the large mirror in the hall. With sure steps he made his way to his room and readied himself for bed. He thought of the duel in the morning and vowed to watch her brother fight Montjoy. It would kill several hours at the very least. He pulled back the hangings on the great old bed and lay down, his eyes staring at the canopy above him. He thought of Alistair and his assertion that he would kill him if he knew that would end the curse. Justin didn't doubt that Alistair meant it; his brother had lost most of his lightness because of what he, Justin, had done. If he hadn't touched what he shouldn't have, they would both be better off. He tossed in the heavy blanket, Alistair was right to hate him. His actions had damned them both and ruined many others. As the oblivion of sleep drew nearer, his thoughts left his brother and turned to Emily and the danger she posed. Still she didn't have much to go on and he had made a promise, it was only a matter of whether he could keep it. At least he only had to worry about his brother and Emily this time. Should any of the others return to England he would have to move on. His last thoughts before sleep claimed him were of a young woman in green with sparkling eyes.

CHAPTER 4

Melissa woke the following morning, convinced that she was responsible for Marcus going to his death. As the first light of dawn stole over the rented London house, she was already awake and sat at the window. Jane remonstrated with her for sitting in a draught without a comforter, but she barely heard the words. Her mind was fixed on the duel ahead, on her brother and Montjoy. As Jane dressed her, she spoke little, moving like a dummy or doll to the instructions she was given.

"It'll be alright My Lady," Jane said as she pinned her hair beneath a filmy bonnet. "Your brother is skilled with a blade. He will win today,"

Melissa did not answer, unwilling to voice the fears

she had. Standing, she turned to the door and headed downstairs to the morning room and breakfast. Her brother was already sat at the dining table eating a hearty repast.

"Marcus," He looked up at her, a forkful of eggs and bacon in his hand and Melissa hesitated. Why did he have to risk himself to defend her?

"Be careful this morning," Her voice was soft and trembled slightly as her fingers dug into the palms of her hands. The desire to ask him to stop the duel nearly choked her but she managed to hold back the words.

Marcus smiled "Don't worry, I am not ignorant of duels, I will certainly try not to let him strike me," He returned to his breakfast as their parents walked in

"Morning," Edward sat at the head of the table and stared at his children. "Marcus, make sure you coat your hands in dust before the duel, it will stop the blade from slipping," He offered the piece of advice to his son with concern, but when he turned his gaze upon Melissa, she was disappointed to see the dissatisfaction and anger still in his eyes. With a huffed sigh, he unfurled his paper and ignored her presence. Melissa bit her lip and stared at the white tablecloth, upset with her father's reaction. She knew from experience that he would not stay angry for long, but she felt angry that he blamed her for something that was not her fault. She didn't ask for Montjoy to attempt to force her from the ball, and he had deserved the slap she had given him, she didn't need to feel as though the situation was her responsibility. Melissa placed a handful of eggs on her plate and took a bite, tasting nothing but sawdust as she chewed. As she ate her breakfast she was aware of her mother watching her, she knew that her mother wasn't in agreement with her father, but that didn't help. Her mother still kept her peace and didn't openly agree with her daughter's actions. She looked down at the congealed mass of food on her plate and pushed it away.

Marcus glanced across and winked, before he stood. "Well time to head out," Melissa stared at her brother with her heart in her throat. Visions of Marcus returning to the house covered in blood flashed through her mind and she felt sick. Rushing across the room, she threw her arms around him.

"Please be careful,"

His hand rested gently against her hair as he murmured, "I will," He glanced up at his father.

"Are you coming sir?"

"Hmm," Edward De Vire returned the paper to the table and stood. Lydia also got to her feet and she lightly tugged Melissa away from her brother before bestowing a kiss on her son's forehead.

"Good luck," She kissed her husband and watched as both men walked out into the hall. The front door banged shut, the sound making Melissa think of coffin lids and she stared down at her feet feeling tears prick the back of her eyes

"Well all we can do now is wait," Her mother noted as she glanced at her daughter, noting the pale cast to her skin. "Come on,"

Melissa nodded and turned to follow her mother from the room. She wished that she would be allowed to watch the duel, but it wasn't done. With a heavy heart she headed to the morning room. The sun streaked through the tall windows and bounced off the brass in the grate. Above the fire, a portrait of George De Vire hung, his sombre gaze staring down at his descendents in what Melissa considered to be disapproval. Her mother sat down behind the desk and began her morning's correspondence, her elegant hand flowing across the heavy parchment with ease. At her mother's instruction she sat on one of the couches and drew out her needlepoint, yet she could not concentrate on the delicate stitch work for worry.

"He'll be fine Melissa," Her mother noticed her nervously shifting hands and spoke up, placing her pen down. "Your brother is an excellent duellist; he will be able to handle Montjoy,"

"It's not just that," Her daughter protested, shoving aside the sewing and standing up. With agitated steps she paced over the carpeted floor of the morning room. "Father just blames me for all this. It's not my fault; I was only trying to be polite,"

"Until you slapped him,"

"What else was I supposed to do? Allow him to drag me out of that room and into the garden? I had no idea what he was going to try then," She stopped pacing and stared at her mother, her face flushed with anger. "And somehow, his ungentlemanly conduct is my fault. I don't feel that is fair or justified. Yes I could have refused to dance with him, but that doesn't mean I deserved to have him try to drag me from the room," Her mother tried to interrupt but Melissa kept on speaking, spilling out the words that had been plaguing her all morning.

"I think he should take the full blame for this. Why should I be considered at fault because he can't control his tendencies? It's not fair and it's certainly not right, because of him, my brother may come back wounded,"

"Melissa," Her mother's voice snapped out, drawing her tirade to a sharp close. "Your father doesn't really feel that you are responsible," She held up her hand to forestall any argument. "But he does feel that the situation would not have occurred if you had taken my advice and avoided Montjoy or if you had behaved like a well bred lady and had the vapours. That is what he finds intolerable. Granted your honour is being defended, but you have become the talk of London for scandalous reasons and given that it is only your first introduction to society he fears that this will harm your prospects for future marriage,"

Melissa turned over her mother's words in her mind and tried to find something offensive within her speech, but unfortunately her mother's words made sense. She knew only too well how fragile a women's reputation could be and even though she never believed it was right, there was nothing she could do about it. Taking a deep breath she tried to calm down and see things rationally, yet with her brother risking his life for her honour, she was finding it hard to do so.

"It is for this reason that we are returning to the country

once Marcus has concluded his duel," Lydia continued, watching the play of emotion across her daughter's face. "Give the scandal time to die down; after all, he did attempt to hit you. Perhaps you will be lucky and this will be forgotten,"

"I suppose.,"

"It will," Lydia continued, picking up the discarded sewing from the corner. "We are returning to the country and the scandal will fade. Now," She held out of the small sampler. "Get to work on that and as soon as your brother returns, we will leave for home,"

CHAPTER 5

The ground was crisp with frost as Marcus walked across the park to the location that had been chosen for this morning's duel. His father walked to his left and on his right stood his second, James Smythe. Up ahead, Montjoy and a small crowd waited for his arrival. As he approached, he felt the excitement of the crowd increase. He took several deep breaths, blowing soft clouds of white into the frosty air before he turned to his left.

"Wish me fortune Father," He was pleased to note that his voice did not quaver as he spoke.

His father smiled and clapped a hand against Marcus' back.

"Keep focused and you'll be fine," Edward replied as he

stepped away from his son and joined the crowd.

Taking a very deep breath, Marcus stepped forward, James at his side. The rapier at his waist seemed much heavier than it should have done and his palms grew clammy with sweat despite the temperature. To banish the worrying thoughts that had begun to nag at him, he nodded towards the group that had gathered about them.

"I wasn't expecting a crowd,"

"Be thankful," James answered back, "they'll ensure that it's honestly done," The pair reached the outer edge of the group, which parted to allow them through. As he reached the middle, he caught sight of Justin Lestrade, the younger man was stood talking to Edward Castlemaine,

"Why is Lestrade here?" He muttered as he finally came to a stop in the centre of the circle and began to unlace his coat. A memory from the night before sprang to his mind. As they had clambered into the coach he had seen Lestrade stood outside the Palace and watching as they left. He couldn't have said with any certainty, but he had felt interest in that gaze and now the man was here, watching him duel for his sister's honour. It was not a coincidence, of that Marcus was sure.

"Interested I guess," James replied as he took Marcus's hat and placed it carefully out of sight. "After all, Montjoy needs taking down a peg, he's probably eager to witness it,"

"I daresay," Marcus shrugged out of his coat and shivered as the cold hit him. "What do you know of him?"

"Marcus," James took the offered coat and laid it flat. "You're here for Montjoy, curiosity about the young cad can wait,"

"Are you ready boy?" Montjoy called from across the circle. He was already in shirt sleeves, a rapier naked within his hand.

"More than ready," Marcus reached across and pulled free his own sword. He held it out and swung it twice, testing the weight of the blade. With smooth, clean movements, the rapier pierced the air and he smiled at the seeming ease of the action. He breathed slowly, calming his mind as he readied himself. On the opposite side of the circle, Montjoy was performing similar exercises as their witnesses began to move apart, allowing the duellists room to manoeuvre.

"De Vire," Marcus stopped moving as Justin's voice broke into his thoughts. Startled, he glanced up and stared at the younger man.

"Lestrade?" He lowered his blade slightly. "What can I do for you?"

"I thought I should wish you luck," Justin replied, stepping closer to him and offering his hand.

"Thank you," Marcus shook the man's proffered palm and shook, wondering just what had prompted this display.

"And to give you some advice,"

"You?" Marcus spluttered after a moment's pause. "Give me advice?" He chuckled, surprise and incredulity mixed together at the offer. The man was barely old enough to hold a sword, let alone give out duelling tips. "I'm older than you boy, what advice could you give me. You really shouldn't seek to correct your elders,"

There was the briefest of pauses as Justin looked at Marcus, and then, as though he had heard some great joke, he began to laugh. Loud raucous guffaws of laughter echoed across the park, drawing attention from the onlookers. Confused and slightly resentful of the younger man's mirth, Marcus stepped closer and muttered.

"What is so funny Lestrade?"

"You wouldn't understand," Justin replied as he dabbed at his eyes with a handkerchief. "Though I do recommend you listen to my advice, despite it coming from such a…" His mouth twisted as he tried to hold in another bout of inexplicable laughter. "Young source,"

"Alright," Marcus held up his hand in surrender and motioned for Justin to continue. "Let's hear it,"

"I noticed that Montjoy favours his left side," Marcus' eyes widened as Justin began to speak and his eyes snapped to Montjoy. "If you aim for that you'll tag him faster," Montjoy swung his blade through the air as Marcus watched, noting with growing surprise that the younger man had seen true. He opened his mouth to thank Justin, but the young man had not finished. "Don't play with him, he's a bruiser and will win out by brute force, if you don't snap him fast," Justin reached out a hand and Marcus shook it, stunned by the man's quick, and from what he could see, accurate assessment.

"Thank you,"

"It's nothing, I just want to see you beat him," Justin released his hand and headed back to the crowd. "The bastard deserves it,"

"So we are aware of the rules gentlemen?" The thin form of Lawrence Carnaby called from the other side of the widening circle, distracting Marcus from his contemplation of Justin's words. "The first to draw blood from his opponent wins. Fight with honour gentlemen,"

Pushing aside thoughts of Justin Lestrade, Marcus moved forward into the rough circle, facing Montjoy. A chill breeze ruffled their hair and they touched blades, a bare gesture of respect before Montjoy lunged. Marcus parried the blow, the shock of metal on metal surging up his arm. Before the sound died, Marcus was moving, lunging, aiming for Montjoy's left side. There was a tearing sound as Montjoy's blade ripped through the fabric of his shirt, tearing a long strip through the white expanse. Marcus gritted his teeth and ducked, sliding beneath the next blow as he raised his sword and struck out. The blades connected again, the metallic notes singing in the clear morning air. He could hear the crowd cheering, egging them on, but it was distant, muffled by the roaring of the blood in his ears.

"Pathetic De Vire," Montjoy hissed at him, as their blades connected again and drew them closer, Montjoy's free hand snaking out to seize hold of his shirt. "Is this the best you can do for that whore of a sister?"

Marcus resisted the urge to snarl and he pushed back, his arm extended and knocking Montjoy to the dirt. Rolling, Montjoy avoided the first thrust of his blade, the second tore a hole in his shirt, but drew no blood. From somewhere behind him he could hear James shout, but the words were indistinct.

"Come on De Vire," Montjoy called again as he made it to his feet and avoided Marcus' strike. "I'm sure you can do better," His blade flashed in the early morning sun as it struck and Marcus parried, the impact jarring his arm. His breath came in short gasps as sweat run down his face. Montjoy pressed again and he found himself falling, his foot snared by a stray tree root. With a shout of triumph, Montjoy moved in for the kill. Marcus parried desperately, trying to gain his footing as the older man pressed forward. Rolling to one side, he avoided a piercing thrust to his upper chest. He struck out wildly with his blade, forcing Montjoy back as he found his feet.

With a shaky hand, he wiped the sweat from his eyes and returned to the guard position. Both fighters drew deep shuddering breaths of crisp morning air, tired from their exertions. Marcus scanned his opponent, looking at the solid frame for signs of weakness as the other man moved. He barely managed to parry the heavy blow, retreating back as Montjoy pressed the advantage, landing heavy punishing hits that jolted his arm with each parry.

Montjoy favours his left side.

Lestrade's words echoed through Marcus' head as he dove from another heavy hit. He was tiring fast, his arm unable to withstand the heavy strikes. Sensing victory, Montjoy lunged forward, aiming for Marcus' head. Desperation lent him a speed that he did not think possible, he parried once more and riposted; aiming for Montjoy's left side. The other man was slow to react. Marcus's blade sliced into Montjoy's upper chest and blood seeped onto the white of his shirt. As Marcus pulled the blade free, Montjoy sank to the ground. On the other side of the circle, Justin bowed his head in respect, turned and began to leave.

"I have satisfaction sir," Marcus called as he sank to the ground, exhausted. From the other side of the clearing, Montjoy struggled upright, fury in each line of his face. His seconds moved close and he pushed them back, regaining hold of his sword.

"We're not done De Vire," Marcus stood, ignoring the tiredness that flowed through his body. With a breath of crisp air, he faced Montjoy, holding his sword arm steady as he watched his opponent drag himself upward. "I'm not through with you yet boy," Montjoy was moving slower, the bright blood seeping across his shirt evidence of a severe wound.

"On the contrary, Montjoy, I'd say you need a surgeon," He watched as Montjoy finally pulled himself to his feet and began to walk forward. "Don't be a fool," He uttered, readying himself for the attack to come. "I don't want to have to kill you. You've lost, now go home and heal yourself up,"

"Curse you," With a yell, Montjoy rushed forward, attacking wildly, angrily. Marcus parried furiously, Montjoy's blows were beating him backwards. He knew that Montjoy now aimed to kill and he fought back, mindful of his life. From the sides he could see the others moving, but Montjoy kept on attacking, blind with rage. Marcus felt the blade sing by his ear and he swore. In desperation he riposted clumsily. He managed to strike Montjoy, skewering the man's other shoulder with a ragged cut, yet the awkward manoeuvre sent him off balance. With a shout of triumph Montjoy kicked out. His foot connected with Marcus' upper leg. Marcus, already off balance, could not keep upright and he fell.

"Marcus," He heard James shout as he hit the ground heavily, knocking the wind out of him as his sword flew from his fingers and landed a few feet away. He looked up to see Montjoy headed for him, blade held high. Montjoy brought up the blade and thrust it down, aiming for Marcus' heart. Marcus flinched, closing his eyes, expecting the blow. Yet it did not come, there was the sound of flesh hitting flesh. He opened his eyes and stared upward. James had reached Montjoy and had pulled him to the ground. He watched as his father reached downwards and wrestled the blade from Montjoy's fingers. As a group, they dragged the older man off. Blood poured from the wounds in Montjoy's shoulders and the older man yelped in pain as the crowd about him pulled him away.

"Another time De Vire," Montjoy yelled, his voice losing strength as his life's blood flowed from him.

"Give it up," Marcus picked up his sword as he drew himself upright. Ignoring the tiredness in his limbs, he levelled the point of the blade at Montjoy's throat. "One more move from you sir and I swear you die,"

"Do you think you can kill me boy?" Montjoy's voice was harsh yet growing weaker as the adrenaline that sustained him began to drop. "I nearly had you,"

"You're broke the rules for this combat," James called out, coming close to the pair and placing a placating hand on Marcus' shoulder. "You have no honour sir and you're not welcome in society. Get yourself to a surgeon and then leave London,"

Montjoy made to stand, but his injuries finally seemed to catch up with him and he sank back to the ground in a faint.

"Get him out of here," Marcus backed up, watching as his father directed several others to Montjoy's side before returning to his son.

"Good fight my boy," Edward called as he reached his son's side. "Mayhap he'll learn something from this," He glanced over as Montjoy's friends loaded him into a carriage. "Though I doubt it,"

"Well it's no longer a concern of mine," Marcus replied, drawing a tired arm across his face. "As long as he leaves the country, I have no further interest in that snake,"

"Come on," Edward tugged at Marcus' arm and drew him away. Exhausted and coated in sweat and dust, Marcus allowed his father to lead him away from the park and back to his carriage.

CHAPTER 6

Melissa spent a wretched morning waiting for news. In her agitation she had ruined not one but two samplers and her mother had insisted that she take a walk to cure herself of restlessness. A spell in the garden had helped somewhat yet she did not fully relax until she heard the front door open just before twelve. Determined not to seem overly anxious, she arranged her hands carefully over her sewing and waited. The clock on the mantle ticked slowly, marking out the time as she chewed her bottom lip nervously. From the hallway came the sound of people talking in low whisper and a fist clenched about her heart. Visions of Marcus being carried injured, pale and bleeding through the house assailed her vision and she gasped in sudden fear. Forgetting her desire to appear calm and collected, she pushed herself from her chair in a rush of movement and headed for the door. Her fingers reached for the door handle as the heavy wooden portal yawned wide. Melissa stopped moving and stared. The figure in the doorway was hidden in shade and a terrible foreboding tugged at her pounding heart. As she struggled to form words, the figure stepped forward and was bathed in the early morning sunlight.

"Marcus," Her voice cracked slightly with relief as she took in the form of her rakish older brother. "Marcus," With a cry of relieved happiness she threw herself into his arms and hugged him.

"You're alright. Thank heaven," Marcus staggered a bit as his sister threw herself upon him, yet he quickly recovered and returned the hug, a tired smile on his face.

"Did you doubt it?" His deep voice was drained of energy yet she could hear triumph in his voice. "It seems you were worried little sister," His hands settled onto her shoulders and he smiled down at the top of her head. "I'm glad you're happy to see me well but, I would like my ribs back now," A soft laugh finished his sentence and flushing with embarrassment; Melissa released him and stepped back.

"So you won?" It wasn't a serious question; she could tell that he had won. There wasn't a single scratch on him. Somewhere within her, she felt great pride at her brother's accomplishment, it was just a shame that this feeling failed to eclipse her worry.

"Oh yes I pinked him well," Marcus replied as he sat down on the brocade couch with a sigh. "Your honour is defended little sister,"

"You didn't have to.," As soon as the words were out of her mouth, she wished she could have retracted them. Marcus was tired and he had less tolerance for argumentative behaviour.

"Oh yes I did. I can't have men feeling that it's acceptable to raise a hand against you," With his left hand, he reached down and picked up the china shepherdess that lay on the small end table. He lightly ran his fingers over its smooth surface, his usual way of calming himself and peered at her severely.

"Would you rather have me well but marked as a cad who cares naught for you?"

She heard the admonishment in his voice. She had not fully thought of what it meant had he not reacted to Montjoy. He would be shamed for not coming forward on her behalf. Even though she didn't want him to be hurt, she realised with a burst of shame that he was right. If he had not come to her aid, others would claim that her honour meant nothing, that her own family would not defend it. "No, I wouldn't have them say that," She answered in a small voice. "I just didn't want him to…"

"What? You thought he could win?" There was a surprised edge to Marcus' voice. "You doubted my skill?"

Melissa couldn't answer that, she didn't doubt him. She knew that Marcus was skilled with the blade, but she couldn't answer for Montjoy and sometimes skill was not enough. She didn't know how to explain that her honour was not as important as his life. In her heart of hearts she knew that Montjoy would have tried to kill her brother as a punishment for his interference. It was a loss she would not have been prepared to make, simply because she had slapped an overly amorous fool.

"Well did you?" Her brother was leaning forward now, all traces of tiredness gone from his face as he searched her features, waiting for her to answer. "Well?" He placed the shepherdess back down on the table and Melissa knew that she would have to answer. Her brother was quite easy going, yet he had his pride.

"I knew your skill but he could have been better…" Marcus snorted in disgust. "No he could have been," Her voice rose as she warmed to her subject, Marcus was clearly not seeing the full picture, he was clearly overconfident in his skills and that was deadly. "If you got killed I… I don't know what I'd do. It was my fault you went into it,"

"Little sister, listen to me," Marcus leant forward and clasped her hands in his, the palms were calloused and she could almost feel the ridges where the hilt of his sword had rubbed. "You were not at fault and Montjoy needed this lesson. He will steer clear of you in future and not just because I skewered him so well that he needed a surgeon. You cannot let people treat you poorly and while you are unable to call a miscreant out, I can," His green eyes fixed on her and he spoke with utter sincerity.

"I will not fight without reason and he gave me a reason. He would have struck you before the entire court. I could not let him get away with that. Besides, if I had not acted, Father would have done," Melissa's head snapped up and she looked at Marcus in horror, her father's duelling days were long over, he would have surely lost at Montjoy's hands.

"Indeed he would have," Marcus had not missed the worried expression in her eyes. "So you see, I had to as you had no other champion," He let go of her hands and sat back, relaxing into the chair.

"There was no need to worry about me,"

Melissa watched him for several moments, conflicting emotions warring within her. She knew that her brother spoke the truth. He had to act on her behalf and yet she did not wish to be responsible should he return home injured or dead. He was the favourite and if he died defending her honour, would it matter that form dictated he should? Would her parents blame her for his demise? It would be so much simpler if she had been born male, then she could take responsibility for her own actions. She would be able to fence, to ride out alone. In fact do everything that a high born lady was not allowed to do until she was safely wed and delivered of a son. The injustice rankled slightly. She raised her green eyes to her brother's exhausted face and wondered. Yes he fought well this time, but what about the next?

"You should teach me to fence," Melissa said suddenly to the quiet room. She had not even been aware that she had been thinking of asking it. In the still recesses of her mind, it made a perverse sense. If she knew how to fence she could defend her own honour, she would also feel able to protect herself. As soon as the words left her lips, she knew that she wouldn't be allowed to. It was not done for a woman to be seen with a sword.

"What?" Marcus looked at his younger sister and laughed openly, glee spreading over his tired face in an instant. "You? Fence?"

"Why not?"

"Because its one thing to know how to handle a pistol. It's quite another to stand there with a sword," Her brother said with laughter still thrumming through his voice. "And father would kill me, I also don't think it's a good idea," He finished with a more serious note.

"I don't see why," Melissa answered, annoyed with his manner, after all he had taught her how to shoot. Why would he have difficulty in teaching her how to fence?

"Because you are female and as such are destined for a very good marriage and a home in Suffolk or somewhere like it. I doubt your future husband wants a sword wielding firebrand,"

"Oh fig for that," Melissa replied with a definite note of sourness to her voice. "I want to learn how to fence. I already know how to sew a sampler with exquisite precision and it's dull,"

"So if I teach you to fence what next? Drinking and swearing like a trooper?" Marcus' voice was losing its humour and a note of annoyance crept in.

"No I just would like to be able to defend myself,"

"Why?"

"Because of all those missing women," She explained, not liking the look of anger that was slowly filtering across her brother's face. "The ones who were taken from their homes," She continued, "I don't ever want to end up like them,"

"How the deuce do you know about them?" Her brother asked with shock. "I mean," he modified his tone slightly and continued. "Who told you?"

"Sarah," Melissa answered wondering why Marcus seemed so angry at her request. He had always been an eager accomplice in her plans when they were younger.

"And are you planning on eloping in the dead of night?"

"Well no.,"

"Then you have nothing to worry about. All of those girls seemed to be leaving their houses on their own. They were not dragged kicking from their beds. There is no need for you to learn how to defend yourself. You are a lady or will be…"

"But.,"

"No," Marcus snapped back, he had definitely lost his sense of humour. "I don't want to hear another thing about you learning to fence," He pulled himself upright and took several long strides towards the door. As he reached it, he turned to face her.

"Be thankful that I won't mention this request to Father," With a last glance over his shoulder Marcus left the room.

Melissa pursed her lips with annoyance and sat back on the couch frowning. When they had been younger, Marcus had delighted in teaching her things that were considered less than appropriate for her sex. Now however he seemed as strict as Father when it came to behaviour. She picked up her sewing and thrust it back into the basket with a snarl of bad temper. It just wasn't fair. She had never doubted that it was her duty to marry well, but it didn't mean she wanted to be nothing but a swooning useless ornament like Mary Westbury.

"Melissa are you alright?"

Her mother entered the room and stared down at the spilled basket of embroidery silks. A crease marred her brow and she walked closer. "Have you and Marcus been arguing?" Melissa looked at her mother in astonishment.

"How did you…?" She stuttered slightly, amazed as always at her mother's almost omniscient powers of perception. Granted she could have been listening at the door, but she dismissed that thought immediately. Had her mother heard the argument, she wouldn't be calmly asking her questions about it. Lydia looked at her daughter without replying and Melissa dropped her eyes to the floor.

"I guess I upset him," she answered, deciding that part of the truth would save her trouble. "I questioned whether he should have risked himself like that,"

"Oh I see," Lydia sat down beside her daughter. She lifted her hand and brushed a stray strand of hair back away from Melissa's face. "Well you know how seriously he takes the job of keeping you safe,"

"I know Mother but…" She shrugged her shoulders once and looked at those familiar blue eyes. "I don't want him to get hurt because of me,"

"Melissa,"

"And I know that Father expects him to stand up for me, but I wish he didn't have to fight duels for me,"

"But that's what he will do," Lydia took hold of Melissa's hand and gave it a squeeze. "Look, you will have men duel for you and over you. Until your marriage is confirmed you will be serenaded and praised. Enjoy it my daughter for this time will never happen again. Have fun and try not to worry about your brother. He is more than capable of taking care of himself," Lydia reached down and picked up the sampler.

"Now I would like you to finish the detailing on this before we make the move to the country," Lydia handed the sampler over to her daughter and stood. She made an elegant figure in cream and blue brocade. "Perhaps a few days out of sight will cloud memories,"

CHAPTER 7

Silver sheets of rain turned the landscape a dull grey as the coach rattled along the roads. Mud sprayed up from wheels, painting the bright livery of the carriage a dull murky brown. Sat beside her brother, Melissa stared out of the foggy window at the dismal landscape, her mood matching that of the weather. She should have been throwing herself into the season with gusto but now she was on her way home, her parents hoped that an absence from court would allow people to forget her indiscretions. The wheels bounced through a puddle and a wash of muddy water splayed across the window, reducing her view to almost nothing. Sighing, she turned back to the carriage and its occupants. Her mother was sat opposite;

hands folded primly in her lap and mouth slightly open in sleep. Her father had stayed in London, trying he said, to smooth over ruffled feathers regarding her behaviour. Leaning back against the slightly hard chair, she tried to relax, remembering her father's words to her before they had boarded the carriage.

"You are on a knife edge my girl. Most would not forgive the display of temper, but luckily for you his attempt to strike you went against him. I will do what I can to mollify certain quarters, but I think it best for you to go back to the country and wait,"

She closed her eyes remembering her father's displeasure with still simmering anger. She was fully conscious of her precarious position in society and the injustice of it, rankled her soul.

"Don't take it to heart," She opened her eyes and turned to face Marcus. His green eyes sparkled with sympathy as he reached forward to squeeze her hand. "They will forget, another scandal will pale yours into insignificance,"

"That's not why I'm upset," She murmured back, conscious of her mother's dozing form.

"Oh?" He raised an eyebrow, inviting further comment.

Melissa looked down at the faded floral pattern on the chairs, her mind running over all that had occurred. She had always known that she had less freedom than her brother and that her life would belong to the man she married, but it had always been a distant knowledge, one that she had never really thought off before. A loose thread in the cushion captured her interest and she picked at it, winding the thin red fibre about her index finger as she struggled with what to say.

"Melly," Marcus leant in close and draped a comforting arm about her shoulders. "I know it seems unfair,"

"It is unfair," She muttered back, fixated on the loop of red thread.

"Is it?" A note of disbelief crept into his voice. "Your entire future rests on you making a decent match; if you don't then you are in far worse trouble,"

"But that is what I mean," She looked up finally, "My future depending on who I marry," She smiled, a bitter twisted grimace. "My husband will get my dowry; he will be able to spend it, to gamble it away. He will take my money because apparently I am incapable of controlling it. How is my dependence on another fair?"

"When the alternative is starvation," Marcus leant back. "I understand Melissa and I sympathise, but what would you do? Father would never leave you independently wealthy and I would have the estate. Whichever way you look at it, you would not be allowed to live as you please. You would be on my charity or Father's," He took in her face and sighed. "Look, father will not make you marry a monster. Be assured of that at least,"

"Marcus," The red loop of thread around her finger slid free and settled on the floor. "Do you think I am a useless decorative ornament, incapable of sensible decisions?"

For a long time, Marcus said nothing, his eyes flicking over his sister as he pondered her question.

"Well?"

"No," He replied finally, his voice soft. "You're not useless," He gave a small smile. "Decorative possibly, but not useless,"

"Then you understand,"

"I may understand, but I also know that I can't change anything. Father would not be willing to allow you sole access to your dowry and I know that I can't leave you helpless," He patted her shoulder. "Accept your lot in life sister, it'll be easier,"

Melissa looked away and back out of the window, the view through the small portal was smeared and hazy. In the increasingly heavy rain, they rattled through the villages that lay closest to the manor. As the carriage rumbled along the familiar roads, she marked each well known sight with increasing depression. The village inn, the church, the green, all went by with a dreary familiarity. With a jolt, they took a left at the mile marker and headed along the roads that led towards the manor. As the carriage jolted and jerked along the muddy thoroughfare, Melissa stared at the damp landscape.

"Marcus?" At her call, he looked up from his light doze. "Look at that," Grumbling lightly under his breath, Marcus stretched across his sister and stared out at the landscape.

"What am I looking at?" He enquired, his sleepy brain finding it difficult to sort out landscape from rain spatter.

"Someone's put a gate up at the ruin next to us," She pointed at the newly acquired gate, as they slowly moved past it. Marcus sighed and settled back against his chair.

"Don't you pay any attention to local gossip?" He

exclaimed as the gate passed out of sight. "That place has been sold for about six months,"

"I don't pay attention to gossip," Melissa retorted, as she craned her neck and tried to see into the overgrown estate.

"Clearly, if it wasn't for Mother, you wouldn't know who the king was," He winced as Melissa thumped him. "Well that's dashed unladylike, you're not supposed to go around thumping me anymore,"

"We're not in the middle of some party now," A mischievous gleam chased away the melancholy look in her eyes that had haunted her all morning. I can slap you whenever you deserve it," She grinned at her brother, who rolled his eyes. "Who would buy that place?"

"Justin Lestrade apparently," Marcus replied, not missing the interest spark in his sister's eyes as he spoke the words. "No one knows why, but he brought the place and is refurbishing it. It's taking an age though, as the debris in the place goes back several decades,"

"I can imagine," She murmured remembering the sight of that crumbling relic of a bygone age. As children they had run through the woods between the estates and run through the overgrown gardens. The house had loomed over the surrounding grounds, its walls ruined and overgrown. Only part of the building seemed standing, the rest was a brooding wreck, its stones scorched by a fire in its distant past.

"Surely he has his family estate?"

"By all accounts that is his family estate," Marcus

replied, leaning forward to stare at the weed choked land. "Apparently after the fire, his family went to the Americas and made more money. He returned last year after the death of his father," The overgrown estates disappeared behind the hedgerows and Marcus sat back in his chair.

"It must be costing a fortune to rebuild that ruin," Melissa mused as they trundled closer to the gates of their estate,"I daresay," Marcus replied, losing interest in the conversation as they drew closer to home. "Still if he wants to waste his money then who are we to argue,"

The carriage turned towards the gatehouse and trundled along the drive towards their home. The house had only been built in the last forty years. Its façade was in pale cream stone and large windows overlooked formal gardens. The carriage rolled to a stop before the main doors and their mother woke. As the footman placed the steps before the door, Melissa caught hold of her brother.

"What is it Melly?" He asked, pushing the carriage door open as he spoke.

"Sorry," She muttered as the footmen reached forward a hand and helped her from the coach.

"For what?" Marcus stepped down after her and began walking to the main doors, shoulders hunched against the rain.

"For this morning, I shouldn't have snapped as I did, you were only trying to.,"

Marcus held up his hand and stopped her. "Don't fret about it," He caught hold of her arm and escorted her to the door. "I know you hate being helpless,"

Melissa smiled as they headed into the hallway and warmth. "So does that mean you'll teach me to fence?" She asked with a grin.

"No," Marcus released her arm and removed his hat. "But if you want, I will target shoot with you," He glanced out at that rain. "If it stops raining,"

"Agreed," Melissa returned as she handed her outdoor coat to her maid and walked towards the dining room and food. "I get to go first,"

Marcus chuckled ruefully and nodded. "Alright," He replied as he began to load his plate with ham and cheese. "Though," He speared a hunk of bread with his knife, "I don't think you'll win,"

"Care to wager on that?"

"No gambling in my house," Their mother's voice echoed from behind them and they both grinned. "I'm not even sure I should let you shoot,"

"Mother?" Melissa protested, picking up her plate and sitting down at the table.

"Don't Mother me; your father would have a fit,"

"He already has," Marcus replied through a mouthful of bread. "Any complaints he may have are a little old hat now,"

"That may be but," Lydia sat in her place and buttered one of the rolls. "Perhaps it's not a good idea to test your father right now,"

"Papa isn't here," Melissa noted as she cut the ham into neat slices. "He wouldn't have to know,"

"Hmm, I'm not sure if I should be encouraging this,"

Lydia continued, staring at her children with a smile. "But you're right, this is a conversation we had years ago," She bit into a roll and chewed thoughtfully. "So I have no objection, just make sure you're far enough from the house,"

"Thank you," Melissa sprang up at hugged Lydia, who smiled and patted her hair.

"I know what it's like, Darling," Her mother whispered as she gently stroked her hair. Kissing her daughter lightly on the cheek, she returned to her food. "Just be careful,"

CHAPTER 8

Melissa and Marcus walked out of the large double doors and squelched through the wet grass as they headed toward the yew garden at the back of the house.

"Perhaps we should have waited for a day or two," Marcus noted wryly as he glanced down at his wet footwear. "I have the distinct impression that I'm sinking,"

"It's only mud," Melissa replied. "It won't kill you,"

"No but Mother might when she sees the state of your dress," Marcus replied with a chuckle as they walked through the majestic line of yew trees and reached their usual practice site at the end of the garden.

"You're not getting out of it," They came to a stop before a target and Melissa turned to face her brother. "I'm still going to beat you,"

"Highly doubtful," He reached her side and handed her one of the two pistols that he was holding. "I bet you won't even touch the target,"

"Getting a little cocky aren't you?" She replied as she began to load the pistol. With steady hands, she loaded the muzzle of the gun with black powder, before placing a small lead shot into the barrel. Using a small ramrod, she jammed the powder and shot into the base of the barrel, before priming the flash pan lid with fine gunpowder. "I'm ready," She looked up at Marcus and smiled. "Do you want to go first?"

"Wouldn't dream of it," Marcus replied, indicated the target with a sweep of his fingers. "By all means, go ahead," He took a step back, holding the primed pistol away from his body and angled upwards, so that the ball did not roll out of the barrel.

Melissa drew back the cock on the gun and aimed towards the target, holding her arm steady, despite the weight of the gun. With a slight narrowing of her eyes, she squeezed the trigger. The flint laden trigger slammed into the fine gunpowder, igniting a small spark that raced into the combustion chamber and fired the black powder. With a deafening bang, the pistol fired, sending the lead shot sailing into the target opposite.

"Not bad," Marcus muttered as he stared across at the target through the drifting curtain of smoke. The shot had left a neat, yet blackened hole quite close to the centre of the target. "Not bad at all," Melissa gave a small smirk as she stepped aside and allowed her brother to take up position. "But I'm afraid," Marcus fired, the small ball of shot rocketing through the air to embed itself into the dense straw. "not quite good enough,"

"How did you manage that?" They reached the target. Marcus' shot was an inch closer to the target than his sisters.

"Practice," Marcus chuckled as he began walking back to the starting position. "What were you saying about wagers?" He drew out some more shot and powder. "I think you owe me a week's allowance,"

"Practice shot doesn't count," Melissa countered as she began to reload her pistol. "I'd say best of five,"

"And give you time to cheat?" Marcus stopped loading and smirked at his sister. "I don't think so, make it best of three and I'm in,"

"I don't cheat," Melissa muttered as she finished ramming her second shot into the barrel. "You can't always be lucky,"

"Not luck sister dearest but skill," He finished priming his pistol and winked at her. "We can't all be gifted,"

"Oh I'm going to love beating you," She replied, pushing a stray strand of hair away from her face. "You can consider your allowance mine," She reached out a hand and clasped his. "I accept your wager,"

"Good morning," As one, they turned to face the source of the call. Elegant in a heavy velvet coat and riding breeches, Marcus' friend, James walked towards them.

"James," Marcus reached forward with a smile and

clasped his friend's hand. "You must have ridden like the devil to get here,"

"Almost," James laughed back as he returned the handshake. He turned his gaze on Melissa, who smiled and bobbed a welcome.

"James, you remember my sister?" Marcus asked, waving in Melissa's direction.

"Yes of course," James took hold of Melissa's fingers and bestowed a light kiss upon her hand. "I missed you at the palace the other night; I heard it was quite an experience,"

"I daresay the entire of London heard," Melissa retorted, wondering if she would ever live down the event.

"I would have liked to have seen it," James continued, "Montjoy is a blight on society,"

"Well you got to see Marcus take him down a peg," Melissa replied, smiling at her brother. "I count seeing blood the best of the bargain," Marcus choked back a cough of laughter at her words and continued to reload his pistol.

"Marcus I had no idea your sister was so bloodthirsty," James called over his shoulder as he leant against one of the hedges.

"Bloodthirsty, a handful and an all round nuisance," Marcus chuckled, ducking a playful slap from his sister. "Really, you can have her for a guinea,"

"I doubt she's that bad," James replied, looking at Melissa with a smile. "She's always seemed perfectly nice to me,"

Marcus glanced up and looked at his friend, noting the direction of his gaze with a small twist of his lips. It wasn't blindingly obvious, but he could read the signs in James' face. His friend was more than interested in his sister. A glance across at Melissa revealed that she appeared to be unaware of his interest. He swallowed the chuckle of amusement and handed his pistol to James.

"Care to join us?"

James nodded and took hold of the pistol. As he aimed it at the target, hurried steps behind drew their attention and all three looked over to see a maid rush to the scene.

"I'm sorry Sirs, Miss," The woman gasped out as she bobbed a curtsey. "But her Ladyship wants to see you Miss," Melissa sighed in frustration and handed her pistol back to her brother.

"Oh well, that'll be me sewing for the rest of the afternoon," She did not bother to hide the frustration in her voice as she handed the shot and powder to James. "Have a good afternoon," Turning, she made to follow the servant. "It's good to see you again James,"

"The pleasure's mine," James answered, almost reaching for her hand and thinking better of it. "Perhaps we can do this another time,"

"Hopefully," She called back as she headed back across the lawns, the hem of her dress wet and muddy from the ground.

Marcus waited until Melissa was out of earshot before he turned to James.

"So tell me why you're out here?"

James aimed the pistol at the target and fired, coming close to the centre. "I fancied a ride and I remembered you had returned to the country,"

"I see," Taking up position, Marcus aimed the pistol. "So it had nothing to do with my sister?" The sound of the shot drowned out James' startled exclamation, but as the smoke cleared and Marcus looked back at his friend, he was gratified to see the shock on the other man's face.

"How the devil did you?" He stopped talking and panic swept into his eyes. "Does she?"

"I don't think so," Marcus began reloading; the movements smooth and practised as he continued to speak. "I only know because I saw your face just now,"

James placed the pistol on the ground and reached Marcus' side. "Are you going to tell her?"

"Why?" Marcus asked, raising an eyebrow as he finished priming the pistol. "I assume you're planning to court her," As the silence lengthened he looked up at his old friend. "I would hope you are planning to court her,"

"I don't think it'll be that simple,"

"If you're worried about our father, then don't," He aimed the pistol and fired again, noting with satisfaction that the bullet seared close to the target's centre. "I will vouch for you. I don't have any objection with you as a brother in law,"

"This issue would not be your parents, but mine. I'm afraid I'm being tilted at other game," He gave a discontented huff and stared up at the cloudy sky. "Also I don't think her performance the other night did her any favours. But even so," He reached Marcus' side and caught his shoulder. "I would like to court her but I don't think she'll accept it, could you put in a good word?"

Marcus shrugged and looked at his old friend. "James of course I would put in a word for you, but I will tell you something about my sister,"

"What?"

"She'd prefer you to talk to her first. Melissa dislikes her life being organised by others. If she thought you and I were colluding to marry her off to you behind her back, I daresay she'll be put out," He gave James a comradely squeeze of the shoulder. "Whatever else you are planning, I'd suggest you try your hand first," He reached for the powder horn and began to reload his pistol. As he finished loading, he pointed towards the abandoned pistol on the ground. "And pick up that pistol, I don't want it to rust.

CHAPTER 9

Melissa walked into the house, the happy mood of that morning evaporated by the summons. Why couldn't she stand in attendance with her brother and James? They were only shooting; it wasn't as though the action would destroy the fabric of society. She swept along the hall and entered the parlour, noting the still form of her mother sat on the chair by the fire.

"Don't you give me that look?" Before she had even time to speak, Lydia De Vire's voice rapped out. "Yes I called you inside away from your shooting. I know you consider it unfair," As Melissa opened her mouth, her mother raised her hand, silencing the protest before it could be voiced. "But think of the potential scandal. Yes your brother teaches you how to shoot, perhaps other young women know how to shoot, but I daresay you don't know any of them," Once again, Melissa tried to speak, yet her mother's words carried on, quashing any possible objection.

"What if James decided to speak about you in club circles and it got out that you know how to fire a pistol. A good many people would consider that unladylike and you would lose a great deal of interest. You must never forget that your reputation is fragile, lord knows you should have realised this after the other night. I don't want Marcus to have to duel again for you and I would hope that you wouldn't wish it either,"

The tirade ceased and Melissa stared at her mother for one long minute, before she started to speak. Her voice was coolly angry and she didn't bother to hide her frustration.

"Very well, if it is that important, I shall go and find my sampler. I feel certain there is a good deal more work that I can do on it. God forbid that I have any other interest,"

"Show me your sampler and I'll decide whether you should be allowed another interest," Another flash of annoyance crossed Melissa's face as she reached across to the sewing basket to pick up her embroidery. Was she supposed to be contemplating marriage as an adult or was she a wilful child? Why did she have to hand her embroidery over for inspection as though she were still under the thumb of a governess? Still she held her tongue as she handed over the sampler. Keeping her face neutral, she waited impatiently for her mother to pass judgement on her stitch work.

"Your stitch work is terrible," Her mother noted as she took the scrap of fabric in hand and stared at the untidy mess. Picking up a pair of ivory handled scissors, she snipped at the offending stitches, unpicking the disorderly muddle with several precise cuts. "There," Her mother handed the small square of silks and tapestry back to her with a satisfied smile. "That's that mess dealt with," Melissa looked down at the unpicked canvas and gave a sickly smile. Her mother had removed a full morning's work from the canvas.

"Yes Mother," Biting back the comments that were teetering on the edge of her tongue, she took back the sampler. "Can I retire?"

"No, you will go to your room and write a composition, expanding on the virtues of patience, chastity and obedience. I will not stand here and take your insolence. You would not say this to your father and you will not say it to me. Do you understand?"

"Yes mother," The words issued from behind tightly clenched teeth as barely repressed anger buzzed in her head. Turning sharply, her feet carried her through the door and out the room.

Hurrying up the stairs, she threw herself onto the bed, trying to still the angry tears that threatened to spill down her face. She stayed like that for several minutes, her chest heaving from the angry breaths that she took.

"It's not fair," Her fist punched into her pillow and she pushed herself upright, trying to stop herself from crying. "It's not bloody fair," She seized her pillow and flung it across the room, giving vent to the anger that had been building since the other night.

"Be good Melissa, don't shoot a pistol Melissa, sew that sampler Melissa," With each complaint, she threw something, jewellery, pots of lead, hair decorations. "Don't forget that Montjoy assaulting you was your fault Melissa," Her sneering tones echoed across her room as she raged, angry beyond words at her lot. From the window she could hear the sounds of pistol fire and it stoked her anger further. Why couldn't she be allowed to stay with her brother and his friend? Why did she have to stay in the house like a useless lump? Her fingers grasped the bottle of ink and she threw it against the wall. It smashed, ink showered over the wall and dripped down onto the floor and she stopped moving, anger turning into guilty horror.

Rushing to the other side of the room, she tried to mop up the spilt ink, but her efforts only spread the mess further and she stopped. Guilt stricken and worried, she moved to the door of her room. Stepping out onto the landing, she rushed along the upper corridor, looking for a servant. Catching sight of her usual housemaid, she called the young woman over.

"I've had an accident with a bottle of ink," She said hurriedly, not missing the other girl's knowing smile. "Could you fetch me another bottle and sort out the mess,"

"Of course Miss," The other girl bobbed a curtsey and hurried away. Returning to her room, she sat down at the window seat and stared out across the gardens. Past the yew garden and somewhere beyond the copse of trees on the edge of the estate, was Justin Lestrade's house. Settling back against the shutters on the side of the window, she closed her eyes and thought back to their meeting at the Palace. Despite his seeming inattention, she still couldn't stop thinking about him. Opening her eyes again, she fixed on the far distance and fantasised about sneaking over there, finding him and having the conversation she so wanted to have.

CHAPTER 10

The room was dark and musty, malodorous with old odours sunk into the very fabric of the furnishings. Dark wooden, exposed beams made the room seem smaller and the semi closed curtains made the place claustrophobic. Katherine Lytchefield waited in the centre of the room for her 'father' to appear. With an expression of distaste, she noted the plate of rotting food on the main table and the pile of stained rags that covered the floor. Stood here amongst the mess made her skin crawl, but he had summoned her and once again she had found herself unable to resist his call. Adjusting her gloves as she attempted not to touch anything, she glanced over at the dirty mirror. Her face stared back, her distaste and nervousness clear on her heart shaped features. Beneath the white mob cap, her chestnut brown hair was arranged in the current style and her dress, though plain, was of excellent quality.

"Still vain I see," Surprised, she turned to face him, her 'father' for all intents and purposes. He walked into the room, tall, broad shouldered and almost handsome. One look at his eyes however revealed the cruelty that lay within. Katherine shuddered and dropped her gaze. "What no comment?" The man stepped forward and grasped her chin, forcing her gaze upward. "And please look at me when I speak,"

"I'm sorry," Katherine breathed, wincing as his fingers dug into her flesh.

"So you should be," He released her and sat down in the chair on the other side of the room. "Now do you have anything to report?"

"Emily's back in the country, she's staying at the Hotel Saint-Clair and affianced to Lord Morton," Her words were clear and concise, her 'father' didn't like mumbling and many painful lessons had drilled the clarity he craved into her. Once again, she wished she had taken up Emily's offer all those years ago. It was far too late to change her mind now.

"I see," The man leant back against the chair back and steepled his fingers beneath his chin. "What about Hugh?"

"I haven't seen him, but I think he's still at court," At the disapproval on his face, she stammered. "I know he's not made contact with either of the brothers," Taking a breath, she tried to calm down; she didn't want to make a mistake. Mistakes had provoked as many painful lessons as mumbling in the past. Katherine was desperate not to bring down his wrath tonight. "Alistair is pretending to be a preacher and he still hates his brother, but he's not doing anything particularly useful with that hate. Henry went to the Americas a few years ago and I haven't heard much more . Abbott, I haven't seen since 1710, so I don't know where he is,"

"Don't worry about Abbott, I have tabs on him. So we only have to worry about Emily," He rubbed his chin thoughtfully. "Has she made contact with Justin?"

"Yes, I saw her carriage at the Palace. I know he was attending that night, it seems likely that they met up together,"

"Have you seen him?"

"No, I don't believe he knows I'm in the country," She had seen him however. It was fairly easy to hide at some of the large events. It had been remarkably easy to observe him, to see who he was with. It was such a shame that she had been unable to attend the Palace event, by all accounts it had been an interesting evening.

"Does he appear to be worried?"

"No," She answered, knowing that their campaign had been slow. It was entirely possible that he was unaware of their activities.

"Well done," A rare smile crossed his features and he chuckled. "Well I believe we move up to the next phase. I understand he has been seeing some noble girl,"

"Is it necessary?" The words were out of her mouth

before she could stop them. She could tell from the sudden set of his shoulders that he did not appreciate the sentiment. Taking a small step backwards, she hurriedly amended. "By that I mean..,"

"Are you suggesting that we spare them?" His tones were mild, but they were enough to make her tremble. "Is that what you suggest?"

"No I don't, I didn't mean, I just thought," She gabbled, trying to scramble away from the mistake she had just made. "I just thought that perhaps we could try something else, something that we haven't done before," He stood up and began to walk towards her. With a small cry of panic she took another step backwards. "Because he might figure out what's happening?" Her voice spilled from her mouth, frantic and scared as he reached for her neck. "Please..," She whimpered as his fingers closed on her throat. "Don't,"

"Say you're sorry for contradicting my will," His voice was cold and made much worse by its very softness. She felt his fingers close, cutting off her breath.

"I.. I'm sorry," Almost choked by the tightness of his grip, she gasped out her apology. "I should never have tried to contradict you," Black spots began to dance before her eyes and she felt herself begin to black out. Gasping for air her fingers reached for his wrist and she clawed at it, feeling the iron hardness of his hand.

"Louder," He muttered and she felt herself choke as she struggled to find a breath. "I can't hear you,"

"I'm sorry," She tried again, but his vicelike grip ensured that her voice never managed more than a croak. "Please,"

A last whisper before darkness shrouded her vision and she crumpled to the floor.

CHAPTER 11

The Castlemaines' study was a long panelled room, filled with books and papers. Lord Edward Castlemaine was a noted scholar and his rooms were filled with maps of far off places and rare documents. It was said in London society that he knew more about foreign places and affairs than both the Secretaries of State for the Northern and Southern Departments. At this particular moment in time, Melissa and her mother were sat eating a late lunch and listening to Lady Edward gossip about society. It had been three days since their argument and Lady De Vire had been insistent about Melissa's attendance at the luncheon and she had complied.

The middle aged woman sprawled on the opposite sofa

was dressed in pale yellow muslin with a puce mantua and blue house bonnet. Melissa, perched precariously on one of the spindly chairs, had used all of her self control to keep her appalled giggles from spilling out and drawing down the woman's wrath. Despite indulging in the usual pleasantries, Melissa had been content to let her mother and Lady Edward talk as she sat, only half listening to the conversation. With uncharacteristic tact, Lady Edward had made little mention of her scandal at the palace and had instead delved into several lurid accounts of various other scandals that had been occupying the doyennes of high society of late. Almost drifting out of the conversation, she eventually realised that her mother was discussing the Marcus' duel and Melissa listened more closely for information that her brother would not impart to her. Not that Lady Edward knew all the details, but her husband had clearly regaled her with some of that morning's events. Listening carefully, her interest was definitely peaked as the older woman revealed that Justin Lestrade had attended her brother's duel.

"Oh you didn't know that Lestrade attended?" Maria Castlemaine cried in a delighted voice. "Well my Edward says he was there,"

"He was?" Melissa opened her mouth for the first time during the conversation. Maria was her mother's friend and though she had a daughter nearer Melissa's age, she was not currently at home. Despite this loss however, Melissa was more than happy with the turn the conversation had taken. Quite a bit of information had been forthcoming from Lady Edward, most of it news that she was sure would have ordinarily be kept from her. Melissa leant forward, interested finally in the conversation.

"Indeed he was," The Lady placed her cup of tea onto the tray and sat forward to further entertain her guests. "My Edward saw the whole thing, apparently Lestrade turns up early, fresh as a daisy, which is of course quite sickening when you consider the amount he was seen to consume that night," Maria took another pastry from the tray and consumed it in several dainty bites.

"And then what?" Biting back her impatience to receive the details, Melissa affected a bored nonchalance and hoped it would deceive her mother. She didn't wish her parents to know that she had a curiosity about Justin Lestrade.

"Well then he proceeded to give Marcus advice," Maria reclined back on the couch and stared at her guests in wide eyed astonishment. "The impertinence of that, the boy can't be all of nineteen. He shouldn't be able to advise your brother," She turned to Melissa, trailing wisps of mousy brown hair from beneath her bonnet.

Melissa started slightly, she wondered briefly why Justin had turned up to advise Marcus, yet that thought was brushed aside as she wondered how her brother had taken to the idea of someone younger telling him how to fence.

"Your brother thought so too," Maria continued as though following Melissa's train of thought. "Stated quite baldly that Justin was younger than him and he shouldn't seek to upbraid his elders. And would you believe that

Lestrade laughed. Edward said that he positively threw back his head and guffawed as though he had heard a great joke. Your brother didn't take kindly to the laughter, but Justin apologised saying that he didn't mean any offence and that he was only trying to help,"

Maria returned her cup to the table and poured another. "According my Edward however, the boy was completely dead on. Gave Marcus some sterling advice," She added a cube of sugar to the cup and stirred it.

"A strange boy that one," She added, lifting the cup to her lips. "He came here to talk to Edward, spent ages in his study. My Edward said that he was impressed by the man's knowledge. Of course he must have a very quick mind,"

"What?" Melissa spoke up, her voice strangely tremulous. "What was he asking about?" Her mother glanced up at her, clearly wondering why she was asking about Lestrade.

"Not a clue," Maria took a sip of the tea. "Now tell me Lydia dear, what do you think of this yellow muslin?" She indicated the pale yellow dress that covered her form. "I wonder if this colour makes me seem washed out,"

Several hours later, Melissa and her mother made their excuses and headed for home. Maria had mentioned little else of interest and the conversation had rapidly become boring. Yet they endured most of the tirade with forbearance and had settled into the carriage with a sigh of relief. The driver clicked to the horses and they moved out through the gates and along the road, a sense of release following them as they travelled. Lydia said little, clearly valuing silence after an afternoon of chatter and Melissa stared out of the window looking out at the rolling landscape.

Maria's information about Justin's presence at the duel had been a revelation. She knew that Marcus would not have thought to tell her. Pressing her forehead against the cool surface of the glass window, she wondered at the mystery of Justin Lestrade. Since his arrival on the social scene a year ago, he had been something of a mystery. He had an old and valued title yet few in society had ever met his parents. He was rumoured to have grown up in the colonies and only returned to his ancestral estates recently. No one doubted his pedigree, the name Lestrade reached back to the Norman Conquest and yet, he was a mystery. At least three of her acquaintances were harbouring thoughts about him and if Melissa were honest about herself, her thoughts about him were more than polite interest. In all her trammelled life she had never found anything as intriguing as Justin Lestrade. He fascinated her, even though she had only met him the once. A vision of him leaning over her, blossom clasped in his fingers as he smiled at her with tender apology drifted into her mind. A small voice wondered whether he had been sincere in his apologies. After all, he was a seducer and an extremely gifted one. It was not beyond the bounds of possibility that this was an exquisite tease; however she did not feel that it was. For all the warnings in her head, her heart cried that there was something genuine about him. Though, her mind retorted, her feelings could be nothing more than hope.

He's a cad and a seducer. Clasping the edge of the window frame, she dismissed the warnings of her mind with a minute shake of the head. They were connected somehow. She had felt that in the brief instant they had talked. And then there was his appearance at Marcus' duel. Despite everything she had heard about Justin, he had helped her brother. That alone endeared him to her.

The coach rattled through a small hamlet and dragged her out of her thoughts. She was being silly, she couldn't be connected to Justin, they had only met the once. Such foolish wonderings were the province of playwrights and poets. Love at first sight did not occur in the real world and her reality was different to that of the bard. Justin was simply a handsome enigma, nothing more. Running her eyes over hedgerows filled with berries soothed her thoughts and she let her mind drift. Soon the landscape and the gentle, rocking motion of the carriage cast their spell and her eyelids began to droop.

She woke to a strange landscape. A long panelled corridor stretched out away from her. Threadbare carpets swathed in dust lay underfoot and small bones were piled up on either side of the hall. The walls were draped with billowing curtains of lace which, on closer inspection, turned into cobwebs. Moving forward with slow painstaking steps, she pushed aside the cobwebs. The spider silk clung to her dress and skin holding her briefly in its sticky folds as she forced her way through. A scampering sound on the floor drew her attention and she watched as a long tailed rat rushed past. That small traveller was the only other soul she encountered as she traversed the seemingly infinite space. In the silent ruin of what was once a rich hall, she found her eyes wandering. There were no doors but in between the cobwebs, portraits hung on the walls. With no exception, each painting depicted a man or woman contorted in pain. One depiction seemed to be in the paroxysms of some fit; another was badly beaten; yet another had been stabbed. Shuddering in horror, she moved away from the paintings, dragging herself from the depictions of agony and anguish. Staring straight ahead, she continued to move onwards, moving faster as she tried to escape from the scenes on either side of her. An unreasoning panic rose within her as she saw more paintings, the rectangular frames seeming endless.

Melissa

The word echoed strangely, bouncing off the walls and overlapping till it hurt. Panicked, she tried to go faster, pulling the skirts up to her knees as she raced. The portraits were fixed on her now, staring at her with accusatory eyes as she tore past them, almost sobbing with the effort.

Melissa

Trying to go faster, her foot finally caught in her vast expanse of skirt and she tumbled over, falling to a floor that was now no longer there. A black pit yawned before her and she fell forward into it with a soundless scream. Cool air rushed past her face, carrying scents of rust and blood.

Melissa

Light flared suddenly in the blackness, illuminating a scene that made her heart stop. Beneath her was a flower. It was large enough to swallow a carriage and its petals were a glossy black. Yet it was not its size that tugged at her breath and forced another scream from her lips. Teeth, razor sharp and coated with the rusty brown of old blood, lined its petals. It reared in one sinuous movement and lunged at her falling body. Unable to do anything but watch, Melissa saw the bloom flex and extend razor sharp petals ready to rend her skin. In a futile gesture she covered her eyes and waited for the blood to flow.

"Melissa," Her name echoed again, yet this time the voice was familiar and welcome. Around her, the dream began to fade and she felt her body return to her place in the carriage. A gentle shaking assailed her as feeling returned and she became aware of her surroundings.

"Melissa," Her mother's voice called again. "Wake up now dear we're home," Melissa slowly opened her eyes and stared to her right. A set of steps had been laid at the door of the carriage and beyond she could see the familiar front door of her home illuminated in the gold of lamplight. It was almost dark outside and Melissa realised that it was approaching suppertime. "You were asleep for a while," Her mother smiled at her."And quite deeply, it took me several efforts to wake you,"

"I must have been tired with all the worry about Marcus," Melissa exclaimed, heading off the questions with a simple explanation as she stepped out of the carriage. It would not do to trouble her mother with stories of dreams and omens. At best her mother would think she was sickening for something and at worst she would wonder if the trials of her debut and the last few days had troubled her too much. Either situation wasn't particularly desirable. It would be best to keep the dream to herself and perhaps a trusted friend.

"Well worry no more about it," Lydia said as they walked across the gravelled surface towards the door. "Your brother lived and your honour is defended. It is about time you put these black thoughts aside and focused on the rest of the season. It's Lady Shearingham's ball in two days and you must be ready for that," They reached the heavy black door, which swung open as they reached it. Jane helped Melissa with her coat and she removed her gloves.

"Lady Shearingham?" Melissa asked as they crossed the hall and entered the parlour.

"Yes. She's holding an event soon and we have an invite," Her mother sat on one of the couches and picked up her sewing. "It happens to be one of the most prestigious events of the season. Anyone and everyone will be there," She threaded a needle with aquamarine silk and began to ply herself to the sampler. "So that makes it the perfect opportunity to start finding a husband,"

Melissa gaped, she knew that the whole point of all these balls was the acquisition of a mate, yet she hadn't realised that she had to start so soon. With a strange hollow sound in her ears she stared down at her own sewing box.

"Oh," Standing up from the couch, she headed for the

doorway.

"Melissa where are you going?" The needle in her mother's hand flickered in the candlelight as she spoke without glancing up.

"Oh umm.. I'm going to write my composition," Melissa lied quickly as she turned around and stared at her mother. "I've done enough sewing today,"

"Very well," Her mother waved her away and Melissa headed through the door with a sense of release. The dream was still fresh in her mind and she wanted to examine it further before supper. Heading up the elegant staircase she reached her room and dismissed the maid. Shutting the door to the house, she pulled out her journal and began to write, trying to sort out her thoughts.

The dream had been so vivid; she could remember the brush of cobweb against her skin and she looked down at her periwinkle blue dress to make sure that she wasn't covered in dust. The gown seemed fine; it was slightly creased from the coach journey but there were no signs of cobwebs or dust on its delicately embroidered surface. She smoothed down the lightweight fabric and stared down at the spiky handwriting that encroached onto the blank creamy parchment.

Such a dream I had...

She dipped her pen into the ink and poised her pen over the parchment, wondering how to continue, how to describe the images that even now were fading from her mind. Her hand moved, the pen scratching the letters into the parchment as she allowed her thoughts to flow.

Without thinking, she wrote of her roaming through the dreamscape, of the cobwebs and dust, the black pit, the portraits. She wrote furiously, noting down all she could remember, yet forgetting the most important. Memories of the blood streaked flower eluded capture and these failed to end up in her journal to be examined later.

Pushing aside her pen, she closed her journal and concealed it at the bottom of her drawer before turning to prepare herself for dinner.

CHAPTER 12

Melissa sat in the parlour, her fingers running over the keys of the harpsichord. She was an indifferent player, but she was always soothed by the melody that she produced. She was due to attend Lady Shearingham's party this evening and she wasn't completely sure she wanted to. It was the first event she would be attending since the debacle at her debut and she wasn't entirely sure of her reception. She had heard of people being frozen out at these soirees and she did not know if anyone would speak to her. Cascading through another set of scales, she wondered if she could convince her mother to allow her to stay home. Visions of being ostracised flashed through her head and she missed another scale.

"Excuse me Miss," The butler cleared his throat as he entered the room, interrupting her practice.

"Yes, what is it Walker?"

"You have a visitor," The sombrely clad man stepped aside with a small bow. In a flurry of sprigged muslin Sarah swept into the room. Sarah's hair was without powder this morning and it gleamed like spun gold beneath a powder blue cap.

"Melissa have you heard?" In a voice eager with excitement, she had started speaking before fully crossing the threshold and Melissa looked up, wondering what had sparked such fervour.

"What news?" Melissa asked mystified by her friend's eager countenance "What are you babbling about?" Sarah only became this excited when there was some great scandal to impart. In truth she was hoping for great scandal, for that was the only thing that would drive her own indiscretion from everyone's mind.

"Honesty Malison,"

"What about her?" Melissa was truly bemused now. She barely knew Honesty Malison, the daughter of a minor baron who had only just made her mark in society.

"She's dead," Sarah's voice was full of ghoulish glee. Next to scandal, death was her subject of choice. "and not just dead… she's been murdered,"

Melissa sat up and stared at her friend in interest, this was indeed news. "When? How?"

"Last night sometime," Sarah settled onto a chaise longue and picked a minute piece of fluff from her dress.

"Her maid found her this morning at the bottom of the stairs, her throat had been cut; they said there was blood everywhere," She looked at Melissa's face as though gauging her friend's reaction.

"That's horrible," Melissa's voice was soft and incredulous. She recalled Honesty Malison as a vision with long golden locks.

"I know, My abigail heard the news from the Malisons' under housemaid. I wouldn't usually listen to servants gossip but the news was far too big to ignore. Also my mother was called on to comfort Lady Malison. Apparently they couldn't hide the sight of the body from her and she had the vapours,"

"I think I would if I saw such a thing. So why was she out of bed in the middle of the night?"

"Ahh here's the interesting thing.," Sarah leant forward and lowered her voice. "Apparently she was fully attired for travelling and there was a note in her hands. She was getting ready to elope can you believe. The door was slightly ajar so they think that whoever she was getting to elope with killed her,"

"My god,"

"Yes," Sarah laughed and brushed a stray strand of hair away from her face.

"Do you know who she was planning to elope with?" Melissa asked as her fingers tightened convulsively. Honesty Malison was a fairly quiet, beautiful blonde with a placid temperament, she couldn't imagine anyone wishing her harm.

"No," Sarah sighed and settled back into the chair. "That's the strange thing; she was never really linked to anyone in that way. It's true that she had flirted with several in society. She had even courted Lestrade," Melissa jumped slightly at her words; however Sarah didn't seem to notice. "Yet she wasn't seriously linked to any of them," A sense of strange relief flooded Melissa as she heard this news. Justin's dark, sardonic expression courted her thoughts and she struggled back to the conversation, hoping that she had not blushed.

"So we don't know who she was planning to meet?"

"Well I don't, but then again I never really spoke with her. She always struck me as a little mouse, but then you always have to watch the quiet ones," Sarah missed the telltale flush in her friend's cheeks as she ploughed ahead with her news. "You have to admit that it's exciting,"

"I would say horrifying," Melissa responded with some heat to her voice. "Honesty is dead after all,"

"Yes I know, but just think. Your scandal will be easily forgotten in the wake of this. None will remember you slapping Montjoy,"

"Hmm.," Melissa wasn't completely convinced at that, she couldn't see that her behaviour would be easily dismissed because of this new gossip. Despite hoping for it, she did not see it happening so easily.

"I guarantee it," Sarah glanced at the clock on the mantel. "Oh Lord," She muttered as she rapidly got to her feet. "I'm going to have to go," Melissa regarded her with bemusement as she prepared to leave.

"Sarah?"

"Oh I'm really sorry Melissa," Sarah apologised rapidly as she pulled on her shawl. "but I promised Edward Marling a morning promenade and I can't be late," She walked across and kissed Melissa on the cheek. "We'll talk again soon, I promise,"

"I look forward to it," Melissa replied with a wry smile. She didn't know why she was surprised, Sarah had never been the best with timekeeping. "Have a good walk,"

"I intend to," Sarah smiled as with a swish of her skirts, she walked out of the room and into the hallway and left the house. Melissa watched as she took her outer coat from the butler. "Have a good day and try not to worry too much, I'm sure everything will be fine," The front door opened and she walked out of the house. "Goodbye," She called as the carriage rattled into view.

"Farewell," Melissa called as she watched her climb into the carriage. She spent a few moments waving farewell until she returned to her desk. Sitting at the heavy wooden table, her thoughts turned to the news that she had just heard. It was troubling, who could have killed Honesty and why? She tapped her fingers on the hard wooden surface, allowing her thoughts to roam over Sarah's words. Honesty was the latest in a long line of gullible heiresses running out into the night supposedly to elope. What did it mean and was Justin Lestrade involved? She was under no illusions that Justin had been involved with Honesty because he seemed to be involved with most of the beauties on the social scene. But Melissa couldn't believe it. For all the secrets she seemed to see in his eyes she couldn't believe him involved in the murder of innocent, if stupid, women. Sighing, she returned to her sewing and attempted to lose herself in the mindless activity, away from the memory of Justin's sardonic smile. Even so, the troubling thoughts remained; thoughts of Justin and Honesty, of Marcus and the other murders. She prided herself on her ability to judge character and her assessment of Lestrade did not suggest that he was a killer.

CHAPTER 13

It was in the bar that he heard the news about his last flame. Honesty Malison had been found dead on the steps of her own home. She had been stabbed several times and left almost on display besides the front door. There had been six murders in the last six months, all women from the upper middle class. He had heard that they had left their homes in the middle of the night and been found in lower class districts several days later to the shame and horror of their families. Yet this murder was prominent, more overt than the others, on the very front steps of her home. A niggling worry fluttered in his mind as he walked quickly along the street. It had not escaped his notice that each of the victims had been old flames of his. Could some of the others be here? Could John be here? Trying hard to dislodge what could conceivably be paranoia, he ascended the steps to his home. The large front door of his London town house swung open to admit him as he reached it. He handed his hat and cloak to a footman and walked along the hallway, admiring the rosewood and mahogany wainscoting. He slapped his gloves onto the hall table and looked up as his butler Hedge reached his side, drawing his attention with a small cough.

"You have a visitor sir," His voice was bland and uncurious. "A Lord Malison, I sent him to the parlour to wait,"

"Thank you Hedge," Justin nodded in acknowledgement, his eyes flickering to the parlour door and wondering what lay in store. Handing his cane to Hedge, he moved through the door and into the parlour. The parlour was decorated in blue, cream and rosewood. The marble surround on the fireplace was a creamy colour and seats decorated in deep blue brocade lay about the room. This room suited Justin well and usually it relaxed him, but at this moment he could not feel calm. Honesty's father stood in the centre of the room, his eyes fixed on him as he entered. The man appeared many years older, his hair was grey and tied back with a single black ribbon. His dress was sombre, as befitted a grieving soul and a long black cane was held in an elegant yet shaking hand. Once again he wondered why he was receiving a visit from Lord Malison on the day of his daughter's death. Still he could not just stand there silently; Justin stepped before his visitor and offered him a small nod of the head.

"Lord Malison what brings you to my home" He asked mildly, noting the pain on the man's lined face. His words had only just finished echoing in the calm air of the parlour before Honesty's father drew back his cane and lashed out at Justin's head, striking him a blow that made his head swim.

"You killed my daughter," His words buzzed dully in Justin's head as he became aware of the second blow, glancing off his shoulder with a dull crack. "You utter swine," Malison drew his cane back for a third strike and Justin reacted, seizing the wooden weapon and pulling it from his hands in one swift moment.

"I most certainly did not," He called back, feeling the pain in his head and shoulder fade as he drew upright. The cane in his hands was heavy and thick, it would have left a heavy bruise. With one swift motion he threw the cane to the floor "Why do you accuse me sir?" As he threw the question into the air, he realised that he had been halfway to the answer earlier. He was the perfect suspect. He was a notorious lover of women and someone that had been linked to all the murdered girls. Unwelcome thoughts of those best left alone, drifted through his mind and he tried to focus on his visitor .

"Because you're the accursed whoreson that she was going to elope with. We knew that you'd seduced her," Malison was nearly shouting, tears standing in his eyes. "I'll kill you for this Lestrade," With a burst of speed he rushed forward seized Justin by the lapels. Malison drew back his fist and punched hard, splitting Justin's lip, causing blood to flow from his mouth. Justin allowed him two more punches before he seized the other man's hand and forced it down. He knew that Malison needed to face this tragedy with his version of action, but it didn't mean he had to make himself a punch bag. Face to face with Honesty's father, he stared him clearly in the eyes and spoke with a clarity and forcefulness that stilled the other man.

"I did nothing to her I swear," His gaze never wavered from Malison's and truth shone through each syllable. "I was at White's until the early hours of the morning, several people saw me there. After that I returned to my home on the outskirts, the publican at the Oak can vouch for my passing in the small hours. I was not near your daughter last night. I will admit that I had a fondness for her…" Malison snorted in disbelief.

"But I swear to you sir that I did nothing to her. I never asked her to elope,"

Malison stared at Justin's dark eyes and said nothing, absorbing what he said. Behind Lestrade, Malison could see Hedge stood near the door. The taciturn butler stood ready to come to his master's aid at the first signal, yet Justin did not summon him. Hedge merely watched as his master wrested control of the situation. For all his apparent youth, Justin Lestrade was in full control of his faculties.

"If you are lying Lestrade," Malison's voice wavered as he collected the tattered remnants of his thoughts and attempted to regain control of his raging emotions. He had no proof that Justin had done anything to his daughter, yet he could not dismiss the knowledge that Lestrade had gotten close to her. He had come to the house, hoping to wring a confession from the young man, yet he was troubled by the boy's reaction. Malison could see Lestrade's eyes and it was clear that he was not lying. He swallowed and tried once again to drag control of the situation from the younger man. "If you are lying I swear…" The threat of violence seemed hollow as Justin seemed to have shrugged off the blows that would have cowed a lesser man. Whatever else Justin Lestrade was, he was no coward.

"I am not lying," Justin peeled the other's hands from his lapels and stepped away. With an unconscious grace he sat in one of chairs, his bloodied face stern yet calm. "However, if you feel that I have," A note of insulted pride crept into his voice, "Please feel free to contact people to gain a perspective on my whereabouts last night," He reached down and handed Malison his cane. "Or you can challenge me to a duel, whichever suits you," He turned to face the fire, dismissing Malison with a wave.

"Either way, I would like you to vacate my home. I feel for your loss but that does not give you the right to come into my house and insult me. I have done nothing to your daughter, yes I like the ladies but I do not kill them,"

Malison opened his mouth and then closed it again, it was clear that Justin was not to be drawn any further on the subject. He had no proof and he was certain that the man's butler would stop him attacking his master further. Vowing to find some evidence to drag Lestrade to the gallows, he cast another glance at the boy's back before he turned to face the door and Hedge.

"This way sir," The butler was polite yet his tone was iron hard and disapproving, clearly he felt that his master's honour had been sullied. As the doors of Justin's home closed behind him, the bitter tang of disappointment soured him and he moved through the courtyard with slow steps. He could feel the eyes of Lestrade's butler on his back all the way down to the street.

"Are you alright sir?" Hedge returned to the parlour where he saw Justin hold a handkerchief to his bleeding face.

"Oh I'm absolutely fine," There was a raw, bitter humour in Justin's voice that Hedge had never heard before. "I just love being accused of murder after breakfast, damn him," Justin held the blood stained fabric over his wounds concealing them from view.

"May I see that sir?"

"No," His voice was emphatic as he turned away. "Just find me a piece of steak for this eye and cancel my trip tonight. I'm not going out like this," He got up in one rapid movement and headed for the door. With light fast steps Justin swept past Hedge and walked towards the stairs. "Send my supper to my room," Taking the stairs two at a time carried him quickly upstairs and towards his bedroom. Like a hurricane he barrelled through the heavy wooden door and into the room, shutting the door as he entered. With deliberate movements, he turned the key in the lock so that Hedge would have to knock before entering. Now he was alone. Beside the large tallboy opposite his bed, hung a gilt framed mirror. He walked forward and stood before the tall, shimmering oval. Concealed by the bloodied white of the handkerchief, his face looked back at him. Beneath the white folds of cloth, he could no longer feel the pain of his beating and he drew his hand away. The handkerchief fell away and he stared at his face, anticipating the sight that met his eyes. Despite the blood that smeared his lower lip and the snowy cotton in his fingers, his face was clean and unblemished. Around the eyes where there should have been a blackening of skin, a bruising of flesh, there was nothing. There was no evidence that he had ever been struck. Pulling open his shirt, he looked at his shoulder, at the unmarked flesh beneath the silk and a bitter, mocking smile inched across his lips.

"Damn him! DAMN! DAMN! DAMN!" The words tore from his mouth as he dragged himself from the image. With a groan of frustration he whirled about and threw himself onto his bed. He would have to stay up here for several days, even if Malison kept his mouth shut about the beating, Hedge would certainly wonder about the lack of markings. It would make the task of staying inconspicuous even harder. He thought about Lord Malison's visit with detachment, he should have known that he would be suspected. After all, he had met Honesty, made her love him. In other circumstances he may have asked her to elope but as the situation stood, he could not. He covered his face with his hands and tried to still his thoughts. If things grew too strange he would have to leave again and the notion disturbed him greatly. He could not leave now.

This society was full of interest and wonder, it changed constantly and he felt alive within it. There was also the matter of Melissa De Vire. Justin's fingers fell away from his eyes and he stared up at the canopy above him. What was the matter with him? He had met attractive girls before and none of them had got under his skin like this, none of them had roused forgotten emotions like she had done. Dressed in that striking colour, she had drawn his gaze as a moth was drawn to a flame. One glance revealed that she was a newcomer and so he had walked towards her, meaning to seduce her as easily as he had done with others. Yet she had seen through his pose and bluster. She had answered him with candour that was refreshing for the vapid society that surrounded her. Beautiful yet restless, he could tell she yearned for freedom and it intrigued him. Her slapping of Montjoy, acknowledged social suicide of the highest calibre, yet he applauded her guts.

"Dear god I'm a fool," He moaned softly as he drew his fingers back to his face, to the unlined and smooth skin. "What am I thinking of?"

He couldn't get close to her; he shouldn't get close to her. It was too dangerous for both of them. And should she get close enough, she would learn his secrets and that could not be allowed. Anna had proved that he could not allow anyone to get too close. He could seduce whoever he wished but nothing beyond that. If John thought it had gone further, then there was nothing he could do.

"Alistair was right. I am damned,"

There was a knock on the door and Hedge's voice

sounded strongly through the wood. "Sir?"

"I don't want to be disturbed," Justin called back, grimacing at the thought of having to spend the next few days pretending to be damaged.

"I have brought the steak you wanted sir,"

"Well leave it outside; I will get it in a moment,"

"You should be looked at sir"

Justin turned to face the door and shouted. "I said I wished to be left alone! Respect my wishes Hedge,"

"As you say sir," Hedge's footsteps moved off down the corridor. Justin waited a few moments before opening the heavy door and picking up the silver platter with the slab of raw steak glistening on its surface. Retreating back into his room, he placed the platter on his dresser. The plate knocked against the enamel lotus brooch and he glanced at it with something akin to hate. Resisting the urge to pick up the accursed thing and throw it out the window, he turned away from the brooch and returned his attention back to the mirror. His reflection stared at him like a stranger.

"She would never understand," He repeated as his gaze roamed over the smooth unmarked skin of his face and chest; skin that should be bruised and bleeding. Who would understand that? Only the others knew and most of them hated him.

"They have more than enough reasons to," He muttered as his gaze slid over to the lotus involuntarily. The black blossom tugged on his mind, drawing him back to that dusty attic. It had been a game. They had been testing their courage against the tales that their family told. They had both seen the engraved box, both heard the stories. They had both climbed into the attic room on that fateful, rainy afternoon to look at the remnants of his Great Grandfather's travels. They had both looked at the box with curiosity. Yet he had made the fateful suggestion; he had dared to open the box. He closed his eyes and dragged himself away from the memory. He had seen that dusty room and that box so often in his mind that he could describe it exactly. He had been a prideful fool and that had led not only to his downfall, but his younger brother's and that of their closest friends as well. Once again he thought back to the dead women and wondered if John had returned to the country, but he dismissed the thought as worry. Had John returned to continue his torment, he would have known it for certain; even Emily could not fail to note John's arrival.

Justin turned away from his reflection and sat down on the edge of his bed. It was futile to think about things that he couldn't change. No matter how hard he searched for the answer, he knew that it wouldn't just fall into his lap. Sighing, he flopped backwards onto the covers and closed his eyes. As he drifted into an uneasy sleep, his thoughts once again turned to Melissa De Vire and he smiled as darkness swallowed him.

CHAPTER 14

Katherine walked back into the foul study and stood before her 'father'. He was smiling today and that seemed wrong. His lips never seemed right for smiling and she suppressed the grimace that threatened to swamp her.

"You seem happy," She didn't whisper, though she felt like it. His last 'lesson' had given her a great deal to think about.

"Indeed, I've discovered something interesting," He got up from the chair and walked towards her. Katherine tried to stay still, but memories of the last time, echoed through her head and she took a step backwards.

"What have you discovered?"

"Well, it appears that our Justin attended a duel

recently," He sounded positively gleeful but Katherine could not understand why.

"And why is that so interesting? I daresay Justin attends a lot of duels," She watched him closely, hoping that his good mood would hold and that her question would not anger him.

"Because," He spoke the words as though she was simple, but she knew not to become offended by them. Her throat still ached, even though there was no sign that he had ever choked her. "Justin usually only attends duels that are for his friends. As my spies tell me, he has no connection with either of the participants,"

"And you find that odd?" She had to admit, she was bemused. Justin attending a duel was not unusual, she was sure he had spent a good portion of time watching men slice pieces out of each other in the past. Why was attending the duel of a stranger such a thrill for her 'father'?

"Yes... you see I know that Justin has not gone to a duel in the last decade or so and Alistair told me that he had lost interest in such things," He positively beamed as he continued the explanation. "No I would take this as evidence that he has found someone to be interested in,"

"Alright, do you know who he was watching?" A flicker of annoyance rushed through her; she knew what she would have to do to know. He would have her scouring the countryside, following whoever he named. Setting her teeth against the scowl that would surely incur his wrath, she waited for his instructions.

"Well I know that one of them was injured and it

happens that he is closer to town," He reached over to a small carved box and opened it. As he picked up the enamel flower, she bit her lip in anticipation. "Now you know what you have to do, get this man's story, find out the reason for the duel and if there is any need," He handed her the flower. "You know what to do,"

She picked up the enamel and felt its cool surface with pleasure. A glance up at her 'Father' however, dispelled her happy feelings.

"And then fetch me Alistair, I want a word with him,"

Nodding, she clasped the small item to her chest and headed for the door of the room.

"And come straight back," She glanced over her shoulder at the man behind her. "You know I can find you if you don't,"

Katherine nodded and headed from the room, clasping the small brooch as though it were made of gold.

CHAPTER 15

"Yes. I hear that Lord Malison gave the boy a thrashing,"

"Is that why he isn't here?"

"Of course, he wouldn't show his face like that. He knows that he is the only real suspect,"

"Yet Malison has not brought him to the magistrate,"

"I think he has his reasons,"

The conversation boiled around her like ripples in a storm tossed pond. Rumours and lies, titbits of gossip and lewd laughter battered her ears as she navigated the sea that was Lady Shearingham's ball. Melissa was dressed in blue today and she moved across the floor in the company of one young bravo, listening to the talk around her. There was no sign of Lestrade this evening, yet that was only to be expected. News of Malison's visit to his town house was the talk of the town and it was anticipated that Lestrade would not be present for some time. In his absence however, rumours flew about the room and he was the talk of the event. As Sarah had predicted, Honesty's death had pushed thoughts of her personal scandal far from those attending and despite a few exceptions, she had not experienced a lack of male company.

"So my angel," Her companion towards her and smiled. Beneath exquisitely powdered hair, his brown eyes watched her with delighted interest. "Do you fancy taking a turn about the room?"

Melissa slowly nodded, in the absence of the one person she would have preferred to dance with; she had flung herself back into the whirl of the night's events. Peter Cornell, her current partner, had snatched her from the clutches of Laurence Baptiste much to her relief for Laurence had been an unmitigated bore. Peter himself wasn't particularly sparkling and he had a tendency to call her angel or beloved yet he was a fount of knowledge. He had filled her in on the latest rumours and had talked with her knowledgably about the current state of the capital. As such, Melissa had spent a fair amount of the evening in his company.

"So is Lestrade going to face charges for the murder?" She asked as he led her through a slow, courtly dance.

"Hmm no," Peter answered quietly as he moved expertly through the movements of the waltz. "He could not have been responsible. He was at Whites until the early hours,"

"Could he not have gone to her after?"

"Possibly but I think not," The music ceased and they both applauded before crossing to a pair of seats in the corner of the room. "Why are you so interested Lady?"

"Oh I'm just curious," She attempted a vacuous smile and was rewarded by the indulgent gleam she saw in Peter's eyes. "All this talk is quite fascinating. Just think we have a killer in our set,"

"It's not something for you to worry your pretty little curls about," Peter answered in a patronising tone. "Just enjoy the party,"

"Of course," Melissa answered prettily enough, yet her thoughts were ranging out over the problem. The rumours were damaging, granted Justin had power yet his lack of parentage, his reputation as a cad and his connection to all the murdered girls was damning evidence. Melissa did not know what to think; in spite of all the talk during the evening she was convinced that Justin was not responsible for the girl's death. It was clear however that she was in a minority. Peter for example seemed to believe Justin was innocent, yet he was practically the only one. During the last half hour alone, she had heard many insist that Justin should be hanged for the crimes; despite the fact the no one could link him beyond his familiarity with the women. Wondering about the dilemma as her eyes roved about the room she found her gaze alighting on the larger than life form of her host, Isabella Shearingham. The lady in question was fast approaching her middle years yet she was a formidable dame who kept up with the latest fashion and trends. Despite the fact that she had given birth to two children, she hadn't retreated from the social whirl. Ordinarily she was the life and soul of the event, greeted newcomers and flirting outrageously with all and sundry, yet this evening she seemed tense. Melissa puzzled at the change in her. The start of the evening had progressed as normal, Isabella greeting her guests with a smile and witty comment, yet as the evening wore on the smile became strained. Keeping this perturbing thought in mind, Melissa ran her eyes over the saffron clad form of her host. At this present moment, Isabella was stood next to a young man and talking. A glance at the fan held in her fingers, revealed the depths of her agitation. Melissa's eyes travelled upwards from the twitching fan towards the smiling yet tense features of her host. Slowly she tracked across and looked at the man opposite Isabella. He was young looking and well dressed. His clothes were expensive yet sombre in tone and his wig was plain and unadorned. Melissa aimed a long searching look at his profile and a stab of recognition found her heart.

"Who's that?" She asked Peter in a hushed tone, nodding over at the strange man with a subtle inclination of her head. She watched as he lifted Isabella's hand to his lips and kissed it. Once again the troubling sensation that she knew the stranger trickled down her spine. The man moved off into the crowd followed by Melissa's eyes, she knew she was being rude yet she couldn't tear her eyes away.

"I don't know," Peter murmured, setting down his

canary and picking up his quizzing glass. Bringing the glasses to his brown eyes he stared at the departing figure for a few moments.

"He reminds me of someone," He ventured finally before releasing hold on his glasses. The fragile collection of wire and glass bounced lightly on his chest as the sturdy chain halted their downward flight. "But I fancy I've never seen him before," Reaching for his glass, he took a long sip of canary and began to lose interest in the stranger.

"I daresay we'll find out who he is soon enough," Peter's hand settled onto her arm drawing her attention from the stranger. "But until we do, would I be too forward if I asked you to walk with me on the terrace?" A smile lingered on his lips as he looked down at her.

"Umm," Melissa stumbled over her words as she looked up at her partner. Indeed she liked his company, he had kept her amused for the best part of the evening, yet she was in no mood to traipse outside on his arm. Searching her mind for a credible reason to decline she settled on the simplest lie.

"I'm terribly sorry but I'm rather fatigued after all this dancing," The words flowed easily from her lips, startling herself with the ease that she lied. "I fancy that I need to sit and rest for a time,"

"Of course my angel," Apparently ignorant of her deception; Peter led her across the floor towards a set of spindly and less than comfortable chairs. He proffered a seat for her and took the one opposite. Gracefully she sat, smoothing her skirts with one practiced motion as she settled unto the hard piece of furniture.

So will you be attending court this season?" Melissa started to speak, her fingers automatically straightening the lace on her sleeves as she spoke. Her eyes still drifted around the room in her search for the strange man she had seen earlier.

"Yes. I find country life remarkably dull after spending time at court. There's never enough to do,"

"Oh? I always find the country most entertaining," Melissa unfurled her fan and began waving it gently before her face.

"Well there is riding to be had I suppose and you can hold your own parties, but you never get quite the same breadth of choice that you do at court. I mean look at Tollchester," He waved his hand towards a short rotund fellow by the punch bowl. "I only see him in London. He's a wonderful conversationalist, wouldn't see him for dust if I were in the country all the time,"

"Hmm,"

"Of course that doesn't mean that I don't have an estate outside of London. My Wiltshire estate is roughly ten thousand acres of prime land…" Schooling her expression into one of polite interest Melissa prepared herself for a long winded conversation. Quite how Sarah could enjoy these men waffling on about their money and eligibility was quite beyond her. Wafting thin streams of lukewarm air about her, she allowed her vision to drift about the room. Over by the punch bowl stood Amelia Danforth and her current favourite, next to them the formidable form of

Lord Asquith ranged over the parquet floor like a restless lion. Behind Lord Asquith and stood between two stone pillars was Emma Dawlish, an old friend. Melissa shut her fan with a snap.

"I'm sorry Mr Cornell," She interrupted his flow of words with as much gentleness as she could muster. "But I've seen someone that I simply must speak to, if you'll excuse me,"

"Why of course," Peter replied with a slightly startled look on his face. "Maybe I can find you later," Melissa smiled and stood up. Leaving Peter with barely a backwards glance, she headed across the floor towards Emma.

"Excuse me," A woman's voice interrupted her mid stride and she turned to face the young widow who had captured Justin's interest at the Palace. A twinge of irritation flowed through her as she stared at the blonde perfection of Emily Saint-Clair.

"Yes?" She asked, looking at the woman with mild curiosity. The blonde was dressed in exquisite and expensive cream brocade and staring at her with an amused expression.

"I'm Emily Saint-Clair," The woman announced, her voice cheery. "And you're Melissa De Vire," Melissa nodded, wondering why Emily had chosen to speak with her. The blonde smiled again and reached for the fan dangling at her waist. Melissa took this moment to properly gaze at her companion. The woman's hair was concealed beneath an elaborate wig and a delicate choker surrounded her throat. With some surprise, she noted that the choker was similar in appearance to the brooch that Justin wore on his cravat. Emily looked up and noted the direction of her eyes.

"My father's," She answered Melissa's unanswered question. "I believe there are only a few of these,"

"Lestrade had one like it," Melissa noted, wondering how close Emily and Lestrade were to have matching jewellery.

"Yes, our fathers were old friends," A note of humour thrummed through her tones that Melissa did not understand. "In fact they were members of a select club. They all had one of these; I wear mine to remind me of my father,"

"Oh," Melissa nodded, convinced that she had not been told the truth, yet unsure how she could pursue the matter. "How did.,"

"I saw you at the Palace," Emily spoke suddenly, cutting off Melissa's questions as her fingers snapped open the fan. "I was most impressed with the way you handled that swine Montjoy,"

"Thank you," Melissa muttered, wondering if she should accept any congratulations for an episode that almost ruined her. Also, Emily's fan was close to her face, hiding the choker and Melissa knew that Emily was attempting to distract her from the enamelled bloom.

"After all, one of us needed to slap him, he's a terror. If he had got you outside of the room and debauched you," Melissa snapped her eyes to Emily's face in shock at the directness of the woman before her. "It would have been more than your ruin," Emily waved the fan gently, negligently as though bored by the entire conversation.

"Others do not think so," She said quietly, hoping that the woman would take the hint and stop talking. The other patrons at the party could hear their discussion and she had no wish for the gossip to flow about her again.

"I beg to differ," The woman leant forward and whispered. "Justin was most impressed," Melissa stared at the woman's blue eyes in shock.

"What?"

"You know, Justin Lestrade, handsome, arrogant," She spoke as though Melissa were a simpleton and that fan kept flapping before her face. "The man who asked you to dance?"

"Yes I know who he is, what are you getting at?" Melissa felt her temper rise as she stared at this porcelain skinned beauty. Was she rubbing in her relationship with Lestrade?

"Nothing," The woman smiled, snapping shut the fan with a decisive snap. "I know he is handsome Melissa and like others, you've probably fallen for him," Unbidden she linked her arm in Melissa's and began to walk. To prevent the room seeing the spectacle of her falling over, she followed the woman to one of the outer corridors.

"And you're here to tell me to leave him alone right?" Melissa guessed as they walked past the gaming rooms and out into the garden.

"No.. no of course not," Emily came to a stop and faced her. The polite, cultured smile dropped from her face and it took on a more serious cast. "I'm here to look at you more closely,"

"Why?" Incredulous now at the strange road the conversation had taken, Melissa stared at the blonde in confusion. Who was this woman and why did she feel it necessary to talk about Lestrade to her? She had only met the man once and that had not been a glowing success. With growing impatience she stared at the other woman and waited for her to continue.

"Because my dear," Emily's vaguely patronising response set Melissa's teeth on edge and she forced down the urge to slap that confident, almost mocking face. "I've known Justin for some time and I haven't seen him this taken with anyone for a while,"

Really?" Melissa finally responded, her patience almost gone. "I only met him the once and he seemed completely bored by the whole experience," Her voice snapped out across the space, waspish and sharp. "I hardly think that he gave much thought to me, he certainly failed to return for a dance," She took a step away from the woman and prepared to move on. "If Lestrade wishes to find his way back into my good graces, then he need not send you to tout for him. I would say that it's been a pleasure making your acquaintance, but truthfully, it hasn't," Taking another step back, she turned and started to walk towards the main hallway. Emily's hand closed once again around her arm and stopped her. "What?" She hissed, her patience gone.

"Miss De Vire, I'm not touting for Justin, I just felt the need to see what had seized his attention," She stepped forward, almost uncomfortably close and whispered. "Now I have seen you and I can understand his attraction," Melissa swallowed nervously as the woman stepped even closer. "It might even be fun to see how this plays out," She released Melissa's arm and stepped back. "Have a pleasant evening Miss De Vire," And with that, she walked away. Melissa watched her go with a sense of confusion and relief, despite the many questions she had, she did not wish to follow.

With several quick steps, she walked back into the room and crossed to a servant, taking a drink from a silver tray, she downed the burning drink in one go.

"Go easy, the night is young and you don't want to pass out," She turned to face Emma Dawlish and she smiled at her.

"Em," She embraced the other girl quickly in joy and they linked arms. "How is it?"

"Utterly dreadful, my abigail insists in putting me in yellow," She waved her hand over the dress she was wearing with a helpless smile. "I really don't suit yellow but I can't seem to get it through to her," The two made their way over a set of seats beside the door to the gardens. A cool breeze flowed through the open doorway, cooling them after the stifling heat from the room. "So how is it with you?" Emma asked seriously as they settled down.

"Oh you know," Melissa replied carefully, her eyes still roving over the room as she watched Emily Saint-Clair navigate the crowd. "It's been better,"

"Well no one has mentioned your debut tonight, that's

got to be an improvement," Emma took a sip of her drink and stared across at her friend.

"I suppose," Melissa replied, she was barely paying attention. Emily had been accosted by the strange man she had seen talking to Lady Shearingham. As she watched the two converse, it was clear that they were both casting glances in her direction.

"Melissa?" She started up to stare at Emma. "What is wrong?"

"I don't know," Melissa uttered finally, tearing her gaze from the pair on the other side of the room. "I was so looking forward to this," She waved her hand about the room. "And now it's here, I don't really want to play," Dropping the goblet onto a side table, she turned from the room to stare at her friend. "Sarah made it sound so exciting, but I can't get away from the feeling that I don't matter. My father gets to decide who I'm with and I know he would not be happy if I chose otherwise. This feels like an upmarket slave block. Whoever can offer the most gets me," She glanced up at the room again and watched as Emily and the strange man continued their conversation.

"Well, you're right," Emma replied, putting a comforting hand on her friends arm. "But it doesn't mean it can't be fun. Enjoy all of those overwrought declarations and try to find someone you can get along with. I doubt your father will throw you to some haggard old bachelor," Emily and the man seemed to have finished talking and the blonde was moving out of sight.

"I know, I just.," She turned back to Emma and tried to

explain the ambivalence she felt. "It feels so false, all of it,"

"Excuse me Miss De Vire?" Melissa stopped speaking and turned, standing before them was the strange man that she had seen talking to Emily only a few moments earlier.

"Yes?"

Melissa stared at the stranger, suddenly taken by a strong sense of the familiar. Beneath a plain, powdered wig, large brown eyes stared at her with disconcerting directness. Beneath an aquiline nose, a full lipped and sensual mouth lay. His face was fresh and young looking; she assumed that he was a year older than her at best. As her mind took in these details, he raised her hand to his lips. A strange chill ran up her spine as his lips brushed lightly across the back of her hand.

"I'm Alistair Lestrade," He said in his soft tones.

"Lestrade?" She couldn't help exclaiming as she stared at him in shock, it suddenly seemed so clear. This was why he had seemed so familiar, the facial features, the way of standing that was so like Justin's. "Are you related to Justin Lestrade by any chance?" She was looking at his eyes as she spoke, those dark eyes that shared the same strange light of maturity that Justin's did.

"He's my older brother," His voice was silkier than Justin's and it echoed slightly as though they were within a cathedral and not in the midst of a crowd.

"Then why have I…,"

"Not heard of me?" He finished the question for her with a smile that seemed frosty. "We don't talk much and I dislike this morass.," He waved a hand at the surrounding crowd.

"So what brings you here now?"

"I was looking for you," He answered with a soft smile, one that didn't seem to reach his eyes.

"Why?"

Alistair glanced about at Emma. "It's a private matter,"

"No," Melissa noted, looking the man squarely in the face. "You can talk here,"

Alistair stared at her for a long minute before he sighed and spoke.

"Very well," He leant close to her and spoke quietly, "I came to warn you,"

Melissa stared up at Alistair, a strange cold hand gripping her heart. The eyes looking down at her were serious and full of concern. "What about?" She whispered almost fearing the answer.

"Justin is…" he glanced around the room and leant closer lowering his voice. "My brother is dangerous to you. I warn you because I fear that he will hurt you,"

"You believe he is capable of murder?" Melissa asked, an appalled note entering her voice. It was true that she had sensed darkness in Justin yet she couldn't believe he could kill.

"If you mean the girls lately, I couldn't tell you," Alistair continued in that soft toned voice. "I do know that his attentions are not pure and they certainly will not bring you joy or wellbeing," He released her arm and stepped back his face blanking out the emotion that had been spilling out over it.

"Now I have warned you and I sincerely hope that you take this warning seriously," He turned and began to walk away into the crowd.

"Wait," She called, pushing herself from the chair and following after him. "You can't just tell me this much and then leave. I need to know," Emma followed behind, worry flowing through her features. "You have to tell me more," She pushed out into the crowd after him, trying to keep up, yet he moved through the crowd with the elusiveness of a wild thing.

"Hey," She crashed into the back of a brocade dress and apologised profusely. She turned back to the chase, yet all she saw was the crowd with not a sign of Alistair in sight.

"You made me spill my drink," Melissa turned at the shrill accusatory note and stared straight into the eyes of Mary Westbury. The girl before her was looking up at her with harsh, green eyes. In one hand she held an empty glass and the other was pointing at her in accusation. Across the front panel of Mary's cream coloured brocade dress, a blaze of red revealed where the burgundy from her empty glass had spilled. It was abundantly clear that Mary had been in possession of a nearly full glass of wine before she had been bumped.

"Oh lord I'm so sorry," Melissa stared at the spreading stain in horror. Forgetting all about Alistair for the moment, she drew her handkerchief from deep within her skirts and ineffectually brushed at the stain. The pretty white handkerchief stained red yet there was no help for the expensive fabric.

"Why on earth are you bothering? It's totally ruined now," Mary's usually grating voice was harsh and unforgiving. "How dare you? First you cause all that upset at the Palace and now you ruin my outfit,"

"I didn't mean…" Melissa's voice trailed off, she couldn't deny that she hadn't been clumsy. The brocade Mary was wearing was the very height of fashion and she had managed to ruin it but, a small rebellious thought burned in the back of her mind. She had tried to apologise for the incident and if she could ever get a word in, she would offer to pay for the damage. Mary handed the glass to her partner and stepped forward, her green eyes boring into Melissa's.

"Well you certainly weren't looking where you were going. Were you too busy chasing after another eligible bachelor that you couldn't be bothered to watch who you were bumping into?" Stunned by this tirade of words, Melissa stepped back and stared up at the blonde's hot eyes.

"Yes I know all about you," Mary, sensing her advantage, proclaimed triumphantly. "We all saw you make a fool of yourself. Quite the little glory hound aren't you?"

Melissa finally found her voice. "I don't know what you mean. I am sorry for ruining your dress, but I do not appreciate your comments. If you don't mind Miss Westbury, I will take my leave of you," She made to move past the blonde witch but Mary's voice sounded out behind her.

"Yes go on, walk off" Mary stared at her in utter

contempt. "Find some other poor sap to wrap in your drama,"

"What the devil do you mean?" In spite of her desire to avoid a scene, Melissa found herself spinning back to face her tormentor.

"I'm talking about Justin you total simpleton," Mary continued her voice a low hiss of outrage. "You certainly have him wrapped around your little finger. You were all he could discuss after your little spat with Montjoy,"

"What?" Melissa was completely baffled now and more than a little angry.

"Don't you try that on with me," Mary snarled in a low tone. "You knew exactly what you were doing. Play the helpless Damsel in Distress and perhaps get the most eligible man in the kingdom standing up for your honour," She gave a cruel smirk and whispered. "It's a shame that your brother took up the gauntlet for you. I bet that hurt, not managing to gull Justin into standing up for you,"

"You're absolutely mad," She breathed the words looking at the livid face before her. "I would never.,"

"Oh spare me your lies," Mary snapped back, her voice never reaching a pitch which could travel over the crowd. "I will say this once and once alone. If you wish to keep my good regard, you will leave Justin alone. He is mine. He loves me and we intend to be married. I am not going to let him be made a fool of by a chit like you," With a flounce of her head, Mary whirled about and headed for the exit attempting to cover the burgundy stain with her hands.

Melissa watched her storm off through the crowd with a

bemused expression on his face. She had known that Mary was smitten with Lestrade, but she hadn't realised how deeply the other girl felt. As she watched Mary's blonde head bounce through the doors at the end of the room, a hot angry feeling began to supplant the bemusement she felt. How dare Mary threaten her? She would be friends and flirt with whomever she wished. It was not as though she wished marriage to Justin, in fact she was fairly sure that marriage was not even a flickering thought in his mind. Despite her recent musings on his nature, she wasn't even sure she considered him as a potential dalliance. Dismissing Mary as a bitter shrew with no value, she turned her thoughts to the more troubling conversations with Alistair and Emily. It was obvious from the way they had talked that Emily had spoken to Alistair about her. That he was Justin's brother could not be denied, his looks were far too similar for him not to be. Yet she could not take his words seriously. No one had ever heard of Alistair Lestrade and his warning, though it seemed genuine, struck her as a little false. It seemed too melodramatic as though he had spent too long watching the stage. It also seemed presumptuous, especially considering how little time she had spent engaged in conversation with Justin. If she received this much grief over a simple talk, how much more would she get with a full blown discussion.

There was also the conversation with Emily to consider, the woman was clearly urging her into something. Emily was disturbing and clearly hiding something. She had not warned Melissa from Lestrade, it seemed to be pure curiosity but she couldn't for the life of her understand why.

She sighed and pressed her fingers to her temples. Both conversations had given her food for thought and she no longer wished to stand here in this vast crowd. Coming to a decision, she headed through the crowd and located her mother. Pleaded a headache, she begged to return home. Her mother agreed and loaded her into the carriage with Jane, ordering her to return the coach upon her arrival at home. Melissa nodded and with the gentle sound of wheel on cobblestone, the carriage trundled off into the night.

CHAPTER 16

The carriage trundled over the rough road and lulled Melissa into a daze. Jane sat opposite, her knitting needles clicking softly as they travelled.

"You seem troubled Miss," Jane noted in her soft voice as she unravelled another ball of wool. "Are you comfortable?"

"I'm fine Jane," Melissa answered, looking out of the carriage window into the darkness beyond. They were travelling between villages and darkness shrouded the countryside like a living thing. Her mind travelled back to Alistair's words and she vaguely toyed with the lace on her sleeves.

"Jane?" She addressed her maid almost absently as they

travelled through a crossroads.

"Yes Miss?"

"What do you know about the Lestrade family?"

"Well Lord Lestrade has a considerable fortune due to his parents' demise and he holds two properties, one in town and they other is near to your parents' estate,"

"Does he have a brother?"

"Yes I believe he has a younger brother Miss. I heard somewhere that he joined the seminary though not a great deal is known about him. It appears that the brothers do not see eye to eye," Jane was not offering her usual wealth of gossip and Melissa straightened up and looked at her maid.

"Is that all?"

"Well you see Miss, not much is known about the family. Very secretive bunch and have been for years. Lord Lestrade brings his valet to the balls but the man is so closemouthed I'm surprised he knows how to eat. I daresay he pays for his servants to keep his secrets," She cast off and started another line of knitting.

"Do you think him dangerous?"

"In what way Miss? Is he a danger to the virtue of a young girl? I'd say so. Is he drawn to vice like a duck to water? True I would say. Is he a killer? That I don't know about but I would not like to see my Lady involved with such as him," Jane looked up from her knitting and stared at Melissa with an intense gleam to her eyes.

"Oh Jane I'm not interested in getting involved with him. I..I'm just curious,"

"As you say Miss," Jane demurred with a slight twist to her lips. Melissa let the conversation drop, unwilling to continue this line of thought. So she was interested in Lestrade and his background, that didn't mean she was attracted to the man. As she settled back against the cushioned seat and stared out the window she avoided listening to the small voice that suggested she was more interested than she maintained. The wheels crunched over the rough ground and she drowsed again. Dozing comfortably in the padded seat, she was unprepared for the sudden lurch that threw her from her seat and pitched her to the carriage floor. A choked breath escaped her lips as her temple slammed painfully into the side of the coach. Continuing to lurch, the carriage jolted crazily and overbalanced, crashing onto its side with a bang. The footman jumped off the back, rolling to avoid damage as the coachman managed to stop the horses from bolting. Within the coach, Melissa careered into Jane as the coach fell onto its side, a scream tearing from her lips as Jane's knitting needles stabbed painfully into her side. The long thin needles tore the expensive cloth of her gown and stained the muslin undergarments with bright red blood. For a moment, stunned silence reigned in the coach as everything stilled and came to rest.

"Miss," Through a dazed fog of pain, she made out Jane's worried face as it bent over her. "Oh dear Lord. Jeb! Franklin," Her maid shouted out as she steadily began to pull the needles from Melissa's side. Melissa gave a small squeak as the first needle moved within her. "Don't worry

Miss, it'll be alright," She touched a calloused hand to the girl's temple before continuing.

"Sorry Miss, We lost a wheel on the bend," A male voice sounded from outside as the coachman unlashed the horses before turning to survey the damage. The coach was on its side, the wheels still spinning from the road. With practised agility he clambered on top of the coach and reached for the door handle. With a heavy jerk, he pulled the door open and stared down into the wreck of the carriage. Jane and his mistress were crumpled in a heap at the bottom of the carriage. A large livid bruise was splayed across Melissa's powdered features and her hair was a tumbled mess. He could also see blood.

"Is she alright?"

"What do you think?" Jane finally removed the first needle, wincing at the blood that stained the pointed object. As she placed it on the floor she glanced upwards.

"Get in here Franklin, the mistress is hurt and I won't be able to lever her out myself,"

"Hold on Miss," Carefully the coachman lowered himself into the coach and leant over the silk clad form of Melissa. "We'll have you out in a moment," He stood up, balancing on the edge of the padded seats and looked out.

"Jeb… come give me a hand,"

Melissa felt them both clamber onto the carriage and glanced across at her maid. Jane's face was set in concentration as she applied pressure to the wounds on her side. The pain in her temple throbbed constantly yet she was sure that it was subsiding. Her vision was clearer now; she could see the devastation in the carriage. "Jane?" She tried her voice, it was shaky but she could still speak.

"Don't worry Miss,"

"What happened?" She felt the second needle being drawn from her side and winced at the sensation. The carriage rocked as the two men manoeuvred their way into a better position on top of the capsized vehicle.

"We went over," Her maid explained as she carefully began to bandage her mistress with thin strips of torn fabric. "And we lost a wheel,"

"Ah," Melissa hissed with pain as Jane pulled tight at the bandage and attached. "Is there any chance of getting back on route?" She asked through clenched teeth.

"I don't know Miss," Jane stepped back and helped from the carriage by the two men. "You can move her now," She said as she hopped lightly from the carriage to the rough road.

"Are you ready Miss?" Jeb asked as he carefully lowered himself into the carriage space. Melissa nodded, determined not to show any weakness before the servants. When she was back home, she would have a good cry, but not here. Jeb's muscular body supported her as he levered her up and through the door into the outside where Franklin waited. With gentle movements, they got her out of the carriage and into the dark night air. Melissa was finally upright and she felt herself sway with the effort of the motion.

"Oh dear Lord," She looked at the toppled carriage with wonder. The livery was scratched and ruined. The axle which held the carriage wheel was buckled and she could see the wheel lying on its side in the ditch. One glance told her that they would not be using the coach any time soon. Jeb and Franklin moved to one side of the coach and managed to lever it upright. Both men moved to inspect the damage. Melissa watched them for a few moments before the pain in her side forced her to lean against the bole of a nearby tree.

"It's no use Miss," Jeb moved away from the damaged coach and came to stand near Melissa. "It's damaged beyond repair,"

"So how are we to get back?" Melissa asked, trying not to make her voice sound like a whine. "We're many miles from the manor,"

"Jeb can unhitch the horses and ride one back," Franklin answered quietly, glancing across at the damage. "He can then return with the other coach and collect us," He looked at Melissa and added. "Only if it pleases you Miss,"

Melissa glanced at the group, at the empty road with the wrecked carriage and nodded. Her only other option was to walk back along the road, not a task she relished, even if she hadn't received an injury. Franklin and Jeb moved to the horses and freed them from the carriage trappings. With a smooth movement, Jeb hoisted himself onto the back of the freed horse and headed off down the road at a heavy canter. A night owl hooted loudly from the nearby trees and a chill wind tugged at her skirts and rumpled locks. There was little conversation. Periodically Jane looked at the bandage on her side and adjusted it but besides that, none spoke. Leaning against the tree, Melissa gazed out at the moonlit night in a daze. Her side ached from time to time and there was a tender spot on her temple where her head had struck the side of the coach. The moon cast long shadows along the fields and a clear night revealed a sky filled with stars, each brighter than the last. Tapping her slippered foot in the dirt, she found herself drifting with the landscape. Her thoughts flowing over the events of the previous days as she waited for the telltale sound of wheels on stone. Not counting Jane's concerns, she had received four separate warnings about the 'dangerous' Justin Lestrade. Her brother had warned her as had Sarah, both warnings she could take with a pinch of salt. Her brother would warn her from any that he could not personally vouch for and Sarah would presume that she couldn't handle a pleasant smile. Yes she could not really take the first two warnings very seriously as they were generic, warnings about being taken for a naïve fool. However the last two warnings were giving her cause for concern. Mary's warning concerned her, simply because it seemed too ludicrous and Alistair's worried her for the shock of it. She had not been aware of the existence of a brother to Lestrade until this evening, yet the looks matched and Jane had confirmed it. So why was his younger brother running around events warning people about his kin. It seemed the height of betrayal, deriding your own sibling. Unless, her mind argued, Justin was extremely dangerous and this overrode any brotherly feeling. Melissa shook her head imperceptibly; she couldn't accept that Justin was the danger. She had looked at his eyes, he couldn't be a danger, could he? Her side ached and she slid closer to the ground feeling the chill seep through her cloak as though it were not there. She shuddered, dragging her cloak around her as her teeth chattered over and over. Around her the sounds of the night continued, yet they faded in and out as tiredness swept over her body and she sank to the strangely comfortable ground. In the nearby copse, the owl hooted loudly as she rested against the tree, feeling a strange warmth flow through her body. In the depths of the cold night she felt tired and drowsy. Clearly her cloak was helping as the desire to drift into what seemed like a warm sleep grew stronger. Her eyelids fluttered and she felt herself dozing as shock finally settled into her bones.

"Miss," Jane was shaking her, dragging her from the warmth comfort of her sleep. "You must not go to sleep now,"

Melissa glanced up at her maid, the face hazy in the darkness and tried to pull away. "Lemme go to sleep," She moaned, trying to slide back into the delicious warmth of sleep.

"I can't let you sleep now Miss. You have to keep awake," Melissa pushed her away and felt her eyes drift close again.

SLAP

Melissa jolted upright as a stinging pain exploded across her right cheek. Jane had slapped her hard.

"You slapped me Jane," She muttered in disbelief as she raised her hand to her throbbing cheek. "How dare you slap me?"

"Forgive me Miss, but I had no choice. It seems the

accident took you harder than I thought," Jane pulled her upright and began to walk her up and down. "You can't go to sleep Miss, It's dangerous for you to sleep when you're this hurt,"

"Listen," Franklin cocked his head and looked down the road towards town. "I hear horses,"

The small group looked up wonderingly as the sound of hooves grew closer. The servant's fingers moved towards their pistols in concern that the horses belonged to highwaymen. The noise grew in volume and presently the riders came into view. Two riders, one a gentleman for his dress and the other dressed in what could only be described as a boat cloak. In a cloud of dust they pulled up and the pair looked over at them. Both wore mufflers high about their faces and Franklin drew his pistol, prepared to fire.

"Well I never," A well remembered and odious voice flowed from beneath the hood of the first rider. "A she devil grubbing in the dirt, how delightfully apt," The first rider pulled down the hood and revealed Montjoy. Franklin lowered his pistol marginally but did not put it away. Montjoy moved his horse forward, a sneer on his lips as he took in Franklin's stance and his eyes once again roamed over Melissa with lecherous intent. "Good evening Miss De Vire," An oily smile crossed his lips as he lent out of the saddle and stared down at the injured group. "Would you care for a ride? I can return you to your home" Franklin and Jane stiffened, a look of dislike crossing both faces.

"I am waiting for my coach thank you," Melissa replied

as politely as she possibly could and not quite managing to keep the dislike out of her voice. She keenly remembered the feel of his rough hands against her back and the look of rage on his face. "I will not accompany you," Franklin raised the pistol slightly higher, expecting trouble.

"So high and mighty," He muttered in a poisonous tone. "You deserve to be taken down a peg or two," His companion cleared his throat and Montjoy sighed. Sitting upright in the saddle he tossed an insincere smirk back at the group. "I hope you won't wait long," He wheeled his horse back to the road and tapped his heels lightly to its side.

The two riders had barely moved out of sight when another sound reached their ears. Montjoy and his companion moved to the side and stopped.

"A coach," Franklin noted with a smile. Melissa and Jane looked up at the same time, listening keenly for the sound of wheels and hooves and thankful that Montjoy had left.

"I hear it," Melissa woke up a little more as the noise of wheels finally reached her ears and she stood up straighter, looking along the road with hope in her eyes. "Looks like Jeb made good time," She murmured with a smile.

The carriage rolled to a stop just before the group and the driver looked down at them, mild curiosity in his deep set eyes.

"It's not Jeb," Franklin noted as he walked forward and spoke to the coach driver in low tones.

"Why have we stopped Coll?" A familiar voice sounded

from the inside of the carriage as a gloved hand pushed aside the heavy curtain.

"There's an accident sir. A Miss De Vire," The driver answered with a soft toned voice.

"What?" The coach door burst open and Justin almost jumped out of the carriage with a look of shock on his face. His dark eyes roamed over their ruined vehicle with concern before they settled on the decidedly unsteady form of Melissa. "Meli.," He collected himself and continued. "Miss De Vire. I am sorry for your misfortune," He ran his eyes up and down the road before continuing in a worried tone. "You are not planning to stay by the side of the road all night?"

"We have sent Jeb back for the second carriage my Lord," Franklin noted as he glanced up at Justin with some deference. "We do not expect him to be long,"

"Nevertheless, I cannot in all conscience leave you by the side of the road," Justin stepped forward, concern etched on his features as he approached her. Mindful of Montjoy and his companion waiting further along the road, he hoped she would accept his help. "I would consider myself ungentlemanly if I did not assist you," He moved forward into a patch of moonlight and looked down at the dark coloured patch on her dress. "Particularly as you're bleeding,"

"I have bound the wound sir," Jane answered with only a modicum of irritation. "It does require further attention though,"

"Then I insist that I deliver you home safely," Jane

stepped forward, her face like thunder and he hurriedly added. "Your maid of course will accompany us. I would not wish you to be without a chaperone,"

"What shall we do about Jeb? He is bound to have arrived at home by now," Melissa answered, not really thinking clearly about the proposed trip with Justin. Staying by the side of the road was not appealing, particularly since their unpleasant encounter only a few moments before, yet a ride in Justin's carriage could be troublesome.

"We shall meet him on route and this one can deal with the wrecked carriage," Justin answered as he turned those disturbing eyes onto her coachman. "Please Lady I insist that you return with me. Here you are at mercy of bandits, not counting the inconvenience of your wounds," He stepped closer, the soft notes of his voice pleading. "I could not leave you here,"

Melissa glanced over at her would be saviour. He was dressed in everyday garb and had clearly not been to a ball that eve. His hair was without powder and his dark locks looked black in the bleaching light of the moon. The throbbing pain in her side reminded her of the damage done by Jane's knitting needles. Memories of her near fatal slide into sleep were fresh and gave her cause for concern. In addition she could see Montjoy still waiting in the distance, if Justin left, he could return to bother her further?

Justin caught her anxiety and leant forward. "I promise you will be safe from him," He nodded across at the watching riders and smiled reassuringly.

"Very well Lord Lestrade. I will accompany you," She noted, watching as his face crinkled with pleasure as she spoke the words. With exquisite courtesy he held out a hand and helped her carefully up the steps and into his coach. After a moment, Jane followed reluctantly. Franklin shut the door behind the maid with a heavy thump, before climbing up and taking the empty footman's position at the rear.

Montjoy moved off, losing interest in the group as Justin's played saviour. His muffled companion stayed in position, watching the scene with interest. As Melissa clasped hold of Justin's offered arm, the figure turned, clicked to his horse and galloped away, a cloud of dust flying into the air as he sped off into the night.

Coll clicked to the horses slowly turning the coach to face the opposite direction. With a reassuring click of his tongue and snap of the reins, he drove the horses into a fast trot, leaving the ruined carriage where it lay. Another flick of the reins and they were soon flying along the road, towards the sleeping hamlets and their estates that lay beyond.

Melissa sat back on the padded seating and stared across at Justin, barely making out his expression in the dim light. Silently he reached forward and handed her a travelling rug, which she tucked carefully about her legs. "Thank you," It felt like an inadequate response for drawing him away from his evening.

"It was the least I could do. I could not leave you there at the mercy of highwaymen or Montjoy when I saw him on the road," He answered tersely, his eyes on her. She could feel them in the dark scoring into her soul. Beside her she could feel the tense body of Jane as she kept her eyes on Justin, playing the chaperone for all she was worth.

"Still, thank you. I'm sorry to keep you from your evening,"

"Do not concern yourself," Feather soft and gentle, his words mollified her and she settled back, feeling better about the situation. "I'm glad to have been of service, particularly as Lord Montjoy appeared to be making a nuisance of himself,"

Melissa smiled and thanked him again. "So how did you come to be travelling home without your family?" He asked politely, the cushions creaking slightly as he shifted to a more comfortable position. The curtains were half closed and even with the moonlight, his face was hidden from view. Reaching down, he plucked a fleck of dust from his breeches. Holding it in the air for a movement as though inspecting it, he smiled enigmatically before he waved it free. Hazel eyes watched the fluff drift lazily to the carriage floor, before he returned his gaze to Melissa and took in the damage. Her dark hair hung in mussed strands, the powder shaken from the long tresses in the accident. A smudge of dirt on her nose, coupled with the state of her dress made her appear vulnerable, a tattered rose lost in the dark. His fingers itched to reach forward and brush the smudge from her face. Controlling the impulse, he arranged his hands carefully on his knees and returned his attention to the conversation.

"I left Lady Shearingham's ball early," Her voice was polite yet shaky, a remnant of the nasty tumble she had taken in the coach. "I had a headache,"

"Ahh," Justin replied, his face unreadable from the shadows. He watched her though; she could not miss the pressure of his eyes upon her. It should have made her uncomfortable, the frankness of his gaze on her, yet despite the odd twinge of unease, she felt safe in his company. The tenderness he showed as he had helped her into the carriage had impressed itself on her mind. Despite the drama of their first meeting, she knew that Justin Lestrade possessed a heart somewhere beneath the mockery. They lapsed into silence for a moment, unsure of what to say to each other, strangers that they were. Jane had returned to her knitting. She had picked up a spare set of needles from her basket and the clicking sound they made sounded loud in the carriage.

"Why were you not at the ball?" Melissa broke the silence boldly, ignoring the hiss of surprise from Jane at her elbow. It was a direct question, one that should be danced about or garnered from friends. It was not done to ask outright news from a stranger, yet she could not keep quiet. She wanted to know if the rumours were true and this was the best way to go about it. Her green eyes stared straight at him and she could almost feel him smiling at her boldness in the dark corner opposite.

"I had a visit from Lord Malison," He answered directly, with no hint of hesitation. If she could be direct then so could he. "I was given to understand that I was responsible for his daughter's demise," A note of bitter anger entered his voice as he spoke. "Since I am clearly a cad, then I must also be a murderer,"

Melissa stared at him, trying to find his face in the darkness before she answered.

"I don't think you are a murderer,"

"Really?" A note of incredulity entered his voice as he finally leant forward, his eyes shimmering with pent up emotion. "How would you know?" A mocking quality flowed through his tones and she shivered as the notes stroked down her spine.

"I don't, I just feel that you aren't,"

"Then you don't know, you only believe," He settled back against the chair, his face stormy in the darkness. The air in the carriage became still, Jane watched carefully from the seat opposite, her placid face still and watchful. Throughout the hushed stillness, the sound of wheels sounded loud, almost deafening as they looked at each other. His fingers were curled lightly on his knees and she regarded the elegant digits with a detached feeling.

"I could be anything and you would never know," His voice was soft, almost hushed and full of a bitter anger that she felt more than heard. In the gloom of the carriage, he became as a statue, immobile and quiet, save for his eyes which searched out her face with an intensity she found unnerving. For several moments, tense quiet reigned in the carriage, save for Jane's needles and the noise of wheel on stone.

"I'm sorry," She apologised, more to break the silence

than for anything else. From the seat opposite, she heard him draw a deep breath before he spoke, his voice far more gentle than it had been.

"Don't apologise, you have nothing to apologise for. I'm out of sorts this evening and liable to be terrible company. For that I apologise to you," He smiled then, a strange tremulous smile as though he was dredging it from deep memory. "I must also apologise for my lack of regard, the first night we met. It was beyond rude," His voice was quiet, genuine and missing the mocking confidence that had characterised their first meeting. Melissa looked at him sharply, wondering if this were a joke or some kind of trick, yet he stared back at her clearly. Beneath his frank and open gaze, she found herself re-evaluating their first meeting.

"I accept your apology," He inclined his head at her words and she stared across at him, curiosity overcoming her good manners. Beneath his chin, the lotus brooch glimmered lightly in the moonlight and a tremor of apprehension trickled slowly up her spine. Disturbed by the enamel bloom, she wrenched her eyes from it and stared up at his face, noting the smooth planes of skin, seemingly untouched by damage.

"I heard you'd been badly beaten," She noted, her eyes roaming over his face with surprise.

"He did attempt to damage me but that was a few days ago," His lips twisted into a humourless smirk. "I heal quickly,"

"Ahh," She answered, trying to find a way to speak

more candidly though she was overly aware of Jane's eyes and ears on them and she dared not talk more animatedly. Justin watched her, his eyes travelled over her face as she tried to formulate some small pleasantry.

"How was Lady Shearingham?" He asked, rescuing her from her dilemma as the silence lengthened between them.

"Oh she was well, the ball was a triumph," Melissa seized the change of conversation like a life raft and clung to it. "Several members of the court and a good portion of the nobility attended. It was a fair evening,"

"Hmm," He sent a sideways glance at Jane; the maid was relaxing as the conversation moved to courtly gossip. "So who else was there?"

"Lords Baptiste and Asquith as well as Emma Dawlish," She hesitated momentarily wondering whether she should discuss her encounters with Alistair and Emily. What if Justin wished to know what they had spoken to her about? The silenced lengthened and she felt Jane's eyes upon her, the sharp gaze full of curiosity.

"It sounds like a dismally attended soiree," Justin's voice drawled, drowning out her thoughts. Her head snapped upright and she stared across at him, a spark of irritation entering flickering like summer lightning across her features.

"Oh it wasn't that," She answered with a little heat, annoyed that he had interrupted her train of thought. Her green eyes stared into the gloom and sought out the face before her. Its smooth youthful features were calm and she felt the annoyance flare into genuine anger. What did it take to ruffle that countenance? Her thoughts fluttered around the events of the evening before settling on Alistair. She didn't know how Justin would take the news, yet she was rattled and it wasn't a feeling she relished. She took the smallest of breaths before plunging ahead into uncharted waters. "Your brother made quite a splash,"

"My brother?" Justin's head snapped upright and his eyes fixed on hers with an intensity that was unnerving. He looked shocked and more than a little disturbed as though she had brought unwelcome news.

"Yes," She clarified, pleased to have rattled him so thoroughly. "Your brother Alistair. He made quite an impression on the room,"

Justin did not reply, he was running his mind over Alistair's habits and haunts. A late soiree at the home of a society giant was not one of his amusements. A troubling thought brushed briefly at the back of his mind and he looked at Melissa, noting the slight smug gleam in her eyes. She was happy that she had garnered such a reaction from him and he did not grudge her the victory. He would have silently applauded her gumption yet he could not. Alistair changing his habits so thoroughly was disturbing.

Melissa watched as the silence lengthened once more, Justin had leant forward, revealing a face suspiciously free of his usual calm and a wary, troubled look coated his features.

"Lord Lestrade?"

Justin finished his mental wanderings at the sound of her voice and dragged his mind back to the carriage and

Melissa's curiosity.

"Alistair at a ball," He commented dryly, visibly dragging his emotions back under his practised smooth mask of control. "How very unusual. He was never one for the court," He brushed an imaginary speck of dust from his coat and seemed to lose interest in the doings of his brother. "I must speak to him later and see how he enjoyed himself,"

"He was rather soberly dressed," Melissa noted as Justin seemed to return to his usual frame of mind. She dearly wished to ask what was troubling him, yet she could not with Jane sat beside her, eyeing them carefully.

"Well my brother is always soberly dressed," Justin answered with a soft chuckle as a more animated smile crossed his face. "Did he strike you as being particularly entertaining?"

"I'm not sure," It was a truthful answer; there hadn't been enough time to gauge Alistair's foibles due to the dire nature of his warning. Melissa wondered whether she should inform Justin of his brother's words, yet, her eyes drifted over to the side and captured Jane's disapproving look. She couldn't say anything, not here, not with the chaperone sat at her side, paying attention to every word.

"My brother is a sombre fellow," Justin continued, noting her sideways glance towards Jane. "He feels that social events are a waste of his time," With an elegant finger, he straightened his cravat before resting his chin languidly in his cupped hands. "I feel differently," A purring note entered his voice, turning his mocking voice into dulcet notes of velvet. "If I did not attend such festivities, I would not have met you. I count Alistair all the poorer for his denial of such an opportunity," Melissa flushed as his words flowed across her ears. The timbre of his voice resonated deep within her and she stared straight at him, Jane forgotten for the moment as his eyes captured hers and one look from his hazel gaze sent shudders down her spine. Justin was looking at her, intensity burning beneath his dark lashes. In all her life she had never received such a heated glance. It was clear that he wished they were alone and the naked emotion within his dark gaze made her catch her breath. He was nowhere near her and his long fingers lay still beneath his sensuous mouth, yet she could almost feel those elegant digits flowing across her skin. She caught her breath and stared into his eyes, wishing that she could touch him. Beside her, Jane stiffened at Justin's tone, a cold gleam entering her eyes as she regarded the young man before them.

"I did not know you had a brother until he spoke to me," Melissa spoke hurriedly, aware of Jane's frown as she struggled to mask the turmoil that was rushing through her. What was she thinking of? Justin Lestrade was not someone she should desire yet she did. He was a cad, a bounder and the most charming man she had ever met. It was infuriating. All that had occurred between them confused her. His behaviour at the ball had insulted her and his sincere apology softened her heart. Watching him retreat to Westbury's side had annoyed her and now this. This coach ride was turning out to be something surprising and she wasn't sure how to handle it. Her voice stammered to a stop and she stared at him, confusion and hopeless desire warring in her face.

Justin settled back and chuckled inwardly at the emotion he could read from her. Melissa had clearly not learned to mask her feelings that well and he could follow each change of mood with ease. At this moment she was struggling to deal with his words and her own interest. Despite his best intentions, he could not stop himself from trying to seduce her. She was beautiful and enigmatic, a prize for any man and he desired her. With a mental shake he stopped that train of thought. Melissa De Vire was more than just a conquest; he had seen a core of steel within her. He found that he did not wish to woo her so easily. Call it boredom or a sudden strike of conscience but he felt that he didn't wish her to get too close. She could only be a distraction, a small dalliance within his life and he found that he did not wish to subject her to that. It still did not stop his flirtatious nature from coming to the fore however.

"Forgive me for being forward," Reaching forward he captured her hand and drew it to his lips in an apologetic gesture that still contained the heat of his desires. He felt her shiver as his lips brushed across the back of her hand. Moving back against the cushions, he caught sight of her maid glowering at him from the other side of the carriage. Putting away his mischievous play with some difficulty, he returned his attention to the last question she had asked.

"I'm afraid my brother and I do not see eye to eye," It was an understatement, yet he could hardly spill his tale of woe in the back of a carriage whilst under the wrathful stare of her abigail. "We tend not to think about each other,"

"I'm sorry for you," Relaxing now that the conversation had lost that sensual buzz, Melissa gave her full attention to Justin, wondering what had caused such enmity between the two men. Despite his mild words, Melissa was sure that whatever lay Justin and his brother was far more potent than mere squabbles.

"Don't be. We've been at war for a considerable amount of time,"

"Have you ever considering making peace with him?" Her eyes reached out to him, concern plain in their emerald depths, causing a small ball of happiness to sing within him. It was not quite pity or sorrow, yet he could feel her worry for him and his brother and at that moment he knew why he had attempted to stay away. Her compassion and empathy were dangerous to him. She would care about him, worry for him and she would love unconditionally. For many reasons, he steered clear of tender emotions, sticking only to the baser desires of his soul. He could fall in love with the girl before him and that would do neither of them any good.

"I..." His voice was interrupted by a shout from the coachman's box.

"There's a coach coming toward us sir," Coll's voice drifted into the carriage, carrying easily over the noise of the wheels. "I think it belongs to the lady,"

"Well bring us to a halt," He ordered, a mixture of gratitude and annoyance flooding his mind as he felt the carriage slow to a walk.

"It looks as though we'll be parting company," Melissa nodded; her eyes displaying a disappointment that made him feel unaccountably happy. She was sorry to leave his company and he did not wish to see her go. Of course there was no polite way to beg her to stay. Her maid was preparing to leave and he had no doubt that the old battleaxe would raise Cain if he tried to make them stay in the coach. No, the sensible decision was already made. The carriage slewed to a halt and he heard the other carriage's wheels scrunch to a stop outside. With practised ease Coll let down the steps. Moving quickly, Justin climbed out of the coach and helped Melissa to the road. It wasn't for any gentlemanly impulse, he merely wished to take her hands and feel the warmth of her skin.

"Thank you for your assistance," She smiled up at him, stoking the tiny embers of happiness within him.

"It's the least I could do," He kissed her hand again, not allowing himself to linger over the smooth flesh. "I will talk to you again," He promised in a low whisper as watched the coachman release the steps on her coach and wait.

"Promise?"

"I do indeed," With her maid at her side, she ascended the steps and settled into the carriage. The tongues of the whip flickered over the heads of the four horses and the black carriage drove off into the night. Justin watched it go, the back of the carriage fading off into the distance. So deep in thought was he, that he didn't notice the rider riding across the fields, trailing Melissa's carriage distantly.

"Ready to go Sir?" Coll's warm voice echoed slightly in the air. The manservant was standing ready on the box.

"Yes," Justin turned back to the carriage and settled down. "Home Coll," He ordered as he looked across at the empty seat. "It's too late to go out now,"

CHAPTER 17

The curtains moved in an imperceptible breeze before the closed windows. The moon shone fully on the formal gardens, highlighting the yew trees in a ghostly silver light. Melissa sat on her window seat and stared out at the scene. Since returning to her home, she had patiently endured a lecture from her nurse, the ministrations of a doctor and she was now supposed to be asleep. Yet despite the laudanum that coursed through her veins, she was unable to doze off. Justin Lestrade was preventing her rest. His voice mocking and velvety echoed through her thoughts and his eyes. She closed hers, visualising the look he had given her, the heated stare that had started her pulse racing. It was unthinkable, he was a cad and under suspicion of murder. Jane had made it very clear that, if she valued her reputation; she would steer clear of him. Melissa sighed and re-opened her eyes, she wasn't getting anywhere with this train of thought. She snuggled into the blanket she had dragged from the bed and moved away from thoughts of Justin himself. Instead she focused on the mystery that surrounded him. Why would his brother attend a soiree simply to warn her away from him? Justin could be a murderer, yet it was a thought she steered clear of. She did not like to think of him as a killer, yet she knew that something encircled him. Whatever the Lestrade family was embroiled in, Melissa knew it was serious. Justin had gone pale at the mention that his brother had attended the ball and his calm dismissal of a feud sparked her interest. The curtain brushed loosely against her arm and she pushed it aside. There was also the matter of Justin's family; she had not heard a single report about his parents, though there was ample evidence to say that he was due his titles. The knowledge of duelling that he displayed and the education that he appeared to have received all seemed at odds with him. He was young, barely older than she and yet he gave all the signs of someone much older. The boredom he revealed on odd occasions at these events spoke of a malaise that she often saw in her father's friends, certainly not amongst those of her age.

Then there was the matter of Montjoy and his companion. She had not seen the face of the man who rode so quietly beside the jaded rake, yet she knew that Montjoy deferred to him. It was his friend who had drawn him away and yet, something about that still figure worried her. She had felt the intensity of his gaze as she had mounted the coach steps, a guest of Justin. Without really knowing why, she knew that her trust of Lestrade had sparked some strong emotion.

A draught whispered across her bare arm and she shuddered. She was not dressed for sitting at the window like this, her nightgown was thin and the chill went through her despite the blanket around her shoulders. Tucking cold feet beneath her, she relaxed back against the wall, feeling the shutter bounce slightly at her weight. A yawn rippled her features as she leant back to survey the splendour of the yew garden at night. A dreamy expression entered her gaze as she looked down at the long avenue. In the day these carefully pruned trees stood green and proud along the trimmed lawns and now they were silver with black shadows that loomed long and thin across the grey and silver expanse. A breeze tugged at the branches sending small tremors of movement through the leaves as she wondered about Alistair. He was younger than Justin and possibly even her age and yet he too seemed older than he looked. She recalled his reactions at the ball. Like the disapproval of a maiden aunt or preacher his contempt for the proceedings had been clearly written over his features. Why then had he come? Even though he had told her that he had attended the soiree in order to see her, Melissa still had trouble believing it. It didn't seem possible that Alistair would be present at Lady Shearingham's purely to see her. After all she barely knew Justin, surely Mary would be a better choice for any warnings. Then there was Emily, she had almost forgotten that intriguing little discussion amongst the drama that evening. What part did she have to play in all this? Yawning again, she decided to return to bed. The knitting needles had done little damage except to cause her to bleed excessively, yet the doctor had recommended rest for the bump on the head. Jane would be insufferable if she fell asleep on the window ledge and besides she was cold. Reaching across the ledge, she reached for the opposite shutter and started to pull it closed.

Movement on the lawn caught her gaze. She stopped and stared out into the moon splashed night. For a moment, just a moment, she had seen something move between the yews. Had it been a man? Perhaps the man who had slain Honesty Malison? Swallowing quickly, Melissa wiped the condensation from the window and looked out again. Pressing her nose against the cold glass and straining her vision, she stared out across the gardens. Her pupils widened as she attempted to squeeze as much light as possible from the moon drenched landscape. From the yew avenue to the start of the flower beds she stared neglecting no part of the garden. At the edge of the yew avenue, she glanced over at the white marble statue of the muse Terpishore. If anyone had ran across the garden to hide, it would be there. Fixing her green gaze on the statue she waited. Cramp crept up her leg but she stayed still. No sounds save that of her breathing and the wind encroached on her hearing. The cold made the hairs on her arms stand up and she began to shiver. It was pointless. Whatever she had seen from the corner of her vision was clearly not there now. There was nothing and no one out in the garden. If there had been anyone in the garden, they would surely have moved by now. Shaking her head in disgust at her own imagination, she moved and tugged at the shutter opposite, finally pulling it closed.

Sliding beneath the covers of her bed, Melissa stared up at the canopy above her and continued to think. It was no good; she had to find out what Justin's secret was and if he was a murderer. Her toes warmed slowly as she focused on her memories of the man. For the beating he was rumoured to have received, there was surprisingly little evidence of it on him. He wasn't even mildly bruised. It was another minute detail that made up the mystery of the man that she would have to discover. She was drifting into sleep when another thought insinuated itself into her brain. The brooch he and Emily wore, the enamelled lotus, seemed to strike a chord within her. She had felt a twinge of unease as she looked at it and yet every time her eyes fell on its gleaming black surface, a jolt of fear ran up her spine. She pushed her thoughts away from the brooch and felt herself drifting off into sleep as the laudanum finally claimed her.

Out on the lawns, the figure she had seen moved out of its hiding place and moved closer, looking up at the window where it had seen her sitting. With quick light steps, the figure moved closer to the house, running between the yews like a gazelle. Stopping for a moment beside the last tree, the figure stared up at the window it knew to be hers, wondering if they had been spotted. Relieved at the lack of sound or light, the figure moved forward, crossing the last bit of garden with ease. Reaching the wall of the house, it moved along slowly, hugging the wall until her window was above. Once more it waited, keeping still with a patience that would have shamed a saint. The clock in the churchyard struck the quarter hour, releasing the figure from its moonlit vigil. With catlike grace it reached upward and began to scale the wall of the house. Within moments it was within reach of Melissa's window. Carefully the figure slid a thin bladed knife beneath the edge of the window and with the ease of long practice, slid it upwards.

The room was opulent, as was to be expected and there, lying asleep and helpless, lay Melissa De Vire. Taking a satisfied breath, the figure edged forward, reaching for the heavy parchment envelope that lay under several layers of clothes. Grasping the envelope between steady fingers, the figure slowly and softly moved forward.

Melissa was dreaming. She was running through a garden, plants tugging at her legs as she went. Overlaid it all was the scent of death. Her breath was coming in sharp gasps as she struggled over the lawns, the overly bright sunlight a mocking sop to the vile scent that assailed her nostrils. A tendril wrapped itself around her legs and she fell to the ground, face level with the first of the living flowers. A lotus, velvet black with a maw of sharp, jewel bright teeth faced her. It spat towards her, teeth aiming for her eyes.

The figure was almost at the bed when Melissa moaned piteously and bolted upright, a shriek on her lips. The figure jumped back and lay prone on the floor, startled as Melissa woke and stared blindly into the dark. From the hallway behind, sounds of movement could be heard. Apparently the nurse did not sleep far from her mistress. Silently cursing and grateful for the girl's disorientation, the figure scrabbled beneath the bed, just disappearing out of sight as the door swung open to admit Jane's worried figure.

"Miss are you alright?" Melissa stared blindly into space for several moments before Jane's words finally got through. Turning her bright green eyes onto her maid, she stopped herself from throwing herself at her former nurse.

"Oh Jane," Melissa breathed as Jane placed an arm about her shoulders. "I had the most horrible dream," In her mind, she could still see the bloodthirsty flower reaching out for her.

"It's okay Miss, t'was only a dream," The maid's words were soothing and quiet aiding the spell of sleep. "You just settle back now, you've had a long night and you need your sleep,"

"I don't want to dream. I was going to be eaten," Melissa's voice was slurred and dreamy.

"Don't think of it Miss," The nurse was tucking the covers around her mistress tenderly as though she were still a child. "And.," She glanced up at the open window. "It's no wonder you can't sleep with that draught," With purposeful steps she crossed the room and shut the window, cutting off the stream of cold air that wafted through the opulent suite.

"Now you just settle back down and try to sleep," A sigh answered her and Jane returned to the door, an indulgent lift to her lips. Beneath the heavy wooden bed, the figure waited for the movements above him to cease before he finally rolled out from beneath the bed. Getting to his feet he stared down at the sleeping form of Melissa De Vire. In the moonlight she looked peaceful, innocent, her dark hair spread across the pillow like a dark cloud. A feeling of power rushed through him as he gazed upon her helpless form. The sensation of being so close to his prey thrilled him and he reached forward, fingers seeking her smooth skin. He brushed a stray strand of hair from her cheek and leant closer.

"It would be such a shame to mark you," The voice was low, barely a whisper as he moved closer resisting the urge to cup her cheek. Leaning over her, he placed the envelope on the pillow beside her and moved back.

"Take the warning," He muttered as he backed away slowly. Melissa moaned in her sleep and rolled over as he reached the window. Stepping out onto the ledge, he slid the sash shut and was gone as quietly as he had arrived. Melissa slept on unaware of her late night visitor and the danger that had suddenly entered her life.

CHAPTER 18

Justin collapsed into his favourite chair by the fire and pondered the night's events. His decision for a late night carouse had brought unseen consequences. He had certainly not expected to run into Melissa De Vire on the road to the capital. That unexpected yet delightful coincidence had proved to be an education to his jaded palette. Of course he had met charming women in his past, yet none had sparked his interest as much as she. He reached forward, picking up the brass poker to strike life into the dying fire when pain blossomed suddenly across his chest. Grunting as the stomach churning pain roiled through his body, he managed to sit upright.

"Goddamn it not now," He hissed as the sensation faded

from raw, nerve wracking pain to a dull throbbing ache. With shaking fingers, he reached for the enamel flower at his neck and pulled it free. The black enamel bloom sprang open as the small metal catch on its side was depressed and the innards were revealed. It was a locket, carrying two small cameos; one was of Justin, small, perfectly painted and lifelike, the other cameo caused a bitter smile to cross Justin's lips for it was empty. Where there should have been a picture there was merely a blank space.

"Excuse me sir," Coll interrupted his thoughts and he stared up at his servant. "I'm afraid I have some bad news,"

"I know Coll," Justin closed the lotus flower and stood. "We'll deal with that presently, now however," He reached for the chest that stood in the corner of the room and began pulling clothing from it. "We need to go out," He dragged a ragged cloak and two shirts from the wooden chest and threw them on the floor. A pair of breeches so rank in appearance and odour that he nearly gagged followed the shirt and finally, he drew a pair of poor rag shoes into the light.

"My god I hate this," Justin muttered as he pulled off his rich garb and threw them onto the chair. Beneath the white silk his smooth skin seemed paler than before and it glistened with a fine sheen of sweat. With impatient gestures he pulled on the rough garments and mussed his hair. He now no longer resembled the courteously seductive host of parties and instead looked like a street rat.

"Where to sir?" Coll watched the transformation with little surprise, since becoming Justin's coachman he had become privy to all his secrets and aided him in keeping some of the more deadly ones.

"St Albans," The terse answer sounded as Justin reached into a drawer and pulled forth a vial of laudanum. Placing the vial into a pouch along with the enamel lotus, he reached down into the chest and armed himself with the rusty knife that lay there, scant protection but enough for his purpose. "I can find what I need faster there," Pulling his heavy cloak about his shoulders, he marched from the parlour into the damaged hallway and from there out into the cool air. It would take most of the night to return to the city

He hitched two good horses to his phaeton and taking charge of the reins, drove the fast buggy out of the stables and into the crisp night air. It was after three and tendrils of mist drifted from ditches along the sides of the road, tugging at their clothing and drenching their hair so it hung in limp strands. The noise of the wheels sounded loud in the silence, both men were too focused on the future to idly chat.

Dawn tinted the horizon a steely grey as they reached the city. Justin pulled the phaeton to a stop as they reached the slum district. Handing the reins to Coll he stepped into the muck strewn streets.

"Drive round for a bit," He murmured, gazing about his with a note of distaste in his voice. "I won't be long," Stepping away from the carriage, Justin turned and walked into the raucous, cluttered district.

The slums were alive at this time in the morning as

tradesmen and workers trudged wearily through the pre-dawn light. In the alleys by the taverns, drunks staggered, slept or urinated freely into the stinking road. Within minutes, his rag shoes were awash with muck and sewage. Moving deeper into the warren, his eyes flickered over the people huddled in the streets. Clothed in rags and reeking of gin, they looked up at him through befuddled eyes as he stepped over them.

"Care for a ride?" The whore appeared from nowhere, her crude red dress cut low revealing startlingly firm breasts. Her teeth were rotting, yet she was young, perhaps seventeen, he could not be sure. For a brief moment, he considered choosing this one. She was young, strong and would waste away on the streets of the city. A flicker of uncertainty creased her features as he looked at her with a speculating, calculating glimmer in his handsome face. "Only a copper.," She continued, a trembling note entering her young voice.

"Not tonight luv," he altered his tones, bringing a rough burr to his once smooth tone. "I'm on me way home," Stepping around her blowsy frame, he moved deeper into the morass. Pink tinged the sky as the sun began to rise as he reached the very heart of the slums and looked back. He would have to find something soon before the sun truly rose and bathed the twilit streets with light.

Shouts erupted from up ahead and he sped up, heading for the noise. The sounds of scuffling grew louder and he could see the fight. Two men against one as a baying crowd gathered around them. The man was holding his own despite the bloody nose and contusions. Justin reached the edge of the crowd and watched. The first man lunged, punching wildly as he rushed forward, his fist making a satisfying crunch as it connected with a jaw. One of the men staggered back, his hand reaching for his belt and the knife that hung there. The crowd gasped as one, Justin amongst them as a satisfied feeling rushed through his body. He watched the man attempt to circle away, only to career into the arms of the other, watched as he was held still for the shining blade that descended without mercy, listened as the crowd gave up a scream and scattered as the murderers finished their work before robbing the man of all he owned. Both men took off at a run and Justin followed at a slower pace, keeping track of the man holding the knife as he did so. Sliding into the shadows with practised ease, he followed the men and watched as they split up and headed down two separate streets and away from the main press of humanity. Justin did not hesitate; he turned to the right following the man with the knife. In the maze of quiet streets he sped up, catching up to the man with ease. His feet made little noise on the cobblestones as he sped up behind the man and struck out with his fist. Justin's fist slammed into the back of the man's neck pitching him forward. The man yelled and turned, slashing out wildly with his knife. The rust spotted blade tore across the Justin's throat as the man let out a yell of triumph. Justin felt the warmth of blood spray across him as the blade struck yet he pressed forward, watching the man's face change as he reached for him.

"Devil," The man watched him come forward, watched the handsome faced youth ignore a cut throat as he marched forward. With a contemptuous almost negligent thrust, Justin punched again, sending the man to the floor. Slowly he walked forward and pressed his knee against his chest.

"I am the devil," Justin murmured softly as he pulled the small vial from his rags and uncorked it before he poured half of it down the man's throat. Grasping hold of the man's nose and mouth, he forced the ragged thug to swallow. The laudanum acted swiftly, sending the man into a lethargic doze. Once done, he stared down at his garments, the top layer of clothing was soaked with blood and he could tell that his throat yawned wide with what would ordinarily be a fatal wound.

"You…" He snarled at the man as he peeled the top shirt from his body and tossed it over the nearest wall. "You've done it now," He pulled the lotus flower from the pouch and flicked it open, holding the inside before the man's eyes, he slapped his victim awake. He couldn't return to his home like this. His victim's eyes fluttered open and fixed on the locket. On the blank side of the locket, colours began to flow and swarm over the plain surface. The uneducated lout began to tremble as a face began to form, a rough face, a face he recognised. Justin forced himself to watch as the man began to whimper at the sight of his portrait flowing into being before him. It would not be long now. Justin felt the connection snap into being and he moved away from the man as he felt the skin on his neck pull together. He watched from a distance as the man's neck tore and broke open, spilling blood over the alley floor. Within moments he was well and whole, yet his victim. He stared down at the thug and swore, the man was now dead and he would have to find another. Turning, he took off down the alley at a run, there were bound to be other candidates. He couldn't do this to someone who didn't deserve it. Murderers, rapists even a mugger would do. Moving deeper into the maze of alleys, he felt panic touch the edges of his resolve. He could do without finding a host for a few days and then he would wither. He had tried to stop taking life before, yet each time the feeling of his body rotting had made him crumble. He didn't want to live like this, yet he couldn't stop.

Barrelling round another corner he travelled deeper into the warren where life was cheap. He was looking for the man's partner, he knew which way he had gone and the fight with the other had not taken a great deal of time. He ran along the streets, his body carrying him round corners almost in a daze. It was futile; he was never going to find the man's partner. He stopped and took a breath, tasting the heavy air as it rolled down his throat. What could he do now? It was far too late. There was little chance of finding someone, much less getting them home without being seen.

The press of humanity grew as he waited on the corner. Flower sellers, servants, workmen, all passed him as he stood there thinking. He garnered a few stares, yet no one spoke to him. The sun had crested the horizon and slender rays of gold flowed across the cobblestones, shining off the puddles in the road.

The carriage rattled up beside him and Coll stared down at his master. Without a word, the man helped him up and clicked to the horses.

"I take it you were unsuccessful sir?" Coll mouthed the formula phrase as his eyes flickered over the pale form of his young master.

"I'm afraid so," Justin responded, his voice morose. "I did find one but he cut me across the throat and I was obliged to use it,"

"Ah," Coll didn't feel the need to respond any further than that. The coachman knew that he should feel more pity for the men and women that his master used, yet he found that he could not. Justin tried not to take those who were blameless or innocent; in fact he deliberately searched for those who had committed vile acts. Alistair had been another matter; the younger brother had a cruel streak in him that he frequently gave rein to. It was not Coll's place to say so but he felt that Alistair was overly enamoured with the power that his station gave him.

"Will you be staying in the city sir?" He asked after several moments of silence, the phaeton moving slowly through the streets thronged with people.

"I should," Justin replied as he pulled the stinking garb off and threw it under the seat. "But I don't want to sneak past Hedge," His fingers grasped the silken shirt laid across the seat and pulled it on.

"We won't have to sir," Coll replied as he handed a

comb back to his master. "I recommend you returning to your London home and I will find you what you need,"

"Oh wait Coll…" Justin protested holding up his hand.

"I insist sir," His manservant answered. "I know more of the seedier dives and am far more able to blend in," Justin gave a snort of laughter.

"I have had many years experience at this Coll,"

"Indeed you have sir.," Coll argued. "But you haven't the time to linger in the city proper and what you are looking for takes time. I can assist,"

"I can't just let you take the responsibility. I will still need to be there for the end," He drew a tired hand across his face. "Look," He sighed, hating each word that came out of his mouth. "If you are willing to find them and bring them to me then," With a disconsolate wave of his hand, he conceded defeat. "Fine, do what you can,"

Coll nodded and moved to the carriage door, as his hand closed on the handle, Justin's fingers closed on his wrist.

"Remember Coll, pick those who have sinned,"

The coachman bobbed his head once more and clambered out of the carriage. Climbing back onto the box, he clicked at the horses and the carriage moved off down the street. In the back, jolted by the motion on the cobbles, Justin stared at the fabric interior and once again cursed his luck.

CHAPTER 19

It was late afternoon as Justin let himself through the door of his London home. Having changed in the carriage, he was once again in his finery, but the black mood that had followed him from the slums still held a grip on his mind. Handing his hat and gloves to Hedge, he walked past the butler and stepped into the parlour. Sinking into a richly upholstered chair, he leant back and closed his eyes. It was always the same despite the justifications he made to himself. He could not control the visions that came to him, the images of all his victims. Despite their sins they did not deserve what he had done to them.

Lost in his thoughts, he almost didn't hear the door to the parlour open. Without opening his eyes, he called out.

"I want to be alone,"

"Really?" He opened his eyes as Emily's soft voice echoed through the room. Turning his head, he stared at the blonde. Today she was dressed as a proper lady of the town in cream and blue and as desirable as always. With a flick of her wrist, she closed the parlour door and turned back to face him. "I can tell," She removed the bonnet on her head and dropped it onto a small table by the door before walking toward him.

"This isn't a good time," With a sigh, he pushed himself out of the chair and moved to the sideboard and a stiff glass of whisky. Taking the measure in one swallow, he returned to the chair and sank back into it. "You should leave,"

"It never is a good time Justin," Emily's fingers fiddled distractedly with her bracelet, a slender delicate affair of gold and diamond. The bracelet he suspected was new; possibly a gift and that told him other things. It explained her agitation and her reason for being here. "And I don't honestly care if you want to be alone, I know I don't," She stopped playing with the links of the bracelet and walked closer to him.

"What do you want Emily?"

"What do you think I want?" She replied as she stopped just shy of him. He felt the fabric of her skirt brush against his shins and he looked into her face. Those blue eyes stared at him, the flirtatious sparkle gone from their depths, replaced with an intensity of emotion that he recognised all too well. "I want an end to it,"

"We all want that," Justin replied, anger bubbling just

below the surface. "It's nothing new Emily and if you're here to add more guilt to my plate, then please," He stood and pointed at the door. "Feel free to leave,"

"Do you think I'm here to blame you?" Anger to match his own, rose in her voice and she faced him, her eyes meeting his, challenging him.

"Aren't you?" He stepped forward, anger carrying him closer to her than he planned. Gooseflesh prickled along his skin, triggering old memories. "Then why are you here? Do you want sympathy or a shoulder to cry on?" He snorted derisively and moved to turn away. "I'm not in a sympathetic mood today so why don't you find my brother or any of the others to weep to,"

"I don't want your brother and I don't want your sympathy," She snapped back, stepping closer to him as she spoke. As her body moved nearer, he could feel the tension between them increase. Emily was now staring directly into his eyes and he caught his breath at the emotion within them. Anger, desire, fear and want warred within those eyes and he knew why she had sought him out. His anger twisted and other emotions, more primal ones began to sing in his bones.

"Then what do you want?" The answer was clear, but he wanted to hear her speak the words. He needed her to say it and ask it of him, for if he were being truthful, he wanted, no needed, the release that passion would bring.

Something in her gaze broke and she reached for him, her arms wrapped about his neck and pulled him close. The kiss that followed was brief, yet he could feel the passion trapped and caught behind it. She pulled away, almost daring him to push her free. Instead his hands wrapped about her waist and he pulled her in close.

"What do you want?" His voice was husky, he knew this dance and its conclusion, but it didn't stop him from playing. Feeling her breath ghost across his lips, he tried not to lean in. "I want you to say it Emily," Her eyes widened and she almost smiled.

"You," Her other hand caught the back of his head and secured itself in the dark strands of his hair. "Just now, that's all I want," She moved closer and he pulled back, escaping her lips. "You,"

"That's all you had to say," He replied, pushing aside the anger and sorrow of that morning as he pulled her into a rough embrace. It wasn't love that drew them or even passion; it was something more powerful and intense than that. A desire to forget and push aside dark thoughts and memories drove the need that enveloped them. Justin pushed her against the wall as her arms wrapped about his back. His lips explored hers, passionate and bruising. Her fingers caught the lapels of his jacket and began to tug it free from his shoulders. Shifting slightly, he let the jacket fall as he continued the kiss, his own hands moving to the fastenings on her dress. He tugged on the lacing at the bodice as he felt her hands on his shirt. As their clothing fell to the floor their need overrode everything, the pain, memories, anger. All that drove them fled against the onslaught of passion.

Later, when the heat had fled and passion was spent,

they lay together on the rug before the fire. He glanced down at Emily's blonde curls as she slept and gave a wry smile. It had not been love, just desire and distraction. Still it was preferable to hate.

"Em," He whispered softly, stroking her blonde curls. "Wake up," She moaned and sat up, looking at his bare chest with a small smile.

"We always do this," She murmured as she pulled back and began to dress. "I don't even care for you,"

"I know," He stood and began to drag on his clothes. "Does it matter?" He watched her try to fix her stays and walked forward. "Here let me," He pulled on the laces and drew the stays closed.

"Did you rip anything this time?" She asked mildly as he picked up her dress and drew it upward.

"No, not this time," He retorted, watching as her fingers closed the fastenings of her gown. "You look slightly mussed, but nothing else is out of place,"

"Makes a change," She found the mirror and began to place her hair into some sort of order. They lapsed into silence as they finished dressing, both lost in thought.

"Justin?" He turned as she spoke, "I think you should pursue Melissa De Vire,"

He dropped what he had been holding and walked towards her.

"What?" Utter shock permeated his tones and he stared down at her as though he could not believe what he had just heard. "You must be mad,"

"No, just practical," Unconcerned by the anger on his

face, Emily reached down and pulled the gold bracelet back onto her wrist. "You like her, that much is obvious and she seems to have some interest in you, despite her transparent denials,"

For a long moment, Justin said nothing, stunned by the words that were coming out of Emily's mouth. "Haven't you just convinced me that this existence is so much hell, that you would lie with someone you don't care for just to rid yourself of it? Why would you ask me to pursue someone I couldn't be with? Do you hate me that much?"

Emily turned away and sat down in one of the chairs. "I don't hate you Justin, but if you don't take her and make her yours you will regret it," She picked up her bonnet and began pulling at the flowers set into it. "Alistair already knows about her, give it a little time and she will be linked with us. I'd much rather you drag her along rather than leave her to be fodder for John,"

"So how does my brother know about Melissa?" Justin's voice was dangerously quiet as he stood opposite her. "Have you stirred the pot again?" He turned and slammed his fist into the wall. "I thought you were past these petty games. Real people are at stake,"

"Yes," She stood and faced him. "Real people are at stake and if you do not act this time, John will merely take her from you in the same way he took Anna," She grabbed his fist and brushed the drops of blood from the knuckles. "Do you not realise yet that there is nothing that you can do to hide her from him,"

"I've spoken to her once," He hoped that she did not see

through the lie, "And that has been all. God curse it Emily, she may only be intrigued, do not turn this into a grand love affair on the basis of one conversation," He pulled his hand free and seized the back of her neck. "If you start this, you'd better be prepared to face the consequences,"

Emily laughed in his face. "Don't threaten me darling, I won't take it," Her hand snaked around his wrist and she pressed hard on the joints, causing him to gasp in pain. "I will not spend the next few decades suffering from your ill temper. Don't forget love, that I know you almost as well as you know yourself,"

Justin allowed his hand to drop from her skin and whispered. "Then why would push this? I am interested yes, but I know that I can't have her. John need only know that I flirted with her, as I do with many women,"

"I push because John will know regardless. He has his spies and he will find out,"

"There's no guarantee that he's here,"

"Maybe not, but what if Katherine is? She reports to him and Alistair," She pulled on her stocking and secured it with a garter. "He won't clam up, if he has any suspicions he will voice them. Remember Alistair hates you, he may not go as far as murder but it doesn't mean he won't make it easy for you,"

CHAPTER 20

The rattling of the chambermaid stoking up the fire woke her from the depths of dreamless sleep. A pale golden light permeated the room, its softness rousing her steadily. Comfortable and warm as she drifted into consciousness, Melissa snuggled further within the depths of the bed only to be woken by a sharp pinch to her side. Unpleasantly reminded her of her recent injuries, she shifted position and buried herself again, drifting back into the pleasant oblivion of sleep. The coal scuttle rattled loudly and her eyes snapped open with annoyance. Grunting lightly with effort, she dug herself from the blankets and sat upright. Pushing her hair back from her face, she scowled lightly before throwing a glance towards the source of the noise.

Kneeling before the large fire was a young woman, brush and dustpan in hand. Dressed in the simple yet hardy garb of the upper housemaid, the girl was industriously sweeping ash from the depths of the fireplace. It was this activity that had rousted Melissa so thoroughly from the bliss of sleep. Suppressing a hiss of pain as she shifted position, Melissa studied the maid carefully. Beneath the simple cap wisps of chestnut hair escaped and brushed against a slim neck. About to chastise the maid for waking her, Melissa stopped and looked again, her sleep fogged brain finally making connections. The hair that whisked through the air before the fire was a rich brown and not the colour of mud.

"Where's Martha?" Melissa called out finally, her voice husky with sleep and curiosity.

"Martha's had permission to visit her mother Miss," The maid answered as she leant back from the fire and picked up the scuttle with soot covered hands. "I'm looking after the upstairs today," The girl bobbed hurriedly and continued. "Miss,"

"Hmm," Feeling more alert, Melissa sat up further and glanced into the room. The shutters were pulled open and the long curtains tied back, revealing the green lawns beyond her window. Sunlight danced through the window and glittered on something in the corner of her eye. Looking about the room revealed a covered tray sat on a small table near one of the windows. Near the grate, the maid was now placing a fresh stack of kindling in the heart of the fireplace.

"So it's breakfast in bed this morning?" Her voice called out softly as the young woman pulled away from her work and sat back on her heels.

"Doctor's orders Miss," The girl turned to face her, revealing clear hazel eyes within a sweet heart shaped face. "He left orders that you rest up today," Standing up from the fire, the girl picked up the coal scuttle and rested it carefully on her hip.

"Would you like me to contact your nurse?"

"Not at the moment," Melissa stared at the covered dish, pangs of hunger tugged at her. She moved to stand and a wave of dizziness, after effects of the liberal doze of laudanum she had received, swept over her.

"Are you alright Miss?" The maid was at her side in an instant, concern washing from her in waves. "Shall I fetch…"

"No I'm fine," Melissa held up a hand to forestall the girl and waved a hand at the table. "Can you bring my breakfast to me?" Carefully the maid placed the scuttle onto the floor before picking up the tray and crossing the room. Setting it across Melissa's legs, the maid removed the cover before heading back towards the door.

"Thank you," Melissa looked down at the loaded tray, her stomach growling in anticipation. "What's your name?" It was a casual question, asked as she looped the napkin over her bodice.

"Rachel," The girl looked mildly confused; she had not been expecting to talk with the young mistress that morning.

"Well Rachel, can you please be a little quieter in the future in the mornings?"

"Yes Miss," The girl bowed her head and waited, fidgeting only slightly as she waited for her mistress to dismiss her. Picking up the knife and fork, Melissa finally indicated the door and with a bob, Rachel turned to go.

"Oh Miss," Halfway to the door, Rachel stopped and turned around to face her mistress. "I hope you don't mind but I moved your letter,"

"My letter?"

"It were on your pillow Miss," Unheeding of the bafflement in her mistresses voice, the maid continued. "I didn't want to see it crumpled, so I placed it on your tray," An unsure look crossed over the maid's features. "Did I do right Miss?"

Melissa hadn't the faintest idea of what the girl was talking about but looking back down at the tray confirmed the existence of a long creamy white envelope, an envelope that she certainly didn't remember having in her room the night before. The maid was waiting by the door, her hazel eyes staring at her mistress with mild unease.

"Oh yes that was fine," Melissa finally spoke, waving the young girl from her room with a flick of her fingers. Truthfully she would have questioned the girl further about the envelope but she didn't want to become the subject of servants' gossip. Relieved at her dismissal, the maid left the room, leaving Melissa to stare at the envelope. The envelope was plain without any name inked onto its virgin surface. Its creamy parchment piqued her curiosity despite the growling calls from her stomach. Sighing in frustration, she returned her cutlery to the tray and reached for the letter, tearing it open in one angry motion. A single parchment slid out to land on the eiderdown and Melissa picked it up, flicking it open with one hand.

WHORE

STAY AWAY FROM JUSTIN

The words screamed at her from the parchment, a warning striking into her brain like the sound of a fuller's hammer. Melissa dropped the parchment; it fluttered to the bed like the broken wing of a dove. For a long moment all she could hear was the frantic drumming of her heart as she stared at the note.

It were on your pillow Miss

The maid's words echoed through her mind as she read the words again. She knew she had not seen this the night before, which meant that either the maid had placed the letter or that someone in the night had slid it into her chambers. Either way, the implications were troubling. If the maid had been asked to deliver it, she would not have lied and said it were on her pillow. Unless. A chill ran down Melissa's spine, unless this new girl had been planted to send her this? She shook her head in disbelief at the thought. It was troubling enough that someone was threatening her without adding further complications. Pushing aside the tray, she clambered out of bed and checked about the room. At the window, she spotted the small scuff marks where her visitor had entered and she sank onto the window seat sudden fear coursing through her body. What if her visitor hadn't wanted to place a letter? What if? She remembered the tale of Honesty Malison, killed on her front porch and she lifted her hand to her mouth stifling a cry of horror. Her visitor the night before could have been the killer. Deep in thought, she gnawed on her knuckles as scenarios played endlessly through her mind. When had he entered? She felt slightly ill at the thought of him being so close to her as she slept.

He had to have watched the house. She recalled the night before, the movement she had seen on the lawn before she went to bed. Had he been watching her then? Had he waited until she had left her window before making his move? Her eyes shifted over towards the bed, towards the parchment that lay in plain sight. She should tell her parents. They would be horrified at the thought of someone breaking into her room and they would certainly take steps to protect her. She pulled her hand away from her mouth and stared out of the window. Yes they would protect her but their protection would almost certainly involve total exile from society. Granted she could deal with a few weeks in the country, but that wasn't all. The letter had warned her from Justin and her family would take that threat seriously. At the very least they would ban her from seeing Justin just on the threat from the letter. And though she could understand the reasoning, it didn't seem right to her. She was still convinced that he was innocent. The very fact that Justin had been so close to all those murder victims felt set up to her. If Justin were a murderer, it made little sense that he would be so obvious about it. There was also the note she had received, Justin would not have sent such a threat. If someone were trying to frame Justin, they were doing a bang up job yet she didn't think someone genuinely involved in murder would be so careless.

No she couldn't involve her family, they would help but they would also jump to the wrong conclusions and she wanted to make her own decisions about Lestrade. Removing her hand from her mouth, she leant back against the recess and stared at the edge of the shutter. Justin was not the only Lestrade she had to worry about. Was it a coincidence that on the very night Alistair had warned her about Justin she had received a threatening letter? Granted such an action seemed almost clumsy, threatening her twice in the same evening. She nibbled her nails thoughtfully, slipping into an old childish habit as she ran over the events at Lady Shearingham's ball. Alistair hadn't been the only one to warn her about Justin. Mary had practically struck her over him. Though she couldn't imagine Mary having the gumption to leave her father's house, cross several miles of country and climb to her window. Of course there was Montjoy. The nail on her index finger tore painfully as she shuddered, remembering her encounter with him on the road. He had been heading away from town towards his estates which were quite close to hers. Montjoy was supposed to be badly injured and yet there he had stood, seemingly unharmed. And what about the strange figure with him? She stopped chewing and stared at the hangnail. Something about that figure worried her. All swathed in that concealing cloak, he was unidentifiable. He could easily have traversed the boundaries and climbed into her room. Rubbing her temples she turned away from the window and stared at her room. Despite its familiarity, she felt cold looking at it; picturing the intruder stood over her while she slept. Perhaps she would suggest moving closer to town.

Her musing was interrupted by footsteps along the hallway outside her room. They could only belong to Jane and in a panic she sprang upright and almost ran back across her room. Diving into bed, she managed to hide the letter just as the door opened. If she were keeping this from her parents, she would certainly hide it from Jane.

"Are you feeling better Miss?" Her old nurse crossed the room and stoked up the fire, clucking a little at the small amount of mess left by the new maid.

"Much better thank you Jane," Melissa replied, pulling the plate towards her and starting to eat. Beneath her leg, the parchment crackled unpleasantly against her skin and she hoped that Jane did not hear it. "I was wondering about moving to our rooms in London. Do you think that mother and father would allow it?"

"Well Miss, I think your mama and papa would wish to come with you,"

"That is what I mean Jane," Melissa answered, swallowing the cold breakfast with some difficulty. "I can't be expected to travel there alone," She shifted slightly, pushing the parchment further beneath her. "You see this is quite a distance to travel when attending court or other functions," She explained, practising her speech before she had to try on her father. "It's too far from here,"

"Well that may be so, but you know your father doesn't like the town,"

"I know but it is my first season and I can't be travelling to and fro all the time," She stared straight at the maid and played her trump card. "How am I expected to find a husband if I am kept away from court?"

Jane looked at her mistress and nodded. "That is true," She agreed readily as she crossed to the bed and pulled back the sheet. Melissa gave a small sigh of relief as she realised that the note was out of sight. "However you won't be travelling anywhere until these are healed," Her calloused fingers indicated the bandaged puncture wounds. "The doctor has recommended bed rest," She checked the bandages and dosed Melissa with another spoonful of Laudanum before removing the tray and heading for the door. "Get some sleep Miss," She murmured as she left the room and shut the door behind her.

CHAPTER 21

Melissa lounged indolently on a couch in the upper sitting room, a book propped open on the arm of the chair. On the small table opposite, the remains of a late luncheon was spread. Her nurse had finally allowed her to leave her bed that morning, under the condition that she moved into the upper parlour and lay under a coverlet. Agreeing with the restriction purely to leave her bed chamber, Melissa had spent the majority of the morning lying on the couch. It was dull and lonely. Her father was off making social calls and her mother was arranging for the entire household to move into their city lodgings. Jane was out on her morning off and Marcus was out with some friends. Melissa was thankful for their absence. With the house free of distractions, she could think clearly about the events of the last few days. When Jane had left the room, she had tossed the parchment onto the fire and watched the words burn. The flames had consigned it swiftly to ash, yet the threat was still impressed solidly on Melissa's mind. In all honesty she knew that she should inform her parents about her late night visitor so that they could protect her. However she knew the trouble it would cause and though she was usually overburdened with sense, she didn't want the suffocating attentions of worried parents. Sighing, she closed the book on her knee before reaching out for the last solitary pastry on the tray. Holding the crumbling pastry in her fingers, she stared across the room at the china knick knacks lining the shelves on the dresser opposite. Every night since, she had personally closed the shutters on her windows and ensured that they were locked. This behaviour had drawn suspicious glances from Jane and she was sure that her maid had mentioned her suddenly cautious habits to her parents. At any day now she could expect a seemingly innocuous questioning about her disposition. Her fingers nervously shredded the pastry into crumbs. It would not do to have to answer that she had received a threatening letter about Justin Lestrade. Her parents would deduce that he had an interest. That interest, coupled with the beating he had received and her own botched debut would ensure that she never left the house.

With a discontented sigh she pushed herself upright and paced nervously across the room. As the only daughter, she was to marry well and secure her future. Without the stability offered by a good marriage, she was doomed to a career as a spinster, living on the charity of her brother. Not for the first time, Melissa wished she had been born a boy and without the suffocating rules that ruled her life. Her brother would inherit the estate on her parents' death and she would be left to his mercy and though Marcus would look after her, she didn't wish to burden him. Even should her father lay a fair dowry on her marriage, any legacies, estates or monies would revert to her betrothed. Sighing, she sat down on the deep window seat and stared out across the estate. Despite all the negatives of marriage, staying single was not the better choice. If she failed to capture a husband in the five seasons, she would be considered past it and all she could hope for was a job as a governess or the charity of family. Tired with pacing, she settled down onto the deep cushioned window seat and stared out of the window onto the rolling lawns. The sitting room overlooked the front of the house and the main drive. On either side of the pebbled driveway, tall elms swayed in a delicate breeze framing the approach to the house. Beyond the drive, long lawns stretched down towards the ornamental lake and small copse behind that. Bored, Melissa leant forward and rested her chin on her hand, staring out at the familiar landscape. At the extreme edge of her vision something moved from the shade of the trees and moved swiftly across the lawns towards the house. Concerned that it was her visitor of three nights ago, Melissa shrank back against the shutter, watching as the figure came nearer. Her green eyes followed the shadowy outline, the nebulous fear in her mind dissolving as the figure morphed into a distinctive form. To her curious gaze, a lone rider tracked across the lawns, the bay chestnut loping easily at a steady canter as it and its master moved towards the house. Moving even closer, the figure became clearer; his features still blurred to her curious gaze yet a sense of familiarity tugged at her.

"He can't be my visitor," She murmured softly to herself as she returned to the window watching more openly as the horse loped forward. "He would not be so open with his approach," Her breath misted the window and she wiped it clear, gazing at the figure that became more familiar with each passing stride of the horse.

"Justin," She stood up from the window seat in a flurry of motion and rushed to the mirror. Beneath the light cotton bonnet, her hair hung in a tangle of strands.

"Oh lud," She swore aloud, attempting to push some of the more stubborn strands beneath the bonnet.

"Rachel," She shouted, calling for the new upstairs maid who seemed to have settled quite happily into the hierarchy and now handled her toilette on Jane's days off.

"Yes Miss," The younger girl entered and bobbed a curtsey.

"Do something with my hair," Melissa ordered, pointing at the approximation of a birds nest on her head. "And make it snappy, I have a visitor,"

"Yes Miss," The maid bobbed and began to remove the pins from her head.

Outside on the lawns, Justin rode easily across the

springy grass towards the large demesne. He had returned from London that morning having finally obtained what he travelled to the capital to get. He had spent the morning ensuring that the stink of the slum did not follow him and then he had decided to take a ride. Much to his own surprise, he found himself riding for the De Vire estates and despite the small sarcastic voice informing him that he was almost certainly making a mistake, he had kept going. It hadn't taken long to cross the boundary from his land to hers and now he rode through the crisp air with a light heart. It took several minutes to cross the vast lawns and clatter onto the pebbled drive. Pulling the horse to a halt, he swung down from the saddle and waited. Several moments passed as the grooms in the stables realised that they had a visitor. Without a second glance he handed the reins to one of the servants.

"Is Miss De Vire at home?" He asked as the tall form of her butler walked from the house.

"She is Milord," The butler hid his distaste for Justin well as he showed him the way towards the main doors.

Upstairs, Rachel finally finished tidying up her mistress's hair as Justin walked through the main doors. The tread of footsteps on the stairs heralded the approach of the butler. Melissa shot a quick glance at the mirror, checking her appearance carefully before waving the girl away.

"Miss," The butler entered and bowed stiffly. "A Lord Lestrade is here to see you," Hidden beneath the courteous tones, Melissa could hear his disapproval. "I've shown him into the morning room,"

"Thank you," She turned to the maid. "Can you please accompany me Rachel?" Melissa called as she stood and headed for the door, slight prickles of anticipation rippling down her spine. On light feet she moved down the heavy staircase, her fast footsteps revealing her eagerness. Stepping into the hall she bypassed the butler and slowed down.

"And yourself Walker," She called, remembering to ensure that there were sufficient chaperones. As the butler nodded, she turned right and walked into the morning room. Justin was stood before the window, lounging almost insolently against the frame. His face was in shade yet she fancied that his eyes lit up as she walked forward with measured gentle steps. Walker took up a position by the door, whilst her maid stationed herself by the window, with her face in shadow.

"Miss De Vire," He nodded before stepping forward to kiss her gently on the hand. Melissa felt the shiver of his breath against her skin and a warm tingling glow spread through her. Acutely aware of the nearness of the butler, she ruthlessly suppressed her emotions and acknowledged the kiss with mannered politeness.

"My Lord Lestrade," She stepped back away from him and lowered herself onto a chair, fighting the school girl grin of delight that was threatening to break out across her face.

"What brings you here this morning?" Settling against the soft cushions, she felt calmer, more focused and able to deal with the unsettling sensuality that he exuded.

"You," Melissa could not suppress the tiny sigh of shock at this simple answer.

"You came to see me?" She knew it was a trite and foolish response, yet she could not help herself. She wanted to be sure that she had heard the words correctly. Despite her earlier intention to treat him with caution, she felt elated at the thought that he had travelled purely to see her.

"I did," He raised his head and looked directly at her. "I wanted to tell you that…" Melissa felt herself straining forward in anticipation, surely he was about to launch into some impassioned declaration of love. A noise from the other side of the room drew her attention to the fact that they were not alone. Justin glanced at the company in the doorway and lamely finished his sentence with.

"I wanted to see if you were well," Disappointed, Melissa sank back into her chair, suddenly furious at the necessity for having a chaperone. Fervently wishing that a crisis in the kitchen would pull them away, she returned herself to the conversation.

"I am tolerable," She answered in the stilted speech that passed for polite converse. "You did not have to travel all this way to enquire about my health,"

"I know," Justin scuffed his toe against the carpet as though frustrated. He took another look across at the butler and an audible sigh escaped his lips. "But I wanted to," He gave a small smile. "And I did promise to see you again,"

Melissa's heart gave a tiny flutter as that smile drifted across his face. Warm eyes, their depths no longer mocking, stared at her from across the room. "I try to keep my promises," He finished as he sat in one of the chairs opposite, settling into a pose that seemed composed yet relaxed at the same time. A silence settled over the pair of them, neither wishing to break the quiet with banality. The quiet stretched for several long seconds. Melissa settled her hands delicately in her lap, stilling the telltale nervous twitch of her fingers. Her thoughts drifted back to that fateful carriage ride, the tender way he had helped her into the coach. However, thoughts of that evening inevitably drifted onward, toward her visit and the letter that followed. She swallowed nervously and tried to return her thoughts to the present.

"Did I thank you properly for your assistance the other night?" Melissa finally broke the silence, her polite cultured tones echoing lightly in the still parlour air. It was a faltering and paltry attempt at conversation and her words sounded weak and feeble. Fervently she wished she could blurt out her troubles, yet it was not done to reveal so much. So instead she fell back on manners.

"You did," Justin watched her as he spoke, his practised gaze taking in the tense way she held her hands, the yearning look that was in her eyes. Something wasn't right here; she was troubled. Yet he could not ask with company in the room. Running a finger thoughtfully over his lips, he cast his eyes towards her butler. It wouldn't gain them that much time, yet it would be enough. "I could do with a drink," He announced lightly, hoping that Melissa had caught on to his ploy.

"Of course, how rude of me," Melissa sounded dismayed at her lack of manners, yet the tiny twitch at the corner of her mouth indicated that she was fully aware of his ruse. She raised her head and looked over at Walker. "Fetch Lord Lestrade a drink," The old family retainer stood stiff for a moment, the skin around his eyes creasing lightly.

"Very well Miss," He answered, before moving through the door and out of earshot.

"I thought he would never go," Justin murmured lightly, his face livening as he leant forward. "Now we can talk," He cast his eyes towards the door, checking that the butler had gone. Satisfied that they were indeed alone, save for the maid, he returned his gaze to her face.

"What would you like to talk about?" Melissa's voice stammered lightly as she spoke, nervous excitement flowing through her voice. Though Rachel was within the room and a supposed witness, they could talk more freely than before.

"You," He replied simply, leaning forward in his chair all playfulness gone. "What has happened?" His voice was soft, too low to be heard by the watching maid.

"I don't know what you mean," Melissa felt her heart give a violent start at his words. Was she that obvious in her moods? Did everyone realise that something was wrong?

"You're unaccountably nervous and I don't think I'm the cause," He clarified smoothly, his voice flowing like soft velvet as he dropped into a soothing tone. "It might help to talk about what's bothering you. I swear that I will not betray a confidence," Sincerity dripped from every word and he stared at her with serious eyes, the usual mockery missing from his gaze.

Melissa felt the hard knot of fear in her heart twist as he spoke, felt the impact of those soft promises loosen the heavy weight.

"You swear?"

"I do," It was simply spoken and without drama. Melissa sensed that he meant those two straightforward words with all his heart.

"The other night I had a visitor," Her voice dropped low, tense with worry and lingering fear. "He left a note on my pillow," Justin's mouth dropped open with shock yet he said nothing, fearing to stop her story before she had begun. "It was a warning to stay away from you," Her arms crossed her breasts and she clutched her upper arms as though cold. "And he called me a whore," A single tear trickled from her eye and she brushed it away impatiently. "He managed to climb into my room and leave me a note to warn me away from you,"

"Have you told your parents?"

"No.," She denied it vehemently, shaking her head as though angry. "I would lose what little freedom I have and you would never be allowed near,"

"Some would think that a good thing," A trace of his old humour flooded back into his tone as he struggled to keep the anger from his voice. It would not do to be angry here, despite the fact that he knew who had broken into her room. It looked as though Emily had been right again.

"It's not," Her words were low, almost whispered and

he looked up from his dark musings. "I want to know you,"

"That may be a mistake," Of that he was certain; John would relish destroying her before him.

"I don't care. I won't get that much choice with my life and I want to choose something,"

"That doesn't matter," Justin replied angrily. "Someone threatened you and that is serious. You should tell your parents and they will look after you. As for you choosing danger over me, that is not even a consideration. I am not the most considerate of men, yet even I won't bring harm to you by my presence," He stood and headed for the door. "Thank you for your company today, I will now leave you in peace,"

"Justin," Melissa stood and caught his sleeve. "Don't. It's not your fault that this happened and I won't be warned off,"

"Then you're a fool," Justin pulled away from her grasp and turned to stare at her. "I am not well thought of, it may be better if you leave my company. Certainly your reputation would not suffer if you stayed clear. I am considered a poor choice" A tendril of hair drifted languidly drifted free from the black ribbon tie, Melissa watched it settle against the chocolate coloured riding coat before turning her attention back to him.

"I think that is the fault of others," She said finally, twisting her hand in the soft folds of her muslin dress. "You are seductive but I do not see you as a rake. I would feel poorer without your company. Whatever anyone says, you have a good heart and I will not be warned off,"

"You have a high opinion of me lady," A mixture of surprise and mockery flooded his voice, as though he were unsure of what he had just heard. "I have a fearsomely poor reputation, both at the gaming table and in love and it is not all falsehood,"

"But I do not believe that you seduce those unwilling," Melissa argued back, sure that her reading of his character was right. "You do not corrupt,"

"You seem to be so sure," He murmured as he leant forward, his eyes bright with some unnamed emotion. "I am not an angel, lady," His eyes captured hers and she found herself frozen by the depth of feeling she saw deep within them. Suppressed desire and restraint warred within their dark depths and she felt herself biting her lip nervously. His hot gaze set something buzzing in her veins and she was keenly aware of how close he was. Almost without realising, she leant closer, wanting just once to taste his lips on hers. Justin saw her muscles tense as she moved and he smiled wryly. Carefully he pulled back, taking himself away from her and potential disaster.

"Do not forget my reputation. These others you speak of will not be as kind as you," He murmured gently as he restrained the side of him that wanted to pull her into his arms and keep her safe. "Your reputation is far more easily tarnished and I would not want that to happen,"

"Why?" She felt cheated as he moved away. He could touch Mary Westbury with impunity and yet with her he seemed reluctant. She recalled his teasing of several nights before and wondered why had done so. Yes she knew that her father would never let her marry one such as Justin, yet, she wanted so badly to try one thing that was wild and unconventional.

"Why?" He echoed her question and chuckled deep in his throat. "You wonder why I seduce the ball butterflies yet consider your reputation?" A harsh mockery laced through his words and he turned back, startling her with the sudden movement. Crossing the room in a short step, he reached her and leant forward, eyes burning. "Do not doubt lady," His voice was smooth, a seductive purr that flowed through her like honey. "I could treat you with less regard if you should wish," His fingers slowly ran over her cheek, the motion sending a rush of feeling through her. His eyes were holding hers and they were dark with desire, he leant closer, his breath ghosting over her lips as they came nearer. Melissa caught her breath, anticipating the press of his lips with a mixture of desire and fear. For a long moment he hovered close to her mouth, before he pulled away and lightly brushed her cheek with his lips. The next moment he had gone, moving back across the room to stand beside the window, his eyes watching her carefully.

Melissa let out a breath and looked up, her heart pounded painfully in her chest and heat suffused her face.

"But I do not wish to ruin you," Justin's voice was calm yet beneath the matter of fact tones, Melissa could detect some slight strained emotion.

"I don't.," She started speaking yet he interrupted.

"Is it not obvious?" He asked, harsh anger back in his

tone. "Just that one kiss could tarnish your chances of a good match. Even my presence here could affect your reputation. With each scandal you would be affected and while I care little for Westbury and others of her ilk, I would be distressed if I caused your ostracism from polite society. As to the other matter, I would not be the cause of any harm to you. Not when my absence would prevent it,"

"You care for me?" She looked at him, her eyes puzzled and lost at the revelation.

"Yes I do," Justin sighed and slumped back into the chair, a weary and heartsick pain in his gaze as he sank against the cushions. "And believe me, no good will come of it,"

"Why?"

"Why what?" his dark eyes drifted over her again. "Why do I care or why is this a bad idea?"

"Both," Melissa paced in agitation. "Why me and not any of the others?" The nagging feeling that he was playing with her tugged at her mind.

"Why you?" He threw up his hands and sighed. "Not because of how you look, though you are very attractive. Not because you are new and innocent, though sometimes that does please my jaded soul. You have something within you, a restless spirit, strength of character and compassion. Believe me Melissa, nothing in the world is more rare than that," He drew a handkerchief from his sleeve and stared down at it. Melissa followed his gaze, noting the yellow age of the lace with curiosity. For a long time he stared at the scrap of fabric, his face blank. The silence lengthened and

Melissa ventured to speak.

"But.,"

He started at the noise and looked across at her. "It wouldn't work," The lost tone in his voice was gone, replaced by the devil may care mockery that she had come to associate with him.

"My father could be persuaded," She started, thinking that Justin's fortune would serve as an inducement to the match. "If you change…"

"Ahh but there's the rub my dear. I wouldn't change," He stood, tucking the handkerchief back into his pocket with a flourish. "I'm not the marrying type. Your father is right to keep you away from me. I will leave you in peace now and I strongly recommend that you forget about me,"

"How can I?" She shot back, angry at his laissez-faire attitude and mercurial moods. "You came to see me remember. You helped my brother at his duel and you treat me differently to all those others that you play with. You say you care and then you push me away. And let's not forget that warning from your brother.," It was a random shot in the dark, fired out by anger and the only logical explanation, yet the look of shock on Justin's face confirmed her suspicion.

"How do you know it was Alistair?"

"I saw him at the ball the other night when he warned me from you. It was an absurd coincidence that I received a warning note later that same night. I want to know why he's frightening me and I want to know why you push me away," She stopped speaking, her breath coming in sharp gasps fuelled by emotion. Bright tears of anger glittered unshed in her clear eyes and Justin felt something twist within him.

"What do you want me to say? That my brother would see me lonely, that though I would dearly love to play court to you, I would hurt you more than any other," He walked forward and ran a finger along her smooth cheek.

"I have played with you Melissa and for that I am sorry," He leant forward, cupping her chin in his hands and raising her face to face him.

"Justin," His touch burned across her skin and despite her anger, she felt herself moving closer, drawn to his eyes like a moth to flame. "Tell me.," she whispered, low and urgent as he pulled her gently forward, his other hand cradling her cheek.

"If only I could," He murmured softly, warm breath ghosting across her lips as he finally gave in and kissed her. Melissa felt her eyes close as his lips met hers. For what seemed like an eternity they stood together, sharing a kiss that was both tender and warm. A cough from Rachel pulled them apart and Melissa hurriedly stepped back from further temptation.

Ah hem," The butler's polite cough drew their attention as he walked through the door, carrying a drink on a silver tray. "Your drink sir," He held out the tray, his old face creased with barely concealed dislike.

"Take it away," Justin said, looking at the man with contempt. "I'm leaving now," He reached for his hat, fingers closing round it with agitation.

"Lord Lestrade," With difficulty, Melissa managed to modify her tone to something more standard. "Are you sure you won't be staying?"

"Quite sure," He drew his hat from the side, catching the edge of a sewing set as he did so. Grasping the bundle in order to return it to the side, he failed to note the shears concealed within the scraps of embroidery. The sharp implements slashed into the ball of his thumb, drawing a cry of pain from his lips and sending bright drops of blood over the white fabric.

"Justin," Melissa reached for him. "Walker! Get a bandage,"

"Yes Miss," The butler placed the tray on a table and left the room.

"Let me see," Melissa seized hold of his hand and dragged it toward her. For a moment all she could see was blood, slick and vivid across the palm and then she saw the wound. A deep yet clean slice dominated her vision. Stunned for only a moment by the shock of her interference, Justin had the presence of mind to draw his hand back and close it but not before Melissa saw the flesh begin to close.

"What?" Her voice was disbelieving and fearful as the image of rapidly healing skin burned into her mind.

"I have to go," Justin pulled away from Melissa and nearly ran for the door. "Forget me,"

Melissa ran after him, yet to no avail, Justin reached the main doors and headed out of the house. Hindered by her long skirts, she arrived outside just in time to see Justin ride from the stables at a gallop. Troubled deeply by what she had just seen, Melissa returned to the parlour and stared at the bloodied sewing. Who was Justin, why did he pursue her only to push her away and had she really just seen his hand heal? She settled into the chaise longue once more and determined to find out about him, about his secrets and what he meant to her.

CHAPTER 22

Melissa stared across the gardens in the aftermath of Justin's hurried exit. Her fingers still grasped the bloodied sampler and she kneaded it carefully, trying to convince herself that she hadn't seen his flesh knit together.

"It's utterly ridiculous..," She murmured aloud as her eyes once again sought the horizon and the boundaries of Justin's land.

"Miss?" Rachel spoke quietly from the door.

"Oh nothing," Melissa looked up from her brooding to see her maid set a tray of cold cuts onto the sideboard. As the woman set the tray in place, Melissa stood and stepped before her.

"Thank you for the warning Rachel,"

"That's quite all right Miss, the woman replied. "He seems like such a handsome man,"

"That he is," She replied as she turned back to her chair. "You may go now," As the maid left the room, she sat back down. Settling back into the seat, she resumed her perusal of the garden. If only she could have spoken to him alone, without the interference of Walker. Perhaps then she could have garnered some answers. She crumpled the sampler into a tight ball in her fist and stared at nothing. If she could talk to him alone than she could find out some answers, yet that would never happen within her home. There would always be staff nearby keeping a watchful and gossipy eye on her. Walker might even tell her father about Justin's visit and he would never be allowed near the house again. Nervously she nibbled her bottom lip and weighed up her options. At the moment she was alone and without a chaperone, a state that wouldn't happen again for a long time. Justin had added further puzzles to be unravelled and she wanted to know more. Her fingers tapped the arm of the chair in a staccato beat as an idea bloomed within her mind. Her eyes focused more on the horizon. His house was beyond those trees, her eyes widened slightly as she thought it out further. His house was within an easy ride and she was allowed to ride out alone as long as she stayed on the estate. A small smile played about her lips. Turning from the window, she looked across at Rachel.

"Rachel can you tell the grooms to have my buggy made ready, I would like to take a drive," Her maid nodded and left the room, leaving Melissa to sort through her outdoor clothes. A ride across the estate was permitted and as long as she took a chaperone she could travel further. The idea strengthened further as she reasoned it through. Rachel would accompany her to Justin's house as a chaperone. Once there she could confront the man. Rachel would not presume to question her orders once they had left the house and she could be relied upon to keep silent if asked. It was a perfect arrangement.

"You're buggy's ready Miss…" Rachel bobbed a curtsey as she entered the room.

"Good," Melissa reached forward and picked up a pair of kid leather gloves before heading towards the door. "Fetch your outdoor clothing," She said as she walked past Rachel and out onto the upper landing. "You're coming with me,"

In no time at all, the pair were loaded onto the small two wheeled buggy. Designed for a woman to handle and drawn by a pair of placid horses, the small two-seater rolled easily across the landscape. Melissa handled the reins easily, feeling the wind whip the stray wisps of hair about her face.

"Now Rachel, I am going to visit a neighbour," Melissa announced when they were out of range of the house. Rachel said nothing, yet a curious gleam entered her eyes as her mistress steered the horses away from the gravelled drive and across the rolling lawns.

"I do not wish Jane or my parents to know about this," Melissa risked a look to her side and Rachel's face. "Do you understand?"

"Where are we going Miss?"

"To Lord Lestrade's," Melissa answered tersely as they bounced over the terrain towards the small thoroughfare that marked the boundary of lands. "You are to be my chaperone but I do not want people to know that I came here,"

"Miss I.," The young maid stammered. "I can't lie to your father,"

"I'm not asking you to lie," Melissa responded as they entered the tangled woodland and moved through at a steady pace. "I'm asking you to not tell him, there's a difference,"

"But what if he asks?"

"He shouldn't," Melissa drew the buggy to a halt and turned in her seat to face the maid. "But I don't want to explain my visit to them. If you manage this successfully then there is every chance that you will come with me when I marry," Rachel's eyes widened.

"Really?" Hope tinged her words as she looked at her mistress. It was the best position that Rachel could have hoped for, personal maid to a member of quality.

"Yes, but I want to know I can trust you," Melissa looked closely at her. "Can I trust you?"

Rachel stared at the horses before them, desire for a new position warring with her duty to Melissa's parents in her face. After several long moments, she turned to her mistress and replied in a soft, almost inaudible voice. "Yes Miss. You can count on me,"

Melissa smiled in relief and clucked at the horses,

heading through the woodland with trepidation. The woodland separating the estates was tangled and dense, a bridal path barely visible in the tangled undergrowth. Despite the brightness of the day it was dark within the confines of the forest. As the track grew rougher and more indistinct, doubts began to crowd within Melissa's mind. What was she doing risking her reputation like this? It was guaranteed to ruin her if it became known that she visited Lestrade's home with only a maid for company. Even though she could swear Rachel to secrecy, what of all the staff in Lestrade's retinue? They could gossip and her father would hear. The horses slowed down to a slow walk, carefully picking their way through the rough track. The forest grew darker, wilder and a trickle of fear flowed down her spine. The forest was a perfect spot for brigands and she had failed to bring a pistol with her. She sat stiffly in the buggy, directing the horses mechanically as she struggled to suppress the fears that threatened to stifle her. Beside her on the buggy, Rachel stirred nervously, the darkness of the woodland affecting her also.

"Miss?" After several minutes tense silence, Rachel spoke into the heavy air.

"Yes Rachel,"

"I think there's someone watching us," The girl's blue gaze was fearful as she stared about her.

"Where?" With difficulty, Melissa managed to make her voice sound level. It was one thing to be scared, it was another to admit it before the servants.

"I think they're in the bushes to the right," Rachel

shrank back against the hard seat of the buggy and began to nibble nervously on her fingernails. Melissa reined in the horses and stopped. "Miss?" Startled, the maid glanced up as her mistress swung down from the buggy, wielding the large whip she had been driving the horses with.

"It's alright," With a confidence she did not feel, Melissa strode to the bushes indicated and pushed them aside. The greenery rustled as she fanned open the branches revealing the empty interior. At the sight, a sigh of relief escaped her lips and she mentally berating herself for being overly nervous. "There's nothing here Rachel," Melissa drew away from the bush and headed back to the buggy. "You're scaring yourself," Her maid glanced into the still moving bushes and sighed.

"Are you sure?"

"Positive," Melissa replied with some emphasis as she hoisted herself back on the buggy and flicked the tip of the whip over the backs of the two horses. Shaking on the rough ground, the buggy moved off. As the two women disappeared from view, a figure stepped out from behind a large oak, his odd eyes watching as the buggy crested the next rise and went out of sight.

The trees thinned and the buggy left the woodland, Melissa and her maid sighing with relief as they rolled free of the last trees and stopped on a small hill overlooking the house below. Once it had been a castle, yet now it was ruined and heavily damaged by fire. The east wing however showed evidence of recent repair and appeared to be more liveable than the rest of the building. A trail of smoke drifted lazily from the only intact chimney in the roof.

"Are you sure Miss?" Rachel stared down at the devastated castle with obvious consternation. The state of the building did little to alleviate her fears about her mistress's intentions.

"Quite sure," Melissa directed the horses down the gentle slope and towards the looming ruin at a steady pace. The castle's bulk filled her vision and the remains of its towers soon blotted out the sun, leaving them in a cold shade. Drawing to a halt before the building's newly added doors, Melissa stepped down from her seat and walked forward. Above the doorway, the leering face of a gargoyle stared down at her. Discomfited, Melissa raised her hand and banged the heavy knocker against the wood. The noise echoed loudly for several moments before fading into silence.

"It doesn't look like there's anyone here Miss," Rachel couldn't quite keep the relief from her voice as her mistress turned disappointed from the door. "Shall we go?"

"A moment," Melissa turned to her side and walked towards the large windows to her right. Staring through the murky glass, her eyes wandered over the furnishings of the room beyond. A blazing fire roared in the grate and a plate of bread and cold meats lay on the table.

"He is here,"

"But he's not answering the door Miss. We should go," Melissa ignored her and returned to the front door. She knew that Rachel was right, but she couldn't just leave now, not when there were so many questions to be answered. It was likely that she would never get the same opportunity again. Taking a fortifying breath, she boldly depressed the door handle and quietly pushed open the large wooden door.

"Miss," Startled, Rachel jumped off the buggy and rushed forward. "What are you doing Miss?"

"I need to find out something," Visions of that closing wound filled her mind and gave her courage. "Stay and watch and warn me if anyone comes,"

"But Miss,"

"No buts Rachel. I have to do this one stupid thing before I become just another man's wife," Her voice was tremulous yet strong. "Please keep watch,"

Rachel bit her lip as Melissa spoke, her mind a jumble. She should not let her mistress do this, yet she could not stop her that much was clear. "Alright," She murmured, returning to the trap and turning it round ready to leave. "Be careful,"

A grateful smile edged across Melissa's face as she turned back to the open door and tentatively walked through. The air in the hallway beyond was cool and slightly musty. Walking slowly to minimise noise on the flag stoned floor, she moved towards the door on the right. A grand staircase arched to the next floor and she could see the minstrels' gallery above. The walls of the hall were wood panelled in dark mahogany, the heavy wood adding to the oppressive atmosphere as she slowly moved through. Her initial determination fading as the decayed ruin impressed itself on her. Stepping carefully, she reached the door and depressed the handle. Taking a breath to compose herself, she pushed herself into the ruin. The fire she had seen from the window burned cheerily in the large fireplace and the light was brighter here than in the hall. Above the fire's mantle hung a large tapestry, the colours in the threads faded through age. Strewn carelessly across the back of a nearby chair was the brown riding jacket from that morning. Crossing the room, she ran her fingers across its suede surface, the motion releasing small bursts of scent across her nostrils.

"Where are you Lestrade?" She murmured, softly, her voice tremulous and tiny in the vast parlour. Turning from the jacket, she left the room and headed for the door at the rear of the hall. Quietly, she turned the handle and walked in. Beyond was a library, its shelves groaning with books. Dazed she turned in a slow circle, her eyes taking in the sight. The shelves reached to the ceiling and each shelf was full of books and papers bound haphazardly with string. In addition to the stacked shelves a large table in the centre of the room was spread with papers and journals. It looked like the workroom of some mad librarian. Melissa turned to the stacks first. Some were titles she recognised, a heavy bound bible and several recent printed works, yet there were many that she did not recognise. There were tomes in Latin and Greek, German and French and languages that she had never seen before. She ran her fingers over the heavy bound titles, reading them with increasing unease. There was a copy of the Malleus Maleficurum and several French treatises on magic and the devil. Turning away from the stacks, she moved to the table, her fingers idly turning the pages of the journals to reveal reams of spiky handwriting. Looking past the battered volumes, her eyes fell on the piles of parchment and paper.

"What is all this?"

Her muttered exclamation sounded fatefully loud in the still air of the library as she carefully moved the top piece of paper from one stack and stopped dead. The parchment below held only a rough sketch. A sketch of the lotus that adorned Justin's neck lay before her in painstakingly detailed glory, from its outward appearance to the revelation that the ornament was in fact a locket. The air in the library stifled her; the heavy, leaden atmosphere grew charged with tension as Melissa read the notations on the side of the picture.

Unable to break the hinges or even remove the picture... will blacken with fire yet this has no other discernable effect... The curse still holds true and I am unable to free us from its grip.

Curious, she pushed aside the picture and began to leaf through the pages beneath. Notes written in the same spiky handwriting that ran through the journals flowed across each piece of parchment. Each page detailed a test or effort to destroy the locket that he wore at his throat. With increasing bewilderment she read on, the passages becoming more unbelievable and disturbing. Moving swiftly to another pile, she carried on; thoughts of finding Justin pushed to one side as she read the sprawling piles of text. Within the papers and journal lay a terrible history, of a life lived too long and without the release of death.

"What are you doing here?"

Melissa gave a shriek and jumped away from the table. Her startled movement sent a small stack of papers to the stone floor and she looked up towards the sound of the voice. Justin walked from the doorway towards her, his feet making little sound on the stone floor as he approached. She watched him approach, her heart rate increasing with each step he took and she swallowed nervously. His handsome face was creased with shock and anger burned in the dark depths of his eyes as they raked over the papers that she still held in her hands.

"Justin," A tremulous whisper escaped her lips as he stopped just shy of the table. The papers in her hands crackled as her fingers twitched in fear and she swallowed, trying to rid her voice of the fearful squeak that dominated it. With blood roaring in her ears, she waited for him to speak, waited for the understandable anger at her trespass. Silence stretched uncomfortably across the room as he said nothing. Only his eyes were alive as they roved over the mass of paperwork on the table and those that lay in her hands.

"Justin?" She spoke again, dragging his attention from the mess and to contemplation of her. "I'm sorry... I..." She started to babble, trying to salvage something of the situation. In the back of her mind, she hoped that she could bluff her way free. "I didn't mean to.. I shouldn't have,"

"What did you read?" He finally spoke. His voice was terse and clipped as he stepped forward and began to tidy the pile of papers back into place. "What did you see?"

"I…" She stammered as he turned aside the picture and looked down at it. "I just saw the picture,"

"You saw more than that," He noted dryly as he turned to face her. "You've seen my notes, you were reading quite devotedly when I came in,"

"I'm sorry I… I'll go," She backed off towards the door, a prickle of fear travelling down her spine as he stared at her with those unfathomable eyes. If half of what she had read within that spidery mass of parchment were true, she knew she was in trouble.

"Why? I'm sure you have questions," He pushed aside a stack of papers and revealed a chair. "Please ask away,"

"I'm intruding.. I don't know what came over me," She backed away further only to stop as the round knob of the door handle pressed into her back. Hindered by the shut door behind her, she began to panic.

"Melissa," He sighed then and leant forward, his gaze softening as he watched the panic in her eyes. "I won't hurt you,"

"Do you promise?"

A look of pain briefly chased across his features at her words and he nodded. "I promise you are safe with me,"

Melissa tentatively stepped forward and lowered herself into the chair. Justin uncovered another seat and sat down to face her. For several moments neither spoke. The atmosphere was fraught with tension and in Melissa's case fear. A minute passed and eventually Justin spoke, his face breaking free of the dark shroud of angered shock that he had worn since entering.

"I will not hurt you Melissa. I swear," His voice was soft and soothing as he stood. He headed for the door. "If you wish to leave..," He pushed the door open and revealed the empty hallway beyond. "You may. I will not stop you and once you go I promise to never bother you again,"

Melissa hesitated, her fear of the unknown clashing with her desire to know more. Lestrade and his secrets drew her in and she could not leave without getting close to the mystery of the man before her.

"Is it true? Are you really..." She blurted out, giving in finally to the clamouring voice of curiosity that pulsed through her mind. Justin shut the door and returned to his chair, waiting for her to continue in calm silence. Melissa took a long breath, unsure of how to continue with a statement that was patently ridiculous. She bit her lip, tasting the coppery warmth of blood and steeled herself to continue "Are you really immortal?"

"I see you read that far," He considered, looking at her carefully. "And how should I answer? Will I lie and pretend that you are foolish for considering such fairy tales?" He moved a stray piece of paper to the middle of the table and continued. "Or shall I pretend that I have a morbid fascination? Or shall I tell you nothing at all?" He ran his thumb and forefinger over his lips as he finished, his eyes not leaving hers. "Yet..." He sighed and leant forward, "You deserve the truth,"

"Then you are immortal?"

"Yes," Melissa heard the word, simple yet sincere, the

tones echoing lightly in the dusty air of the library for an instant before dying in the quiet.

"How?"

"It's a long and complicated tale," Strands of his familiar humour drifted into his voice as he spoke, notes of a mockery that she was only now beginning to understand.

"Tell me,"

"Are you sure you want to know?"

"Yes," She barely considered the response, only knowing that she wanted the truth, the truth of Justin's manner and history. His eyes caught hers and she felt her breath catch at the intensity in his gaze.

"Very well," He pushed a hand through his hair and sighed. "I was born in Wiltshire in the year of our Lord, fourteen hundred and ninety five. My father was of good stock and a fixture at the court of Henry the Seventh. My younger brother Alistair and I spent much of our time hawking, jousting and hunting until we were called into service at Flodden. We covered ourselves in glory and returned home…" He paused, staring off into the distance, searching for the painful remnants of his past. Melissa waited, stilling the impatient questions that waited on the end of her tongue and wondering just what he saw beyond.

CHAPTER 23
LATE OCTOBER 1515

"Christ's blood I'm bored," Rain pattered across the shutters and a cold draught whistled through the long hall. The two brothers lounged at the far end of the table, idly tossing a pair of dice between them. It was late autumn and the chill of winter had begun to permeate the castle. Justin stared at his younger brother and answered his complaint.

"Don't let the priest or Mother hear you blaspheme,"

"I'm still bored Justin," Alistair rolled the dice carefully and sighed as it landed on yet another unfavourable role. "You're the eldest; find us something entertaining to do,"

"We could check out the attic, have a look at Thomas'

chest," Justin suggested as he pulled himself upright. "

"Isn't that cursed?"

"Supposedly," Justin answered with a careless shrug. "When he brought it back from the last crusade, some witch of a woman told him never to open it," He chuckled and started to walk towards the door. "I don't know whether I believe it though. There's possibly some gem or treasure in there, yet nobody in this family has yet been brave enough to risk the curse,"

"You don't believe that it's cursed?"

"Let's just say that the word of a witch who couldn't keep her own head doesn't frighten me. So are you coming?"

Alistair slowly got to his feet and they crossed the hall and headed for the wide stairs that led to the minstrel's gallery that ran around the edge of the room. Slowly they made their way to the stairs and headed up. The dark wood was smooth beneath their calloused fingers as they held onto the balustrade.

"Justin, Alistair," A light girlish voice interrupted their progress and both turned to see the slight figure of a young girl head towards them. "Where are you going?"

Alistair turned to his brother and rolled his eyes. Neither felt like entertaining their younger sister this morning.

"Somewhere you don't want to go," Justin said smoothly as he knelt down to her level. "Listen, Nan's making almond paste in the kitchens. She said that she'd keep a piece for you,"

"Almond paste?" Eleanor's eyes lit up in delight and she turned away and headed down the stairs. Justin looked at his brother and winked. Hiding a chuckle, Alistair continued on up the stairs and began to look for the hatch into the rafters. After some investigation they heaved their way into the low ceiling room that wasn't much more than a crawl space.

"So you say there's a chest up here?" Alistair asked as he pulled himself through the hatchway and stared about him. "You can barely swing a cat,"

"It's in the corner.. hold on," Justin felt forward, his vision not much use in the dim hazy light. His searching fingers touched cobweb, cloth and remnants of old armour yet nothing that felt like a chest. He moved deeper into the crawl space, the darkness deepening as he moved away from the feeble light offered by the hatchway.

"Hurry it up Justin," Alistair urged uncomfortable crouching low in the darkness. Cobwebs brushed the back of his neck and he scratched absently. "There is a chest right? It's not just some family myth?"

"Yes…" Justin grunted in response as he crawled onwards. "I found it when I was a child. Nan caught me however and she made sure I couldn't sit down for a week," He shuffled forward, feeling the route with calloused hands. "Ah hah," His fingers closed on the edge of something solid and smooth "Here it is," Reaching forward with both hands, he caught hold of the sides of the box and began to pull it backwards towards the hatch. "Move then," He ordered as he reached Alistair's side.

"Are we looking at it here?" Alistair asked as his brother moved into a more comfortable position and laid the box before him.

"I don't fancy explaining to father why we're running around with this. Do you?" Justin replied as he shifted into a lotus position and stared at the dark shape in his hands.

"Well I can't see anything," Alistair complained as he moved to enable more light to spill through the hatch. It didn't help; the chest lay shadowed in darkness. Alistair shrugged and turned to Justin.

"I still can't see anything,"

"We can't move it downstairs," Justin answered, nettled by his younger brother's impatience. He shuffled about, looking for something, anything to increase the light level. A quick glance upward revealed the answer. "There's a loose tile up there," Justin exclaimed as he reached up and poked hard at the ceiling. A spattering of dust or mortar showered their heads as weak daylight lit the small space and the box between them. The sides were smooth and made from some lustrous wood that even smeared in dust retained some of its glory. Over the lid and hinges, ornate and fabulous carvings held the eye, their strangeness offset by their beauty. Neither dared to breathe, both looking at the box with rapt attention, scarcely aware of the time as they drank in the exquisitely carved lines.

"Shall we open it?" Justin murmured finally, his voice breaking the hushed silence.

"No…" Alistair's voice followed, equally hushed, awed by the beauty of the box. "The devil has cursed it,"

"Nonsense. Good God-fearing souls fear nothing of the devil's traps and besides, it's probably a rumour to stop people from getting at what's within," He reached for the latch and lifted the lid. Motes of sunshine danced in the air and bounced off the contents of the box. Laid on a bed of blood red velvet was a black enamel flower. Exquisitely carved and painted, the brooch lay like a discarded bloom against the fabric.

"Is that it?" Disgusted, Justin reached forward and pulled the brooch from its resting place. As his fingers closed around the blossom, he felt it cling to his flesh, the smooth planes of metal and enamel fusing to his skin. A lassitude spread through his body and he pitched forward as the blankness of unconsciousness claimed him.

"Justin," Alistair grabbed his brother and pulled him upright. "Justin," He reached for the brooch, meaning to wrench it free yet as his fingers closed round it, he found it fusing to his hand. As he too fell into a dreamless darkness, his eyes focused on the newly formed second brooch that now lay within his fingers.

CHAPTER 24

Justin fell silent, still able to remember those fateful moments when his life had changed forever. He could recall the first time his fingers grasped that brooch, it was seared into his memory and no amount of time had dulled that image. He had woken first, seen Alistair lying as though dead next to him. He had tried to wake him, but to no avail. He could only wait and watch. The light dimmed further, rendering him blind in the darkness of the attic.

"Justin?" Melissa's voice pulled him from his thoughts.

He pulled his mind free of the memories of that dusty attic and returned to the now and the ruins of his old home. He looked at her face and tried to smile. "So there you have it, my tale, convoluted though it may be,"

"The brooch gave you immortality?" Her voice was hushed, incredulous, half believing and half chalking him up as insane. Well he couldn't blame her for that, if he had not lived it, he would find it hard to believe also.

"You could say that," He did not wish to mention the price of this life; she would turn from him in disgust if he spoke of the horrors that had filled his life since. It would not matter if he did not tell of it, she was ephemeral and he would have to leave her behind. "Neither my brother nor I have aged since that day,"

"It's incredible," Melissa sank back into the chair, her thoughts full of his tale. She should not believe it, dismiss it all as fancy and yet. "It explains so much about you," She said finally, running her mind over everything that had seemed strange about Justin. His mocking laughter, his studied boredom and his knowledge, all were explained by this simple yet absurd tale.

"Really?" Justin raised an eyebrow and looked across at her. The perpetual mocking expression had vanished from his face and he seemed gentler, more open than he had ever been. A thrill of excitement rippled down Melissa's spine, glad that he could trust her so far. "How so?" He continued, curious to know what had intrigued her about him.

"Why you seem so much older than you are and how you know so much,"

"It's an occupational hazard; you must do something to fill up the days in a long life," He stood and crossed the floor to stand before her, his face calm. "I'm relieved in a way that you found out,"

"Why?"

Justin reached forward and captured her chin. Melissa felt her heart skip a beat as his eyes stared down at her, eyes that were naked with raw emotion.

"Don't you know?" His thumb delicately brushed against her lower lip; she shivered with anticipation as he leant forward. His breath wafted softly against her lower lip and she closed her eyes.

"JUSTIN!"

A loud voice from deeper in the house startled them. Justin pushed himself away from Melissa. "By all the hells it's Alistair," He glanced round rapidly and pushed aside one of the long curtains beside the nearest window. "Hide here," He pushed Melissa gently behind them and pulled the fabric closed. No sooner had the curtains swished together when the door to the library swung open. Melissa held herself rigid as several loud footsteps crossed the stone floor.

"You do know that there's a maid and trap outside?" A slow drawling voice rang across the quiet space as the footsteps came to a stop. Melissa drew closer to the curtain and pressed her right eye against the small gap in the middle. Barely daring to breathe, she watched the unfolding drama.

"I had noticed yes," Justin replied laconically to his brother as he settled back into the chair behind him. His long fingers rested on the arm of the chair with apparent ease as his dark gaze took in his visitor. Alistair was playing the role of preacher this day, all black and white. It was a disguise he had used on numerous occasions in the past century. Justin privately thought that Alistair hoped to be healed by continued devotion to God. From behind the curtain, Melissa watched Alistair approach, taking in the details that she had missed during their brief meeting. He was tall, like Justin and he walked with the self assurance of a soldier. His face was handsome, though at this present time his features were twisted in contempt. His gaze raked across the table with its reams of notes and his lips sneered with barely concealed distaste. With a swift movement he reached across and pushed aside a stack of paperwork. Justin flinched slightly as his precious stack of papers cascaded across the table, yet he controlled the impulse to shout.

"And what is she doing here?" Alistair sat on the cleared edge of the table and carelessly flipped open the nearest journal. Justin's eyes hardened slightly as Alistair's fingers idly leafed through the book.

"Asking for a favour from her mistress," Behind the curtain, Melissa heard the chill coating Justin's mocking tones and she bit her lip. Alistair was smirking openly as he skimmed the rough pages, his fingers lingering on the detailed notes, smudging the writing.

Don't get angry.

Melissa silently pleaded with Justin to remain calm as she watched Justin's knuckles whiten as they gripped the arms of the chair with suppressed tension.

"What favour?" Alistair finally asked, his fingers

running along the flowing script of the book with casual insolence as though daring Justin to say something.

"Her mistress left a scarf in my carriage," Justin swallowed the angry words that threatened to overwhelm him and fell back on calm nonchalance. Ignoring Alistair's studied efforts to annoy him would drive his younger brother mad.

"And she came all this way to retrieve it?" Alistair snapped the book shut with a decisive motion and stood. "Oh come now Justin, you can think of a better excuse than that," His eyes swept across the room and lingered briefly on the shut curtains. Melissa jerked backwards, hoping that he hadn't seen her.

"Explain what you mean Alistair,"

"Nobody comes here," Alistair replied with exaggerated patience as though he were talking to a child. "No one has been to this house in a hundred years, no one except for us. You honestly expect me to believe that you have been handing out this address as a contact?"

Melissa held her breath as Alistair pushed himself upright and paced the floor between the table and Justin's chair. "So why don't you tell me where your latest fancy is?"

Justin laughed, a short sharp sound of mockery. "Really Alistair, do you think I would invite someone here, to our home and only sanctuary? You are deluding yourself,"

"Then what is that maid doing out there? Hmm?" Alistair was still pacing the floor, his eyes travelling back and forth between his brother and the closed set of curtains at the far end of the room. Melissa shrank back against the cool glass of the window, hoping that Alistair would soon lose interest. A wrought iron handle pressed into the small of her back and she fumbled with it, wondering if she could make a run for her carriage.

"As I told you Alistair, she is returning a scarf. I was writing a note for her to take back to her mistress. That is why she is waiting," He watched Alistair pace the floor for a few moments more before he too stood up. His voice became hard, less mocking and infinitely colder. "I am no longer interested in discussing this Alistair, now why don't you tell me why you are here?"

Alistair went quiet, ceasing his movement across the floor as he looked across at his brother. Justin was gambling that the reversion to strict, older brother would cease Alistair's faltering efforts to find out about Melissa. Of course there was no guarantee that this would work.

"Well?"

Alistair took a breath. Melissa bit her lip and silently prayed that Justin's gamble would pay off. She seized hold of the window latch, preparing to clamber out and run should Alistair come any closer towards her hiding place.

"You could never lie very well," Alistair retorted as he turned fully to the curtains and took a step forward. Justin moved to intercept him as Melissa groped clumsily at the iron catch. "Your slut can come out now," Justin seized hold of Alistair's arm, face incandescent with fury as Melissa finally pushed open the window. In a panic, she fell over the ledge and landed hard onto the weed choked ground. Pulling herself upright, she hitched up her skirts and ran.

"How dare you?" She heard the words clearly through the open window and she risked a glance over her shoulder. The open window sent the long curtains billowing and she clearly saw Justin strike his brother across the face.

"What?" Alistair replied mildly, ignoring the thinning trickle of blood from his nose. "Are you telling me that she isn't your whore? Because it certainly seems that way to me," He released himself from Justin's grip and headed to the window.

"It will do you no good to run Miss De Vire," He called in a cruel, amused tone. "So you visit my brother illicitly? Do not fear, I won't tell," Melissa stopped moving and turned back to the window, clenching her fists tightly as her panic slowly turned to anger.

"Who are you to call me such things?" She demanded, her voice quavering only slightly as she faced him. "What right do you have?"

"What right?" Alistair threw back his head and laughed. "I have every right. He gave me that right when he destroyed everything I held dear," With one smooth movement, he climbed out of the window and stood before her. His dark eyes roamed over her body and he gave her a broad, leering wink. "And am I really saying anything so terrible, forgive me for not knowing that this…" His hands flailed in the air. "This meeting was fully chaperoned and sanctioned by your family. Oh," He stopped speaking as the colour rose in her cheeks, tinting her face a delicate shade of rose.

"Does that mean that you are not supposed to be here?"

"Leave her be Alistair," Justin had reached the window and he climbed out after his brother.

"But why Justin?" Alistair turned to face his older brother and gave a mock smile of concern. "I'm terribly afraid for her. After all it takes so little to destroy a reputation and I'm sure her parents would be so delighted that she has decided to take up with an old rake like you?"

A knot of anger twisted deep within Melissa and she stood a little straighter, her fists clenched so tight that she could feel the nails digging into her skin.

"What do you want?" She threw the question into the clear air, each word tense with suppressed anger. "Are you here to warn me once again to stay away from your brother? Are you here to gloat about your night-time excursion to my chambers and the lovely note you left?" Alistair stared at her, his face registering shock at her words, yet Melissa wouldn't let him speak. She kept talking, a torrent of repressed anger spilling from her tongue as she poured out her frustration.

"Yes.. I know all about it, all about you and Justin and your curse. I know why you want me to steer clear. Well here's something for you to chew on, your brother seems to think the same thing. He seems to think that I should be happy to spend my life at the mercy of my parents, my brother and my future husband. He won't even countenance the thought of a relationship, so really, your warnings and disgusting invasion of my bedroom were completely unnecessary. I have done nothing to be ashamed of, save hoping for something that was foolish," Alistair flinched slightly as her words raked the air between them and he opened his mouth to reply.

"Unless that's an apology, you can hold your tongue, you sad, pathetic excuse for a man,"

And with that, she turned and ran, back towards the front of the building and Rachel. She heard Justin call out behind her, but she kept going and did not stop until she reached the side of the buggy.

"Miss?" Rachel asked with alarm as her mistress pulled herself into the small cart. "Are you hurt?"

"Never mind that just give me the reins," Melissa called back as she settled into the seat and took hold of the leather strands. Clicking to the horses, she started to turn the carriage.

"Miss DeVire?" Justin appeared around the side of the building and raced to the slowly moving carriage. Melissa kept the carriage turning, ignoring his cries and the prickling tears of anger that were slowly flowing from her eyes. In the seat beside her, Rachel huddled into the confines of her cloak, almost hiding herself in her fear.

"Please Miss?" His voice was soft, gently pleading and Melissa relented, pulling the carriage to a stop. "I'm sorry…"

"You can't apologise for him," She snapped back, her eyes flashing. "That's for him to do,"

"I wasn't…" Justin reached forward and placed a hand on hers. "I'm apologising for me. It was wrong of me to bring you into my life, to expose you to him,"

"Then why did you?"

"Why?" He sighed and glanced over his shoulder. Alistair appeared around the corner of the house and began to walk across the space between them. "I can't talk of this with you now. I will be at Lord Horvath's party and I hope I will see you there. We'll talk then," He stepped away from the buggy and smiled at her. "Get home safe," Melissa hesitated for a brief moment.

"Miss?" Rachel gently prodded as she watched Alistair slowly head towards them.

"All right Rachel," She murmured, before turning back to face Justin. "I'll see you at the party," Casting a disgusted look at Alistair, she lightly flicked the lash across the backs of the two horses and steered the buggy away from the house.

Justin watched the small vehicle trundle clear before turning to face his younger brother.

"Did I ruin your little tryst?" Alistair noted with a vicious glint in his eyes. "Terribly sorry and all that, though I can certainly see why she has your interest. Has a spark about her, she reminds me so much of Anna,"

"Was there something you wanted?" Justin asked, coolly, cutting off Alistair's words with a biting note to his voice. His hands moved to his cuffs and with careful, precise movements he straightened them. "Or did you just wish to play?"

"Why there was actually," Alistair replied, heavy emphasis in his voice. "But if you're busy," His voice fairly sparkled with malicious glee. "I'm sure it can wait," He turned back towards the house and began to walk away.

"Alistair," Justin snapped. "Out with it,"

"Alright," Alistair reached down and plucked a swaying weed from the choked ground. "But you're not going to like it," Justin hissed with exasperation and Alistair hastily continued. "I saw John the other night,"

Justin's hands stilled as his eyes found his brother's face. "Are you certain?" He asked slowly, gauging his brother's reactions as he hoped that Alistair was joking.

"Positive," Alistair replied, his voice amused and fearful at the same time.

"Did he see you?"

"No. Do you think me that much of a fool?" Alistair turned and began walking towards the house. "But it's a safe bet that he knows that we're here. You haven't exactly made yourself inconspicuous,"

Justin ignored his brother and stared out across the estate, watching the buggy roll out of sight.

"So will you be running brother?" Alistair called back over his shoulder as he reached the front doors of the house. "I would,"

"What and leave you here?" Justin finally turned to face his brother. "You've already caused enough trouble,"

Alistair whipped around and marched forwards, his face dark with anger. "So you're blaming me for your lady love's problems?"

"Well it was not I who broke into her room,"

"And you think it of me?" Alistair retorted as he stopped just shy of his brother.

"Frankly yes," Justin responded, his voice calm and untroubled.

"Have I fallen so far in your esteem that you would accuse me like this?" Injured pride rang through Alistair's voice.

"Oh stop. Don't forget I know about Paris and what you did to Claudine," Justin stepped forward and seized hold of Alistair's shirt. "Innocence does not become you brother. And you've pulled this stunt before, I take it you've become bored with the appearance of piety,"

Alistair sniffed disdainfully as he glanced down at Justin's hands, unimpressed by the strength that held him. "So what if I warned the whore? It's bad luck to get involved with you. Consider Honesty and all those other blue blood sluts connected to you that have tragically died," He raised his eyebrow at his brother. "I consider it my duty to remove these unfortunates from your path. Though," He smiled cruelly. "I do admit it's entertaining watching your women flap about like injured ducks after receiving my missives,"

"Well stop or.,"

"Or what? You don't frighten me Justin. You're too tender hearted to do anything to me properly and let's face facts, you can't,"

"Don't test me brother. John is not the only immortal you should fear," Justin released his brother's lapels and headed to the stables. After a few moments Alistair followed, a thoughtful expression on his lips.

CHAPTER 25

Melissa finally pulled the buggy to a stop once they were out of sight of the large ruin. Her heart still beat at an increased tempo and she took several breaths before she felt able to continue. Around them the trees swayed lightly in a low breeze.

"Are you well Miss?" Melissa glanced at Rachel and nodded, barely able to trust herself to speak. The things she had discovered flew through her mind in delirious circles, making her head swim, Could it really be true? Was Justin immortal? She wished she could deny all she had seen, but the facts had been laid before her in black and white. His skin had knitted together before her eyes and she couldn't forget that image. Then there was Alistair, his words made her blood burn with indignation and anger. He had not the right to chastise her.

"Miss?" Rachel asked, her open face curious and concerned. "Did Lord Lestrade do anything?"

"He was a perfect gentleman," Melissa answered. "It was his brother that caused the problem," She slowed the horses as they moved deeper into the copse. "That man is vile," Like the shutting of a keep door, her voice signalled the end of the conversation. Both servant and mistress lapsed into silence as the gloom of deep woodland descended over them. The trap trundled over the rough ground in a bone rattling jarring motion and all of Melissa's attention was on guiding the animals across the hard mud.

"Miss," Rachel's startled cry caused Melissa to jump, pulling the reins tightly and drawing the horses to a sudden halt.

"God curse it Rachel, what the devil is the matter?" Incensed at the abrupt stop, Melissa turned to her maid.

"I'm sure there's someone out here," Melissa took a breath, remembering her late night visitor, and slowly cast her gaze out around them, taking in the gently swaying greenery carefully. Silence settled once again on the pair as they looked into the cool dim forest. After several moments of careful speculation and seeing nothing out of the ordinary, Melissa turned back to the girl beside her now thoroughly annoyed.

"It's probably the gamekeeper or a stray pheasant. For heaven's sake girl there's enough trouble at the moment without you jumping at shadows," She clicked to the horses and the trap moved off. Rachel slumped back in her chair, her eyes all over the forest. She was convinced she had seen someone following them, someone who stayed back out of sight, yet Melissa was in a foul temper and she dared not annoy her further. So Rachel kept a careful watch on the surrounding woodland until they broke from the tree line and trundled over the smooth lawns of the De Vire estate. As the horses moved into a rolling trot, a dark form detached itself from the upper branches of a nearby tree and watched as his quarry reached her home.

The trap drew up before the large doors and Melissa pulled the buggy to a stop. As the footman helped her down from the cushioned seat, a loud cry echoed from the door.

"Where have you been girl? I've been waiting for an age," Melissa lifted her face to the door and smiled as Sarah hurried from the main house to see her.

"Out for a drive,"

"Well I can see that, I'm not blind," Sarah caught Melissa's arm in hers and they moved towards the house together.

"What brings you here?"

"Well Mother is going to the country for her nerves," Sarah snorted as she spoke the last word. "And I hadn't seen you for several days, so I asked to visit. And what happens after I trudge all the way over here? I find you gallivanting around the estate and not ill at all. You utter fraud,"

Melissa chuckled as Sarah's well meaning gush of words

drowned out her thoughts and worries about her trip out. "I am not. Jane managed to stab me in the side with her knitting needles. I still have bandages,"

"Hmm," Sarah replied. "I'm not convinced, but whatever you say," They moved through the doors and headed towards the parlour. "I have had a wonderful few days and I must tell you all about it,"

"Oh ho, I knew there was another reason for your visit. So who are you romancing now?" Melissa chuckled as a look of chagrin crossed her friend's features. They traversed the long hallway and Melissa removed her outer coat, handing it over to a servant.

"Don't be so nasty. It's not a romance,"

Melissa raised her eyebrows, disbelief implicit in every line of her face.

"Oh all right," They moved into the parlour and Sarah sat on one of the long couches. "It is a man, but it's not a romance," She shifted excitedly on the brocade seat, clearly eager to impart her news. Melissa waited, knowing that silence would be intolerable to her friend.

"Well go on make a guess,"

"I wouldn't even know where to begin,"

"I'm getting married," A delighted shriek poured from her mouth and Melissa found herself smiling in return. Behind them, a tray of sweets, cakes and tea were placed on the nearby tables.

"Oh I'm so glad. Who to? Henry Wickford or Anthony Cornridge?"

Sarah waved her hands dismissively as Melissa said

both names. "Neither, Percy Chalmsford,"

Melissa found her mouth dropping open in pleased surprise. Percy Chalmsford was Sarah's preferred choice and not one that had particularly pleased her mother. "Oh Sarah I'm so pleased for you,"

"Oh so am I," Sarah rattled on, about how he had spoken well to her father. How he had made a good showing of himself, despite not having quite the fortune that Sarah's ambitious mother had hoped for. As her friend babbled on, Melissa found herself tuning her out as her thoughts finally turned inward and what had happened to her that morning.

"Of course Percy isn't exactly what Mama hoped for but still it's the best offer I've had… "Sarah's voice stopped in mid flow and she stared across at her friend with an exasperated sigh. "You're not listening…"

"Oh Sarah I'm sorry," Melissa pulled herself out of her reverie and smiled apologetically at her friend. "I was somewhere else,"

"I'd say," Sarah took a long look at her friend and began to smile. "You're thinking about a man aren't you?"

"Sarah…"

"Come on you can tell me.," Sarah hunched forward and stared eagerly across the room at her. "I tell you all about my loves, its time you told me about yours,"

"That's not it,"

"Rubbish," Sarah pushed aside the small pile of needlepoint and looked directly at her friend. "You've been in your own dream world all afternoon. Either it's a man or.," she shrugged as though she could not conceive of anything else taking up her friends attention. "Well?"

"All right," Melissa finally said with a sigh of exasperation, "since you're so insistent. I was thinking about Justin Lestrade,"

"Really… but you've only seen him the once,"

"Well not quite," Melissa admitted as she tidied her skirts. "You remember the carriage accident several days ago," She certainly wasn't going to admit that she had travelled out to meet him that morning.

"What about it?"

"Justin saved us from a long wait on the road. His carriage stopped and picked us up,"

Sarah was focused now, her attention now fixed on her friend. "And?"

"He was a perfect gentleman,"

"Oh lud Melissa do I have to beg for details?" Sarah dragged across the bowl of sweetmeats and delicately tasted one. "This is the first thing of interest that has happened to you, granted it is with that boorish fool but still.. You have to let me know what happened,"

"Nothing happened, Jane was there and we talked," Melissa was reluctant to pass on details of her carriage ride, yet perhaps Sarah would understand more if she told her. She took a sip from the glass beside her and launched into the tale. She left little out save her trip that morning.

"So he then came here. Oh what did you talk about?" Sarah was gripped now, the sweetmeats forgotten on the arm of the chair.

"Nothing really," Sarah clucked in impatience. "He does feel for me, but he doesn't want to stain my reputation by courting me. Father would never allow his suit, so he doesn't want me to be ruined by his attention,"

"I wonder," Sarah settled back in her seat and stared at her friend. "I think you're being startlingly naïve," As Melissa went to speak, she held up her hand peaceably. "Think of it. He just wants you both to sneak around. It makes it easier for him that way. He gets what he wants and you feel that your reputation is safe. You'll probably be the talk of the clubs,"

"No that's not it at all," Melissa stood up, colour flooding her pale skin. "You don't understand him at all. I know that I can never be with the one I want to be with, I've accepted that," She pushed aside the little voice that taunted her about her trip that morning. "But I can dream,"

"But Melissa, that's all it is. A dream and while you have that dream, you won't give another man a chance. Believe me I know. This one will take advantage of you,"

"I don't believe he will. You did not see the change in him,"

"Ahh yes, he changed out of sight of others. A calculated plan to gain your sympathy and eventually your virtue, I'd bet," As Melissa shook her head, Sarah pressed her advantage. "Think. He is a seducer and a cad, I know the temptation of those but they are cruel in their schemes. I would not see you hurt Melissa. Please forget about Justin Lestrade while you still have a chance,"

Burning with humiliated anger and the feeling that she

had been treated like a child, Melissa sat back down and swallowed the torrent of angry words that hovered on her lips. Taking several deep breaths, she took a mouthful of tea and tried to calm down. Sarah did not know what she knew and couldn't understand what she had seen. Quietly she fumed as Sarah moved rapidly onto other topics. As the afternoon wore on, the tense atmosphere faded as Sarah wisely steered clear of Justin Lestrade for the remainder of her visit. As the sun began to drop towards the horizon, Sarah made her apologies and headed home, leaving Melissa alone with her thoughts.

Stepping back into the parlour, she thought about what Sarah had said. Could this be an elaborate ploy to seduce her? Could Lestrade be playing the honourable soul with her, purely to ease her fears? She stopped that train of thought because that certainly did not include his claims to immortality. Troubled beyond thought, she ate a light dinner and headed to her chambers. Jane, having returned from her day out, fixed her a warm drink and tucked her into bed. Beneath the heavy cotton sheets, she tossed and turned as her mind refused to settle. As stillness descended over the large household, she gave up and sat on the window ledge, staring out across the grounds towards the boundary between their estates' and his home beyond.

CHAPTER 26

The music swelled as dancers twirled on the dance floor, filling the space with bright colours and extravagant wigs. Sat along the edge of the dance floor, Melissa twirled a crystal goblet absently between her fingers and lost herself in thought. It had been two days since her fateful visit to Justin's house, two days of fretful wondering about his motives and history. His revelations should have scared her yet somehow she found herself more intrigued by them. A priest would have claimed he was possessed by a devil and perhaps he may be but, she sighed and took a sip from the glass, she could see his heart and it was good. Even with all his dissembling, he could not hide from her. Motes of candlelight danced off the fine crystal and she gently flicked the edge of the glass with her finger. A whisper soft, clear note flowed through the air and she focused on it, cutting out the sights and smells of the crowd. Maybe she was a love struck fool as Sarah claimed. He was a master of seduction with a list of conquests as long as her arm, he could be lying in order to claim her as another one. She nibbled her lip as she tried not to hunt about the room for sight of him. Could he have decided to not come this evening, despite his promise to? Had Alistair prevented him from attending somehow? The last thought hardly bore thinking about and she fidgeted in her seat, discomfited by the thoughts that roamed through her mind. Sarah's words echoed within her, maybe she shouldn't pine in the corner and wait for Justin but drag herself back into the social whirl and move on. It was the most sensible option, but not the most thrilling. Her life stretched before her, inflexible, planned and without any ounce of real personal choice. First society and its balls, then marriage to a suitable bachelor followed by children and whatever came after. She could decide not to marry, but without a reasonable allowance she could only become a governess. Choices were few and while she knew that Justin could never be hers, it was nice to dream at least for a little while.

"A beautiful girl like you should not be without a partner," Startled by the voice close to her ear, Melissa looked up. Hovering near her, was a pair of laughing blue eyes beneath an exquisitely powdered and ornate wig. Her eyes travelled over the unfamiliar countenance with appreciation. He had strong chin with high cheekbones and eyes that laughed beneath pale gold brows. He was solidly built beneath a set of clothes that squarely proclaimed him as a dandy. From the exquisitely embroidered rose coloured jacket and lavender waistcoat to the lace handkerchief that he waved delicately from his left hand, he declared his status to the room. In a flash she noted his high heeled shoes, the well padded calves and expensive watch chain. Hanging from his right wrist, an ivory fan dangled from a silk strap. The effect of all this fashion on such a solid frame tickled and stirred a hefty desire to laugh. Determining that laughter would surely be the wrong opening for a conversation, she swallowed twice and tried to regain her composure.

"Forgive my intrusion into your thoughts," His voice was clear and crisp with the slightest trace of an accent. "And for shocking you," A faint trace of humour tinged his words as though he knew what she was thinking. He indicated one of the spindly chairs nearby. "May I?"

Melissa nodded, her struggle between laughter and politeness had not yet finished and she didn't fully trust herself to speak.

"I'm Lord Tarlington," He announced with little preamble.

"It's a pleasure to meet you," Melissa murmured after finally getting her emotions under control. She had heard of Lord Tarlington only in passing, he was a notorious dandy and follower of fashion, yet beyond his known love of outlandish garb he had never garnered a reputation for anything else..

"And you're Melissa De Vire," He bent over to delicately place a kiss on her hand. "The girl who is being such a burden to our dear Justin," His words were softly spoken and breathed over her fingers, yet she heard them as clearly as though he had talked to her face. Stepping back, she stared at the exotic stranger, consternation in her face.

"How do you know Justin?" Or me? She wondered to herself as her fingers gripped the goblet a little more firmly. Granted she knew that her behaviour with Montjoy had garnered her some gossip, yet she had only been seen with Justin once in public. How could this dandy know of Justin's attentions toward her, when she barely knew them herself?

"Oh my dear girl, everyone knows Justin," He pulled the seat close and leant forward. "He's a cad but a delightful cad. But enough of him let's discuss you,"

He settled back in the chair and smiled merrily at her. Melissa watched him with interest. Despite the foppish clothing, his mind seemed to be razor sharp and she regarded him with mild concern. There was little reason for him to approach her and yet the possession he attached to Justin's name intrigued her. It suggested an ownership of or a familiarity with him that she was unaware of. Despite her misgivings, she decided to stay and find out as much as she could about the garishly dressed stranger.

"Me? Why would you have any interest in me?"

"Oh my dear girl, you're so delightfully modest," He chuckled as he spoke. "And quite entertaining," Melissa smiled nervously as he spoke, wondering what she had done to garner his interest.

"I don't think I follow you sir," Her voice was crisp, cold and icily polite. She was feeling more and more uncomfortable. The dandy sat too close and his manner was too familiar for her ease of mind.

"Of course you do," Tarlington insisted drawing himself closer to her. "You slapped Montjoy, which in itself was quite amusing and then you snare our Justin's interest," The minuet ended and the orchestra struck up again. "But rather than sit here and let me stroke your ego, I believe you should accompany me on the dance floor," He stood up and held out his hand. "Will you do me the honour?" Melissa sighed and looked at the stubby fingers of his right hand, toying with the thought of refusal.

"Please come and dance lady," His voice was softer, cajoling and Melissa saw an entreaty in his eyes which softened her resolve. Reaching up, she caught hold of his hand and he led her onto the dance floor. The music swelled about them as he led her expertly through the steps of the dance.

"So what did you mean when you said 'our dear Justin'?" At a lull in the dancing, she leant forward and asked the question that had been nagging at her for several minutes. There was a momentary pause and Tarlington looked down at her, eyes appraising.

"Well you are a bold one," He murmured as executed a neat turn. "What would you say if I told you that we were related?"

Melissa started and looked up at him. It was not possible. Everything she had heard in the last few days, made a relationship between Justin and this man unlikely at the very least. Once again she ran her eyes over the stocky form and found nothing familiar in either his features or gait.

"I'd wonder how you were related," She answered finally, dropping into a deep curtsey as the music ended. "I thought he only had a brother,"

"Oh he does," The other replied as he offered her a deep bow. "But he does have a family of sorts," Holding out an arm he drew her towards a set of chairs on the edge of the dance floor. Settling down opposite her, his face creased into a warm smile.

"Really?" She rearranged her skirts and raised an enquiring eyebrow. "How are you connected then?"

"Not by blood, though we may as well be," He answered obliquely, neatly sidestepping her direct questions in favour of evasion. "Let's say that I know Justin well,"

"Oh?" Many questions flooded through her mind. How well did this dandy know Justin? Had Justin mentioned her in the clubs that Gentlemen frequented? Was she the talk of the town? "Does Justin.," She hesitated, wondering if she were breaking protocol with undue curiosity. Lord Tarlington tilted his head questioningly and waited for her to continue. "Does Lord Lestrade speak of me often?"

"On the contrary my dear, he barely speaks of you at all. Which is an intrigue all on its own and quite delicious in its way," He leant closer, causing her to pull away sharply. "What is so special about you?" He dropped his voice even further as he wondered aloud. "Perhaps you can enlighten me?"

"Lady DeVire," A familiar intruded into the discussion and Melissa looked up in relief. Justin stood mere feet away from them and his eyes flashed a warning as they alighted on Tarlington.

"Don't worry dear boy, I'm going," Tarlington announced as he stood up. "It was delightful to see you my dear. Perhaps we will become better acquainted in the future?"

"I doubt it," Justin's voice whipped out and ended Tarlington's musing. "Miss DeVire is destined for better things,"

Melissa raised her eyebrow and watched as Tarlington nodded in resignation. What was going on? As quietly as he had approached, Tarlington left the scene, leaving her with Justin and her welter of thoughts.

"Please Lord Lestrade take a seat," She offered, feeling the familiar thrill of excitement as she took in his garb of burgundy and cream. The lotus adorned his neck and she found herself staring at it intently as he slowly lowered himself into the chair opposite.

"Are you well?" It was a formal question, sterile and cold somehow. Melissa felt some of her excitement seep from her as his words weaved around her mind.

"Quite well," She confirmed in polite tones. "Justin… I..," He held up a hand and glanced to one side. A couple sat close to them, close enough that they could hear the conversation. Cursing herself for her lack of observation,

Melissa clamped her mouth shut and lowered her head, hiding her embarrassed blush beneath layers of white powder.

"Care to take a turn?" He offered his arm and she took it gratefully, rising from the chair and heading into the crowd with him. Slowly they walked, moving through the crowd towards the foyer in silence. His fingers gently held her elbow and tiny shocks of excitement flowed through her at his touch. Her mind whirled with reams of unspoken questions and as they found a quieter corner, relief flooded through her.

"Now we can talk," His face was hidden in shadow, yet she could feel his eyes upon her. "I understand that you will have many questions and I will try to answer them as best as I possibly can,"

Melissa stared up at him, her thoughts twisting chaotically as she tried to read his shrouded face. "Why are you relieved that I know the truth?" She recalled their interrupted conversation and though many other questions clamoured to be heard, this was the one that she needed answering first.

A ripple of motion ran through his body as she felt him relax. With languid grace he leant back against the wall and considered her face. "Because lying is not something that comes easily to me. I have spent years learning to believe this farce of a life and it is good to feel open for once,"

"Very politic," She answered acidly as she looked at him. "Now tell me the rest," Melissa knew she should be calmer, less antagonistic but she could not help it, he had ensnared her in his secrets and she needed the truth.

"I am glad you know because I see a kindred soul in you," Justin spoke in a low tone as his fingers reached out to brush hers. "You have a spark that cannot be dimmed even by the hemmed in life that you lead," Melissa stared at the long fingers, felt their soft pressure as he clasped the tips of hers. "I saw you across the room at the Palace and you drew me in," A couple walked through the foyer door and he drew back into the shadow, removing his hand reluctantly from hers. "At first you were a pretty face and only that, something to be wooed," He lifted his chin and those dark eyes stared off into the distance as he struggled with speech. "Then I spoke with you and something tugged at me," Pushing himself from the wall in a flurry of motion, he looked down at her face. "Understand it was not love at first sight. Understand that I did sit with you in order to seduce you,"

"What stopped you?" In a voice as hushed as his, she demanded the answer as her fingers worried at the French lace on her sleeve.

"You started to speak and I could see that you were unlike the rest. You have a restless spirit and…" He gave a bark of low laughter. "So refreshingly honest that I found myself disgusted with my selfish desire. You also managed to see straight through me. I am a hedonist Melissa," He uttered simply, with little guilt or apology in answer to her bewildered face. "My amusements keep me sane but I do not love or even care for those I use. If a girl is willing to offer herself to me, then more fool her," The words spilled from him in a rush as rapid as water from a burst dam. "Now do you see? I could not seduce you as though you were one of those blue bloods that I see each and every night, because to me you are worth more than a simple dalliance," The torrent had finished and in the sharp silence that followed only their breathing could be heard. Melissa stood like stone before him, her fingers coiled round the French lace as though it were a lifeline.

"But you would never let it go further," She whispered into the stillness born of a knowing despair. "You would soon leave because of your secret," A crushing weight settled on her chest, was this heartbreak? She could scarcely believe it possible, she barely knew him and yet he seemed to hold her heart in his hand.

"I would leave you because I have no choice," His voice grew soft; all traces of harshness gone from his tones and Melissa could hear the longing deep within. A hand reached forward and caught hers, sudden warmth capturing her cold fingers. "I never meant to go this far. But when I saw you on the road that night, I couldn't in all conscience leave you there and I had to make sure you were well," He released her hand and stared at their surroundings as though in turmoil.

"And then I called," Melissa finished the narrative and a small laugh escaped her lips. "What a pair of dolts," They laughed together for a short space of time before the reality settled back in on them. "I wish.," She could not finish the thought and Justin did not press her for details. He had not wanted to draw her into his world, yet circumstance and her own curiosity had placed her squarely in his path and he had to be strong once again.

"Melissa. You know we cannot go on. You know why I cannot woo you properly and I cannot in all conscience ruin what reputation you have," Melissa felt tears prick the back of her eyes and she bit her lip, trying to hold in the emotion. "Much as I would like to, I can't stay. You deserve better than me,"

"Why though? Surely we can…"

"What can we do?" He asked softly, wearily, as though the question drained him. "You will age my love and I'm damned if I will subject another to my hell. You will age and I will not. If we stay in England, I would have to fake my death in a few years, if we move abroad; I deprive you of your family. I am not as selfish as that," He chuckled bitterly and continued. "Besides, you will be free of my brother's attentions once I move on," He picked up her hand again. "Live and be happy. Your father is not a tyrant; he will ensure you have a suitable match that won't distress you unduly. Forget me, it is the best way,"

Melissa bowed her head. In her heart of hearts she knew he was right. It was only in fairy tales that love found a way and she had to live in reality. Justin was a dream and always had been. Comforted though she was by his desire to save her reputation, she couldn't help but wish she had her own choice.

"It looks as though we have company," Justin nodded towards the end of the foyer and the thunderstruck form of Mary Westbury. Melissa groaned as her supposed rival pulled herself together and headed for their direction with the determination of a charging bull.

"Justin darling," She simpered as she approached, her excessive flirtation gaining a raised eyebrow from her supposed paramour and a barely concealed sigh of derision from Melissa. "I believe I have you on my card for a dance later. You aren't going to disappoint me are you?" Casting a poison filled glance at Melissa, she caught hold of Justin's arm. "Only you did promise,"

"Indeed I did," He responded, the devil may care mockery back in his voice and manner. "But I may have to pass I'm afraid. I have a splitting headache. I was explaining to Miss DeVire that I would be unable to attend her brother's jaunt to Somerset this weekend,"

"Oh my poor Justin is there anything I can do to help?" Melissa bit her lip in an effort to suppress hysterical laughter as she reached for her fan to hide her expression. Justin on the other hand, managed to contain his amusement perfectly and he adopted a tragic expression.

"I'm afraid not, but thank you for your concern," He turned from Mary and looked back at Melissa. "Miss DeVire," He dipped his head and kissed her fingers lightly. "I must bid you adieu," Melissa felt the thrill of his kiss run through her body and she watched him walk away with increasing sorrow.

"Hussy," Mary waited until Justin had left before she rounded on Melissa. "You've bewitched him and he is not for you," Mary's face was flushed even through the layers of powder that she wore and she advanced on Melissa with hatred in her eyes. "I warned you to leave him alone,"

"Oh grow up Mary," Upset and angry, Melissa stared at the other girl. "He will never marry you and even if he would, your father will disallow the match," She closed her fan and pointed it at Mary's chest. "Whatever he said to you, he lied. If you were foolish enough to believe him then it is your own misfortune,"

"And you think you can do any better?" Mary sneered into Melissa's face. "You? Whose only claim to fame is the striking of a Lord?" Her laugh tinkled off the parquet floors. "It is not I who has brought shame upon my family and forced my older brother into a duel he did not want. Who is the fool here, me, with my several offers of matrimony or you?" Mary paused and looked over Melissa with repulsion twisting her elegant features. "You only have the reputation of a Docklands fishwife following you. I'm sure a wonderful match is waiting for you this year," Mary stepped back with a vicious, triumphant smile creasing her lips. "Enjoy your season Melissa; I'm sure it'll be a wonderful memory in the future when you're a governess or some lady's companion," Mary turned away and took several steps before glancing back over her shoulder. "As long as you know that Justin will be my husband and if you continue to turn him from me, you will regret it. I promise you that,"

Melissa watched Mary stalk off into the main ballroom and rolled her eyes. She had not thought it possible to see such foolishness. Relaxing the vicelike grip she held on her fan, she left the alcove and moved toward the exit and her carriage. As she moved into the cool darkness of the street, the figure of Alistair Lestrade moved from his hiding place in the shadows to stare after Mary, who was chasing Justin through the crowd. A thoughtful expression creased his features and he moved into the ballroom, following Mary and Justin at a discrete distance. Moving through the chattering throng, he followed his quarry, watching as Mary finally reached his brother's side. Stopping beside a tall fern, he feigned interest in the green leaves as he focused in on the pair. Their conversation was low, beneath his level of hearing yet Alistair was an adept lip reader and though he could only see Justin, he was more than capable of following the discussion. Without a doubt, Mary was attempting to charm his brother in her simpering, simplistic fashion and, he smiled cruelly, Justin was clearly breaking his flirtation off. Alistair watched carefully as his brother severed his ties with Mary Westbury and moved away from the devastated girl before him.

"Something interests you?" A soft voice sounded beside him and Alistair turned to face the woman at his elbow,"

"Katherine," Alistair turned and smiled, his gaze drifting over the woman with approval. The woman's face was pale and she wore periwinkle blue. Fine silver embroidery and beading on the bodice and skirt flashed in the candlelight and exquisite French lace trailed from each sleeve. A fan dangled from a fine boned hand and a bracelet of silver and pearls encircled her slim wrist.

"I haven't piqued your interest, so don't lie," The woman's voice was gravely serious and familiar as Alistair bent over her fingers, gently kissing the pale skin with his smooth lips. "So what has got you all serious and concerned?"

"As if you don't know," He replied, smiling at the woman with a crooked grin, noting the sadness within her eyes. "You were there,"

"Oh the De Vire girl," Katherine moved out from behind the pillar and stared at Justin. "Do you think he will take her?"

"Not if I can stop it," Alistair replied, moving back into the alcove and drawing Katherine back with him. "Don't be so obvious Kat, I've seen Tarlington already and you can bet that if he sees you, he'll be straight to Justin to warn him,"

"Am I that dangerous Alistair?" Katherine's voice was soft, almost regretful as she regarded the young man.

"Yes my dear, you are, both you and your pay master," He watched Justin stride towards the gaming room and he turned back to his companion. "Now why don't you tell me why you were posing as a maid of all things?"

"As you say Alistair, I have my pay master and he has orders," She fumbled in her pockets and drew out a fan. "He's asked me to talk to you,"

Alistair sighed and leant back against the wall. "What about?" His asked in a low tone.

"He wants a meeting," She waved the fan slowly before her face as she spoke. "He needs to talk to you about your brother and the others," The fan snapped shut and she leant forward. "I wouldn't advise saying no to him,"

CHAPTER 27

Justin finished drowning his sorrows and headed from the card tables. Since his talk with Melissa, he had found a game of piquet and gambled recklessly, losing a small fortune in the process. After an hour and a half of play, he excused himself from the table and left the party. Retrieving his cloak from the servants, he walked through the doors of the great house and turned right. Despite the alcohol he had downed he moved with considerable alacrity along the gravelled driveway and towards the stables. The great house and grounds were bathed in the milky light of a full moon turning the exquisitely planned lawns and arbours into a silvery fantasyland. It was indeed a night for lovers and lunatics. He snorted derisively at his romantic notions and hurried through the covered alley that led to the stable yard. Distracted, lost in his thoughts, he was unprepared for the hand that snaked out of the darkness and pulled him into shadow.

"What the blazes," He yelled and punched free, fist meeting solid flesh as he turned to face his assailant, his hand reaching for his sword.

"There's no need for that Justin," A familiar voice drifted from the mouldy recesses of the alley and Lord Tarlington walked into view. Free from the light of the ballroom and beneath the silvery moonlight, Tarlington's dandyish clothing seemed less of the mode and more outlandish and strange. The man's gaze swept across Justin coolly and he seemed quite unlike the charming fop that Melissa had spoken with.

"What the devil do you want?" Justin got his breathing under control and he stared at the other man with barely concealed contempt. Tarlington did not answer instead he pointedly stared at Justin's fingers, still curled about the hilt of his rapier. "Oh heaven forefend," Justin exclaimed as he released his sword and stepped back. "As if this would harm you,"

"Not me dear boy, my jacket," Tarlington replied with a gentle rebuke as he reached into a pocket and withdrew a snuff box emblazoned with an enamel lotus. He lifted the lid and delicately took a pinch of snuff before returning his attention to Justin.

"Well your desire for unmarked tailoring aside, what do you want?" Justin's voice was low and filled with venom.

"I thought we had an agreement that you steer clear of England when I'm here," The moonlight picked out the silver embroidery on Justin's frock coat and threw his face into sharp relief. His handsome features were harsh and angry beneath the harsh silver light. "Particularly when you interfere in my affairs,"

"If you mean your fancy, then I'm terribly sorry for that dear boy, but I thought some things were more important than our little feud,"

Justin drew a sharp breath and stared across at Tarlington with suspicion. "Like?"

"I thought you knew," Tarlington sighed and headed back into the alcove. "And there was I counting on your omniscience,"

"Tarlington," Justin snarled, his frustration finally boiling over. "Enough of the games and tell me,"

"If you think this is an example of my games, then I worry for you," The dandy bemoaned as he removed one of the kid gloves and revealed a ring set with a blood red jewel. "But as I believe in helping those that least deserve it, I'll ignore your rudeness,"

Holding in his impatience with superhuman effort, Justin waited quietly. Past experience had taught him that Tarlington would get to the point in his own time and rushing him was not advised. Stilling his questions, he watched as the lamplight played on the other's face, waiting for him to continue.

"Oh very well," Tarlington finally spoke, a tinge of disappointment colouring his tones. "John has returned,"

"I knew that," Justin replied, irritation bubbling over. "Alistair has already warned me,"

"Oh I knew he had already warned you,"

"Then why for the love of all that's holy have you…" Justin snapped, his patience almost gone.

"He likely didn't tell you all of it. Don't forget I know you and your brother. Alistair is known for half truths," Tarlington smiled as he looked at the older Lestrade brother, he liked to needle the other man but it wasn't really malicious. He had known both Justin and Alistair for a very long time and while they were both responsible for what had happened to him, he did not really hold a grudge.

Justin sighed and ran his fingers along his chin, feeling his irritation subside as he weighed up the issues in his mind. "Alright," He murmured finally. "Tell me,"

"It's not just John,"

Justin felt sick as the words settled into his thoughts. John was bad enough but the others; he closed his eyes briefly and whispered. "Who else?"

"Katherine," He spoke simply, dropping the names as though unaware of their impact on Justin.

Justin's eyes popped open. "Not Abbott or Henry?" He asked with obvious relief.

"Not that I'm aware of," Tarlington adjusted his cravat and walked towards the main courtyard. "That doesn't mean they aren't here," He looked back over his shoulder. "You boys really made a mess of things didn't you,"

"We didn't mean..,"

"I know," Tarlington placed the tip of his cane to the cobbled ground. "That's why I get along with you," He stepped out into the courtyard, the moon painting him in silver and grey. "I would watch for your lady friend my boy. Your interest has been noted and I would venture that John will be taking steps,"

These words galvanised Justin into action. "He can't. I've left her; I've put aside those thoughts,"

"Doesn't make much difference as you know," The dandy whirled round and stared at Justin with hot eyes. "Or have you forgotten what you did to Anna already?"

Justin bowed his head, pain creasing his features as he struggled to respond. "Anna was…" He swallowed. "I loved her.,"

"Not enough to leave her in this life as I recall. You were spoiled, selfish and entirely too sure of yourself. I warned you and so did Abbott and you ignored us both, convinced that true love would conquer all," Tarlington stepped closer until his face was mere inches from his. "And Anna paid for your flawed desires with her existence,"

"Hugh," Justin's voice was a broken whisper. "Don't.,"

"Why should I not remind you? I see the same signs in you now that I saw back then," Tarlington's icy blue gaze stripped through to Justin's very core, puncturing the pretences that he had so carefully constructed.

"Don't you think I don't know how foolhardy such thoughts are? I made a promise Hugh and I will stick to it," Justin stared back into the other's eyes, his own warm eyes as cold as the stones beneath their feet. "I have told her that

I can not woo her. I have asked her to move on with her life. John should have no issue with that,"

"But she is aware of your nature," The point of Tarlington's cane pressed into Justin's chest as though to punctuate each point.

"How did you?" A look of horror crossed Justin's face and he stepped back. "He had me watched,"

"Of course he had you watched," Tarlington replied with a sneer of derision. "John is determined to punish you, like your brother is determined to punish you. And both would not stop at warnings to bring their point across. He sees you and this girl and knows that she is tempting for you. He wonders if you will break your vow and bring her into this select group of ours and he means to stop you,"

"Hypocritical of him though isn't it?" Justin countered his voice harsh. "His errors are as manifold as mine yet he buries his own complicity and blames me for all. It is insanity that he revels in and whatever reason he spouts to cover his cruelty does not alter the fact that John likes to kill,"

Tarlington stepped back and lowered his cane. "Indeed he does and I do not agree with the direction he has taken. You've been a fool boy, but you're not malicious," The tip of his cane tapped the ground lightly. "I know you mean to keep your promise," He turned back to the courtyard and spoke nonchalantly to the air. "I saw him enter the stables not long after your lady was seen to leave. It's quite possible that he knows where she lives,"

Justin moved like a scalded cat, a frenzy of action

and barely concealed panic. He rushed into the stable yard, startling a stable boy and kitchen maid kissing in the corner. The maid gave a small shriek of shock at his agitated appearance.

"Saddle my horse boy," He called to the stable lad as he stammered apologies. "And quickly now," Stumbling over his feet, the young man leaped to do his bidding and headed into the stables. Justin paced impatiently across the straw strewn cobbles, sparing barely a glance for the girl straightening her garments in the corner. The heels on his boots made tapping noises over the dusty stones as he moved back and forth.

"Can I get you a drink sir?" The maid asked tremulously after several moments of watching him stride up and down. He turned to face her and she swallowed a gasp at the bleak look of anger on his features. He stared at her for a few moments before answering, trying hard to restrain his fear fuelled anger.

"No, thank you," A clattering of hooves announced the arrival of his horse and he turned. Seizing the reins from the stable boy's hand, he vaulted onto its back. Touching his heels to the horse's side and raising a cloud of dust, he raced out of the stables towards the road. The maid and her lover watched him pass, curiosity and concern etched onto their features.

Justin barely felt the movement of the horse beneath him as they galloped through the moonlit landscape. His thoughts raced with the beat of the hooves as they passed through quiet villages and turnpikes. Hooves thundered over the rough ground and the horse ate up the miles as though they meant nothing. He knew that the horse could not sustain the pace indefinitely and he was forced to slow down as he passed through villages. It was ten miles to the De Vire estate and time was not on his side. John was probably at her house already and who knew what he had planned. He recalled the murdered heiresses and cursed himself for not thinking of it sooner. In renewed fear, he touched his heels to the horses side and increased the pace, trying to make it there in time.

CHAPTER 28

The carriage drew up before the great doors of the house and Melissa stepped free, her heart leaden with what she had heard. As her mother chattered on about gossip, Melissa was thinking of Justin. She knew well that there was no hope, even if he had been able to stay there would be none and yet she felt shattered. Justin represented excitement and adventure, more than the stifled world she currently lived in. He made her feel at ease, she could be more herself in his company.

"Melissa," She turned to face her mother. "Is everything well?"

"Yes," She forced a smile onto her face. "I'm just exhausted. I'm going to head to bed,"

"Very well," Her mother placed a hand on her arm. "Your father won't stay angry for much longer. He'll let us return to London soon enough,"

Melissa nodded but did not reply. Turning back to the staircase, she headed towards her room. At the bottom of the staircase her mother watched her progress anxiously, she was not completely blind and she knew the signs of an infatuation. She just hoped that her daughter had found someone suitable. Setting her wrap onto the banister, she left the hall and walked into the cosy comfort of the study.

Melissa slowly walked upstairs, past the glowering portrait of her grandfather, James De Vire. As always, she walked past the painting with her eyes lowered, afraid somehow that her grandfather's stern gaze could follow her from the depths of canvas and paint.

Slipping into her room, she closed the door and leant back against the smooth wood. What had she been thinking? Justin Lestrade was a pointless choice. He could not stay and her brief dalliance could cost her dear. What if her servant blabbed? What if someone had seen them talking and made the necessary connections? What if Mary exposed her to her father? A sigh escaped her lips and she closed her eyes. Why did she have to be so conscious of her duty?

"Miss?" Jane's voice sounded as a soft knock reverberated through the door. "Are you ready to retire?" Melissa opened her eyes and stepped forward into the centre of the room. The gilt mirror caught her profile and she grimaced, she was never very good at hiding her emotions and her face was a picture of misery. Taking a deep breath, she attempted to school her expression into one of calm nonchalance.

"Enter," She carolled, not turning as the older woman bundled into the room, carrying a bed warmer. Settling the long handled pan between the bedcovers, Jane turned to face her mistress.

"Let's get you out of that dress shall we? Raise your arm please Miss," Melissa complied and stood like a stuffed dummy as Jane undid the laces and ties that cinched her into the elaborate dress.

"Are you alright now Miss?" Jane asked as she began working on the corset stays at her back. "You seem a little upset tonight,"

"I just feel tired that's all Jane," Melissa lied smoothly as the corset was drawn from her body and she stood facing her maid in little more than a linen under gown.

"Well the bed'll be warm enough Miss," Her maid dropped the clothes onto a chair and reached for the long linen nightgown. As the crisp, white fabric settled into place, Jane drew a brush free and motioned her towards the dresser. "And you'll be fine once you've had your sleep," With the ease of long practice, she drew the soft bristles through Melissa's dark hair. "Don't worry Miss, love doesn't always answer the first time," Melissa stilled and turned her head. "Oh you think I didn't see? Well Miss if he can't see the prize before him, then he's not worth the trouble," She drew the brush through one last time. "Done, up you get," Jane turned back to the bed and drew back the bed sheets.

"Hop in then Miss," Melissa clambered between the white sheets, feeling the warmth emanating from the bed warmer at her toes. Settling into a comfortable position, Melissa stared up at the ceiling as Jane fluffed up the pillows around her before she left the room. For several long moments, she watched the flickering candle flame send obscure shadows up the walls. Her thoughts were chaotic, keeping her from sleep. Minutes passed and she still did not roll over to snuff out the candle. She was still staring at the canopy above her bed when a soft tap sounded on her door.

"Yes," The door creaked open and her older brother entered the room. He was dressed casually in his house clothes and had clearly been home all night.

"Mother said you had come home," He crossed the room and sat on the edge of her bed, looking down at her. His green eyes, so like hers, pierced her pretences. "What's wrong?"

For one long moment the temptation to blurt out all her troubles was almost too much to bear. But she couldn't, Marcus was easier to deal with than her father, but he was still bound by tradition. He would not understand. "I'm just tired Marcus," She lied, trying to bring a smile to her face. "It's been a long night,"

"You can't lie very well sister," Marcus replied with a small shake of his head. "Who's broken your heart this evening?"

"No one," She answered, turning her head away, so she

faced the solid armoire on the other side of the room. "I'm just tired,"

"That excuse may work on Mother but not me," He moved forward and took her hand. "You can talk to me about it you know," She turned back to look at him, he was looking down at her with a gentle beseeching look in his gaze. "It won't get back to Father, I promise," She bit her lip but nothing could stop her eyes filling with tears.

"Oh Marcus," She sobbed finally and sat up, flinging herself into his arms. Marcus wrapped his arms about her, rocking gently as a drenching rain of tears soaked into his shirt. "It's not fair," Her voice, muffled against his shoulder was raw with heartbreak.

"It's alright," He murmured softly, letting her cry. After several moments of silence save for her sobs, Marcus eventually spoke. "What happened?" His voice was mild and soothing, disguising the outrage he felt for the person who had made her cry.

"There was someone I was hoping for and he... he doesn't want to consider me," It was close to the truth, hiding the lie within those simple words.

"Then he's a fool and not worthy of you," Marcus whispered against her hair, his voice calming. "They'll be others far more deserving of your attention,"

"But I really cared for him,"

"What does that matter?" Marcus held her at arm's length and stared into her eyes. "Love is not a requirement for marriage. I know the romance is wondrous but it's not essential. You think I love the woman I will be marrying?"

Melissa stared up at him in shock, her tears forgotten in the face of his news. "You're getting married," It was the first she'd heard of any forthcoming arrangement. "I hadn't heard…" Melissa was bewildered now, how could her brother be this close to an arrangement and she not know of it.

"It hasn't been finalised yet," Marcus replied with a rueful smile. "But yes, I will be marrying Lord Layton's daughter," Melissa cast her mind over the women she had seen with Marcus yet no one stood out. "I don't love her," He continued speaking, not noticing Melissa's far away gaze. "And she doesn't love me, but we do not despise each other," He smoothed a stray strand of hair away from Melissa's face, drawing her attention back to him. "It's a marriage of convenience, nothing more. As most of these things are,"

"When?" Melissa could not conceive of her brother marrying and leaving the family home. Marcus had always been a fixture in her life. He had taught her to shoot and ride; he had tolerated her prattling questions about life in the city and hadn't insisted that she restrict herself to purely female pursuits. With Marcus married, she would be left here alone with her parents and her father's disapproval.

"Sometime in the next few months but not much longer than that," He caught sight of Melissa's stricken face and smiled reassuringly. "I'm not going to abandon you, little sister. I'll still visit,"

"I bet my match will be sorted soon after," She stared down at the bedspread, noting how the intricate embroidery blurred when seen through a veil of tears. Trying hard not to think about life without the steady presence of her older brother, she turned the conversation to other things.

"Most certainly," Marcus raised his hand and brushed the stray tears from her cheek. "Don't worry about your lost suitor; there will be others for you. Love isn't always the best way," He kissed her forehead and stood up. "Get some sleep Melly; things will be better in the morning," Turning, he headed for the door.

"Marcus," Melissa called him back; the desire to tell him about Justin was almost suffocating.

With his hand pressed against the door handle, Marcus turned back to his sister, his eyes questioning. "Yes,"

It wouldn't take much, just a few words and Melissa would feel lightened from the weight of Justin's secrets. The words teetered on the edge of her tongue, threatening to spill out into the open and change everything. Yet as she stared at her brother's open face, she knew she could not tell him. Marcus would comfort her but he could not understand and Justin would suffer. She had discovered Justin's secret and he had entrusted her with it. No matter how much she wished to unburden herself of it all, she would take his secrets to her grave.

"Thank you," Simple words of gratitude filled the air, sealing away secrets that were not hers to tell.

"Anytime," Marcus smiled over at her, missing her silent moment of struggle. "Sleep well," He opened the door and left the room, leaving Melissa sat upright in bed, staring after him.

For several moments, she stared blindly into space, thinking over the conversation. What Marcus had just said was true; love was not a requirement for marriage and in some cases had proven to be a liability. Of all of her acquaintances, only one had married for love and the others had settled for their families' choice. She fell back onto the bed with a heavy sigh. Rationally, she knew that Justin was off limits to her. Even before discovering his past, he would be forbidden to her, yet her feelings for Justin surpassed anything she had ever felt. Foolish perhaps but, she rolled onto her side and stared at the flickering candle flame, she felt real around him. Even with his disconcerting ways and mockery, he encouraged her to be herself. If only she could have chosen him, what a life they could have had. Blowing out the candle, she snuggled into the bedcovers and eventually drifted into an uneasy sleep.

On the edge of the vast gardens, a shadowed figure watched the lights in the house die one by one. Concealed in the shrubbery, he waited for all to fall silent before he made his move. Careful observation had revealed her room to him and patiently he gave time for her to fall into a deep sleep. Clouds scudded across the moon and eventually the man moved, his feet making little sound on the springy lawn as he headed through the ornamental gardens towards the house. Reaching the wall, he reached up a hand and began to climb. Her room was on the first floor and with the grace of a cat, he reached her window.

Melissa was dreaming, the same dream that had woken her several nights before. She struggled against the confining roots that were bound about her legs, trying to shield her face from the vicious maw that snapped just inches from her nose. As she pulled towards wakefulness, the figure opened the window and slid within the room.

He crossed the carpeted floor, marvelling at his ease of entry as he slowly drew a knife from his pocket. It was an old blade, the hilt spotted with old blood. A smile inched across his lips as he reached her bedside. One swift thrust and her fate would be sealed. As he bent forward, Melissa gave a loud cry and jerked upright, waking as though from a nightmare. Startled, the figure froze for a moment. Shocked into immobility by her movement, yet this did not stall him for long. Making up his mind, the figure lunged forward.

Disorientated, Melissa almost missed the attacking figure. Her eyes were heavy with sleep and the near dark of the room made it hard to see. Yet even as she struggled towards wakefulness, she could sense that something was wrong. A cool breeze played off her skin raising gooseflesh and she turned looking for the source of the draught. Then she heard it, the hissed snarl that drew her eyes up in time. Glancing up, curiosity turned to shock as she watched the dark figure dive at her. As though in slow motion she took in the details, the black, featureless clothing, a scarf wrapped around the face so it hid all but the eyes and the last feature, the one that drew her eyes more than any other, a knife, glimmering dully in the moonlight from window. Fully awake now and reacting instinctively, she managed to roll to the left, avoiding the slashing blow from the thin knife as she tangled herself in the bedclothes. The sleeves of her nightgown however were not so lucky and the sharp blade tore through the fabric.

"MARCUS!" She shouted for her brother as she rolled again, struggling to manoeuvre through the sheets which were wrapping around her legs and slowing her down. A hand, strong and pitiless reached out and closed around her nightshirt pulling her forward. She felt the cotton rip as she was dragged across the bed. "MARCUS!" She screamed again almost sobbing as her fingers frantically reached up and scratched wildly. A muffled oath burst from her attacker as she raked her fingers into his eyes. With one powerful blow he pushed her back onto the bed before raising the knife again.

"NO!" Almost crying with fear, she threw herself forward, seizing hold of his wrist in a vain attempt to forestall the descending knife. She could feel the strength in his arms as they wrestled and she knew she could not hold him for long. Biting and punching, the will to survive lent Melissa more strength than she thought possible, yet it would not be enough. He was stronger and once more he pushed her back, his fist connecting with her jaw and sending her reeling. He dove onto the bed and pinned her, raising the knife once more.

"Miss?" The door burst open to reveal Jane, who let out a scream at the sight of her mistress in danger and raced across the room. Throwing her matronly frame onto the man, she seized hold of his arm. The brief struggle that ensued between her attacker and Jane gave Melissa time to reach the edge of the bed. Stretching out with grasping fingers, she reached for the only weapon available, an unlit candle in its metal cradle. Jane gave a scream as she was thrust off and thrown to the floor. He turned back to the bed and Melissa, who had just whirled around. Grasped in her fingers was the metal holder and candle. Without hesitation Melissa thrust the candleholder straight at her attacker's head. A grunt of pain escaped the figure and the knife slashed out wildly.

"MELISSA," Her brother rushed into the room and the attacker took flight, diving from the bed and racing across the room for the window. Without even breaking stride, the man dove out, moments later they heard the muted thud as the body hit the floor outside. Jane let out a shriek of pure horror and Melissa gaped, staring at the window in disbelief. The figure hadn't even paused before the large panes of glass.

"What the deuce," Marcus rushed to the window and stared out. "God's teeth," He swore, pulling his head back inside.

"Is he dead?" Melissa spoke, her voice trembling and out of breath as she pulled the shredded nightgown closer to her body with shaking fingers.

"No," Marcus pulled away from the window and strode across the room, his rapier loosely held in his fingers. "The bastard's running away,"

"What?" Melissa flew over to the window and stared out. Beneath the window, the broken remnants of the window shimmered in the moonlight and there was no sign of a body. Casting her eyes around in disbelief, Melissa caught sight of her assailant running along the yew path.

"Impossible," Watching as the figure headed across the lawn with not even a limp to show that they had dived from a first storey window. "How?" Turning, she caught sight of Marcus heading for the door.

"Where are you going?" Melissa felt her heart leap into her chest. Her assailant had walked free from a fall that should have broken his legs. What could her brother hope to do against someone like that?

"Jane," Marcus stopped her flow of words as he called to the maid. "Fetch Jeb and Simon, we're going after him,"

"He just dived out of the window," Melissa called after him,

"And?" He glanced over at her, at the torn nightgown and tangled hair. "He would have…" Casting his eyes downward, he stopped talking. "No arguments Melly, you stay here with Jane," He nodded at the shattered window. "Close those shutters and move into a safer part of the house," He watched her start forward. "At least until we make sure that he isn't left on the grounds alright,"

"Melissa," Her parents rushed into the room, eyes wild. What the devil is going on here?" Her father's thunderous voice rose above all, as he took in the broken window, Melissa's state of dress and Marcus's rapier.

"Someone broke in," Marcus answered shortly as he pushed through his parents to the door. "They had a knife,"

"Oh lord Melissa," Her mother clasped her hand to her forehead and sank into the chair.

"I'm going after him,"

"Not alone you're not," Their father uttered shortly as he turned with purpose towards the main body of the house. Marcus looked as though he would protest, but after a moment he nodded and followed his father out of the room. As they left, a strange silence settled over the room. Melissa took several deep breaths, feeling the adrenaline from the struggle fade slightly as normality kicked in. Were it not for the shattered window and tumbled bed covers, she would have thought that the whole episode was a dream. Behind her, her mother finally got herself under control and stood up.

"Come on dear, let's get you downstairs," Melissa's mother slid her arm about her shoulders and led her towards the door. Nodding, Melissa followed; a strange numb sensation drifting over her as the realisation of what had happened began to sink in. In silence, she traipsed downstairs after her mother to await the return of her father and Marcus.

CHAPTER 29

Justin reached the edge of the De Vire estate and cantered over the boundary, heading for the large manor in the distance. The moon flooded the grounds highlighting each yew and elm in silver. He cast his gaze over the gardens, heart beating hard within his chest as he looked for his quarry.

A loud meaty thump drew his attention and he turned towards the sound. On the gravelled walkway that ran the length of the house, a man lay broken. Justin took a step forward and the man stirred, slowly dragged himself to his feet and started to move. A fast walk turned into a loping run and then the man was sprinting. "John," He murmured, watching the familiar figure run across the garden. Justin glanced up at the second floor window and his heart stopped beating. "Dear god no," He whispered brokenly as he watched the figure head through the hedges with uncanny ease and speed.

"Come on," He nudged the horse forward and broke into a canter. Beneath the dappled moonlit, he urged the horse onwards, catching up with the figure as he reached the yew avenue.

"John," His voice whipped out angrily as he vaulted from the horse's back, slamming into the shadowed figure. They both fell to the ground, rolling over and over in the dirt.

"You bastard," Justin managed to drag himself upright and he aimed a heavy kick to his opponent's stomach. "How dare you come here? How dare you draw her into this?"

"I?" John ignored the searing pain to his stomach and stood up. In the silvery light, his dark brown locks appeared almost black. "I didn't bring her into this, you did, the moment you turned your corrupted eyes on her," They circled each other warily, both looking for openings in the other's defence. "You don't deserve a moment's peace," Noise distantly erupted from the front of the house and John moved, his right hand slamming into Justin's nose making his eyes water as his left dove for the lotus at his throat.

"No," Justin struggled through the watering eyes and numbing pain in his nose to seize John's hand. For a long moment they wrestled, John's clenched fist holding the enamel brooch tight within his fist as Justin aimed punches at his side, face and stomach. With a sharp twist, John wrenched the brooch free, tearing Justin's shirt at his neck. His right hand snaked around Justin's throat closing into a deathlike grip.

"You're not as strong as me Justin and you know it," John ignored the blows that rained down on his side as leaned in and whispered softly into his ear. Justin raised his hands to prise himself free as John's grip grew stronger making spots dance in his vision as he began to black out. Through the haze of he saw John flick the lid of the locket open. Beneath the silver and gray light of the moon the pictures within were dark and indistinct. He knew what John was about to do and in desperation he used all his strength to claw at the hand fixed at his throat. Teetering on the edge of consciousness, he succeeded in freeing himself just in time to see John tear through the picture on the left hand side of the locket with his thumbnail. Justin gasped, the shock of the connection between him and his donor breaking, catching him like a punch to the gut. "Especially not now,"

John released him and let him fall to the floor as he threw the garments he had been wearing at Justin's feet. Shaking from the separation, Justin tried to pull himself upright, but John placed a foot on his chest and forced him back to the floor as he glanced back towards the house and smiled. "Enjoy yourself Justin," He smiled as he reached up and seized the reins of Justin's horse. Vaulting his way onto its back, he waved the lotus locket in Justin's direction before touching his heels to the horse's sides.

"John," Justin dragged himself upright and started after him, a staggering figure in muddy and dishevelled clothing. Behind him, the sounds of a pursuing crowd grew louder. John disappeared into the copse, leaving him alone for the baying mob that followed.

"That's him," Within moments he was surrounded and seized, several heavy punches landed on his already battered body and he fell to the ground, unable to heal from the wounds without the charm. He was pulled upright and struck again, fists flying in from all directions as he tried to protect his head and body.

"Alright that's enough," From the depths of the crowd, Marcus De Vire pushed his way to the front and stared down at his captive.

"Lestrade.," His face was grave as he stared down at Justin. "I might have known," Marcus drew back his fist and the blow sent Justin's head into a spin. "That's for my sister," He looked at the men holding Justin and nodded. "Get him into the stables,"

"Marcus" Justin found his voice. "It wasn't me. I would never hurt her. Please let me know she's alright?"

"Don't you dare speak to me about my sister," Marcus whirled around and there was hate in his eyes. "I should kill you right now but I think you have a date with a noose. You can't wriggle your way out of this one,"

Justin struggled futilely against the hands holding him as he urged Marcus to listen to him. "I saw the real assailant; he beat me and left me here. Damn it man, I'm being set up.

"You must think me a fool," Marcus replied, turning back to the house. "We saw no one but you. Your estate is next door; don't conjure phantoms to explain away your guilt," He turned to the stable hands and waved them away. "Get him out of my sight,"

As one, the grooms pulled Justin to his feet and they dragged him across the ground towards the large stone building that housed the De Vire horses. Bodily they threw him into an empty stall and lashed his hands and feet together. Leaving him in a heap on the floor, they walked out, leaving a man on guard. Justin tried to move, but the grooms had skilfully hogtied him, leaving him little room to manoeuvre. As the reality of his situation sank him, he wondered how he could have been such a fool. Alistair would have played mind games but even he would not have murdered innocents purely to inconvenience him. Really that's all it was, John meant to see him hanged or sent on permanent exile, depending how De Vire wished to handle it. Whatever the odds, it would make it impossible for him to continue operating in England. Even if Edward and Marcus De Vire allowed him to run to France, he would not be able to return to England for many years. He closed his eyes and felt his head hit the stable wall. Melissa was in terrible danger now and the only way he could save her would mean an uncomfortable death.

CHAPTER 30

Melissa lay on the chaise longue, a blanket wrapped around her frame and a glass of brandy clenched in her fingers as her mother fussed about her.

"I don't understand it," Her mother muttered as she paced up and down the parlour in agitation. "Why would anyone want to kill you? Why?" Plucking agitatedly at the sleeves of her robe, she continued to pace, as if she could walk the answers out of the floor.

"Mother, I'm alright," Melissa's voice shook slightly, a lingering reminder of her frenzied fight for life. "Marcus will catch him,"

"But who would do this?" Her mother stopped pacing and she stared down at her daughter, concerned tears filling her eyes. "There's no reason for it,"

Melissa bent her head; she had no answers for her mother, for she wanted them for herself. She had an idea of who it might have been, but she couldn't tell her mother about Alistair, after all she had not mentioned the letter that she had found on her pillow. She took another sip of the burning brandy and stared into the freshly stirred flames of the parlour fire. Why was Alistair doing this to her? She and Justin were finished, if indeed they had ever started, what was Alistair hoping to accomplish by attacking her? The loud bang of the front door drew her from her thoughts and she stared at the parlour door, wondering what state her brother would be in. The handle turned and Marcus walked into the parlour, his hair mussed and bruises across his knuckles.

"Well?" Their mother broke the silence as Marcus headed for the drinks cabinet and a stiff brandy. "Did you catch him?" Her son glanced over his shoulder as he poured the drink, he stoppered the bottle and turned back to face his mother and sister.

"Hmm," Marcus nodded in affirmation as he knocked back the slug, savouring the burning sensation as it travelled down his throat. "It was Lestrade," He sat on one of the chairs and leant back, closing his eyes, suddenly exhausted by the night's events.

"Justin Lestrade?" A horrified note entered her mother's voice and she reflexively squeezed Melissa's hand. "That cad?" Lydia racked her brains and finally came up with an image of the man.

"Yes," Marcus left his eyes closed as he replied, the empty glass of brandy hanging loosely from his hand. "He's in the stables. I have the grooms watching him,"

Melissa did not hear the rest of his sentence, her mind had stopped working when he had confirmed Justin's name. The room swam before her eyes and she had to struggle not to faint. This couldn't be true, Justin wouldn't, he couldn't have been the one to attack that evening.

"Are you sure it was him?" Her voice was low, frightened and Marcus opened his eyes to stare at her.

"I'm positive," Marcus replied as he finally gave the empty glass in his hand to Walker. "He was on the edge of the estate and that disguise he wore was on the ground beside him. Of course he claimed he didn't do it,"

"It might not have been him," Melissa argued, her heart in her mouth as she tried to process what her brother was saying. A strange sick feeling settled over her and she gripped the arms of the chair tightly, steadying herself.

Marcus glanced at her sharply, his green eyes measuring her reaction. "There was no one else there, he was bruised and in a mess," He sighed and continued. "I have no doubt in my mind that he was responsible," Moving to the edge of the chair he pushed his hair free from his face with a distracted hand. "But I don't understand it," He glanced over at Melissa, noting the tense set of her shoulders. "You barely know the man. All the others have been his fancy,"

"Walker," Melissa's mother turned towards the servant, her voice bell clear and sharp. "Send for the constable. I want him here as soon as possible,"

"Yes Miss," The butler nodded and headed out of the parlour.

"Melissa my dear," Her mother was once again at her side, her hands shifting the coverlet with agitated motions. "It will be fine. When the constable gets here, Lestrade will answer for this night's work,"

"Mother I don't think it was him," Melissa argued, throwing aside the blanket and standing up. "I'm sure my attacker was heavier set. You can't hang a man because you hope it's him,"

"And you can't save the man you desire from lawful justice," Marcus' voice drawled from the corner of the room, turning Melissa to stone and drawing a wrathful glare from her mother.

"Marcus you're not suggesting.," Lydia De Vire's voice was shocked and taut with fear. "That Melissa has…" Her eyes darted to Melissa and her daughter was shocked to see shame mingled in with the horror in her gaze.

"No that's not what he's saying," Melissa cut across her mother's words, her eyes sending a silent plea to her brother. "Justin saved me from a horrible accident on the road and that is all. If you must search for someone to blame for this then why not look at Montjoy? He definitely had a grudge against me,"

"Because much as I personally despise the man, Montjoy was not discovered at the edge of our estate, armed with the instruments used to terrify you," Marcus pulled himself upright. "I know you don't want to believe it Melly but you must face the truth. This is not his first offence…"

"That has never been proved," Melissa was almost shouting, her voice cracking with anger. "In fact we know that he could not have killed Honesty. He could have fought with the real attacker.,"

"Enough the pair of you," Lydia's voice snapped over their bickering and they both looked at their mother in surprise. "I believe it's time for bed. Melissa you will sleep in the parlour and Marcus.,"

"I'll sleep in the hall," Marcus interrupted as he dragged himself out of his chair. "Keep an eye out,"

"If you're convinced you have the right man," Melissa's retort sizzled across the room. "Then you will not need to keep an eye out," She sank back onto the cushions and crossed her arms. "Because the danger is apparently locked in the stables,"

"Don't be sharp dear," Her mother reprimanded as she fluffed up the pillows on the long couch. With gentle but brisk movements, she tucked Melissa into the makeshift bed. Turning back to her older child she directed him out of the room with an imperious gesture. "Go to bed Marcus. In a couple of hours the constable will be here and Lestrade will be off the property. I'm sure the grooms and those ropes will stop him escaping," Marcus opened his mouth to protest. "Not another word Marcus, your sister will be quite safe here," She stood with a swish of fabric and walked toward him. "It's been a long night and you need to sleep," Resting her hand on Marcus' shoulder, she squeezed gently. "I'm proud of you," Gently, but with firm determination, Lydia ushered Marcus from the room and shut the door. Turning back to her daughter, she sighed and sat in a chair.

"Now what about Lestrade?" The glance she gave her daughter was piercing and Melissa bowed her head, unable to stare directly at her mother.

"Mother I," She started to speak, wondering how she could lie her way out of this. Lydia was not a fool; she could pull the wool over her eyes for only so long. As Marcus had planted the seeds in her mind, it was only a matter of time before her mother dug the truth out of her.

"When I was younger," Her mother interrupted and she looked up, surprised to see compassion and understanding in her gaze. "I fell in love with Lord Jonathan Gabardine. He was a scoundrel of the highest order but exciting and different. I was madly in love with him. When he asked me to elope I jumped at the chance," Lydia's voice was soft, kindly and lost in an old memory, Melissa listened enraptured, wondering what had occurred to prevent her marriage and why she had never heard of the tale before. "It was almost the scandal of the year,"

"Almost?" Melissa leant forward, alight with curiosity. "What happened?"

"Your grandfather," Lydia replied, an undercurrent of old anger buzzing through her words. "He found my night bag and realised what I meant to do. He waited for John and thrashed him within an inch of his life. He only let him live if he promised to leave the country and settle in France," A hiss of old hurt escaped her mother's lips. "I remember thinking as my father issued that ultimatum that John would never obey him; that he would rise up and take me away," She stopped talking, her thoughts in the past and far away. Melissa tugged on her sleeve, bringing her back to the present and urging her to continue.

"I never saw him again," Lydia uttered with brutal directness. Melissa glanced at her mother's face and was shocked to see the gleam of tears in her eyes. "He knew he was doomed and he ran,"

"Mother," Melissa placed her hand on her mother's arm, trying to offer some comfort. "I didn't know,"

"It was a long time ago and though he broke my heart, I have never forgotten," She looked at Melissa full in the face and her words flew forcefully across the space between them. "This is why I beg you not to make the same error I did. Whatever feelings you think he has for you, understand that they are not real," Melissa opened her mouth to argue but her mother continued, determined to say her piece. "You are a rich catch for a rake like him. Yes he may be more pleasant than Montjoy but underneath he is the same. Don't let your wishes cloud your judgement. I nearly eloped to Gretna for a foolish rash love. And you are nearly dead..."

"But I know Justin would not attack me like this," Melissa pleaded, trying to get her mother to see what she knew but Lydia held up her hand, stopping her before she could begin.

"How do you know?" Her mother interrupted, gently but firmly pushing her back on the bed. "You barely know him beyond your girlish dreams," Lydia stood and pulled the coverlet straight. "He's been implicated in several deaths before being caught on the edge of the estate, clearly damaged by the fall from your window. See sense Melissa and see reason. Lestrade is a dangerous man,"

Melissa settled back beneath the covers and pressed her lips closed. It was no use arguing, her mother had clearly made up her mind. At dawn or earlier, the constable would be called and Justin would be taken away in disgrace. Her only chance to save him now was to wait until the house were asleep. As she feigned a large yawn, her mind began plotting how she could reach the stables and set him loose.

"Sleep well," Her mother leaned over the bed and pressed her lips lightly to her cheek before turning to leave. "Think about what I said," She called over her shoulder as she reached the door.

"Hmm," Melissa replied in what she hoped was her sleepiest voice. Through half closed eyes, she watched her mother turn the door handle and leave the room. Left alone in the lounge, she sat up and pushed the blanket free of her legs. Whatever else happened this night, she wanted to be awake in order to save the man she loved, for without a doubt, she knew that she did. It may not seem sensible but she could not deny her feelings. When had she swopped curiosity for affection? Melissa stared at the clock on the mantle and pondered her feelings. No matter how she looked at it, Justin had seized a place in her heart and she couldn't let him die for her. Around her, she could feel the house fall back into silence, its inhabitants slowly relaxing after the night's events. As the candle burned lower, she watched the clock slowly tick down the time. Three O'clock arrived and the house had finally settled back to sleep. Standing up from the chaise longue, she pulled the blanket about her shoulders and crossed the floor. Pulling apart the curtains, she opened the window and carefully clambered out. Clouds had finally covered the bright shimmering moon and the grounds were dark as she hurried towards the stables, her feet making little noise on the lush lawn. She passed the main entrance of the house and crossed the courtyard towards an archway in the wall. On light feet, she headed through the arch and made for the large darkened building on her left. The gravel crunched slightly beneath her slippered feet and she slowed down, looking up at the house in worry. The only windows that overlooked the stables were dark and with a sigh of relief she walked forward.

"So what you thinks' going to happen to him then?" A voice echoed loudly nearby. Melissa stopped dead, her heart pounding in her chest as she stared through the gloom towards the stable.

"Dunno," A second voice answered and Melissa let go off the breath she was holding. She recognised Alun and Tom, two of the stable hands and with a sinking heart, she realised that her brother had placed guards. They were now between her and the stable door.

"Reckon he'll hang?" Alun continued, his feet crunching to a stop on the gravel. "Attacking the mistress an' all?"

"Nah..," The other answered, sniffing as he did so. "Cause too much scandal. They'll pin summat else on im or drive im to Southampton and put im on a boat. If word gets out that he was in her room, then that's it for any marriage for 'er. Poor little lass,"

"Heh," Alun grunted with no real humour. "'ow about poor us? I got to be up tomorrow early and they have me guarding a stable door. They've only trussed 'im up like a turkey. 'E ain't going nowhere,"

Melissa backed up until her fingers hit the rough stone of the wall. Pressed back against the hard surface, she struggled to think. Justin was only a few feet away and she couldn't get to him. Biting her lip in frustration she stared up at the sky, watching the shades of light and dark that made up the clouds above. Even with the cloud cover, they would see her if she got too close. For several long moments, she stood in the darkness, pondering her options. The main door was barred to her, but that didn't mean they had guarded the door from the servant's quarters. Gritting her teeth in determination, Melissa left the scene and hurried back to the house.

CHAPTER 31

Justin lay slumped against the back of the stable, arms lashed to rings on either side of the box. His ribs ached and he could feel the blood slowly crusting above his eyebrow. John had known what he was doing when he ripped out that picture. Whatever damage afflicted Justin from now on would remain unhealed. He sighed and shifted position, hoping to alleviate some of the pressure on his arms, but to no avail. Marcus De Vire's grooms were extremely thorough and there was no give in the bonds at all. In all honesty he couldn't blame the young man for casting the blame his way. Had the situation been reversed, he probably would have done the same. The minutes slipped into hours and he drifted into an uncomfortable sleep.

A noise in the corner of the stable jolted back to full alertness and he stared into the gloom. Had Marcus come to deal with him? Footsteps, light and quick, hurried nearer as his eyes strained to see. A blur of movement to his right and a slender set of fingers pressed against his lips, stilling his mouth.

"Hush," Melissa's voice breathed softly against his ear, sending shivers down his spine. "I'm getting you out of here," Her fingers slowly left his mouth and began pulling at the tight hemp knots that held his wrist. In the dim light of the stable, she was a pale blur as her fingers worked furiously at the rough rope Stunned by the sudden turn of events; he did not react as she tugged free the first knot. The ropes loosened and feeling rushed back into his arm. Released from its bondage, his arm dropped limply to his side, sending ripples of pain through him as his muscles returned to a more natural position. Grunting with satisfaction, Melissa switched her attention to his other wrist. Fighting an uncomfortable wave of nausea, he reached for Melissa with his free hand, dismayed at his weakness.

"Melissa," His hand brushed her shoulder, feeling her skin beneath the soft cotton of her nightgown.

"Shh," She whispered, a tremor running through her at his touch. "You don't want to rouse the guards,"

"This isn't going to work," He hissed back, his fingers reaching for her wrist and drawing her hand away. "You can't let me go,"

"Why not?" Melissa turned to face him and her breath

ghosted across his lips. "They won't know it was me," A desperate hope sounded in her voice and he wished with all his heart that he could make that hope come true.

"They'll know," Justin argued, his voice low yet urgent. He felt her toss her head in annoyance and he reached forward, holding her chin with a strength he did not have. "You have to leave me here,"

"My father will have you hanged," Melissa whispered back, her voice breaking with emotion. "It wasn't you who attacked me. I know it wasn't and I can't and won't let you take the punishment for it. If they think you broke free?"

Justin shook his head sadly, hating himself for the being the voice of reason. "Your brother tied these ropes himself and he'll know how tight they were. He won't accept that I broke them or worked my way free," Melissa stiffened and he could feel the warm wetness of her tears on his hand. "He'll know it was you. Your reputation…"

"I don't care about my reputation," Pulling her head free, she reached once again for his bonds, only to be stopped by Justin's free hand snaking around to seize her wrist. "I can't let you be killed,"

"Melissa think," Justin urged, his whispers sounding hideously loud in the quiet of the stable. "Your father cannot hang me for assaulting you. If he did, your reputation would be damaged beyond repair. There would be those who would say that you invited me and that there was no assault. You know how this works,"

She bent her head, feeling the tears slide down her cheeks, grateful for the dark that hid her grief stricken face. "But… they will send you away. I won't ever see you again," His hand reached up and cupped her chin, drawing her closer as he wiped the tears from her cheeks.

"It's for the best. You know I can't stay with you and now you can find someone else," He felt her jerk back in dissent and he chuckled blackly. "It's not as though you don't have admirers. You would have had to choose one to suit your family eventually,"

"But I wanted to be free.," Her words rippled in the space between them, heavy with tears and regret. "I wanted you. You're the one I…"

Justin pulled her close, his lips brushing hers. "You don't know how long it's been since I felt alive enough to want more. But it was a dream," He kissed her delicately, brushing her soft mouth with exquisite tenderness. She folded against him, her body soft and warm against his. With effort, he broke the kiss and gently moved her away from him. "Now you must retie me and go to bed before we are discovered,"

"Justin," A soft plea entered her voice and she sat there, her body a pale flame in the dark. "I can't,"

"The man who attacked you will know that you freed me," Justin uttered into the space. "He will make it his life's work to see you killed and in the worse way possible,"

"But why?" Her voice rose in shock and Justin winced. For several moments they froze still, listening for the sounds of the guards on the door. One long minute stretched by, broken only by the sounds of their breathing before Melissa spoke again. "Why would he do that?" Her voice sounded lost in the darkness of the stable. "and why did he attack me?"

Justin drew a deep breath; his mind was working overtime, trying to decide how much to tell Melissa in case it terrified her. Once again, he cursed his own stupidity for failing to leave before things got out of hand.

"John is punishing me," His voice was softly apologetic and he stared blankly into the darkness. Melissa shifted beside him and he could almost hear the question teetering on her lips. He sighed and continued to speak, reluctance coating every word. "Alistair was not the only victim of this curse," Melissa sucked in a breath, stunned by the revelation. A bitter chuckle escaped his lips and he leant his head back against the wall, ignoring the stabbing pain from his ribs. "There were others.,"

"Tarlington?" Melissa's voice sounded softly in his ear and he nodded, gratified that she had made the connection.

"Yes. Tarlington was one, there were two more," He threw back his head and laughed softly, cynically. "We experimented on our friends, only to find out too late what we had done," He fell silent, lost for a moment in recrimination and old memories. "John was once a friend but that all changed once we realised what the curse meant. By then he had cursed others and it was far too late. He blamed me for it, led no doubt by my brother's example,"

"But why does he blame you? You weren't to know," Her fingers squeezed his upper arm and he smiled sadly in the darkness. He wondered whether she would be so accepting once she knew the full truth about the danger he had put her in.

"Blame doesn't need a reason. Suffice to say that he's determined to make my life a misery. Alistair can be an irritant but John is dangerous in his passion," His free hand reached for hers and he took a deep breath before launching into the meat of his tale. "He decided that no punishment would be sufficient, so he improvised. Once every decade or so, he tracks me down and makes it impossible for me to settle. He could set my house afire or mark me a killer,"

Melissa choked back a shocked breath as the meaning of Justin's words finally hit her. She thought of Honesty and the other girls whose demise was loosely laid at Justin's door and she felt sick.

"You mean he kills people so you would be blamed," Her voice was a horrified whisper and cold fingers of dread trailed across her spine. "That's inhuman. How could he kill another purely to spite you?" Outrage tainted every word and she clenched her hands into fists, her anger roused by what she had just heard.

"I know," He breathed the words, wondering how she would take his own abuses, would she be forgiving? Would she be able to understand what he had to do to survive? He shook away the maudlin thoughts and continued with his tale. "I should have left the moment the first body surfaced, but I wasn't sure that it was him, I have been wrong before and I selfishly didn't want to leave. I had not seen John in sixty years and I foolishly hoped that I was wrong. I was too enamoured with this life that I forgot about him," His voice trailed away in shame as he revealed his reasons for not packing up and moving on.

"What about Honesty?" Her voice reached his ears, filled with reproach, not that he could blame her. It was his fault that Honesty was targeted and sent to her death. "And what about me?" Her voice broke on the last sentence and he raised his fingers to stroke her cheek reassuringly only to have her pull away. "He attacked me because I was close to you?"

"Yes," He replied in simple and matter of fact tones even as he felt his heart lurch in pain. "He attacked you to spite me," As his words rang across the space between them, he stared across at her face, wishing he could see her face. Did she hate him? Had he killed what love she had professed for him? Should he grieve if she had? It was the last thought that caused him trouble. Logically, he knew that Melissa should hate him and leave, it was the best course of events, the one that caused the least harm and yet, he did not want her to go. Selfish though it was, he wished that she could be by his side; join him in his hunt throughout time. Even knowing that he was saving her from hell, he could not help but hope for her to follow him.

Melissa remained silent, taking in his words with disbelief. He had known John was targeting people close to him and he had still courted her. He had knowingly brought her close to death and yet, he had made her feel more alive than she ever thought possible. A horse whickered in a nearby stall and she started towards the noise in confusion. What could she say? She brought her fingers to her mouth and nibbled her nails absently, the old childhood habit betraying her inner turmoil.

"You knew I was in danger," She whispered brokenly, her fingers trembling near her mouth. "You knew and you said nothing,"

Justin reached for her, his fingers blindly seeking her cheek. "No.. no. I didn't know he was here," His voice cracked on the words as her words shattered like glass against his mind. "I should have realised, but I didn't know until Alistair told me and I immediately tried to end things, but it was too late," Panicked, he tried to move closer to her, yet the remaining ropes and several cracked ribs put paid to his desires. He didn't know why he was trying to explain, he should let her leave in a fog of anger but he had to try to fix this. "I didn't want harm to come to you,"

"But it has," She pushed herself away from him and stood. "And Honesty died because of you," Her fingers seized his hand and she began to tie his wrist back to the wall as tears began to flow freely down her cheeks. "I have never felt this way about anyone before Justin. I loved you. How could you do this to me?"

"I'm sorry," He winced as she pulled the knot tight against his raw wrist and pulled his arm back against the side of the stable. "Melissa please understand. I made a mistake. I thought he was not here and when I finally understood that he was, I made ready to leave. I couldn't let him bring any harm to you because of me," Raw desperation tinged his voice and he almost winced at the plea he could hear in his tones. "I never wanted this. Please hear me out?"

"No," She stepped back and fumblingly she found the edge of the stall. "I can't believe you let Honesty, the others die like that, never mind what you've done to me…" With tears blurring her vision, she staggered back the way she came, leaving Justin alone in the stable.

"God curse it," He hissed as the stable once again rang with the sound of silence. "I'm so sorry; I never meant to hurt you. By all the hells, I didn't," He spoke to empty air; half wishing she would return to hold him, forgive him for his offences. His head flopped onto his chest and for the first time in two hundred years, he sobbed. Tears fell silently from his eyes and soaked into his breeches. "But at least now, you will be safe from him,"

Melissa staggered blindly from the stable and through the servants' quarters, tears flowing like rain from her green eyes. Moving on light feet, she reached the main part of the house and slipped back into the parlour. In the dim light, she collapsed onto the chaise longue and buried her face in her hands. The tears flowed freely and she rolled over, pressing her face against the pillow. For an age she lay there, tears soaking into the fabric of the cushion as she cried.

"How could he do that?" Her voice, muffled against the pillow, echoed in the empty room. "How could I love him? Why did I?" She raised her hand and balled it into a fist. "Stupid! Blind! Fool," With each word, she punched the ornate cushion beneath her head, feeling the gold embroidery scratch across her knuckles with each blow. In a blind fury, she attacked the cushions, expelling her rage in frenzied anger. "How could I have been so stupid?" Her next blow flew wide; her fist slammed into the wooden arm of the chair and she yelped in pain. Drawing her hand free, she stared at her skinned knuckles and felt her temper dissipate as she contemplated the tiny beads of blood that collected on the graze. Sniffing, she reached for her handkerchief and dabbed at her eyes, composing herself. Pulling herself upright, she stared about the room, the shapes of the furniture milky and indistinct in the low light. Shivering in the chill of early morning, she pulled the blanket about her shoulders and reached to light the candle by her side. The flame ate the wick greedily and she watched the orange light dance up and down the walls.

Her rage expended, she stared at the candle flame watching it stretch and grow as she recalled her visit to Justin. In the still of the parlour, the events of the stable could be analysed more thoroughly and by dawn her anger had faded, only to be replaced with a guilt that gnawed at her insides. She sat back, leaning her head against the back of the chair as her thoughts milled crazily within her head. Thoughts of Justin roamed through her head, a myriad images that tore at her and left tears of a different sort. How could she have not heard him out? Why had she let fear and anger ruin their last moments together? It was not his fault that John killed Honesty and he wasn't responsible for the assault earlier; no matter what he had done in the past, he had not wished John to attack her. She was acting like her father after the ball, blaming Justin for something he had no control over. A small part of her knew that she would have been safer without him in her life, but that wasn't his fault. Yes he should have warned her earlier but she would not have listened. She chuckled bitterly, playing with her hair as once again Justin's parting words echoing through her mind.

"What a fool I am?" She hissed to the ceiling as she closed her eyes and pressed her fingers against the lids. "How could I have done this to him?"

She opened her eyes and sat up, thrusting the blanket from her shoulders and moving to the edge of the seat. In a frenzy of movement, she got to her feet and headed for the door. Almost heedless to the noise she may have been making, she hurried down the hall and moved towards the servants' quarters.

"Can I help you Miss?" A voice spoke from the darkness on her left. Melissa gave a small gasp of surprise and whirled round.

"Alice?" Melissa stared at the face of the Upper Housemaid and almost swore in frustration. The servants were up, it would now be impossible to get to the stables. Swallowing her frustration, she attempted a wan smile. "I woke with a stiff neck," She said, trying to fob off any unwarranted attention. "What time is it?"

"It's gone five of the morning Miss," The woman bobbed a small curtsey and continued. "Martha will see to your fire in a moment Miss. Would you like anything?" The woman's sharp eyes were alive with curiosity and Melissa was sure that she would be the subject of much speculation in the kitchen.

"No that's fine Alice. I'll go back to the parlour now," With a dead weight settling over her heart, Melissa turned and returned to the parlour. Shutting the door behind her, she sat back on the chaise longue and stared out at the lightening sky, counting the moments until her father arrived.

CHAPTER 32

"Will you stop all this nonsense Melissa," Edward's voice snapped across the breakfast table with a violence that she had rarely heard before. "It's quite clear that this Lestrade has broken into your chambers and attempted to hurt you," Resting both hands on the table; he leant forward and towered over his daughter. "Your brother found him outside, almost red handed and you would have me believe that this some coincidence?"

"He said it wasn't him and I believe him," Melissa ignored the warning glance from Marcus as she plunged ahead with her reckless defence of Justin's character. "Why can't you accept that you could be wrong?" Marcus drew a sharp intake of breath and Melissa glanced across at him.

One fleeting look at her brother's face informed her that she had gone too far.

"Damn your eyes girl," Edward stood and marched around to her side of the table and seized her by the arms. Pulling her to her feet with one angry motion he forced her to face him. "If he wasn't attacking you, then what was he doing on the estate? Hmm?" He shook her, making her teeth rattle. "Was he making a call? Was my daughter acting like a common whore and inviting men to my home?" Another shake and his fingers dug into the bruises on her upper arms. "Well?" Melissa could not answer as her head swam as the shaking continued. Her teeth bit down onto her tongue and she hissed at the sharp spasm pain rocked through her. Out of the corner of her eyes she could see Marcus moving to stand and she wished she could tell him not to interfere.

"Father I didn't do anything," Her words tumbled from her lips, jumbled and incoherent through a mouth rapidly filling with blood. Her protestations were cut short as her father raised his hand back and let fly with a stinging slap to her cheek. The sound echoed through the room, shocking the room into momentary stillness. Edward had never raised his hand to Melissa before.

"Edward stop it," Lydia voice snapped out and she stood, seeing her son ready to place himself into the fray and not wishing a further scene, she reached up and caught hold of her husband's arm, pulling him back. "Melissa is saying nothing of the sort, she is confused," Edward let go and Melissa slumped back into the chair, the taste of blood swirling through her mouth as she pressed her hand to her reddening cheek. Marcus crouched beside her as Lydia continued to speak; she was pulling her husband away from Melissa with gentle but firm movements. "She thinks that her attacker was larger than Justin and that is all. I feel she is frightened and confused. You know that she would never invite a man to her room,"

"I don't bloody know anymore," Edward's voice stormed over all them, making the crockery rattle. "She wished to fire a pistol as a child and then she acted like a common housemaid at the Palace. Who knows what she thinks is acceptable behaviour?" He pulled away from his wife and stood over her, his face almost violet with rage. "I warned you Lydia about allowing her too much latitude and look what happened," He waved across at Melissa, who flinched back from the hostility in her father's voice. "This affair will ruin our reputation. No one will want her with this scandal attached and she could even ruin Marcus' match. I can't see the Layton's accepting a son in law with such a sister. If she had any shame, she wouldn't be speaking at all this morning,"

"That's enough Father," Marcus finally snapped out as he stood. He faced off against his parent, seizing hold of his father's shirt with one strong hand. "Melissa did not invite Lestrade to this house," He pushed his father back, his grip on the shirt rigid and unforgiving as Lydia moved to help Melissa back into a chair. "You should know she has more propriety than that," His eyes stared straight into Edward's, their green depths jewel bright and harsh. "I believe that she would have been killed if she had not woken. Would you prefer her to be dead?" Edward moved to free himself from his son's strong grip, but Marcus shifted his weight and held firm. Beside her mother, Melissa looked at the confrontation through tear blurred eyes, holding a hand to her stinging cheek. "Well would you?" Marcus demanded, his voice shaking slightly with outrage as he stared up at his father.

"No," Edward finally admitted, staring across at Melissa with a tortured gaze. "But she will not survive the scandal," He shook his head and stared at his wife, "we will not survive the scandal,"

"I didn't invite him Father," Melissa shook off her mother's fingers and stood, facing her father with new found resolution. "I went to bed and woke to find a man in my chambers ready to kill me. I don't believe it was Justin," Edward snorted with derision yet Melissa continued, determined to say her piece. "I have no idea how he came to be so close to the house but I did not invite him,"

"Whether you did or not, the scandal still exists," Edward snapped, yet making no move to advance on her again. "There will be those who say that you invited your attacker,"

"Then we say nothing of this night's work," Lydia interjected her voice calming as she walked forward to brush her husband's arm. We will tell Lestrade to leave the country quietly. The reason can be gambling related, an excuse that all will accept," Marcus nodded, his eyes not leaving his father's face. "There will be no mention of what happened here. No shame to infect the family,"

"And what about the servants?" Edward's voice snapped across Lydia's calm solution. "What if they talk?"

"They should know that any mention of this night's doings will cost them their position," Marcus retorted as he slowly released his father's shirt. "I need not tell you that," Edward stared from his son to his daughter and gave a huff of disapproval.

"So be it," He uttered shortly as he straightened his cravat. "But I won't forget this in a hurry," he glowered down at Melissa before seizing a slice of toast and marching from the room. Lydia cast a disapproving look at Melissa before following her husband, leaving the two siblings in the room alone.

With Edward and Lydia's departure, silence fell over the morning room; a silence that had the clarity of glass. Melissa reached for a small mirror and stared at the reddened mark on her face. Deep shuddering breaths rippled through her and she bent her head into her hands.

"It's alright," Marcus' arm slid round her shoulders and she leaned into the hug, sobbing into his shoulder. Marcus patted Melissa's back with gentle taps, comforting her as she cried out the events the events of the past twelve hours. He could feel the sobs shaking her frame and he tried to calm his own anger. He had seen Melissa the night before, had seen what her assailant had done to her. How could his father think that she had brought it on herself? Whilst he was certain that Lestrade was involved, Melissa was so adamant that he was innocent. He could blame it on the simple throes of a first crush, but Melissa was rarely so easily swayed. Granted she had been excited about her first season, but she seemed so unmoved by the exploits of her friends. It seemed inconceivable that she would lose her head over a man, especially Justin Lestrade. He felt her sobs subside and he pulled back, handing her a handkerchief from his pocket.

"Better?" He asked as she dabbed at her face and blew her nose. Beneath the snow white of the handkerchief, her face was streaked with tears and her eyes were red. She still drew in gulping gasps of air and he wondered if she were about to cry again.

"Uh-huh," Melissa could not find the words to speak, her head pounded from the sudden rush of tears and her face stung from the blow. The lingering taste of coppery blood still drifted through her mouth and she couldn't help but think about the blind fury on her father's face as he swung his hand towards her face.

"What on earth possessed you?" Marcus asked, pouring tea into his cup and handing it to her carefully. "You should have known how father would take your defence of that man,"

"I know it wasn't him Marcus," Melissa retaliated, her voice growing stronger as she spoke. From somewhere within her, a great burning sense of injustice flamed into being, helped in part by her own feeling of guilt.

"And how do you know that?" Marcus poured himself a cup and stood opposite her. "We found him on the outskirts of the estate in some disarray," A snort of disbelief escaped her lips and he took another sip of the lukewarm drink. "If he had nothing to do with your assault then why was he there?"

"His estate borders ours," Melissa argued, getting to her feet as she warmed to her subject. "And he's not as tall as the man I faced or as heavy set," Her fingers gripped the cooling cup of tea as she stepped closer to her brother. "I know it wasn't him Marcus, why can't you believe me?"

"Because I don't know how much of this fancy is generated by your feelings for him," Marcus said as he returned the cup to the table with a heavy thump. "You think I don't know who has stolen your heart?" He pushed a tendril of dark hair away from his face and drew in a deep breath. "Melissa, he has broken the hearts of many women," Marcus took a step closer and caught hold of her upper arm gently as he stared into his face. "He knows how to twist words so that each woman feels something for him. I understand that he has charmed you," Melissa looked away, not wishing to hear the words that fell from her brother's lips. "But you must understand that he lies," Melissa flinched as he finished uttering the very words that she had said to herself in the cold darkness of the night. "Surely you have considered this?" His other hand reached up and cupped her chin drawing her eyes back to his.

"Marcus I know how this sounds," She finally spoke, her voice soft yet firm as she met his eyes directly. "But you can't blame him for something he has not done, yes he is a philanderer but I know that he would not hurt me,"

"How can you know?" Marcus insisted, confusion

running through every line in his face.

"Because I was the one attacked," She retorted, finally pulling away and throwing herself back into a chair. "That man tried to end my life, I felt his weight as he threw me across my own bed," Despite her best efforts, her voice rose as her anger flamed once again into being. "I have danced with Lestrade and he is at least a hand span shorter that the man who attacked me. This I know," She stalked away from him and headed across the room to the door. "You should trust my instincts Marcus, you know I'm not a foolish child given to obscure fancy. You have the wrong man," She reached the door and pulled it open, "But I daresay that will not aid matters now, for the good of this family's reputation, an innocent man is to be sentenced to exile and the real culprit goes free," She threw the handkerchief onto one of the end tables and turned to leave. "At least my future husband is assured and that's really all that matters," With a flounce of her head she headed out of the door allowing her last words to drift in bitterly as she reached the stairs. "Isn't it?"

Marcus watched her go and made no effort to follow; he knew that she would not welcome any further talk this morning. He settled down at the table and stared at the breakfast on his plate. The egg had congealed on the white china and though he had reached for his fork, he threw the utensil down in disgust, sending it clattering across the plate. For what seemed like an eternity, he stared down at the detritus of the breakfast table, his thoughts on Melissa and Lestrade. The clock in the hall chimed the quarter hour and pushed his chair back, a decision forming in his mind. Standing, he left the table and strode across the room with rapid footsteps. Heading from the breakfast room, he passed the lower parlour and the sounds of his parents arguing before reaching the main door of the building. Pushing open the heavy door, he strode out onto the morning air. With sure steps, he reached the stables and nodding to the two men on either side, pulled open the door. Hurrying to the stall which held Lestrade, he hunkered down into a crouch and stared at his captive.

"What the hell have you done to my sister?" He demanded, looking at the ragged, bloody figure with disgust. The straw crunched loudly beneath him and the scent of horse enveloped his nostrils, causing him to sneeze.

"Absolutely nothing," Justin stared up at Marcus with bloodshot eyes, trying to gauge the emotions of Melissa's older brother. "If you're about to launch another assault on my person, I would have to advise you that my left rib is possibly cracked should you need a target,"

"No that's not why I'm here," Marcus pointed a finger at Justin's prone form. "Melissa sent me," Justin drew a small breath and listened more intently. "She is convinced that it was not you," Marcus chuckled cynically and ran his fingers across his top lip. "How on earth do you manage to inspire such devotion Lestrade?" He leant back against the side of the stall as he spoke.

"I have no idea," Justin replied, "Just my stunning good looks I fancy," He twisted his gaze upward, ignoring the screaming pain in his upper shoulders as he stared at Marcus in curiosity. "Is that why you're here De Vire? Are you after tips for the ladies or…" A trace of leering innuendo rippled through his words as his eyes slowly raked across Marcus' frame "Are you after something else entirely?" Marcus' lips curled back into a snarl and he jerked free of the stable wall as though he had been shot.

"Don't you play with me Lestrade," His usually soft voice tore from his lips in a vicious growl as he launched himself at Justin and seized hold of his shirt. With his left hand wrapped in a fistful of fabric, he pulled the man forward, drawing a ragged cry of pain from Justin as he did so. Ignoring Justin's gasp, Marcus jabbed his right forefinger into his captive's chest. "Right now we are banishing you," His voice hissed into Justin's face, sending a small spray of spittle across the other's skin. "it won't take much for me to change my mind, drag you outside and put an end to your existence," He was too angry to see the tiny roll of his captive's eyes. "Why were you here last night? And I want the truth,"

Justin sighed and rolled his head back, away from the sparkling green eyes that were so like Melissa's. He was regretting his comments of a few moments ago. Marcus was a decent man who cared for his sister; he did not deserve either Justin's caustic temper or poor imitation of wit.

"Why do you care?" Justin finally spoke, a husky tired whisper as he rotated his head to face the younger man. "You were fully convinced of my guilt last night, I still have the bruises to prove it," He glanced down at his bruised and bloody frame. "It is a little late to wonder at my innocence,"

"My sister insists that you could not have assaulted her," Marcus said, looking at the bruises on Justin's body with a pang of guilt. With slow movements, he released Justin's shirt and the other sank back to the floor with a sigh of relief. "She claims that you are shorter than her assailant and therefore it could not have been you in her bedchamber," Marcus' voice continued, low and urgent, demanding answers that Justin did not wish to give. "Now either my sister is lying or mistaken," He pushed an agitated hand through his hair and clasped his hands in front of him. "As Melissa rarely lies, she could have made an error," He stood and walked away from Justin, pacing his words to the speed of his walk. "She is however, quite insistent that it was not you," Marcus reached the stall opposite and whirled around to face Justin once more. "So I am here to ask you the truth," He leant back against the closed stall door and folded his arms across his chest. "What happened?"

Justin glanced at the ground as he struggled to come up with an answer. He was perfectly willing to let Marcus believe that he was responsible for the attack. However he did not wish to tell lies to Melissa's brother, the man was too amiable to lie to. Granted he was practised in lying, but he was tired of the constant deception. In another time and place; he could have counted Marcus as a friend and ally. He shuffled his feet against the dirty straw and bit his lower lip. He wondered why Melissa had declared his innocence and though he was pleased that she seemed to have forgiven him, it would not serve her reputation if she continued to champion him. Marcus, frustrated by his silence, stepped forward and waved his hand before his face. "Lestrade," Startled out of his thoughts, Justin returned his attention to the other man.

"Alright," Justin uttered finally, staring up with blurry vision at Marcus. Shifting his weight slightly to reduce the pain in his upper arms, Justin leant forward as best he could. "I'll tell you what happened, but I must ask you to promise me something,"

"That depends on what you want," Marcus replied, hunkering back down beside his captive.

"It's nothing beyond your power," Justin assured, wincing as a twitch developed in his shoulders. "I only ask that for your sister's sake, you exile me as you planned, regardless of what I may say,"

Marcus started, looking at the other man in shock. "What?" He asked in a hushed tone.

"I'm serious," Justin continued, looking at Marcus intently. "No matter if you believe me or not, you must still continue with your plan to exile me," Had his hands been free, he would have seized Marcus' arm. "I will not bring any shame to Melissa," Marcus stared at him, confusion paramount on his face. Justin almost roared in frustration at the blank look on the other man's features. "Promise me Marcus that you will still tell people that I am exiled,"

Justin stopped speaking and for a long moment, neither spoke. The horses shifted uneasily in the nearby stalls and the distant conversation of the grooms rumbled indistinctly in the background. Eventually the cloud of confusion lifted from Marcus' face and reluctantly, he nodded. "I promise," Justin gave a sigh of relief as the other gestured impatiently for him to speak. "Now tell me,"

"I was on my way home," Justin began, staring with utter sincerity and conviction into Marcus' eyes. He would have to employ every method he knew in order to convince Marcus of the half lie he was about to impart. "I returned late from a ball and as I headed for the stables, one of my staff mentioned that he had noted a cloaked figure move cross country towards your estate. Realising the late hour and knowing that visitors would not call so late or so suspiciously, I took it upon myself to follow,"

"Why?" Marcus pressed, his voice still holding the stunned shock of a few moments ago.

"Because of the others," Justin replied, staring into Marcus's face with complete honesty. "I know that other women have been assaulted and I was concerned about your sister," His trapped shoulder muscle fired into a painful cramp and he gasped as waves of agony tore through him. Through gritted teeth, he continued his story, determined to say his piece "I came onto the estate but I was too late to prevent what had happened," Marcus moved as if to speak, but he subsided and waved for Justin to continue. "I ran into the real assailant as I reached your gardens. I saw him run from the wall of the house and I gave chase. However he saw me approach and," He nodded down at his damaged body. "Dealt the injuries that you saw,"

Marcus rubbed his bottom lip between his thumb and

forefinger and regarded Justin with curious eyes. From the thoughtful look on his face, Justin concluded that he had Marcus half convinced.

"You have to admit that the injuries I have," Justin mentally thanked John for removing the link and therefore leaving him with visible wounds. "Are not the type sustained in a fall. They show all the hallmarks of a beating," He smiled ruefully and continued, "Beyond the beating that you and your grooms gave me that is. I have no damage to my legs or lower body only to my face and arms," Justin stared at Marcus intently. "I would never bring harm to her Marcus and if things were different I would ask for her hand, but I know that cannot happen. I did not assault her and I can't bring shame upon her,"

Marcus stared at him for a long moment and finally reached forward to release the bonds on Justin's wrists. Justin's arms fell to his sides like lead weights and pain raced through his body. A long drawn out moan of pain escaped from between Justin's bloodied lips as his shoulders screamed in agony.

"Thank you," he muttered tautly, fire surging along his arms as circulation slowly returned to his limbs.

"You understand why I believed as I did," Marcus finally spoke as he watched Justin slump to the floor of the stable in pain.

"Yes, I understand fully," Justin replied, attempting to lever himself upright with limp, pain wracked arms. "I was on the estate and the real assailant nowhere in sight," He grunted as he finally gained purchase on the wall and pulled himself into a sitting position. "Had I been in your position, I would have done the same,"

"You're taking this awfully well," Marcus muttered,

"How should I take it?" Justin straightened his legs beneath him and grunted at the effort. "I can't deny that I was somewhere unwanted, I can't blame you for a conclusion that anyone would have come too," He placed his hands on the floor and pushed lightly, feeling the prickles of pain run up his arms as he moved.

"Do you really care for my sister?" Marcus asked, leaning back against the wall and watching the other man with curiosity.

"Yes I do," Justin moved to stand, yet his legs gave way and he slumped back to the floor. Marcus reached forward and offered him his hand. "thank you," Justin caught hold of the outstretched hand and pulled himself to his feet. His unsteady legs swayed beneath him and he seized hold of the top of the stall to keep himself from falling.

"Then why have you not offered for her?" Marcus placed an arm around Justin's waist and kept him upright.

"Because my suit would not be welcomed by your father," Justin replied, his breath whistling painfully from behind his teeth. "I know that Melissa is due for a good match and sadly I am not that,"

Marcus' lips twitched at Justin's words, he knew that his father was angling Melissa towards bigger game, but he didn't really think it was what she wanted. He glanced across at the man stood beside him. With what he knew of Justin's reputation, he should be sceptical of anything that the young man said, but Melissa believed in him and she wasn't usually a fool.

"You're probably right," He conceded finally, moving Justin to the wall and allowing him to lean against it. "But you have money and a title,"

"But no history," Justin responded, resting against the wall with a sigh of relief. "My family is not around and my reputation is against me. My home is a ruin; no one would want that for their daughter," Justin's voice trailed off as a wave of dizziness rushed through him.

"Lestrade?" Marcus looked at the other man with worry. "Are you able to stand?"

"I'm able to walk," Justin replied, a familiar mocking grin on his lips. He drew in another long breath and stared directly at Marcus, the grin fading into seriousness. "And I do apologise for my comments earlier, they were churlish and unworthy,"

"Well forget it," Marcus replied, answering the grin with on of his own. "I daresay if I had spent the night on a stable floor with my arms bound, I would be crotchety,"

"Hm," Justin chuckled and winced as the movement sent ripples of pain through his body. "We could have been good friends De Vire," With effort, he pushed himself free of the wall and stood, swaying, in the centre of the stable. "Now its time for you to see me off," He glanced at Marcus and continued, "You'll have to thrash me within an inch of my life,"

Marcus stepped back and stared at him. "No, you're battered enough; I could kill you if I strike you again,"

"Then limit your fists to my face," Justin replied with some heat. "Remember that they don't know of what's occurred and we need to make it look real,"

Marcus bowed his head, staring at the man before him. "Why are you putting yourself through this?"

"Because I can't have her, but I won't be responsible for the damage to her reputation and this is the best way," Justin nodded to the stable door, "Now are we going?" Marcus glanced at Justin's set features and nodded. With a resigned look, he reached forward and took hold of his upper arm. Justin stepped forward and whispered "Remember to take care of Melissa, Marcus,"

"I will," Marcus led Justin to the stable door, beyond the wood, they could hear the chortles and talk of the grooms. Reluctantly, Marcus reached for the handle.

"Marcus," The other man turned to stare at him, "Make it good,"

Melissa's brother nodded and he turned back to the stable door. Placing his hands on the grainy wood, he hesitated for the briefest of moments. Glancing back at the wounded man, he smiled grimly. "Take care Lestrade," He whispered as he pushed open the stable door and let them out into the light.

CHAPTER 33

"Do you really think that you should watch Miss?" Jane's mildly disapproving tones resonated through the parlour and interrupted Melissa's contemplation of the scene below her.

Sprawled in the dust of the stable yard floor and with a bloody nose and lip, Justin lay. Her brother, who had just dealt the blows that had bloodied Justin's face, stood over him, his face twisted into an expression of utter loathing. Something twisted within Melissa as she stared at her beloved brother and Jane's disapproving tones did nothing to dispel the growing knot of anger that was building within her breast.

"And why not Jane?" Melissa's voice, hushed and

angry whispered in the space between them. "This is all for my benefit after all," Marcus delivered a solid kick to Justin's midsection and Melissa winced, her nails bending painfully as she gripped the windowsill in a in a death grip. "Never mind that Justin is innocent," She watched the blood pour down from Justin's split lip and nausea flowed through her. How could her brother do this to him? Was he not injured enough? Blood dripped from his chin and spattered onto the dust of the yard, turning the sand a deep brown. Melissa watched with morbid fascination. Something about that darkening pool of blood held her gaze and sounded a note of discord deep within her bones.

Jane derisive snort recalled her attention and Melissa whipped round from the window to face her, eyes bright with angry unshed tears.

"Oh I'm so sorry Jane," Melissa declared, her voice saccharine sweet and cutting. "I forgot that you know all of this matter," Jane stared at her mistress' bright eyes and, undeterred by her rage, began to speak.

"Lestrade is a bad lot Miss," Jane spoke with the surety of age and familiarity, few others could speak so freely and Jane used her position without qualm. "He attacked you in your bed and now he's paying for it,"

"Really?" Melissa walked forward, rage filling her voice as she spoke. "You could really see that it was him?" She stopped just a step away from her maidservant and challenged her with her eyes and voice. "For I did see who it was, only a masked assailant with a knife," She shrugged her shoulders and continued. "Perhaps you were privy to a completely different assault,"

Jane harrumphed with exasperation and stared at the girl she had brought up from childhood. Her mistress's moods were well known to her and at this moment, she was displaying all the charming qualities of an ox, stubborn and intractable. "What I know Miss is that he was found outside in the garden, it could only have been him. We know what a danger he is to respectable women,"

"No you don't," Melissa snapped back, trying hard to keep a leash on her temper, yet failing at each word from Jane's lips. She drew a deep breath and briefly closed her eyes, mentally counting out the digits from one to ten. "The man who attacked me was clearly taller than Justin,"

"It were dark Miss,"

"And he stood on a box to assault me, ahh well that explains everything," Jane winced at the cutting sarcasm that dripped from Melissa's mouth. "Jane," Melissa looked at her old nurse's face and tried once more to explain. "Justin may be a cad," She ignored the grunt that escaped Jane's lips and continued. "He may be a cad, but I swear he is innocent of this and I should know," She ran an agitated hand through her hair. "Yet everyone appears to disregard what I have to say, even though I was there and know what happened,"

"If you forgive me Miss, it was quite dark and confusing. How could you tell height in the dark? And he was discovered on the edge of.,"

"Oh yes, I know all of this already," Melissa interrupted, her calm voice seething once more. "Justin was on the edge of our estate, so clearly he must be responsible. However I know that my attacker had a completely different build and height to Justin. I told this to my father and he took my testimony to mean that I was not attacked, that I had invited Justin to my room," Melissa cradled the darkening bruise on her cheek and she curled her lip in anger. Her words tripped out of her mouth, falling over themselves in their haste. "He's only believing the attack story because of Mother and she," Her voice broke on the last words and she whirled away and began to pace the length of the room.

"My mother believes that I was attacked but feels that I am a weak minded fool who is blinded by a pretty face and my brother," She stopped pacing and turned back towards Jane who took a step back at the sheer fury she saw in Melissa's eyes. "My brother is beating him senseless because he also believes me love struck and foolish. No one is listening to a word I say and I know he didn't do it," Melissa drew in a deep shuddering breath and sank into a nearby chair.

"And you," She whispered softly, the rage draining slowly from her as she spoke, "You who know me better than anyone, believe that I am wrong," She stopped speaking and leant forward, sinking her head into her cupped hands. Silence built between them and Jane shifted uncomfortably on her feet. Melissa was not crying, she could see that, but she could tell from her rigid position that she was not very far from tears.

"Miss," She began tremulously, her old voice soft and calming. It was a voice she had used to Melissa often as a young child.

"Just leave me alone," Melissa's muffled tones issued from behind her clasped hands. Jane stared for a long moment at her old charge and gave a curt nod, before she finally turned and left the room. Melissa heard her footsteps echo away down the stairs and she stood up and turned back to the window.

Marcus and Justin now stood before the open stable doors. Her brother's back was to the house and she had a clear view of the horrendous injuries that covered Justin's face. Once again a sense of unease, of wrongness shuddered through her. Taking a fortifying breath of air, she watched her brother berate Justin, who stood stoic and unspeaking throughout it all.

"Why Marcus?" Melissa's voice was a long drawn out moan of despair as she watched him seize Justin's bruised and unsteady form and face him away from the estate. As Justin took his first faltering step, Marcus shoved him forward, nearly throwing him back to the floor. Justin staggered and picked up the pace, running with limping ragged steps across the gravel drive and towards the park. Melissa watched as the grooms, laughing and joking, headed back into the stables and her brother finally walked back towards the house.

Melissa turned away from the window and sat in the chair, composing her face in a hard mask as she waited for her brother's footsteps to ascend the stairs and reach her. She didn't have long to wait. In no time at all, Marcus made his way into the parlour where he stopped at the sight of Melissa's stony face. He lowered his gaze as she stared at him.

"You saw?"

Melissa nodded, her eyes accusatory and fixed on her brother. "How could you?" Her voice was low, the anger in her too extreme for shouts. Marcus shuffled his feet and did not answer.

"Well talk to me?" Melissa's voice was brittle as glass and he could feel the contained fury that she held within. "I'm sure you have something to say after you battered an innocent man,"

Marcus opened his mouth, closed it again and slowly shook his head. Melissa got to her feet, her eyes flashed dangerously and her face grew livid with rage.

"I never would have thought it of you," She hissed at him, anger fuelling every word. "After everything I said to you this morning, you still went out there and…" Her voice stammered to a halt, strangled for the moment by her seething emotions.

Marcus just watched her, his face impassive as the silence lengthened between them. He wanted to say something, but he had given his word, Justin had been willing to take that beating for her honour and he couldn't renege on his oath. Yet he wished he could take what he had done back, regardless of the circumstances, he had still beaten a helpless man into a pulp. It was not something he was proud of and Melly, he stared at her raging face and wished he could say something, anything to her, but anything he could say would be inadequate and so he stood there, taking her rage and pain.

"You're not the person I thought you were," Melissa uttered finally before sweeping past him and heading out onto the landing. Marcus watched her go, following the hem of her mint coloured day dress as it brushed through the doorway and out of sight. With a heartfelt sigh, he sank into the chair that his sister had just vacated and he rubbed his bruised hands across his eyes.

"I'm so sorry Melly," He whispered, the words barely audible in the empty room, "but he asked me to,"

Melissa ran to her room and threw open the door, the shutters were still closed, yet the glass had been swept up and fresh sheets now adorned her bed. Pushing the door shut, she threw herself onto her bed and sank her face into the pillow. Her eyes remained dry as she breathed in the scent of rose water and down. Swallowing back the tears that she so wished to shed, she forced herself to remember the events of that morning. Her father striking her across the face, her mother's disapproval and Marcus, she balled up her fists and punched the pillow, Marcus as he slammed his fist into Justin's face.

She had been watching from the moment Marcus had headed outside, she had seen him enter the stable and stay there for some time. Hope had found a place in her thoughts as the doors opened and they spilled out of the darkness together into the grey early morning light. Justin was badly wounded, a state that triggered a sense of outrage and also vague unease. She had known that he had been hurt yet she had not known how badly, but a glance at his swollen face had tugged at her heart. For the briefest of moments she had thought that Marcus had mending relations with Justin, yet that forlorn hope had been banished as Marcus turned and punched the other man. She had watched as his fists slammed into an already damaged body and face and she cried aloud as fresh blood spattered his shirt. She clenched her fist around the down filled pillow and tried to focus away from his wounds. How could Marcus have done this, after all she had said? It was not like her brother at all, she knew that he had attacked Justin the night before and that she could understand. He had thought that Justin had been her assailant, but this, she drew a deep breath and forced away the tears that seemed so present, crying would not help. What had Marcus and Justin been talking about for Marcus to attack like that, what had Justin said? She closed her eyes as thoughts of the night before settled into her mind.

"You have to leave me here,"

Justin's words echoed once more through her thoughts and her eyes snapped open, appalled by the revelation that accompanied the memory.

"You made him," She whispered to her pillow, the voice muffled by the soft down and cotton. "Dear Lord, you said enough to force his hand, why?" Even though she could attain no answer, she pushed herself upright and sat up. "Damn my reputation Lestrade, I don't want to be protected at the expense of your skin," Once more, visions of his bruised, bloody form paraded though her mind. "As if you weren't damaged enough, you had to goad him into brutality," She stopped and stood up, the vague sense of unease that had followed her since she first seen him leave the stable, now returned with a vengeance. Her thoughts drifted back to a single event, one that had changed her perception of the world. She recalled his hand picking up his hat, the shears slicing into the ball of his thumb and the wound closing as she watched.

"Why is he still wounded?" It came to her then, in one solid flash, what had bothered her as he had walked free from the stable. Blinded by the rage that had accompanied Marcus' first blow, she had failed to notice that Justin was still injured from the night before. He was covered with injuries that shouldn't still be there, injuries that the enamel lotus was supposed to heal. Yet the lotus was not fastened to his neck, and had not been since last night. Marcus had not mentioned taking his jewellery and she wondered if the grooms had removed the enamel bloom. She shook her head, dismissing that thought, if the grooms had removed one piece of jewellery, they would have not stopped there. Justin was wearing several pieces of expensive decoration and from what she could see from the window, he was still in possession of most of them. Someone who knew about the blossom had torn it from his shirt and now held it hostage. She had read enough of Justin's notes to understand that his wounds would not heal, that he would be in agony from his injuries until he received the brooch back. She recalled what Justin had said about John, if he had taken the brooch, he would be sure to keep it on him in order to prolong Justin's suffering.

He would also mingle more fully with society as Justin would not now be admitted to certain functions thanks to this morning's work. John could hide out at the Palace for the next six months and Justin would suffer. Coming to a decision, Melissa yanked at the bell pull beside the door, summoning Jane to her room in a flurry of action.

"Yes Miss," Jane cautiously entered the room and stared at the animated features of her mistress with shock. The maid servant had been expecting tears and anger, not this cool eyed, determined young woman that now stood before her. "You rang?"

"I did yes," Melissa replied coolly, witnessing Jane's surprise but paying little attention to it. "I understand there is a party at Lady Hawthorn's this evening,"

"Yes Miss, it's one of the largest parties of the season,"

"Very good," Melissa replied, turning to replace her soiled handkerchief within the sleeve of her gown. "Could you also tell me if a Lord Tarlington will be there?"

"I believe so Miss, I don't know the full guest list, but I believe he is due to attend,"

"Good," Melissa turned back to face her old nurse. "Then make me ready, for I will be attending,"

"But Miss, your parents,"

"I'm certain my parents would be happy that I am forgetting Lestrade and attempting to re-enter the marriage mart. I feel certain that one or both of them will accompany me. Certainly my father owes me a debt for this," Melissa pointed at her cheek and sneered lightly. "After all, they want me to find a good match and I can't do that locked up here. Tell them for me and then arrange for my clothes," And with that, Melissa pointed at the door and turned away from her maid, dismissing her with a single look.

CHAPTER 34

Justin crossed the threshold of his home and he slumped to the floor, finally unable to stand upright. His ribs felt broken and he was quite convinced that at least one had splintered. He coughed once and a small amount of blood smeared across the back of his hand.

"Wonderful," He murmured, looking at the bright bloom of blood with a sneer. "That's just what I want, a pierced lung," Taking a deep breath, he reached up and began to pull himself upright. It was hard going; his body did not want to cooperate. The pain of the beating and residual damage from a night chained to a wall ensured that he could barely move. After the third failed attempt to stand, he sat back and shouted.

"Coll," His broken scream echoed through the halls of the ruined mansion and he waited, pain wracking his body, for his servant to arrive.

"Sir?" After what seemed like an eternity, Coll appeared at the top of the steps, he took one look at his master sprawled across the stones of the hallway before he raced downstairs. "Are you alright?" He wrapped his arms about Justin and pulled him to his feet. "What the devil happened?" He grunted as he guided his young master into the parlour and laid him on the chaise longue.

"John happened," Justin replied tersely, tiredness and pain making him short tempered. "Where's my brother?"

"Your brother has not returned since yesterday," Coll replied as he stoked up the fire.

"Typical," Justin felt his eyelids begin to droop with the onset of unconsciousness. "Very well, go to London and visit 18 Swan Street. Tell Emily that I want her here,"

Coll nodded and began to stand. Justin's fingers snaked out and grabbed his servant by the wrist. "As fast as you possibly can Coll and don't take no for an answer. Tell her that John has stolen my brooch,"

He heard his manservant rush down the hallway and leave the house. He tried to move unto his side, but the pain in his chest prevented all movement. Wincing at the pain, he opened his eyes and stared around the room. It was so different from in his childhood, the furniture was heavier, the drapes missing from the walls and the rushes missing from the floor. He had to admit that in some cases, this curse was delightful; he could never have imagined the progress he had seen. He only had to walk through the houses to see just how things had changed. A snort escaped his lips at the thought of owing this curse something when it already took so much of his soul. These injuries he had sustained would not heal unless he found his brooch and another vessel. Giving up on moving, he settled back against the cushions and closed his eyes. In the quiet, his mind ranged back to the night's events. He hadn't anticipated Melissa sneaking down to the stables to talk to him, a bold move and one he appreciated, despite how the conversation had gone. He supposed he could not blame her for the reaction, his secrets had endangered her and he hadn't seen fit to warn her of them. He shifted into another position and tried again to settle down. Drifting towards sleep, he thought back to his conversation with Marcus and what he had said about Melissa and he dared to hope that she had forgiven him. It was the last thing he thought before sleep finally claimed him.

"Justin," He jolted awake and looked up into a pair of bright blue eyes. Emily stood over him, concern etched on her features. "What the devil happened to you?"

He would have chuckled at her startled concern, but it hurt far too much. "I sent the message with Coll, John stole my brooch,"

An exasperated tut escaped her lips as she took in the bruises, livid on his face. "Did John do this to you?"

"No as a matter of fact," He coughed, tasting blood. "It was Marcus De Vire and his grooms,"

"Why would?" She stopped her question and stared

down at him with a wry smile. "Oh of course," The light of revelation flooded into her face. "You couldn't leave her alone after all," Dipping a cloth into a basin, she began to cleanse the blood from his face.

"It wasn't quite like that," He protested, closing his eyes as her fingers tenderly dealt with the damage.

"Then what was it like?" She rinsed out the cloth and returned to his wounds, slowly and softly daubing the bruises and cuts in cool water.

"John found her," Her fingers stopped moving and she stared down at him, a mixture of pity and smugness in her features.

"I told you to take her with you," She dampened the cloth once more and returned to his face. "I did say that John was going to find her,"

"Yes you're extremely clever," Sardonic tones flowed out from between his bloodied lips. Emily being right was not a pleasurable experience.

"Don't get like that darling," She whispered as her fingers slid gently over his skin. "I am sorry for what has happened to her,"

"Did I say that she's dead?" He glanced up at Emily and was gratified to see the shock in her features. "It appears she woke up and fought him off. I arrived after he'd thrown himself from her window,"

"You confronted him?" Her fingers began to check lower parts of his body for damage.

"Hmm," He winced as her hands slid over angry bruises and she whispered an apology. "He then took my brooch and left me for De Vire,"

"And he naturally assumed that you were the intruder," Emily gave a slight roll of her eyes as she undid his shirt and gave a small whistle at the damage. "Did De Vire do all this?"

"Well his grooms did some of it, I asked him to do the rest,"

"Why?" Delicately she began to sponge his chest, watching him cringe with a worried expression.

"If John feels I have been banished he may leave Melissa alone,"

"Hmm," She didn't answer as she continued to sponge down his body. The water in the bowl became redder and redder as she continually washed out the soft rag. Concentrating on his bruises, Emily ceased conversation and Justin saw no need to speak. Eventually her fingers stilled on his skin and she drew the blanket up to his chin.

"There,"

"Thank you Emily," He whispered, grateful that she had come to take care of him.

"Think nothing of it," She disposed of the bowl of water and turned back to face him. "So you've left her,"

"Yes, I've promised to leave the country," He indicated his battered body with a sigh. "As soon as I can heal, I'll be leaving for France. John is sure to follow me there,"

"Well if that's your decision," Standing, she pulled a short cape about her shoulders. "I'll talk to Katherine and see if we can get your brooch back. Stay here and get some sleep," With a slight smile on her lips, she turned to face the door.

"Em," She turned back to face him, "I mean it, thank you,"

"I'm glad you called me," She smiled at him as she turned to leave the room.

CHAPTER 35

"She won't hate you forever," Lydia De Vire stated to her son as they sat within the parlour. The remains of a late lunch lay on the tables nearby as Lydia finished off some embroidery.

"Are you sure?" Marcus replied. His face was dark, brooding and not at all like his usual self. The events of that morning were burned into his mind and he wished that he could have taken it all back. "You didn't see her face mother, I've done something unforgivable," Standing suddenly, he began to pace the floor.

"No, she will understand," His mother soothed, laying aside her embroidery to stare at her oldest child. "You were protecting her,"

"Are you trying to convince me or yourself?" Marcus turned to his mother and continued. "I know that Lestrade was innocent," He nodded with a bitter smile at the look on his mother's face. "He asked me to beat him and I did," He ran an agitated hand through his hair. "Damn me I did,"

Lydia was silent as she watched Marcus pace, watched the torment in his features. Her son was a good man, always had been and this had hurt more than she had ever seen. After a few moments she stood and crossed over to him.

"Marcus," Her arms extended and wrapped about her son's tall frame. As her hands flowed around him, he leant into her embrace, sobbing the way he had done when he was still a child. "It's alright,"

"It's not alright; I beat an innocent man and made my sister believe that I am a monster," Lydia patted him on the back, allowing him to cry out as she had done so many times in the past. Silently they stood there in the centre of the room as Marcus softly cried out his sorrows.

"She will forgive you son," Lydia whispered as Marcus' tears finally dried up. "You're her brother, she will find in her heart to forgive,"

Marcus opened his mouth to speak and stopped as Melissa walked into the room.

"I'm going to the Hawthorn ball," She announced loudly, her gaze falling anywhere but on her brother.

"You are?" Lydia's voice was bemused; she had not been expecting Melissa to be attending any parties so soon after the events of the night.

"I am and I will need you to accompany me,"

"I'll go with you," Marcus stepped forward, looking at her with apology in his eyes.

"That's quite all right," Melissa's voice was cool; remote and Marcus felt a further stab of guilt at the implied accusation in her voice. "Mother can accompany me, she was going anyway,"

"Well I was," Lydia glanced at her two children and inwardly sighed, it would take a long time to defuse this little war. "Very well, arrange the carriage for five,"

With a curt nod, Melissa left the room and headed upstairs, barely sparing her brother a glance.

"I told you," Marcus spoke as he reached for his riding hat. "She won't forgive me," With a sigh, he left the room and headed out towards the stables, hoping a ride would clear his head.

CHAPTER 36

Melissa strolled through the wide hallway in a dress of cream brocade, her real hair hidden by an extravagantly designed wig. She moved through the crowd, dispensing hellos and platitudes as though nothing troubled her, yet the palms of her hands were clammy and her eyes raked over her fellows guests as though she were a hawk.

"No, puce is a wonderful colour if utilised properly," Familiar, drawling tones flowed from a side room and she turned her head, staring through the door at the small group that stood within. Tarlington stood in the centre of the throng, holding court with a mixed group of men and women. A quizzing glass was held firmly in his hand and he gestured with it grandly as he held forth with his views on fashion.

"Whatever you say Tarlington," One of the others responded, his voice laughing. "But I don't find puce all that appealing; it turns my stomach, particularly on someone who does not have the colouring for it,"

"Well I suppose we all have our fancies and mine is…" Tarlington stopped speaking as his gaze fell onto the form of Melissa stood within the doorway. "Well I see we have an interloper," He declared as he stepped forward and held out a hand. "It is lovely to see you again my dear," Melissa entered the room, drawn in by the gentle pull of his fingers.

"Well my dear are you ready to discuss the finer points of fashion," He ran an appraising look over her form.

"Err no," Melissa stammered, looking at the eyes on her with some trepidation. "I wanted to speak to you about jewellery,"

"Jewellery?" Tarlington responded, confusion colouring his features. "What could I tell you about jewellery?"

"Not any old jewellery," she clarified, staring him straight in the eyes and hoping that he would take the hints. "Enamelled jewellery; brooches to be precise,"

A gleam of understanding flashed through his eyes and he nodded slightly. "I see, what exactly do you want to know?"

"I believe Justin Lestrade has such a brooch,"

"He doesn't move in my circle, but I daresay you're right," Tarlington held out a hand and led her towards a set of seats in the corner of the room. "What of it?"

"It's missing," She declared, unable to find a more

oblique way to inform him of the fact. "He mentioned that he last saw it when in the company of John,"

Tarlington took a deep breath and stared down at the young woman before him. "My dear, Justin's possessions should be none of your concern," His voice dropped in volume and he held her gaze with a look of complete seriousness. "And if John did see Justin's brooch last, then it is up to the two of them to sort it out," He reached for a goblet and long a sip, all the time his eyes resting on hers. "But you're not going to leave it are you?"

"I can't, Justin is indisposed and unable to visit,"

"I do advise you Miss De Vire to drop this enquiry," Hugh leant forward and took her hand. "It's not your concern," He pitched his voice so that only she could hear and moved closer. "Whatever happened is between them and please do not get involved, it's far too dangerous,"

"But he saved my life," Melissa retorted, staring at the older man.

"Even more reason why you should stay far from him," He placed the goblet down on the table and moved to stand. "I don't want him to finish the job he started, so no Melissa, I'm not going to help you,"

Melissa blinked back two warm tears and pulled herself upright. Reaching for the sleeve of Tarlington's jacket, she arrested his movement and pulled him back to face her. "Tarlington," Her voice was harsh yet brittle, "Please help me,"

"You should be ashamed Tarlington, not helping this lovely young woman," A new voice declared from the doorway as Emily, dressed in a daringly cut, blue dress sashayed into the room. Melissa felt Tarlington freeze beside and he turned his elaborately coifed head to face the newcomer.

"What is your interest in this matter?" Tarlington's voice was cold and disapproving as the woman made her way across the floor.

"My interest is my own," Emily responded airily as she took in Melissa's troubled face. "Oh dear this will never do," She muttered as she reached forward and handed Melissa a handkerchief. "Wipe your eyes dear and then we can sort things out, but not here," She stared round the room, noting the other guests. Catching hold of Melissa's arm, she began walking with her from the room.

"Emily," Tarlington caught hold of the other's arm and dragged her to one side. "Now is not the time for your games, John has made an appearance and things are far too dangerous at the moment for whatever amusement you have planned,"

"And who says I'm planning anything?" The blonde answered carelessly as she turned from Tarlington and returned to Melissa's side. "I'm just interested in aiding the cause of justice," A bark of laughter escaped Hugh's lips as he watched Emily take hold of Melissa's upper arm. "Now then Melissa, I'm going to help you," With Tarlington following, she walked Melissa into an empty room and shut the door.

"No you're not," Hugh caught Emily's other arm and forced her face towards his. "John took Justin's brooch but as I tried to say to this overly emotional idiot," he nodded at Melissa, who glowered back at him. "It is not her business, neither is it ours. John and Justin have been battling for a while now and they can sort it out themselves. If anyone else gets involved," He threw up his hands in disgust and paced across the room to the tray of drinks. "If anyone else gets involved then it's going to get very messy," He picked up a glass of brandy and downed it in one swallow. "Justin has decided to not tarnish this one's reputation, which means that he at least cares about her, if we put her in John's path then I daresay he'll be a tad put out with us,"

Emily threw back her head and laughed. "Oh Hugh, Justin's been a tad put out with us for a very long time now. I wouldn't know how to handle things if he wasn't,"

"No Emily," Hugh retaliated, his usual dandyish tones, serious and completely disapproving. "You remember what happened to Anna?" Emily glanced at Hugh and grimaced, her lovely face suddenly stricken with a pain that Melissa didn't understand. "John is ruthless and he won't stop, don't encourage foolishness and let this girl get on with her life,"

"Anna?" Melissa finally broke into the argument and both looked at her. Hugh glared at Emily before finally returning to Melissa's side. "I understand that I'm a late arrival at this party, but will someone explain?"

"Very well," Tarlington caught hold of her hands and took a deep breath. "Anna was a girl Justin had feelings for about one hundred and fifty years back. As you're no doubt aware, Justin is a ladies man, always has been, but when he met her, he saw something that pulled at him. He wondered if he could find some peace with her, but," Tarlington sighed and reached out for one of the glasses of canary. "He was wrong,"

"What happened?" Melissa asked, listening to the hypnotic quality of Hugh's voice with interest. His hands were warm about hers and the sympathy in his gaze tugged at her heart.

"It was both of them," He replied, squeezing her hands lightly as he spoke. "Justin let her into his life and put her at risk, John took advantage of that and..,"

"He killed her?" Melissa whispered in response, trying to visualise Justin in the past.

"Worse," Hugh replied, his voice angry. "He decided that the best way to hurt Justin was to force Justin to kill her,"

Melissa moved forward, wanting to hear and yet wishing that she could not. Behind her and to the left, Emily stood stock still, her face set in stone. "How?" Melissa breathed lightly, wondering if she really needed to know the answer.

"How much do you know about these brooches?" Hugh asked, watching her face with interest.

"I know that they make you immortal,"

"It's a bit more than that," He answered carefully, "You have to take the life force of someone to keep alive," he watched as horror slowly dawned on her face and smiled sadly. "And not only that. If you don't take someone's life, you'll still live, you just won't heal. You will be fully aware, even if you take a mortal wound. You can die and still be in your body rotting. So we have to steal other people's energy,"

"Then what happened to Anna?" Melissa whispered.

"John broke into her house and took her. He then killed the one Justin was draining, drugged Justin and dragged him unconscious into a cellar. He placed Justin's brooch in his hand and used Justin's own fingers to open it," His voice was low, breathless with bitterness as he related the tale. As he spoke, he looked down at her fingers; they were clasped together so tightly that they were white about the knuckles.

"And then what?" She whispered, almost fearing to hear the end of the tale.

"Then he forced Anna to look in the locket and she became Justin's life," Emily wrapped her arms about herself and stared straight ahead, listening intently to Hugh's voice. "Justin then woke up, right before John slit his throat," Hugh slammed his fist into the table beside him, startling the pair of them. "Justin had to watch as Anna took the damage from him. John gloated and then blamed Justin for what had happened to her,"

"Justin took it to heart," Emily finished and looked down at her. "He never let himself get that close again, there are times obviously when one of us wants more human contact than what we have, but it isn't possible,"

Melissa stared down at her hands as Emily finished speaking and chewed her lower lip. She couldn't quite take it in; it was too big for her. This tale, this tragedy was larger than anything she had faced in her life and she wanted more than anything to hide until it was all over. Out of the corner of her eye, she saw Tarlington's face. He was paying close attention to her reactions. He wanted her to run, to go home and continue her mundane, safe existence. But could she do that? In her mind she saw Justin's battered body lying on the floor of her stables and remembered his determination to push her away from this. If she just walked away, she would be safe, it was what he and Marcus and everyone else wanted, but it would feel wrong. Safety at the expense of another was cowardice and she wasn't a coward. She remembered the terror of the other night, of that heavy frame pressing her into the bed and once again, deep anger boiled within her. If she ran, John would win, his assault would define her forever and that too would be unacceptable. With a brisk jolt of her head, she drew her face upwards and stared at the two before her.

"Why do you want me to help him?" Melissa demanded of Emily, her clear green gaze wanting answers.

"Because when he doesn't care, he turns into the shallow womanising idiot you saw at the ball," Emily returned as she sank into the chair opposite. "I've had to put up with this rubbish for one hundred years and I'm sick of it," She reached for Melissa's hand. "I'm not saying he loves you, but he could. You make him feel again and that is worth more than anything,"

"Emily," Tarlington finally stepped forward and seized hold of her upper arm. "What are you thinking? Lestrade promised that he would not consider drawing another into this mess"

"I do not want him to admit her into our company, but if she does this for him, he'll have some fond memories for the future, memories that won't make him brood or send him into a flurry of meaningless..," She broke off and stared up at Hugh with a plea in her eyes. "She wants to help and I think she should,"

The dandy rolled his eyes and rounded on her. "You don't care about her and you don't care about him. This is another one of your games, don't play with her life like this," His voice was low, threatening and Melissa suppressed a shudder.

Emily laughed, a silvery, tinkling laugh that bounced off the walls and ceiling. "Oh my dear Hugh, how can you think that?"

"Because I know you, you're not an altruist,"

Melissa watched the impending argument with a mounting fury. Standing abruptly, she faced down the pair of them. "I don't care," She announced finally, her words ringing in the sudden silence. "And I'm not scared," Melissa stared at Emily and beckoned her forward. "You will take me to John and we will take that brooch back," Tarlington moved to speak and she rounded on him. "Whatever you may say Tarlington, John will not make me run. He owes me satisfaction for the other night, if I run and hide behind my skirts, then he gets away with it," Her voice hardened and she stared up at the older man's face. "I'm not going to let him get away with it," Flicking her gaze over to Emily, she continued to speak, her voice growing stronger with every word. "I'm not doing this just for Justin; I'm doing this for me," She held out her hand to Emily and beckoned. "Well are we going?"

The blonde stared at her outstretched hand and nodded. With one movement she had reached forward and clasped her hand. As their hands met, Melissa froze; Emily pressed an object into her fingers. It had a hard, glossy surface; cool and smooth against the skin of her palm. Recognising the shape and feel of enamel, she raised her head and looked at Emily. The blonde was smiling that perfect beautiful smile, a smile that held a tinge of mischief.

"What?" She managed to gasp out, aware of the black lotus against her skin dragging her down into darkness. Until the last remnant of consciousness fled from her body, she focused on the blonde, betrayal thrumming through every vein as she stared at that perfect visage.

CHAPTER 37

She did not know how long she had been out, did not know how long she had laid on the floor. All she knew was the reality of that brooch in her hands. As Tarlington waved the snuff box beneath her gaze, as she felt the smooth planes of the brooch within her hand, she knew what had happened. Through the cloud of darkness, she remembered, focused in on that moment when Emily had pressed the brooch into her fingers. With hatred searing through her, she stared up at her.

"You bitch,"

Emily smiled in response and stepped away, ignoring Melissa's incoherent rage. In an instant, Tarlington had caught her by the shoulders.

"It's alright Melissa, just take a breath," He urged, throwing an exasperated glare at Emily. "Come on now," Tarlington placed his arms about her shoulders and helped her to her feet. "It'll be fine," He sat her down in a chair by the fire. For a long moment she said nothing as she drew in vast gulps of air, trying to make sense of what had just occurred..

"What did you do?" She finally asked, staring at Emily with something akin to hatred. "You've cursed me," She couldn't stop looking at the brooch in her hand, the simple innocuous item that had signalled her fate. "After all you've told me about this thing, after all the harm it does; you've decided to put this on me,"

"Believe me, you'll thank me," Emily chuckled, taking a sip from one of the glasses on the other side of the room.

"I doubt it," Melissa was fuming, angry almost beyond reason. The glossy, shimmering planes of the lotus sparkled in the light, hiding its violent nature beneath its beauty.

"Oh you will, at least you're now safe from John," She downed the liquid in the glass and smiled. "Let me tell you Melissa that I do care for Justin and what he would go through if you had died," She placed the glass on the table and drew herself to her full height. "I've just left him in a mess. Cracked ribs, no ability to heal and he took it all for your benefit," Leaning forward to stare at Melissa, she continued. "You do realise that he told your brother to beat him to spare your reputation,"

"No," Melissa drew a stricken breath and sank back against the cushions, bewildered by what she had just been told. "He couldn't have done,"

"Why do you find it so hard to believe?" Emily snorted back at her, "I've heard about your brother, by all accounts he's a pretty decent fellow," She gave a snort of derisive laughter. "Wait, are you saying that you believed your brother capable of beating an innocent man?"

Melissa did not answer the question as she felt her heart sink. Tarlington took one look at her face and faced down Emily.

"Enough of the antagonism," He stated blankly, the persona of cultured dandy completely missing now. "And please do go on with your reasons for doing this? I'm fascinated to know why,"

There was a pause as Emily took in Tarlington's grim visage. "Justin is an optimist by nature," Her words were slow, almost as though she were talking to a child. "He believes that John will leave you alone if he runs," Giving a snort of laughter, she turned back to the fireplace and stared at the flames. "He's an idiot; he waffled over Anna and look what happened to her,"

"Are you saying you have altruistic motives?" Hugh asked, his voice clearly suggesting that he didn't believe it.

"No," Emily turned back to the room, her eyes clouded by sudden anger. "When he's unhappy, he doesn't care. He seduces his way through the world or he shuts himself off,"

"Oh don't tell me you care," Hugh snorted as he walked up to face. "I'm trying to work out if you even know what the truth looks like," He stopped just in front of Emily and stared down at her. "Let me make an alternative hypothesis," Emily's face twisted into a mockery of a smile. "You just like to make trouble for your own amusement, much like Alistair does. Whatever you say to me will not be the truth," He sighed and turned back to Melissa. "Regardless of the explanation, you're stuck, like the rest of us,"

"So what do I do now?" Melissa dragged her eyes away from the enamel brooch and stood. Her fingers were twisted about the thing that had completely altered her life. Hugh's heart twisted with pity at the desperate plea he found in her face and voice. Once again he shot a look of disapproving anger at Emily, who merely sniffed and looked away.

"Melissa," The group glanced up as Lydia De Vire walked into the room. Melissa's mother ran a quick measuring gaze over the small group before her. "I'm just getting the carriage ready, that's if you're ready to go,"

Casting a questioning look back at Hugh, Melissa hedged. "Just a few moments more mother," She hoped that her voice was steady and that Lydia did not see the fear in her heart. "Lord Tarlington was spinning us an amusing yarn,"

Lydia sized up Hugh, who responded with his most winning, empty headed smile.

"Indeed Lady De Vire," Emily chimed in, her face swept clear of mischief. "Only a few moments more, it is a fascinating tale,"

"Very well," Lydia gave a tolerant smile "Just a few moments more," And with that she swept back out of the room, leaving Melissa to stare at Hugh in panic.

"What do I do?" She took several agitated steps forward. "What happens now?"

Hugh reached her side and caught hold of her upper shoulders. "Don't worry," He whispered, hoping to soothe her. "It's not a problem yet,"

"It will be if you get injured," Emily interjected as she sank into a chair. Melissa glowered at her, trying not to scream abuse at the calm, almost flippant woman before her.

"Indeed," Hugh continued, shooting Emily a stern look. "For now there is no real problem," He pointed to the locket. "You can find a vessel from now, but there is no need at the moment. You are fit and healthy,"

"So I can go home?" Melissa tried not to think his words. She doubted she could find it in her heart to steal another's life. Once again, she bit her lip, keeping her anger from spilling out into the open. Casting a hate filled glance at Emily, she tried to focus on Hugh and what he was saying.

"You may go home," He uttered, not missing the silent struggle that was going on behind her eyes. "You don't have to leave your family yet,"

"Yet?" Her voice was faint and scared. "What do you mean?"

"You're going to have to leave them sometime," Hugh fervently wished that he did not have to impart this sentence and not for the first time, he wondered why Emily had gone against Justin. "After all you've now ceased to age," He let the words sink in. "People will eventually notice,"

"I see," Melissa swallowed nervously, a reflexive gesture as she tried to sort out just what had happened.

"We'll talk more later," Hugh promised, conscious of Lydia De Vire waiting just outside the room.

"What about Justin?"

"We'll think of something," With a gentle push, he urged her towards the door. "Now go home and for the love of God, don't show that brooch to anyone," *Not just yet*. He added silently, trying not to frighten the girl any further than she already had been.

"Thank you," Melissa reached up and brushed her lips lightly against his cheek.

"Think nothing of it," He smiled sadly at her. "We'll visit you tomorrow," He stepped back and kissed her hand. "Get some sleep; you're going to need it,"

Melissa nodded and stepped back, ignoring the nonchalant figure of Emily in the corner of the room. Nodding to Hugh, she turned, walked back through the door and joined her mother.

CHAPTER 38

"Well that went well," Emily chuckled as the door swung shut behind Melissa and Lydia De Vire.

With a snort of disbelief Hugh rounded on Emily. "Of all the cruel things I've seen you do over the years. I believe this is the worst,"

"You exaggerate," Emily chuckled airily, dismissing Tarlington's anger with a shake of her head.

"You think so?"

"I know so," Emily pulled herself out of the chair and stared at Hugh. "Listen to me Tarlington," For the first time that evening, Emily was completely serious. "I made the best choice, in fact, I made the only choice," She reached his side and faced him down. "Justin had already signed her death warrant by his very interest. John has already been busy murdering Justin's regular girls. By the very act of leaving her, Justin has placed her in a very special niche," She removed a handkerchief and dabbed lightly at her neck. "Unfortunately that special niche brings her to John's attention,"

Hugh took a deep breath, forcing himself to consider Emily's words. For once, the blonde was making perfect sense.

"You're saying that once linked to Justin, she was already dead and the only difference would be the means of her death,"

"Precisely, though I don't see why you need me to spell it out for you so neatly," Emily replied as she reached out and plucked a long stemmed glass from a nearby table.

"Why don't you humour me?" Hugh retorted, staring at her in dislike. "Perhaps I'm feeling especially slow today,"

"As you wish," Her fingers caressed the stem of the glass in her hand, moving slowly over its smooth surface, finding the flaws in the glass blowers art. "If Justin had seduced and left after, she would still be dead," She swirled the glass, watching the amber liquid slosh like a mini whirlpool. "John would want to make sure that Justin got the message," Cupping the bowl of the glass, she lifted it to her lips and took a swallow of the amber wine. "However, because he was noble and tried to mask his interest, he's only insured the depths of John's cruelty," With a sneer at John's methods, she took a long drink. "Whatever Justin did, she would be damned," With that, she drained the last drops of wine and relaxed, confident that she had Hugh's attention and support. "At least this way, he has a chance to spare her,"

"Not that much salvation," Hugh picked up the decanter and poured two more glasses. "She's still cursed,"

"True," Emily noted, removing her fan from her skirt pocket. "But at least it's a fighting chance. Even if John does attempt to kill her, it won't take,"

"It might have been kinder in the long run to kill her ourselves," Hugh mused, settling into one of the other chairs with a sigh.

"What makes you say that?" Opening the fan with a snap, she began to fan herself slowly, the very picture of a bored noblewoman. Only her eyes betrayed her intelligence.

"John can kill her several times over now," He took a long drink from his glass and stared into space. "And if he gets hold of the brooch…" A long sigh escaped his lips. "Regardless of your intentions Emily, I don't think they'll forgive you. You may see Melissa De Vire taking the romantic opportunity, but I don't," He tapped his cane lightly against the parquet floor, almost tuning out the conversation as he declared his thoughts aloud. "Like all the rest of us, she will despise what has been done to her. I foresee a few centuries of recrimination. "

"Not if Justin finally discovers a cure," Emily interrupted, leaning forward in her chair. "He certainly has a reason to now," She closed the fan with a snap, anger building up in her face again. Taking hold of the glass, she took another swallow.

"Are you saying he has been holding back all this time?" Hugh snorted, quaffing a swallow of drink in derision. "I've seen his library,"

"No," Emily laughed as she returned her glass to the table. "I'm saying that he now has better incentive," Hugh listened to her laugh, noting the bitterness that belied the light notes. "He has a lover to return to humanity," The mockery in her voice was unmistakeable and Hugh raised an eyebrow.

"Nevertheless, you won't have made any friends today,"

"If that were my only reason for my actions then I would be upset," Her response was flippant, unconcerned, only Hugh could hear the anger that lay behind her words.

"So what actions are these?" They both turned as Alistair's voice broke into their conversation from the door.

"Alistair," Hugh stood up and walked toward Justin's younger brother. "I had heard you were in London again,"

"Don't change the subject Tarlington," Alistair walked by Hugh and stood before the still seated Emily. "What actions have you taken that might not win you friends," His voice, while civil, was low and threatening. Emily glanced up at the younger Lestrade brother and began to laugh.

"Alistair," She chortled, watching his face twist with rage as she laughed at him. "How sweet of you, you're showing off your baby claws?"

"Don't laugh at me Emily," He reached for her, his hand curled, fingers grasping. He heard the gasp of horror from Hugh somewhere on the other side of the room, but gave it no mind as he reached for her. Emily was still smiling as his fingers dug painfully into the creamy skin of her shoulder. "I won't have a whore like you laugh at me,"

"Then you shouldn't be such a fool," Almost negligently, her fingers curled about his and settled there. For a brief moment she clasped his hand, her skin soft and warm against his. "I don't like threats Alistair," She whispered before, with one wrench, she pulled his middle finger backwards. He heard the bone break at the same moment the pain hit. That was shortly followed by a pain in his wrist as she leant forward, and pulled his hand back toward his forearm. "I also despise insults," A choke escaped his lips as he struck out at her with his free hand. With a bored smile, Emily leant back out of reach and, using the bone handle of her fan, struck him across the wrist joint. "Behave Alistair," Her voice was soft, lethal and he stared down at her in shock. "Did you thing I was a weakling?" She stood, keeping the pressure on his hand. "Did you think I hid behind your brother or Hugh?" Through the haze of pain, he nodded. "Well it would appear you've learnt a lesson," Without releasing him she leant in close, her lips mere centimetres away from his ears. "I do not take threats or bullying, please remember that. And if that is a hard task for you, I will be happy to remind you of it again,"

"Enough Emily," Hugh's voice rumbled from the side of the room. "You can hurt him later. Right now I want to know why he's here,"

"Very well," With a shrug, she dropped his wrist and walked across to the door. She watched him nurse his injured wrist with a small smile. "What are you doing here Alistair?"

CHAPTER 39

Melissa walked into her room and sat down on her bed. The return from the party had been quiet; she had barely noticed her mother's conversation, lost as she was in contemplation of the night's events. Once she had passed the front door, she had excused herself and headed for her room. The change of venue did not help. Over and over, she remembered Emily's fingers pressing the brooch into her hand. Drawing her hand across her eyes, she tried not to relive the horror of what had happened next. It hadn't felt like sleep or faint. The darkness had stolen up on her and she had felt drained, altered, her skin had crawled as the darkness swamped her. Gasping, she opened her eyes and tried to still her breathing. She could feel the brooch within her pocket, the weight of it at odds with its size. Slowly, she drew it from her skirts and regarded it. The flower was exquisitely worked, the enamel smooth and bright. It was beautiful. On the left hand side of the bloom, a small gold catch drew her attention. Carefully she undid it. Inside the locket lay two small ovals, much as you would find on any other locket. Swallowing nervously, she examined the ovals before her. On the right hand oval, she could see a small cameo of herself. The picture was perfect, as though her reflection had been captured by the artist. Hesitantly, she ran her gaze across the second oval. The oval was empty, a blank canvas waiting for another's picture. With a small cry, she dropped the brooch and scuttled up the bed to huddle in a ball of terrified misery against the headboard.

She did not know how long she sat there; clinging to the headboard in fear, trying to find some distance between her and the brooch that ruined her life. Visions of her future rushed through her mind. A future spent hiding and lonely. A fresh storm of sobbing swept over her and she cried, heartbroken and afraid. Lost in her misery, she did not hear the knock at her door. Moments passed and the knock sounded again. When she did not answer, the portal swung open without invitation and Melissa glanced up, straight at her brother.

"Melly?" He took in her stance, the tears and he crossed the room in a flash. "What the devil happened?" His arms wrapped around her and she hugged him, crying into his chest as though her heart would break. "Did someone hurt you?"

"No," She whimpered, trying to contain the sobs that were overpowering her. "It's just…" She stopped; unable to lie once more to the brother she loved. "I can't tell you,"

"Melissa," His hand stroked her hair gently, setting off a fresh storm of weeping. "Please what is it?" He pulled away and stared down at her face. "You can tell me," He paused, "Is it about Lestrade?" Melissa looked up at him, tears running tracks through the lead powder on her face. "I'm so sorry I had to beat him like that," He caught hold of her hands and squeezed them. "I didn't want,"

"Marcus, I know what you had to do," Melissa finally spoke, her voice cracked by grief and horror. "It's not your fault, never think that. You've been wonderful," She seized hold of her handkerchief and blew her nose. Her head began to ache as she continued to cry, the emotion blocking her nose and throat. "I don't want to lose you. You're my brother and I love you," The lotus on the floor dominated her thoughts, its presence a malignant force on her mind.

"Melly" He hugged her again, his familiar embrace sending a fresh wave of misery through her body. "I'm not going anywhere, at least not just yet," Rocking her gently, he tried to calm her, yet the tears kept coming. "What happened Melly? Please tell me?"

She shook her head, the desire to tell so strong, that she did not trust herself to speak. Gulping another breath of air, she tried to calm down. She felt her tears soak into his shirt.

"Melissa please?" His voice broke slightly as he felt her

sobs ripple through her body. "What is it?" She pulled back from him and lay face down on the bed. Helplessly, he looked down at her. "I'm getting Mother," He announced finally, pulling away from the bed.

"No," Shaken out of her despair, Melissa sat up and seized his arm. "You can't tell mother,"

"Melly, if you can't tell me what's going on," Detaching his arm from hers, he walked toward the door. "Then maybe you'll tell Mother," He reached the door and looked back at her. "Well?" His fingers depressed the door handle and he opened the door.

Melissa took a deep breath. "You won't believe me Marcus," He let the door close and turned back to face her.

"Why don't you try me?" He returned to the bed and sat down.

Melissa bit her lip as she stared at her brother. She wanted to tell him, needed to tell him. The horrifying turn that her life had taken, needed bringing into the light. Marcus may not fully understand but she trusted him, even if he did not know what to do, he would have advice or comfort. She cleared her throat and took a breath, wondering how she would start this lunatic tale. Marcus sat on the edge of the bed, expectant and encouraging as she tried to formulate the words. Whether she would have told him was a mystery she never solved, for at the precise moment she began to speak, a scream echoed from downstairs.

"What the devil?" Marcus got up and raced for the door, Melissa followed close behind, her emotional breakdown forgotten in the rush of adrenaline. They reached the upper landing and began to race down the stairs.

"Wait," Marcus called as they reached the first landing. "The lamps are out," Melissa glanced sideways and picked a candle from the nearest table. Handing it to Marcus, she followed him down into the hall. At the foot of the stairs, the crumpled form of the upper housemaid Alice lay in grim stillness. "Melissa go upstairs," Marcus ordered, stepping into the hall and reaching for a cane from the stand by the stairs.

"No," She moved forward, staying close to him.

"Don't argue," He seized her arm and propelled back towards the stairs. "Go to my room, take one of my pistols and wait there," She staggered backward and began to climb the staircase, reluctant to leave her brother in the dark hallway. Marcus moved deeper into the hall, watching the shadows carefully as he traversed the familiar space. Glancing back over his shoulder, he motioned her upward. "Go," With a heavy heart she raced up the stairs and dashed across the landing.

Opening the door to Marcus' bedroom, she raced inside, shutting and bolting the door behind her. Without even taking a breath she headed for his dresser and pulled out the top drawer. Nestled within the shallow space was a mahogany box, polished to a high sheen and monogrammed with Marcus' initials. Undoing the clasps, she opened the case to reveal Marcus' duelling pistols. She seized both and laid them flat on the dresser top, before retrieving the powder and shot. Forcing herself to slow down, she loaded both guns and returned to the locked door. For a long moment, she stared at the door, listening intently for any sounds from downstairs. Silence had descended on the house, both comforting and terrifying. No matter how hard she listened, few sounds from the floor below reached her ears. For several minutes Melissa stood by the door, straining to hear through the sound of her heart pounding in her chest. As the silence lengthened, dark thoughts flooded her mind. What if something terrible had happened? What if Marcus had… She shook her head, trying to obliterate the dark thoughts. Yet the thoughts stayed, plaguing her mind with visions of her brother wounded and alone in the dark.

"Damn it Marcus," She swore, "I'm not letting you get hurt," She gritted her teeth and reached for the handle. With a decisive click, she unlocked the door and walked out onto the landing.

It was quiet on the dimly lit upper hallway. The portraits on the walls were in shadow, only briefly seen in the light from a few candles. Taking a deep breath, she crossed the landing and headed for her mother's bedroom. Light from the candles bounced off the barrels of the pistols as she reached her mother's door. Depressing the handle, she walked into the room. The room was dark, her mother's bed shrouded in shadow.

"Mama?" She whispered, leaving the door wide open as she crossed the room to the bed. "Mama?" Her knees bumped against the frame and she stopped. Using the dim light from the door she reached for the bedside candle and lit it, throwing warm, welcoming light across the room. Her mother's bed was empty and it had clearly not been slept in. Fear clenched about her heart and she backed off, reaching for the candle as she did so. With a cluck of annoyance, she realised that she was still carrying two pistols. Looking down, she weighed up the options. Two pistols were better than one, but if she had no light shooting would be a problem. After a moment's indecision, she tucked one of the pistols into a pocket and then reached down for the candle. Carrying the candle and one of the pistols, she headed back out onto the landing and moved towards the stairs. Stopping at the top of the steps, she listened intently. No sound drifted up the stairs. Swallowing nervously, Melissa began to walk downstairs into the darkened hallway.

As she reached the ground floor she stopped, the still form of Alice still lay at the foot of the stairs and she avoided looking at. Listening intently, she tried to work out where her brother had gone. In the dark vastness of the ground floor, there were no sounds to be heard. Wondering where the rest of the servants had gone, she finally stepped into the middle of the hall and looked around. Each of the doors that led from the hallway was open. Choosing a corridor at random, she walked down it, looking for her brother and anyone else.

"Marcus," She reached the first door and opened it, letting herself into the library. The stacks of books loomed over her, only partially lit by the candle she held.

"Marcus," She called again, moving between the stacks carefully. "Are you here?"

Moving around the library slowly, she glanced into each shadowy corner before returning to the corridor and moving on. As she walked deeper into the house, she felt fear clench at her heart. Where was her brother? She reached the next door and pushed it open quietly. Stepping through the door, she gave a little yelp as a hand snaked about her wrist and dragged her to the side.

"God's teeth Melissa, I told you to stay upstairs," Her brother hissed as he dragged her to one side. "Just for once can't you do as you're told?"

"I couldn't stay up there alone," She whispered back, "Mother's not in her room and I can't find any of the servants,"

Marcus sighed and nodded. "Alright, but hand me one of those pistols," Melissa passed over a pistol and took hold of the remaining one. "Let's go,"

They headed back out into the corridor and Marcus directed her back to the hallway. "I've already been down here, there's no sign of anyone. Come on,"

Arriving back in the hallway, they chose the route to the parlour and slowly moved down it, listened all the while. After a time, they reached the morning room and pushed open the door.

"Mother," Melissa pushed past her brother to run to the crumpled form on the floor. Lydia De Vire lay on the hearth rug, her hair bloody from a blow to the head. "Marcus," her brother rushed forward and knelt down beside her.

"What the devil is going on?" He dropped his pistol and picked up his mother. He placed her into one of the chairs and stared at the damage with a wince. "Fetch me some brandy,"

Melissa stood and rushed to the sideboard and pulled out a decanter of brandy. Turning back to the room, she shouted a warning as a man wielding a poker rushed out from behind the door. Marcus turned and avoided the blow that was aimed squarely at his head. With a grunt, he rolled to the side and stood. The man came on and, as light bounced off his features, Melissa finally recognised him as Montjoy. Marcus dove away from another blow and attempted to wrest the poker away from his attacker. Melissa let go of the brandy decanter and raised her pistol. As the older man rushed forward, Melissa fired. The ball sailed true and slammed into his upper shoulder. As the shot hit, Montjoy dropped the poker and it clattered to the ground.

Marcus glanced at his sister in surprised appreciation, but his words of congratulation turned to a shout of surprise as Montjoy continued to advance. The rake chuckled at the look on Marcus' face. Melissa stared at Montjoy in shock and a terrible sense of foreboding settled across her. She could see blood from the wound, but there wasn't nearly enough of it. Her mind flashed back to cut she had seen on Justin's hand and how fast it had appeared to heal. Now, watching Montjoy walk towards her brother, she felt the sickening sensation of dread seep through her bones. Could Montjoy have obtained a lotus? She remembered the meeting on the road the other night, remembered that he seemed well.

I pinked him so well that he needed a surgeon.

Marcus' words echoed through her mind and she stared at Montjoy in fresh horror. Someone, perhaps John, had given him a lotus. He must have used it, for how else could he have been on the road as though nothing had ever happened.

"Disappointed De Vire?" Montjoy spoke as he walked forward, a nasty nice smile playing about his lips. "I believe I said I would have my revenge," He then lunged at her brother.

Marcus dove back out of the way and Montjoy missed, his swing going wide, sending him off balance. Marcus retaliated, his fist punching Montjoy in the ribs and stomach, knocking the man backwards, yet the older man still came on. Melissa scrambled forward and seized Marcus' dropped pistol. Picking it up, she cocked it and aimed at the struggling pair, waiting for a chance to shoot. Even with the dark suspicions running through her mind, she couldn't let Montjoy hurt Marcus.

Marcus and Montjoy's fight ranged across the room, knocking over chairs and tables. Melissa's hand shook as she tried to keep a sight on Montjoy. Despite the blows that were landed on his frame, the older man kept coming. Marcus stepped backwards and fell over a small footstool, landing in a tangled heap on the floor. Melissa saw her chance and fired. The lead pellet smashed into Montjoy's chest and he gasped, the blood draining from his face as he fell to the ground.

"Thanks," Marcus gasped as he stood up. Walking

across the room, he stared down at Montjoy's body in confusion. "What the devil was he doing?" Melissa shook her head, her eyes not leaving Montjoy's prone frame. The suggestion that he was as cursed as she, still lingered in her mind. She kept her gaze on the body, watching for signs of movement as Marcus knelt down, his fingers closing about Montjoy's wrist as he felt for a pulse.

"I think he's dead," He announced after a few moments. Standing up, he walked up to Melissa and clasped hold of her shoulder. "I think you killed him," She did not respond, her eyes still staring at the prone form. Marcus glanced at her stony face and took it for shock. "You had no choice Melly," He muttered reassuringly. "He must have attacked Mother and Alice," He released her shoulder and walked back towards their mother. As Marcus moved away, Melissa darted forward to Montjoy's side. Rolling him over on his back, she stared down at his face. His eyes were wide and unseeing. Taking a sigh of relief, she stepped back from the body and moved over to help her brother.

"Is she going to be alright?" She asked, her voice a whisper.

"I think so," He glanced over at the sideboard. "Fetch some brandy,"

Melissa nodded and picked up the decanter that she had placed down earlier. Picking up a glass, she poured a good measure of the spirit and walked back across the study. Handing the glass to her brother, she waited impatiently while he tried to rouse their mother.

CHAPTER 40

"I'm here on behalf of Katherine," Alistair muttered as he nursed his bruised hand.

"Katherine or John?" Emily asked as she shut the door. "You can't honestly expect us to believe that she is acting independently?" Stepping away from the door she sat down on one of the chairs and smoothed down her skirt.

Alistair sighed as he sat in one of the other chairs. "Alright, I would have to say that I'm here on John's orders,"

"And what pray tell does John want with us?" Hugh picked up one of the decanters and poured another glass of brandy. Sitting down on the couch, he took a sip and relaxed. "More exhortations to join him in his crusade against your brother perhaps?"

"No," A nasty nice smile crossed his features. "He wants you to stay clear of him and not get involved,"

"I believe we already do that," Hugh replied, toying with the glass as he stared at the younger Lestrade.

"No, you skate on the edge of neutrality," Alistair replied, a cold light glimmering in his eyes as he nodded at Hugh. "And you," he indicated Emily with a dismissive wave, "You periodically sleep with my brother. I fancy that John finds that behaviour distasteful,"

"Oh heaven forefend," Emily stepped away from the wall and walked towards Alistair. "I don't care about John or his crusade," She walked towards him, anger evident in the set lines of her face. Stopping just shy of Alistair, she glared straight into his eyes. "I made my peace with Justin long ago," She unfurled the fan and gently wafted it through the air. "I don't particularly care for this curse but I'm living with it,"

"But do you want to make an enemy of John?" Alistair asked.

Emily laughed and snapped shut the fan. "I made an enemy of John a number of years ago. In fact..." She glanced around at Hugh. "I'd go so far as to say that we're all enemies of that psychotic bastard,"

"Then you're not worried?"

"Not in the least," The door opened and Alistair stepped back, schooling his features back to polite disinterest. Emily turned and faced the door, smiling at the people who crossed the threshold.

"I really think you should listen," Alistair hissed to her as she walked past him.

"Talk to Hugh," She whispered. "Thank you however for the warning," She stopped and leant closer. "But if John wants to play his games with me, then he'd better be ready for the consequences," With that she swept past him and out of the room.

"Hugh?" Alistair looked at the older man, who shrugged and crossed the floor. A babble of talk rose from the newcomers, covering the sound of their own muffled conversation.

"Don't talk to me dear boy," Hugh interrupted, shaking his head. "John knows not to mess with me,"

"You don't understand Hugh…"

"Oh yes I understand very well," Hugh chuckled, a harsh humourless laugh. "John is threatening us with the same torment he has meted out to Justin," He glanced up at the mirror and straightened his cravat. "I'm neutral Alistair. Both John and your brother know where I stand. I will assist either one of them or neither of them, but," He turned back to Alistair and a grim line appeared across his forehead. "If John feels the need to threaten me, then I may find my sympathies lying elsewhere," He reached for his hat and placed it upon his head. "Let him know that,"

"Hugh?"

"No," He did not raise his voice, yet there was finality to it that Alistair paused at. "I believe you should work out your priorities. John is a loose cannon and not friendly to his allies, as Katherine discovered to her cost. If you link your fate to John, all you will receive is pain,"

"But what can I do?" Alistair replied with a modicum of panic. "John scares me, even my brother runs from him,"

"Do what Emily and I do," Hugh replied, brushing down his jacket with a careless hand. "Don't get involved," He walked past Alistair then and out into the hallway. Alistair watched him go before leaving the room.

"I take it they ignored you?" Alistair glanced over his shoulder at Katherine and nodded slowly. The brunette walked forward and caught hold of his arm. "No matter," She continued as she led the younger man from the room. "John has another plan of attack,"

CHAPTER 41

Justin woke from deep sleep with a start and he sat up, heart pounding in his chest. For several moments he sat there staring into the gloom of his living room. It was gone midnight, of that he was sure and the room was in almost total darkness. The curtains over the windows shut out the moonlight. There was nothing obviously amiss and yet his heart was fluttering like a caged bird and he knew that something was very wrong. As the covers fell away from his still wounded body, he realised that he could hear nothing within the house. Fear unfurled in his chest as he came to full wakefulness.

"Coll?" He called out, pushing aside the covers as he got to his feet. The glowing embers of the fire gave only the barest of light as he reached for the candle that lay on the table beside his chaise lounge. As he registered that there was no candle within reach, he also became aware of someone walking across the floor of the room toward him.

"I'm afraid your lackey is indisposed," John's silky tones crossed the space as he walked closer. Justin closed his eyes in resignation at the pronouncement. He wondered, or rather he hoped, that John had not taken Coll as a vessel.

"What do you want?" Justin pulled himself to his feet and stared through the darkness at John's shape. "And light a candle, I'd like to see your face when I beat it,"

"Justin," The voice chided as the figure stooped to the embers and lit a candle. "So much violence in you," John stood, the candle throwing light across the room.

"You have this effect on me," Justin pulled himself upright and walked towards John, raising his fist as he did so.

"Ah ah," John held up a hand and smiled. "I wouldn't," He placed the candle down on the table and leant back against the table.

"Why not?" Justin replied with a snort. "You took my brooch and left me for dead. You threatened a woman I care for and killed several innocent ones, I feel fully justified in beating you to a bloody pulp. Granted it won't take but I least I'll get some satisfaction out of it,"

"Justin, you misunderstand," John smiled chuckling slightly as he did so. "Of course you may beat me, but that will only waste you time,"

Justin stopped moving and he stared at John with

growing suspicion. "What do you mean?"

"I mean while you're here beating me, my agent is dealing with your paramour," Justin took a step back and stared at the other man in horror. "Of course," John carried speaking in a conversational tone. "By all means you can start, but unless you want your current beloved to end up like your last one..,"

Justin didn't wait to hear any more. Despite the screaming pain in his ribs he raced from the room. Running through the main hall, he headed out in to the night. Ignoring the agony from his injuries, he raced across the drive towards the stables. Pulling open the door, he stopped. The scent of coppery blood hung in the air and his feet slipped on the slick floor. Looking down he swore as he took in the body of Coll. His retainer lay on the floor, his eyes wide with horror and his throat slit.

"I'm sorry Coll," He whispered as he closed the man's eyes. Pushing open the stable doors fully, he raced back into the building. It smelt of horse, sweat and now blood. Reaching the stalls, he pulled open the first door he came to and reached for one of the horses. Dragging himself onto the horses back, he urged the horse out of the stables and into the cool night air. There was a waxing moon in clear sky and the world was bathed in shades of milky white. In desperation, he kicked the horse into a gallop and they flew across the landscape, heading for the woods and Melissa's house beyond.

CHAPTER 42

Melissa watched as Marcus tended to their mother's wounds. She felt like breaking down from the events of the evening. First there was her disastrous meeting with Hugh and Emily and now, she risked a glance at Montjoy on the floor, now he had come to her home. She bit her lip and tried not to cry, she had done enough of that already this evening.

"Mother?" Marcus stared down at their mother's form with concern. "Melissa,"

Melissa was at his side in an instant, looking at the bloody wound to their mother's head with apprehension.

"What is it?" She choked on the words, fear strangling each syllable. She took a deep gulp of air and tried again, hoping that what she feared was unfounded.

"Give me a hand?" Marcus reached down and took gentle hold of their mother's body. Steadying himself against the dead weight, he picked her up. "Get the doors; we'll take her upstairs,"

Melissa nodded and walked forward. She was stepping over Montjoy's body, when his hand snaked out and seized hold of her ankle. With a scream, she crashed to the ground and watched in horror as the man dragged himself upright.

"It worked after all," The older man sneered as he watched the shock on Marcus' face with a grin. "I believe you owe me boy," Montjoy lumbered forward and reached for Marcus. His body was slow and uncoordinated, but still moving. "And after I deal with you," He cast a glance at Melissa, "I believe I'll have your sister, after all, you can't stop a dead man,"

"No," Melissa grabbed a nearby vase and flung it at Montjoy's head. The heavy ceramic shattered into myriad pieces, cutting into the man's face. He bled freely, rivulets trickling over his skin to drip over his shirt.

"You can't stop me girl," Montjoy gasped out as he staggered forward.

Marcus carefully placed his mother on the ground and advanced on Montjoy, his face bleak. "Get out of here Melly," He uttered in deadly grim tones.

"No! I'm not leaving you to…" Marcus grabbed her arm and propelled her towards the door.

"Get out of here and find the servants," He gave her a push through the door, "If you can't, get to the stables and run,"

"No Marcus!" She shouted as he pulled the door shut and she heard the bolts strike home. "No!" Flattening herself against the heavy wood, she hammered futilely on the hard surface of the door. From within she could hear the sounds of a struggle and she sank to her knees, weeping in frustration and fear as she tried once again to beat on the unyielding wood.

"Please Marcus don't die," She whispered, despair running through her as she imagined her brother lying still and cold. Something large or heavy fell over in the other room and she looked up, wondering if her brother was now lying dead.

"Crying about it won't help," She whispered to herself as she picked herself up from the floor. Looking at the closed door, she pushed aside the desire to curl into a ball and hide. Wiping the tears from her face with the back of her hand she turned and faced the hall, resolve building in her chest as she took stock of her situation. "If I find the servants it may be too late," She muttered. Making a snap decision, she reached out for her father's cane. Her fingers closed around the smooth wood and she pulled it free from its stand in the hall. Clasping the cane tightly in her hand, she ran from the study door. With light steps, she raced to the front door and pulled at the handle. Flinging it open she raced through and out onto the drive.

Heading out into the darkness, she raced towards the side of the building, heading for the windows to the study. Her skirt wrapped about her legs and she fell heavily. The breath whooshed out of her lungs and she scraped the skin on her hands and face. Bruised and almost in tears from fear, she picked herself up. Blood ran freely from a long scratch on her hand and pain radiated through her. She looked down at the long restricting skirt and swore. Reaching down, she grabbed the front of her dress and tore, ripping the fabric from the hem to the waist. As her legs became free, she seized hold of the cane and started to run. Heading for the side of the house, she raced round it, fright fuelling her movements. When she reached the study window, she swung the cane, shattering the window with several powerful blows. In a panic, she clambered over the windowsill, slicing the delicate skin on her hands as she did so.

"Marcus," She called as she pushed herself against the heavy shutters, hoping that the household staff hadn't managed to secure the panels yet. "Marcus," She could hear fighting from within and she pushed again with renewed hope. The shutter rattled in its place but did not move. As she readied herself for another blow, she heard a familiar voice cry out from beyond the shutter. In her fear and worry, she threw herself at the shutters, jarring her bones painfully as they gave way. She spilled through the window and into the room, landing in a heap on the floor. Dragging herself upright, she stared into the room looking for her brother and Montjoy.

"Good evening Miss De Vire," She choked back a scream as Montjoy's arm closed about her throat and pulled her close to his chest. As he dragged her across the floor, she could see her see her brother. He lay before the fire with his eyes closed and shirt bloody. Her cry of horror was choked by his hold on her throat as he dragged her mercilessly across the floor. She could see her mother still unconscious in the chair and took a deep fearful breath.

"How nice of you to get ready for me," Montjoy's voice echoed in her ears as one of his hands reached down to her torn skirt.

"Bastard," She swore and kicked back, feeling her heel connect against his hard shin. He staggered back but did not let go.

"Enough of that," He growled in her ear before throwing her to the ground. "You'll only make me angry,"

Melissa lay on the floor and stared up at him. His shirt was red from where she had shot him and he limped toward her, his injuries clearly slowing him down.

"As you can see, I can't die," He reached into a pocket and pulled a black lotus blossom from its depths. "Such a wonderful thing isn't it," He whispered in a marvellous tone. "I can just keep going," He walked forward slowly.

Melissa rolled and stood, reaching for the mantel and the several large vases that were arrayed there. Grasping one in her hands, she threw it across the room, where it broke against his head. He staggered back, woozy from the blow.

"You're only making it worse," He threatened as he lurched forward.

She threw another vase, this one caught him in the chest and he doubled up in pain. Melissa reached for something else to throw but at that moment, her mother groaned as she started to come round. Montjoy turned and headed for Lydia, flicking open the lotus as he did so. Melissa threw the next vase before racing across the room towards Montjoy.

Melissa grabbed hold of Montjoy's arm, but even as wounded as he was, he was still stronger than she. He pushed her back to the floor as he reached for her mother, holding the lotus blossom in his hand.

Justin reined in outside of the De Vire manor as an anguished scream rent the air. Throwing himself from his horse, he raced into the manor as fast as his legs could carry him. He reached the main hall and caught sight of the dead body in the hallway.

"Melissa," He shouted, hoping that she was nearby.

Melissa stared at the body of her mother in shock. It had taken but a moment. As Lydia De Vire's eyes had flickered open, Montjoy had thrust the brooch before her gaze. Just one look sealed her fate. Melissa had watched as her mother jerked as though she had been shot. Blood poured from wounds that appeared from nowhere as Montjoy stood straighter, the damage leaving him.

"Melissa," She heard the shout from the hallway and screamed out, trying hard not to watch her mother die.

Justin raced through the hall and entered the study, stopping in horror at the sight that met his eyes. Montjoy was reaching for Melissa as her mother lay crumpled and dead nearby and Marcus, he glanced down at the other man but couldn't tell whether he were alive or not. The thing that really drew his attention was the lotus bloom in Montjoy's hand.

"Lestrade," Montjoy turned to face the newcomer. "How kind of you to make it?" He lifted his hand and showed him the lotus. "I hear I have you to thank for this,"

Justin ignored him; he glanced over to Melissa and helped her to her feet. "Are you alright?"

"He killed my mother," She replied, her voice dead and eyes full of hate. "I'll kill him," She lunged forward, taking Justin by surprise. Rage powering her, she struck out at Montjoy wildly, attacking him with her hands, feet and teeth. He pushed her to the floor before slamming his foot into her side. She gasped in pain as Justin moved to place himself between them. He seized Montjoy's arms.

"Don't touch her again," He snarled back, more angry than he had ever been.

"What do you think you can do?" Montjoy smiled back. "You can barely stand, you haven't healed your injuries and you can't heal them," He jerked back and tried to break free, but Justin held on with grim determination.

"True I am injured," He replied with a grim smile, "But I know more about these lockets than you," As he spoke, he viciously twisted Montjoy's arm, causing his fingers to spring open in pain. The locket hit the floor. As Montjoy tried once again to pull himself free, Justin shouted over his shoulder. "Kick it into the fire," Melissa rushed forward and bent down. "Don't pick it up," He yelled in panic as he watched her hand stretch out towards the smooth enamel. With dawning shock, he gaped as she stood, lotus clasped safely in hand and still fully conscious.

"It's alright," Melissa said with a grim smile. "Your

friend Emily already gave me one of these," And with that, she threw the lotus into the fire. Montjoy flinched as though he had been struck and Justin took advantage of the distraction, throwing the man backwards and into the wall. He reached down and picked up the poker that had been dropped earlier. With an almost nonchalant motion, he struck at the man's head. At the first blow, Montjoy fell to the ground and huddled in a foetal position as Justin hit him with the heavy implement. Justin did not stop the blows until Montjoy lay still and cold on the study floor with a bloody mess for his head.

Justin backed off and dropped the poker, his face grey from the exertion. Melissa rushed to his side and stared at the body.

"What do we do?"

"He'll be awake soon, but he will be decaying," Justin muttered as he reached down and pulled Montjoy's body upright. "Help me with him," Melissa rushed over and helped pick up the body.

"What are we doing with him?"

"Burying him," Justin answered simply. He took in the shock that crossed her features and continued, "Or at the very least, making sure he won't move for a while," Together they manoeuvred the body from the study and out onto the grounds. Justin loaded him on the back of his horse and mounted up behind.

"Where are you taking him?"

"My estate," He called back. "It won't take me long," He glanced up at Melissa's house and then back at the girl before him. "I think you should pack some essentials, things that won't be missed. You're going to have to leave tonight,"

And with that he tapped his heels to the horses side and sped off across the grounds at a fast gallop, leaving Melissa to stare after him in shock. Turning back to the house, she rushed into the study and the body of her brother.

"Marcus," She whispered, reaching down to shake his shoulder. "Marcus," His skin was warm beneath her fingers and his chest rose and fell with each slow breath he took Relief that he was still alive was tempered by fear as she failed to wake him. "Please wake up," She pleaded in soft tortured tones as she sat back on her heels and began to cry.

She was still sat there when Justin returned. He reached her side and hunkered down next to her, his arms sliding across her shoulders. With a moan, she turned and cried into his shoulder, feeling his warm arms supporting her.

"Do I have to go before knowing he's alright?" She whispered when she finally gained control of her emotions.

"Yes," Justin replied, his voice low and sorrowful. "Because you will be assumed to have been abducted or killed. When Marcus comes to, he will tell them about Montjoy," He took a deep breath continued, his heart heavy with all the things he had to say. "They will see your mother and assume that he found you and left,"

"But I can't just leave…" He pulled back from the hug and stared her deep in the eyes.

"You have to," He stood up and reached down a hand.

"I'm so sorry I got you into this," Melissa stared at the hand and then back at her brother. "He will be alright," He reassured, stepping closer and laying a hand upon her shoulder. "I should know, I've seen more than enough wounds. It'll take a couple of hours but he will be alright,"

Melissa reached out a hand and turned Marcus over. She brushed the strands off hair away from his face and felt the tears start to come. "I'll miss you," She whispered, weeping through the words. "And I love you," She reached down and hugged him tightly to her. "I'll never forget," Reluctantly she brushed the tears from her eyes and pulled away. Justin watched her stand and head for the door. Without so much as a backwards glance, she left the room heading upstairs to pack.

Justin took another look at Marcus' body before he sat down in one of the unbroken chairs and waited for her to reappear. It would have been better for all if he had never spoken to her, better if he had not returned to court. He thought of Emily and all the words he would have with her once he caught up with her. His ribs and body still hurt and John still had his brooch. By the time Melissa had finally returned with a small case in her hands, he had made his decision. They couldn't go on like this forever. There had to be an end to it, an end to the suffering and bickering, even if it took him many centuries, he would cure them. As Melissa mounted the horse behind him and they headed off into the night, he swore that he would not rest until he found the answer. No matter how far he had to travel he would cure them all.

To be continued…